PAUL RANDALL ADAMS

We Were Giants

First edition

Cover art by Ashley Santoro

This book was professionally typeset on Reedsy.
Find out more at reedsy.com

To dreamers everywhere—

Art is not what you see, but what you make others see.

—EDGAR DEGAS

Contents

Acknowledgement

Without my wife, Sara, this book would be nothing, and I would be nothing. She saw me when I couldn't see myself and continues to make me strive to be better every day. She is my support and lends me strength when I am weak. She showed me what love means, how love can be, and the love I hope all of my characters experience once in their fictional lives. Thank you, Sara. I love you to the moon and back.

To my son, who brings sunshine, life, and laughter to every single day, I hope you know how loved you are. And I hope you remember to never stop dreaming. Dream as big as you want, and then go one step bigger.

To my family, who suffered through countless hours of me sitting alone at night at the kitchen table, furiously scribbling away in a spiral-bound notebook, thank you. Thank you for believing in me. Even when it didn't make sense, and even when I didn't make sense, thank you for supporting my dreams.

To Credonia, my always-in-my-pocket support group who continually has a word of encouragement, who pushed me to publish this book, who build me up time and time and time again, I owe so much to you and your friendship. Thank you for your love and your support. And for always being in my pocket.

It has taken a community to get me to this point, and there is no way I can thank everybody who has influenced my success.

And finally, thank you to you, dear reader. I hope you have loved your time with Cade and Isaiah as much as I have. They are truly special to me, and I cannot thank you enough for spending time with them.

Chapter One

Hey...

That's always bad news. When Kayla ends anything with an ellipsis, it's going to mean a bad day for, well, everybody.

I consider not replying but decide that it's not in my best interest; Kayla's my best friend, and if I don't respond, she'll flood my phone with a thousand angry text messages. It's only 7:00 on a Monday morning. The drama is starting early.

What's up? I respond. Two minutes have passed. In the world of drama, that's hours.

Can I pick u up? We need 2 talk.

Kayla knows that I can't stand it when she types like that. How hard can it be to spell out the word *to*? I mean, seriously.

I find it funny that she waited this late to see if she can pick me up. Had I ridden the bus to school this morning, I would have been gone an hour ago. I'd rather not endure a barrage of drama today, but I concede because she's apparently having a crisis, and sometimes it's nice to be needed.

Sure

Good. I'm n ur driveway.

Great. Now I'm going to have to get dressed quickly and finish my English homework during lunch. I throw on my clothes—rumpled as usual—and run out to meet Kayla.

The car smells of breakfast tacos and fried hash browns. That's never a good sign. Kayla never eats fast food unless she's upset. The bright side, though, is she always brings me food when she's stress eating.

"What's wrong, kiddo?" I ask before tearing into my breakfast taco.

I have called her kiddo since we became friends five years ago. To be honest, I don't know why I do it. Most likely, it's because I have always treated her like a kid sister. She's always needed my protection.

"It's my mom again," she mutters through a mouthful and egg and sausage.

Of course, it is. It's always her mom. Her parents are hard on her—I get that—but I can't imagine what her life must be like. She has two parents who love her. They've been married forever. They both have college degrees, good-paying jobs, and time for Kayla. She and her sisters are their world. Their entire world.

"What'd she do this time?" I ask. I am genuinely concerned. I complain a lot, I know, but Kayla's my best friend. I want to make things better. I want her to be happy.

"It's my grades again. She's mad that I have a B in chemistry." She huffs. I swear this girl is destined for an Oscar in the category of Hurting Teenage Girl. Even the music on the radio is moody and melancholy. I sometimes wonder if she plans the soundtrack for our rides when she's in a bad mood.

"Well," I wince as I speak. She's not going to like what I have to say. "Can you blame her? You have been making straight A's your entire life. You could teach this class. But, instead, you ask Cameron Mathis for help. Then you intentionally throw your grade so that he'll have a reason to help." I hear unintended exasperation in my voice. I know her defenses are going to be raised before I finish talking.

"That is not true, and you know it." Kayla huffs again. I can practically see the fire in her eyes.

"Oh, come off it," I laugh. "It is, too. Your mom would not be mad over a B if it were the best you could achieve. But it's not. You're too smart for that."

Kayla tries hard to hold onto her anger, but I know I've won. She knows I'm right.

Contentedly, I finish my breakfast taco and stare out of the window.

"Okay, fine. But I won't let my GPA drop. I'm gonna get an A." Kayla says matter-of-factly. "And, besides, Cameron asked me on a date this weekend, so it's finally working the way I planned it to."

I don't get everybody's thing for Cameron Mathis. He recently moved to our school, and the entire place is buzzing about him. Guys want to spend all their time with him. Girls stare at him like his skin is made of gold. Teachers dote on him like he single-handedly cured every disease on Earth while simultaneously restoring the Sistine Chapel.

I'm sure Cameron is a great guy, don't get me wrong. He seems nice enough. But I won't be petitioning the mayor to give him the key to the city anytime soon.

"This weekend?" I ask as we approach the school. We're supposed to have plans this weekend. But Kayla is about to bump me. I should be surprised, but I'm not.

"Yeah, he's taking me bowling and to the movies. Really low-key. It should be fun." Kayla's eyes sparkle, and I'm happy for her. Truly, I am. And now I can tell my mom to take the double shift she was offered at work. I guess it's a win-win. Almost everybody wins.

We pull into Kayla's spot at Riverside High School and ready ourselves for the day. I survey myself, noting my rumpled, old clothes and messy hair one more time before climbing out of Kayla's car.

"Are you ready for the best day ever, Cade Swanson?" Kayla smiles at me.

She's asked me this at the start of every school day for five years. If those have been the best days ever, I really fear for the future.

The hallways are loud and bustling, and I do my best to shrink into the noise and disappear. In the hallways, I fear for my life. People are so loud, all trying to talk over each other. It's like some kind of animalistic ritual, like howler monkeys screaming over territory.

During this scene, daily, I am grateful for my superpower. I have this unique ability to turn unnoticeable. It's not invisibility because people can still see me if they want. I just become uninteresting to them, and therefore they don't notice me. It's not a superpower that's of much use to anybody. I'll never have to decide whether to use it for good or evil or anything like that. It just helps me navigate the hallways.

It probably also helps that Kayla is the only person who wants to notice me.

"Hey, short stuff," a voice says behind me. I smile, turning to see Isaiah. Isaiah Rosenthal is the only other person who can see me when I'm slipping silently through the hallways.

I guess he's my other best friend. At least, I enjoy talking to him and hanging out with him, but Isaiah and I rarely hang out like Kayla, and I do.

"How was your weekend?" Isaiah asks, his smile lighting the hallway. He always makes me smile because he's always smiling.

"It was good, I guess." I shrug. "Same as usual. Mom worked. I babysat my brother. Drew some. Nothing special."

Isaiah's eyes grow bigger as we talk. He acknowledges people who greet him in the hall, but he never interrupts our conversation. It's incredible how attentive he is when we talk. Even my mom can't give me such undivided attention.

"What did you draw? Will you show me in class?" Isaiah and I are in advanced art together. He's taking it for fun, but I'm putting together a portfolio. Art school is my ticket out of Riverside. It's not that I don't like my hometown; it's just that Riverside is where all original thought goes to die.

When we get to the art room, I pull out my sketchbook to show Isaiah my latest creation. I always feel nervous when I show my work to him. I know that if I drew a stick figure, he'd praise my talents, but I still want him to like what I've drawn.

"This is your best, yet," he says as if he's stating a fact. "There's so much detail. I don't know how you get so much emotion out of just a pencil. It's really good." He finishes, handing my sketchbook back to me.

The bell rings before I can respond, and Mr. Camplin begins class. For the duration of the class, I can't help but smile. Isaiah is right; it is my best work yet. And an art school will be lucky to have me.

"Okay, class, I have exciting news," Mr. Camplin announces, holding his hands together as if attempting to contain his excitement. "This year, Riverside High School will be hosting the state art show. This is an amazing opportunity for our school because we've never even had an artist qualify for the art show. But the host school is guaranteed at least three entries as restitution for hosting the show. I will be selecting these guaranteed slots from this advanced art class."

Mr. Camplin begins speaking more excitedly about compiling a portfolio for judging, and while he's not looking at me, I know that he's banking on me to enter the show. Mr. Camplin thinks that I have what it takes. And maybe I do. But I wish he wouldn't place all of his bets on me. I tend to disappoint.

As I leave class, Mr. Camplin stops me, looking me in the eye.

"Cade, I hope you'll work on that portfolio. It can be anything you've done in the past four years. Anything from your high school career that shows your personality as an artist. You've got a real shot at the scholarship this year."

And suddenly, I'm sold. That one little word changes everything. Scholarship. It's the only way I'll have a shot at college. I know I could take out loans, but I've seen how hard my mom works to pay hers off, and she doesn't even use her degree anymore.

"I'm sorry, sir. Did you say scholarship?"

Mr. Camplin beams at my sudden interest.

"The student with the best portfolio receives a full scholarship to any state school's art program." He nods. "And if you keep producing the work you've been churning out this year, you'll have a real shot, especially if you borrow some of your best pieces from the past few years. But you'll need to vary your media. You can't just work in graphite if you want to win."

I can't contain my smile. Mr. Camplin would not lie; if he says I have a shot, I must have a legitimate chance at winning. As I walk to my next class, I actually greet people. I guess I won't be going unnoticeable.

"You look different when you smile," Kayla laughs as she joins me. "It's kind of scary. I don't think I've ever seen you smile at school. Especially not this early in the morning."

"Maybe it's your daily affirmations, kiddo. They've finally started working," I laugh. "This is the best day, ever."

As Kayla looks at me with confused curiosity, Isaiah catches up with us, chuckling. "Cade's just excited because he's the shining hope for Riverside High." He answers Kayla's confused look by filling her in with the morning's events. I allow my mind to wander to my portfolio and what I can fill it with to beat everybody else in the state.

I have drawings of nature and sketches of my friends hanging out. I've made a couple of flipbooks, one that showed strange animations of baseball players hitting a baseball into outer space, and the ball turned into a new planet. Mr. Camplin had told me it was a beautiful depiction of the cyclic nature of life. I had just thought it was cool. I didn't expect it to have made a statement.

Before I can stop daydreaming, Kayla and I are at our second class of the day. Chemistry. Chemistry with Cameron Mathis. It's chemistry with Cameron Mathis that makes me wonder if I've turned my self-proclaimed superpower back on. Because chemistry with Cameron Mathis makes even my best friend, Kayla, ignore me. And then I wonder if I'm still unnoticeable. And I know I don't actually have a superpower. And I know that people can see me. But Kayla doesn't. Or won't. And then I remember that I'm the surrogate.

Mr. Barnhill drones on about the table of elements, and I remember the first time I ever called myself the surrogate, the first time I ever realized that I was, in fact, a surrogate. Kayla's surrogate. I was Kayla's surrogate.

"What does that even mean?" Isaiah asked when I told him about my revelation.

"You know," I explained. "A substitute. Like when celebrities want to have babies, but they think getting pregnant will hurt their image."

He laughed his infectious laugh, his broad, toothy smile filling up the room. "So, you're saying Kayla wants you to have her baby?"

I glanced across the cafeteria where we were talking and made eye contact with Kayla. She gave me the slightest of nods but tried not to acknowledge my presence. That's how she always behaved when she had a new boy.

"That's what I mean," I said to Isaiah through a smile, nodding toward Kayla. "I'm her best friend and closest confidante whenever she's single, but the moment a new boy comes along, I'm kicked to the curb."

I shrugged, trying to look nonchalant. "I'm her surrogate boyfriend."

I didn't want to be Kayla's boyfriend. I *don't* want to be her boyfriend. I just don't always want to be kicked to the curb when Kayla has a new love interest. Nobody wants that.

Of course, Isaiah just chuckled.

"It's just the way she is in a new relationship. Everybody's that way a little bit. Once the new wears off, she'll come back." Isaiah was always so optimistic. *Is* always so optimistic.

But he was also correct. Kayla does always come back around once the new wears off. Because once the new wears off, Kayla is through. She just can't seem to commit to a relationship for long after it stops being fresh and easy. Once it starts taking work, she's done.

And then, inevitably, she comes back to me, teary-eyed, and I offer her chick-flick-and-ice-cream therapy. I always pick up the pieces, put her back together, and send her back into the big world.

And though I always complain about it, I know that I'll always do it. Because Kayla's my best friend and because she is the only one who sees me when I'm invisible.

Chemistry ends as boringly as it began, and I duck into the hallways, Kayla's loud, flirtatious giggle sinking into the noise of the hallway, the howler calls.

It's lunchtime now, and I'm glad to find Isaiah already awaiting me at our table with nobody around him. I don't know why there's never anybody around him; everybody loves him. Everybody wants to be his friend. People don't idolize him the way they do Cameron Mathis, but he's definitely not hurting for friendships or admirers.

"I was thinking," Isaiah says as I sit down. "We should have a game night this weekend. Do you play much Xbox?"

I don't. I've never played Xbox. Or really anything.

"I wish," I sigh, digging into my lunch. "But my mom is working all weekend, so I have to watch Thomas." Thomas is my little brother, though sometimes it's more like he's my kid.

"I could come to your house." He suggests through a mouthful of half-chewed macaroni. "If that's cool."

He says it half-heartedly like he's afraid I'll say no (the way I always do.)

Kayla's the only person from school who's seen my house. My rundown, poor, decrepit, falling apart little house on the wrong side of town. But Isaiah is a safe friend. He won't judge me; I can tell. I hope.

"That would be fun," I feel myself smile. "I'll ask my mom, but it should be fine." And it should be. Mom's always ruffling my hair and asking me why I don't have friends over besides Kayla. She never believes that I don't have any friends other than Kayla.

"But you have to promise me," I warn, biting into a fish stick. "You can't make fun of my house. I don't exactly live in the same neighborhood as you."

Isaiah just smiles and nods a little, and I know that he understands.

School ends, and I'm back in Kayla's car, listening to some bubblegum pop song with too much auto-tune and not enough talent. Kayla's in a good mood. Her music choice always reflects her mood.

Despite the Texas heat, the sunroof is rolled back, and all the windows are down. The hot wind is whipping through the car, and I know that I will have to peel myself off of her leather seats. We're not talking because Kayla is too into her teeny-bopper music. When her song ends, she turns down the radio. My ears are thankful for the respite.

"You and Cameron looked cozy at lunch today," I muse, mostly because I find silence uncomfortable.

"He's really a special guy, Cade," Kayla sighs. "He wants to get to know you."

"I'm sure he does, kiddo." Kayla has said different variations of that same thing about her last six boyfriends. "I'll give you time to get used to each other before I add myself into the mix."

Kayla nods in agreement, and I bite my tongue. I always want her to say that I'm always part of the mix. She never does. Kayla's not a bad friend. *She's not*. She's just a little self-absorbed in relationships.

We make idle chit-chat as we ride, talking about our days, and our homework, and our classes. Mondays are always our worst days for conversations. Tomorrow we'll be solving the world's problems. Today we'll do the conversational equivalent of twiddling our thumbs.

Kayla drops me off, and I get in the house to find my mom getting ready for work.

"Cade, you're home?" She calls from the kitchen as she buttons her blue polo shirt. My mom's beautiful. Not in the way Hollywood starlets are with their million-dollar facials and their thousand-dollar haircuts. She's beautiful in the way actresses were in those old musicals from the 50s, when they didn't all look alike, and they still had their original noses.

"I'm home. Kayla drove me." I open a soda from the fridge and drop my backpack by the table. "I wanted to talk to you before Thomas gets off the bus."

Butterflies buzz in my stomach, furiously begging me not to ask my mom what I'm about to ask.

"First of all, Kayla made other plans this weekend, so I can watch Thomas if you still want to take that second shift you were offered." I try to slow my breathing; I can hear myself rambling. "And so, I was wondering if Isaiah could come over this weekend. We'll make sure to involve Thomas and take care of him."

Mom smiles one of those warm, motherly smiles before ruffling my hair.

"Of course, Isaiah can come over. You sounded so nervous. Did you think I'd say no?" She half laughs.

"Oh, no. That's not my big question." I feel the words catch in my throat.

I take a deep breath and tell her about the state art show and Mr. Camplin's faith that I could win it.

"But I can't win with just my graphite drawings. They'll expect other media." I hold my breath for a minute. I try not to ask my mom for art supplies. I know they're expensive and I know we can't afford them. I have some money saved up, but it's not enough for the things I'll need, and I can't use the school's supplies for extra-curricular projects.

My mom runs a hand through her hair, the wrinkles on her forehead appearing as she considers my request. Before she speaks, I know what she's going to say.

"I'm sorry, Cade," she says at last. "We just don't have the money right now. Our budget is already so tight."

She looks like she's going to cry as she says this. It must be hard to be a parent and not be able to give your kids the things they want. And as I think this, I feel stupid for even asking. I know that my mom reacts like this.

I don't expect what she says next, though.

"Maybe you could ask your father." It seems like it hurts her worse to say this than it did to tell me that we didn't have the money.

"No," I try to force a smile. "That's okay," I feel myself deflate. It was a fun pipe dream, but I shouldn't have gotten my hopes up. Because let's be honest, I'd rather sell my organs than ask my father for anything.

"Cade," she starts in that tone that tells me she thinks I've made the wrong decision. "He's your father. You shouldn't feel strange calling him." But she knows as well as I do that her arguing is futile; I won't call him. He abandoned us.

Luckily the front door opens before I have to say anything else, and Thomas comes running in to hug Mom before she leaves for work. They chat a little before mom kisses us both.

"I have to get to work," she says like she does every day. "Thomas, behave for your brother." And with that, she's gone, off to be the best damned night manager Megamart has ever seen.

Mom's not home yet when the night terrors start. Screams like gunshots hang in the air, coming from Thomas's room.

I check my phone for the time and see that I've missed twelve texts from Kayla. I'll have to text her back once I've dealt with Thomas. It's 11:00; she'll still be awake.

Slowly, I make my way into my brother's room. The street light outside filters in through a slit in the curtains. The long band lights up Thomas's face, a twisted expression of fear and pain on his face. He looks so little like this, seven years old and terrified. I grab his hand and whisper softly to him, the way I have since the night terrors started.

"Shhhh," I say softly, my voice barely audible in the night. "It's okay, Thomas. Everything's okay. I'm here." I brush his hair back off his forehead and keep trying to soothe him. And I curse my dad.

With every fiber of my being, I hate my father. Thomas's night terrors started when our father left four years ago. And for four years, I've lost parts of nights'—if not entire nights'—worth of sleep.

After a while, Thomas settles back into a restful sleep. I stay for a couple of minutes longer to make sure things have actually passed before going back to my room.

I read Kayla's text messages. They're full of misspellings, but the gist of her multitude of texts is that she's struggling with our English homework. Poetry has never been her strength, but it's also not something I can explain through a text. So instead, I tell her to pick me up in the morning, and I'll explain on the way to school.

I hear the front door unlock and I'm relieved to hear Mom come home from Megamart. She can take over Thomas duty, and I can sleep. My door creaks open, and Mom's head appears in the crack.

"Hey," I smile and click on my lamp. "How was work?"

The half-light from my lamp casts long shadows on my mom's face, accenting the lines that have been growing across her face in the last four years. At this time of night, my mom always looks so tired. Her smile is always gone.

"Work was fine," she says in a mixture of a huff and a sigh. I gesture for her to sit at the foot of my bed. She does, knowing that I must want to talk about Thomas. I notice, again, just how tired she looks. Working two jobs has really started to take its toll on her.

"Thomas had another night terror tonight," I say softly, not meeting her gaze. "It's the worst one he's had in a long time."

She swallows hard and nods. Her eyes glisten, and I know that she's fighting back tears. She always has to when it comes to Thomas. I wonder if she feels guilty, but I can't imagine what she has to feel guilty for.

"They're getting worse, Mom," I clench my firsts because I dread telling her this. I'm not an adult, and I'm not a parent. I don't know anything about raising children. "I think he needs to see somebody. A doctor or a counselor or somebody."

Mom hangs her head for a minute, and I feel awful. I hate having talks like this with her. Because I'm not qualified to make that kind of statement.

"Or maybe he'd do better if you were here every night instead of me," I suggest, weakly shrugging. I've offered this suggestion before. I could start working nights so that she could be home with Thomas and stop working so many hours.

"Kayla's dad has offered me a job at his pharmacy whenever I want it. Why don't you quit your job at Golden Acres and switch to days at Megamart? And I can work at night."

Mom's hand grabs mine, and I see a tear rolling down her cheek. She just looks so tired. So tired. She keeps shaking her head.

"No," she finally says, her voice just the ghost of a whisper. "No. School is your job, Cade. I already ask too much of you with your brother. But I can't let you get a job. You have to focus on school. You're my retirement plan, remember?" She smiles a weak, sad smile, and I smile with her.

Mom was the activities director for Golden Acres, a senior retirement community, when my father left us. She loved her job, and the residents loved her. She planned dances and bingo nights and brought in Christmas carolers to sing for her residents. And she was home with me every afternoon when I got home from school. It was nice to come home to my mom and fresh cookies and dinner at 6:30 in a big house in a good neighborhood.

When my father left us, though, she had to take a second job at Megamart. I started taking care of my brother, then, at 13 years old. I never minded. I'd do anything to help my mom out. I always told her that I'd work for a big advertising firm and draw artwork for national accounts like McDonald's, and Coke, and Yamaha one day. And then I'd make enough money that she could take early retirement and live in a big house with a picket fence just like she deserved.

"Maybe you could ask Cole for money or to pay for Thomas some help. It's his fault that this is happening, after all."

Mom's eyes shoot daggers, and her nostrils flare out.

"Cade Allen Swanson, I have told you not to call your father by his first name." Mom is stern. Her tone is severe. But I don't care. I keep pushing.

"I'm sorry," I'm not at all sorry. "Mr. Swanson. My sperm donor. Twenty-three chromosomes." I know I've gone too far. Mom doesn't like me to be disrespectful, even if my father did leave us high and dry.

"Cade, enough." She doesn't raise her voice, not even when she's mad. Instead, she grits her teeth and speaks very softly, slowly accenting each syllable.

"I know you're mad at him. I know you think your father abandoned you. It's okay to be mad. It's okay to be hurt." Mom's voice is gentle again. "But you have got to stop being so full of hate. Hate only complicates things. He's your father, Cade."

She sounds like she's pleading with me, and I feel guilty about upsetting her. I don't say anything, but I nod.

"I can't ask your father for money," she finally says. "But I'll figure something out."

We say nothing for a minute, the sounds of our old house creaking filling the silence. I think I can hear our neighbors fighting again, but I can't be sure.

"It's late," Mom squeezes my hand. "You have school in the morning."

She kisses me on the crown of my head before getting up and walking to my door.

"Thank you, Cade," she smiles back at me. "Thank you for taking care of Thomas. It won't always be this way. I promise." I can hear a tear in her voice, and I have to remind myself that she gets this way late at night. She cries more when she's tired, but she'll be okay.

"We'll all be okay," I hear myself say aloud. I climb out of bed to check on Thomas one more time and am relieved when I find he's smiling in his sleep. When I click off my lamp, back in my own bed, I wish I could sleep for a week and not be disturbed.

Chapter Two

The week passes fairly smoothly after Monday. Thomas only has two other night terrors, so I manage to sleep pretty well, all things considered.

Kayla picks me up for school every day. I hate when she comes to my neighborhood; it's embarrassing compared to the gated community where her family lives. But it is nice not to have to take the buses to get to school. Yes. *Buses.*

I don't actually live in Riverside High School district. I'm supposed to attend South River High, a terrorizing kind of place not unlike something from Dante's *Inferno*.

Fortunately, I qualify for Riverside's arts magnet program. The downside is that I have to ride one bus for thirty minutes, get off at an elementary school, and then ride another forty-five minutes to Riverside High. When Kayla drives me, it hardly takes twenty minutes.

We lived in Riverside district when my parents were married, and we lived on the nice side of town. Things were different then, but I never talk about it around Thomas. He was three when our father left, so he doesn't really remember the *before* times. I keep thinking that if he thinks this is the way things have always been, all this will be easier for him.

"Are you ready for the best day ever, Cade Swanson?" Kayla's voice snaps me out of my daze.

"Always, kiddo." I smile, climbing out of her car into the glum morning. The rain has begun collecting in puddles in the school parking lot, and the clouds overhead look like the rain may never stop. I prepare to activate my superpower as we enter the school.

The hallways are bustling as ever, the territorial wars still going strong.

A towering figure appears over me, and I smile at Isaiah's presence.

"Hey, shrimp," he teases. I'm not short. I'm not tall, either, but I'm not short. It just happens that Isaiah is 6'9". He towers over everybody at our school, even the basketball team. He's an entire foot taller than I am. And he's thin as a rail. He's almost hilariously skinny.

"Are we still on for tonight?" We're walking to art class, and I can feel the smile on my face growing. In the craziness of this week, I guess I forgot that Isaiah is coming over.

"Yeah!" I can't hide the excitement in my voice. I'm genuinely excited for a break in the monotony of the week. Of every week. Nothing changes for my family in our rat race. "Just remember,"

"I know, no judging your house," He interrupts. "You know I won't."

I know he won't.

"And don't be surprised if my little brother idolizes you and/or wants to climb on you like a piece of playground equipment." I laugh, but it's true. Thomas will likely want to climb up Isaiah's shoulders and announce how tall he is.

The rest of the day passes slowly. I can't stop counting down to the end of the day and the weekend. I resist the urge to drum on my desk in English. I'm positive the clock slows down the closer we get to the end of the day.

Finally, the stars align, and the second hand gains momentum enough to finally tick and mark the end of school. The bells ringing are like the sweetest music I've ever heard: freedom, sweet freedom. I pack up my bag and go to meet Isaiah by his locker.

"You coming?" Kayla grabs my arm as she passes.

I shake my head almost too eagerly. "Isaiah's taking me home. He's spending the weekend at my house."

I don't know why I didn't tell her before now; it just didn't occur to me. And the look on her face tells me that was a mistake. Apparently, I should have told her earlier.

"Oh," she looks crestfallen. "I didn't realize... I guess I'll just have to give myself my pre-date pep talk." Her face says she's joking, but something in her tone makes me think otherwise.

"You'll be great," I smile. "You always are. And I want to hear all about it on Sunday." I hug her then catch Isaiah's eye.

The parking lot is nearly empty by the time we get outside; nobody sticks around on Fridays. I follow Isaiah to his car and catch myself, stopping to gawk. Isaiah drives my dream car. A sleek, black sports car with all leather interior. It's beautiful. I might be drooling. I don't even care.

"This is your car?" I try not to sound excited or jealous. I am *totally* excited and jealous. I'm beyond jealous. I'm down-right envious.

"Yeah," he kind of chuckles, scratching his head. "My parents insisted. I just wanted a banged-up old pickup truck."

At this point, I don't care who insisted he had that car. All I wanted to do was drive it. And drool over it. And maybe pet it a little bit. If I die and get reincarnated, I want to come back as this car.

Of course, I say none of this. Instead, I just shrug, lamely, like I've seen a thousand cars like this before.

"Cool."

Yeah, I tell myself. *You played it real cool.*

"We just have to run by my house, so I can pick up my clothes and Xbox," he says as he presses the ignition button. The car hums to life like something in a science fiction movie, and for the first time, I understand what it means to hear a car purr.

I try not to seem like this is unusual for me, but I feel like I'm sitting in the literal lap of luxury. It's all too much for me; how does Isaiah just sit there and drive, all relaxed like that?

"Could you not do that please?" Isaiah smiles, turning down the radio.

"Do what?"

"Sit there and half-gawk," he laughs. "You're trying so hard to play it cool, but your eyeballs look like they're going to pop out of your face any second."

I catch myself smiling broadly. It feels like I'm actually smiling from ear to ear.

"I'm sorry." And I am, even though I don't look it. "I've just never sat in such a nice car. I don't mean to obsess. I just. I've dreamed of this car." I'm aware of how pitiful I sound, so I try not to say anything else.

"Tell you what," Isaiah says, chuckling in his infectious way. "I'll let you drive from my house to yours."

"Deal." I'm trying to play it cool again. But on the inside, I feel like I've just swallowed an entire hive of bees hyped up on caffeine and sugar.

We ride the rest of the way without saying much. Instead, we turn the radio up (I've never pegged Isaiah as a country music guy before) and jam out.

It's not until we pull up to the gate at Isaiah's house that I realize just how different our worlds are. When I say we pulled up to Isaiah's gate, I don't mean he lives in a gated community like Kayla. His house sits on some beautiful Shangri-La-inspired property behind a giant iron gate that you need a code to enter.

We drive up the private drive, and a massive brick house comes into view, perfectly trimmed hedges lining the façade. Big windows overlook the property. The whole place reeks of money. Even though it's raining everywhere else, the skies are blue here, like Isaiah's parents pay extra for perfect weather.

Something suddenly clicks in my head. *Rosenthal.* Isaiah's last name is Rosenthal. As in *the* Rosenthals. The family who practically owns half of Riverside. Isaiah's family is wealthy. I don't even try to hide my awe. Isaiah's house could swallow mine whole and still have room for a trailer park. It could dwarf the Parthenon.

"You live in a mansion," I hear myself mutter. "I thought mansions were only real in 90s dramas and fairy tales and stuff."

Isaiah suddenly looks uncomfortable, and I wish I could grab the words out of the air and push them back into my mouth.

"Look," he says pleadingly. "Try not to be weird about this. I don't bring people over because they always freak out. I figured you could be cool. About all this, I mean."

I nod. I understand what he's saying. I just don't know if I can actually play it cool. But I try.

"My mom will have a million questions for you—just a head's up. Since

I never bring people over, she'll want to know all about you and your life and your family. It's nothing personal; she just wants to make sure I'm not hanging around drug dealers or those people who dress as giant hoagies and dance on the sidewalks or anything." Isaiah laughs a little when he sees what a look of terror on my face must be. "Relax."

"Okay, I need you to understand something. My house looks nothing like this. I'm a little overwhelmed by all this." I hand my head a little.

This is why I don't have friends at school. Everybody at Riverside High lives in brick houses with SUVs and designer dogs. Their dads all wear ties to work, and their moms all wear Lululemon and have the same hairstyle. They all vacation in places like Aspen, or Europe, or Venice Beach.

Our lives are so different; the kids at school wouldn't even begin to understand how my life operates.

"I promise it's cool. We're just going to run upstairs so I can grab some clothes and my Xbox, and then we'll be gone. It'll be like we weren't even here." So, I follow Isaiah into his house.

To my surprise (and relief), there is no tuxedo-clad butler at the door or anything. The entryway is very formal, shiny tile gleaming like the foyer of a fancy hotel. I half expect to be turned away because I have no reservation.

"Mom, I'm home!" Isaiah announces into the cavernous hallway, his voice reverberating off walls and marble floors. This house (mansion?) is daunting. I would be overwhelmed to come home to this every day. I'm overwhelmed now.

"In here!" His mom calls back. We follow her voice into a large room covered in books. Shelves and shelves and shelves of books. I thought personal libraries like this only existed in Disney movies.

"Oh, I didn't realize you brought a friend." I'm sure she doesn't mean to, but I notice her eyeing my faded shirt and rumpled jeans.

She looks like every middle- to upper-middle-class woman over forty in Riverside. It's some kind of coming-of-age ceremony, I guess, but every woman over forty gets their hair cut into what Kayla calls "The Mane." They keep their hair at shoulder length, tease it into a general cloud shape, and meticulously dye it with blond, red, brown, and sometimes black steaks. I can imagine it becomes hard to find your mom in the supermarket when they all look alike—all with their new-money lion's manes.

"I'm Cade Swanson, ma'am." I extend my hand to her.

"The artist." She says a flicker of recognition crosses her face. She smiles a dry smile, and I'm not sure if she meant this as a question or not.

"Isaiah has told me about your work. If it's as good as he says, my husband and I may have some associates who are interested in buying some of your work."

The way she says associates unsettles me a little. Most people might say friends. But, despite this, his mom seems nice enough.

She gestures for me to sit in the studded leather armchair beside her. I oblige—mostly because I have manners—and know that I am silently agreeing to answer the multitude of questions on her tongue.

"So, Cade, tell me about yourself." I always hate this question because—honestly—what eighteen-year-old knows himself well enough to accurately identify himself?

"Well," I grasp for enough words to put together a complete sentence. "I like to draw."

I sound stupid, even to myself.

"I, um, I don't really know what to say." I cast my eyes toward the ground.

"Tell me about your family," she smiles at me. Isaiah huffs in the background as if he's already irritated with this whole situation.

"Well, my mom is the activities director at Golden Acres retirement center and the night manager at the Megamart by our house." I shrug, feeling embarrassed. Isaiah's mom probably doesn't work. She's probably the president of the Symphony League or the Daughters of the American Revolution or something.

"Well, your mother certainly keeps busy. How does she ever find time to get to the gym?" Isaiah's mom muses as if that's honestly the first concern in everybody's life. "And what about your father, dear? What does he do?"

"That's enough, mom." Isaiah sounds stern, irritated. "Can we go to Cade's house, now?"

"In a moment, sweetie," Mrs. Rosenthal's voice is sugar-sweet. "Now,

Cade, what were you saying about your dad?"

Isaiah opens his mouth to say something, but I have a feeling that we'll be held captive until I answer the question.

"He's an accountant. His firm, Swanson & Johnson, works for some of the big companies in town." I hate talking about my father. It makes me uncomfortable.

"Oh, yes. I should have seen the resemblance. You're Cole Swanson's boy. My husband's company uses your dad's firm. Do tell him I say hello."

I try to save face, mostly because I'm afraid the Earth will end before I'm allowed to leave this chair.

"I will," I smile.

"Alright, we should get going now," Isaiah says a little too loudly and a little too urgently. Before she can argue, I'm behind Isaiah on the staircase, taking them two at a time.

When we get to Isaiah's room, I'm shocked by the stark difference between the lavish, luxurious house and the minimalism of his room. Inside, Isaiah only has a simple desk with his computer, his bed, a nightstand, and a TV stand with a TV and his Xbox. Compared to the ostentatious house on the other side of the door, Isaiah's room is dizzyingly simple.

Isaiah begins gathering clothes and throwing them into a bag, opening his closet. He pulls a shirt off a hanger and inspects it.

"Will this fit you?" He tosses the shirt to me.

I run my hand over the buttons on the front as I look at the designer label on the inside. Calvin Klein. The tags are still hanging on it. This shirt, alone, will triple the value of my entire closet, maybe even my whole house.

I can't say anything, so I nod.

"Then it's yours. It's not really my style," he shrugs like it's nothing. Maybe to him, it is nothing. But it is now the nicest thing I own. I won't wear it until a really special occasion.

We climb back down the stairs and make our way to Isaiah's car. That beautiful car.

When Isaiah hands me the keys, it's like the heavens part. (I don't actually need the keys since it's a keyless ignition.) When I sit in the driver's seat, I swear the angels sing. And when I press the ignition and it's like an out-of-body experience.

I scoot the seat up, adjust the mirrors, and put the car—no, the work of art, the engineering marvel—in drive. Isaiah's car jumps to life at the slightest nudge of my foot.

I want so badly to take the longest way possible to my house. I want to drive to Oklahoma instead. I want to pay rent and live in this car.

In this moment, I feel powerful and invulnerable, and special. In this moment, I don't feel poor.

By the time we arrive at my house, two things have become apparent:

1. I am a horrible driver.
2. Isaiah has finally figured out just how different our worlds are.

"Welcome to my beyond humble abode." I'm no longer indestructible. I'm no longer powerful. Now, I'm just me—that pitiable boy from the wrong side of the tracks.

"Is your dad really an accountant?" He asks. I know he's trying to ask why we live in this neighborhood if my dad is all that successful.

"I mean, I've never heard you mention your dad the whole time we've been friends. I guess I didn't really think you had a dad."

"I don't," I hand him the keys and grab my backpack from the tiny, half-person-sized backseat.

I see the confusion on his face and can predict his next question.

"My parents are divorced," I explain before he can ask. "My father is an accountant; I wasn't lying. He just doesn't have anything to do with us."

It should be easier to talk about my parents and the divorce at this point. But it still feels like I've swallowed a baseball when I try to speak.

"He just walked out on us one day and never came back. He agreed to give my mom full custody of us in exchange for him not to pay child support or anything."

Isaiah's eyes grow enormous, the grey sky reflects off of his honey-colored irises.

"He traded his children for the ability to pocket his entire paycheck?" He sounds incredulous. He sounds disgusted.

And when he says it like that, I'm disgusted, too.

"He said he had a certain lifestyle to maintain," I shrug. I really don't want to talk about this anymore. And, yet, for some strange, masochistic reason, I want to keep talking about this. It's cathartic, I guess.

We don't ever talk about the divorce at home. Thomas never asks because he hardly remembers our father. And I can't talk to Mom because she either gets angry or cries. Kayla used to talk about it with me right after it happened, but people are so temporal. For her, it was out of sight, so it was out of mind.

"I try not to hate him because I know it's wrong. But I want to. We're his kids, and he knows nothing about us."

I see genuine remorse in Isaiah's eyes. Or pity. Maybe both. He doesn't know how to process all of this, so I just smile and shake my head.

"Don't worry about it. Let's go set up your Xbox."

When we get inside, the house smells amazing. I can't remember the last time my mom baked, but the whole house smells of butter and brown sugar and chocolate and childhood.

"Mom?" I call from the front door. It's not like Isaiah's house where it's actually possible to lose somebody. Our house consists of a tiny kitchen, a tiny living room, and three tiny bedrooms. Isaiah is so tall he can probably walk the entire length of my house in three strides.

"In here!" Mom calls from the kitchen. When we walk in, she's setting a plate of cookies on the kitchen table.

It's been so long since my mom baked that I'd forgotten how good she is at it. But she's the best. And I know it's some basic instinct for everybody to think that their mom is the best at everything, but my mom truly is the best.

Her smile lights up the faded yellow, very 70's kitchen. And not in the way Isaiah's smile brightens a room. My mom's smile is like sunshine and warmth. Her smile is like the sun itself. It's been so long since she's smiled like this. Her hair is down for the first time in months, and, for the first time, I notice just how much gray has crept its way into her raven hair.

"Isaiah," Her dazzling smile turns toward him. "It's so nice to meet you. I'm Teresa Swanson."

It still surprises me that my mom still uses my father's last name. Mom says that a woman only changes her name again once she's remarried. I not-so-secretly wish she'd change all of our names to Moreno, her maiden name.

"It's nice to meet you," Isaiah shakes her hand. He smiles his own warm, dazzling smile, and suddenly it's like I'm staring into the sun. It's like I'm staring into multiple suns, standing between my mom's and Isaiah's smiles, and I feel like I need to rub my eyes.

"Thank you for having me over this weekend. I promise I won't be any trouble." As if Isaiah could be any trouble if he tried.

As I watch my mom and Isaiah try to out-polite each other, I dive into one of my mom's homemade chocolate chip cookies. They taste like summertime. The flavors of chocolate and cinnamon and honey wash over me in a wave that brings me back to my childhood, to a time even before Thomas.

"This is so good," I tell my mom through a mouthful of cookie.

I offer Isaiah a cookie while shoving the rest of my cookie in my mouth. I'm acutely aware that I look like a Neanderthal, but I don't care. I'd drink milk out of the carton if not for Isaiah. Instead, I pour each of us a glass of milk.

"When Thomas gets off the school bus, I'm going to take him to the park to play for a little while, so you boys can have some time to yourselves."

It's only when Mom says this that I remember it's Friday and her only evening off all week. I wish she wouldn't feel obligated to take Thomas out, but I'm also grateful not to be Thomas duty, if even only briefly. I know that my mom will be working a sixteen-hour shift at Megamart tomorrow, and I'll have plenty of time to play father.

"Are you sure? It's been raining," I say, more out of obligation than genuine concern.

"You're so sweet," Mom reaches to ruffle my hair but thinks twice about it in front of company. "But we'll be fine. I think we could both benefit from a little bit of fresh air and whatever sunlight we can get."

In this moment, I can see my mom as the society wife she used to be—charming, endearing, and captivating. She wore black dresses and pearls, and my dad would whisk her away to nice dinners and fancy parties.

I used to stay up late, imagining what they were doing, my dad looking handsome in his suit and tie and my mom so stunning with her gleaming, raven hair. I always imagined crystal chandeliers, and velvet ropes,and VIP lists. I pictured my parents as celebrities, as small-town royalty. They were glamorous.

I used to wait for their headlights to filter in through my window before I'd close my eyes and pretend to be asleep. After they sent my babysitter home, mom would come in, smelling like a mixture of whatever restaurant they had gone to and Chanel No. 5. And she'd lean over my red race car bed and kiss my forehead and ruffle my hair. She'd whisper goodnight in my ear, and I'd have to fight my smile until she left the room. And then I'd fall asleep knowing that I had the best parents on Earth.

This is the woman I see right now when I look at my mom today.

The front door opens, and Thomas's loud singing draws me from my memories. He always sings loudly when he's happy. Today's song is "Here Comes the Sun" by The Beatles, and I mentally pat my own back on, helping to shape his excellent taste in music.

When he sees me, Thomas's eyes light up, and he sprints to give me a hug.

"I made a hundred on my spelling test!" He digs through his backpack and hands me a crumpled piece of notebook paper with a big gold star and a ruby red *100* written on it.

"Proud of you, buddy," I smile and turn to hang his test on the fridge. Behind me, I hear a loud gasp, and I can imagine Thomas's eyes popping out of his head.

"Bub! Who's the giant? Is this your friend?"

The kitchen explodes into laughter, and I turn to see a wide-eyed seven-year-old staring up at Isaiah as if he has just met Santa Claus.

Isaiah bends down to get eye-level with Thomas, and when he does, it looks like he's folded in on himself.

"I'm Isaiah," he smiles, extending his gargantuan hand to take my little brother's tiny one, and shakes it.

"How tall are you?"

"6'9"."

"Do you ever hit your head on things?"

"All the time."

"Did you come from the top of a beanstalk?"

My mom's laughter ends the conversation.

"That's enough, Thomas," she laughs. "Put your things in your room; we're going to the park. We're going to give Isaiah and Cade some time to play their games and have some fun."

She barely has time to finish her sentence before Thomas takes off at a sprint to his room.

"You mean, I get to play in the mud?" He seems so excited. I can't help but smile. For Thomas, it's easy. A kid can have fun in anything. The idea of playing in the mud is like Disney World for him.

When Mom and Thomas finally leave, I realize just how strange it is to be alone with him, with no escape route. What if he hates it here? What if he hates me here?

At school, bonds are built through mutual hatred for the same teacher and lunchroom trades. In my house, will these alliances hold? Or will he turn tail and run at the first opportunity?

Isaiah grabs his bag and Xbox and looks around our citrus-colored kitchen.

"So, where can I set this up?"

Well, he's not abandoning ship yet. That's promising.

I signal for him to follow me to my room. Only now, with Isaiah in tow, do I realize how disgusting our carpet is. It was beige once; you can tell near the baseboards. But now it's a putrid, grunge color.

"Watch it. There's a hole in the floor." I point to a sunken-in spot on the floor. "The landlord is supposed to be out to fix it." He's been "coming soon to fix it" for six months. But I don't say that. I don't want pity.

My room is tiny, I realize as I show Isaiah in. I have a little TV on a little dresser next to a little bed. It's like my room is the opening setting of a fairy tale or nursery rhyme.

On the tiny desk in the corner by the tiny closet, Isaiah eyes my latest project—a pencil drawing of Thomas asleep in his bed. I've been trying my hardest to make it realistic, like a black-and-white photograph, but I've been having trouble getting the folds in the blankets, and the shadows look right.

"Are you doing this for the art show? It's really good. You're so talented." He shakes his head like he's in awe.

"Yeah," I nod. "Thomas was just so cute, sprawled out with one leg out of the covers like that."

"Thomas," Isaiah sounds pensive. "Such a grownup name for a little boy. He doesn't prefer Tom or Tommy?"

I've never thought about this before, but it is unusual that Thomas goes by Thomas all the time. I've never tried to call him anything else. I don't even know if he would answer to anything else.

"I don't think so," I shrug, sitting on my bed. "He's kind of grown-up for a second-grader. But he is small." I catch myself smiling. Sometimes I think I forget that Thomas isn't my own child. We're supposed to fight and stuff, right? I'm supposed to resent him for taking away my only-child status. But I never have.

"Here, let me hook up my Xbox. Do you have a preference of game? Any preferred genre?" Isaiah wakes me from my thoughts.

I don't have a preference. I've never really played any video games. I could feel the heat rising in my cheeks, that panicky feeling that comes when I'm embarrassingly indecisive. Isaiah must have seen it on my face because he just smiles and hands me a controller.

"We're going to shoot some zombies."

Apparently, what he really means by this, is that he's going to shoot zombies while I fumble around with the concept of two joysticks and ultimately meet my demise in the first few seconds because I hit the wrong button, and instead of using my knife, I jump. Right onto an approaching zombie.

Isaiah laughs so hard I think he's going to cry or wet himself. Or both. Surprisingly, though, he manages to take out all of the enemies, and my character is revived for exactly thirteen seconds before I die again.

This time, it's my turn to laugh until tears roll down my face.

"I'm sorry," I say once I've caught my breath. "I apparently should not be allowed to touch this." I set my controller on the bed beside me as if it's made of delicate glass.

"It's cool. You just need to practice." Isaiah makes it look effortless. He's destroying droves of zombies and still manages to talk with me. "Maybe we can do this more often. Maybe by graduation, you'll be able to get to round two without dying."

Chapter Three

When Mom and Thomas come home a few hours later, Thomas is the most excited he's ever been. He comes bounding into my room and launches into the air. When he lands on my bed, he narrowly misses kicking me in the face.

"I wanna play." He is disgusting and smells like sweat and mud. I'm afraid to see the dirty imprint he's going to leave on my bed when he moves.

"Tell you what, go get cleaned up, and you can play with Isaiah." Before I'm finished, Thomas is a blur, running to his room to clean up.

"You're a good brother," Isaiah sounds wistful, smiling into the distance. His golden eyes glint in the light, and, for a moment, I think he's crying. He's not. "I always hoped my brother would treat me the way you treat Thomas."

I cock my head and try not to look as surprised as I feel.

"I didn't know you had a brother." Expect it comes out more like a question than the casual statement I intend it to be. I've always assumed that Isaiah is an only child. I mean, not that I've ever really pondered all that hard on it.

"Yeah. He's in the Marines now, so he's never around. He's five years older than us. And we've definitely never been as close as you and Thomas." He shrugs like it's no big deal, but I've grown to realize when people want to talk about something, it's a big deal.

"He and my sister are twins," He continues. I had no idea he had a sister, either, but I don't say that. "And I guess twins are complete together. They were always inseparable and didn't need me. Lizzie was always nice; she was always the big sister type. I was her adorable little brother. But Logan was always so distant. They both live in North Carolina now. Logan got stationed there, so Lizzie found a college near his base and moved with him."

I guess the protector in me expects him to crumple, but he doesn't and just sets his jaw and looks at the TV. In this moment, I can see just how handsome Isaiah is, and I wonder why he doesn't have a girlfriend. And I wonder if he had a girlfriend, would he still want to hang out with me, or would I be booted to the curb by him, too.

And then I realize just how self-centered I am. Here's Isaiah baring his heart to me, and I'm just thinking about myself.

"That sucks, man," I say because when I don't know what to say, I state the obvious. "I'm sorry."

Isaiah just shrugs, then hits me with that million-watt smile.

"It's okay. It's just nice to see you guys together. I thought siblings like that only existed on 90's TV shows or something."

"Okay, I'm clean!" Thomas appears in the doorway in clean clothes, and I'm thankful for the interruption. I was out of things to say.

When he crashes into my bed this time, he still smells a little like a wet dog, but at least he won't leave a muddy, child-shaped outline on my bed.

"You guys play," I stand and walk toward the hallway. "I'm going to see if Mom needs any help in the kitchen. She hasn't cooked in a long time."

When I get into the kitchen, I hear clanging and clattering from underneath the counter. Mom has practically wedged her body into the cabinets where we keep the baking pans.

"Cade, do you know where the large casserole dish is?" By the way she's shouting, she doesn't know that I've come into the kitchen.

"It's in the dishwasher," A loud, hollow thud tells me I've surprised her. My mom has always been easily startled; it's a wonder she hasn't died of a heart attack with two sons.

I open the dishwasher and hand her the bright red casserole dish. The dishwasher hasn't actually worked since we moved into this house four years ago. That's another thing the landlord has been promising to fix for a long time.

Instead, we use it as a drying rack when we hand wash the dishes. It has always seemed to make sense to me until this very moment, as I'm handing my mom an old pan from a broken machine. I bet Isaiah's mom has never had to hand wash a dish in her entire life.

"You're not in there playing with your friend?" Mom asks as she takes the pan from me.

The kitchen smells like tomatoes and garlic, and there's a pot on the stove bubbling with red sauce. On the counter are ingredients for lasagna, and I'm suddenly overcome by nostalgia. Mom hasn't made lasagna in ages because it was my father's favorite food. I've missed the way it makes our whole house smell.

"I came to see if you needed any help with dinner. Isaiah and Thomas are playing right now."

"I'm going to have to get counseling for poor Isaiah, now, being in there alone with your little brother." She laughs as she fills a big pot with water for noodles. "He's a nice guy. Isaiah, I mean."

I just nod because I know that it's true.

"What does Kayla think of him? Do they get along?" She's now chopping vegetables with the speed and precision of one of those television chefs. It's always kind of mesmerizing to watch her in the kitchen. It's like a perfectly choreographed dance. She makes everything look so easy, so effortless.

"Yeah, I guess." I shrug because I'm not totally sure. "We hang out at school sometimes, but they don't really spend a lot of time together."

Mom just smiles at me, but I can see in her eyes that she's contemplating something. I don't ask because I know that she'll eventually tell me what's bothering her. She always does.

"Are you and Kayla fighting?" She finally asks with a furrowed brow.

"No. Not really," I shrug again. "She just has a new boyfriend-ish thing. Guy. I don't know. Anyway, it's the same stuff she always does when she starts a new fling."

It's true; we're not fighting. I'm too passive-aggressive for us to actually fight. And Kayla doesn't mean to hurt my feelings; she's just trying to find her own happiness.

"You don't have to stay in here and help me." Mom finally says when she sees that I'm all talked out. "I cooked without your help for a long time before you were born. I'm sure I can manage tonight."

She ruffles my hair and nods in the direction of my room. I often think about telling her that I'm too old for her to rub my head like that, but it seems to make her happy.

When I get back to my room, Thomas and Isaiah have abandoned the video game altogether and are play-fighting. I catch myself smiling—almost weepy—at how good Isaiah is with Thomas. This is one of those moments when I feel more like Thomas's parent than his brother, and his giggles fill me with joy.

Isaiah practically overpowers my tiny room with his presence, his height, his bellowing laughter, and that giant smile. He looks like a seven-foot-tall kid with Thomas climbing him like a tree.

"You're back!" Thomas squeals from his perch on Isaiah's shoulders. And then he wraps his arms around Isaiah's head in a tight headlock.

"I'm winning!" Thomas shouts through giggles. "He's gonna tap out soon!"

The next time Isaiah's head is visible, he looks like a swimmer taking a breath.

"Alright!" He laughs. "Alright, I give!"

"I told you I'd win!" Thomas roars triumphantly. Without warning, he launches himself off of Isaiah's shoulders and onto my bed, landing with a little bounce and panting from exhaustion.

Isaiah's face is as red as a cherry, making his blonde hair look bright yellow. He's doing some strange combination of panting and laughing. When the red finally subsides, he looks at me, golden eyes sparkling.

"If you do this all the time, why aren't you on the school wrestling team? There's no way anyone is as strong as Thomas. You'd win every time."

We all sit for a moment in contented silence, smiles stuck on our faces. I keep looking from Isaiah to Thomas, thinking about how different Kayla and Isaiah are. When Kayla's over, she seems like Thomas is a giant imposition.

Granted, her sisters are giant impositions. Whenever I'm at her house, they always follow us around and stare at me with their mouths open. And they demand all of our attention. Kayla says her sisters think I'm cute, making a grand total of two people who think I'm cute. But they're nine and eleven, so I'm not entirely sure their opinions count.

"Do you want to come live with us, Isaiah?" Thomas asks, finally breaking the silence. "You can stay in my room."

"I would love to come live in your room," Isaiah laughs. "But I think my mom would miss me. So, I'll just have to visit a lot." He casts a glance at me, smiling broadly.

I could get used to Isaiah visiting a lot. It's nice having him here and just having fun. He doesn't make me feel uncomfortable being in my house, despite the hole in the floor and the broken dishwasher, and the peeling paint in the bathroom. He just seems to be in his element anywhere he goes.

"Boys!" Mom's voice calls from the kitchen. "Dinner's ready! Wash up and come eat!"

My mom's cooking is as delicious as I remember—it's so rare we get a full meal and not something boxed, quick, and easy these days. By the time we're finished eating, I'm so full I can barely walk. Thomas, Isaiah, and I shovel away two dozen cookies between the three of us, and that was after devouring half of a huge lasagna. I won't be surprised if I'm sick later.

"I always said I wanted three boys," my mom laughs as she surveys the chaos left behind. "But I'm afraid three would eat me out of house and home. Good thing I hid a couple of dozen cookies in the pantry for you boys to snack on tomorrow while I'm at work."

This is the first time I've thought about the amount of food Mom prepared. I'm curious how she could afford to splurge on such a big meal. The fresh vegetables she used in the sauce were expensive, and I know that she had to buy eggs, butter, and chocolate chips for the cookies.

But I don't ask because I know it'll embarrass her—and probably Isaiah—and she really hates when I worry about money. She says it's not the business of a child to worry about adults' finances.

Isaiah and I help clean up after dinner before going back to my room.

Once the door is shut, we both plop down on the ground, our backs propped against my short, twin-sized bed. Our breathing is labored after eating so much, and the last thing I want to do is fail miserably at video games.

So, Isaiah digs through his bag and pulls out a battered old DVD copy of *The Blair Witch Project*. The iconic cover has always frightened me, with the scared-looking girl and the trees over her head. I don't watch movies, but I don't tell Isaiah that. Tonight, I'm game for anything.

Okay. Maybe not anything. Halfway through the movie, when Mom opens my door to leave extra blankets and tell us good night, I nearly jump out of my skin. I didn't think people legitimately wet themselves when they're scared, but I get it now. I nearly did.

Before I know it, it's 11:00, and I'm exhausted. Thomas's cries fill the room, and I stand to check on him.

"Thomas has night terrors," I explain to Isaiah on my way out of the room. "If you're tired, you can sleep on my bed. I'll take the floor."

When I get to Thomas's room, I instinctively take his hand and run the other through his hair.

I get so frustrated sometimes for Thomas. He should be able to sleep like anybody else. I know that he doesn't sleep well through his bad dreams. When he has multiple bad nights in a row, his skin starts to look yellow, and he gets dark rings around his eyes, like the ones my mom permanently sports lately.

"You don't deserve this," I whisper into the dark, shaking my head. And then I think about how selfish I am to be planning on leaving to go to school out of town next year. Mom and Thomas need me. I can't leave them next year. Who would tuck Thomas in every night and make sure his homework's done?

When the yelling has stopped, and it looks as though Thomas is relaxed again, I make my way back to my bedroom to find Isaiah on the floor, buried under the heap of blankets Mom dropped off earlier.

"Is he okay?"

"He's fine. He just has night terrors. They're not uncommon," I say, repeating what the doctor said when we could afford to go to the doctor.

"Why are you on the floor? I told you that you could have the bed."

"No offense," Isaiah laughs from under his mound of blankets. "But I'm not a leprechaun. My feet hang off your bed like five inches."

I'm so tired, I don't even change out of my school clothes. I just fall into bed. My bed smells like sweat, and mud, and Isaiah's cologne, and I can feel a smile cross my face as I slip into sleep.

Chapter Four

When Monday rolls around, I'm still riding the high of the fantastic weekend. I text Kayla early to make sure she'll pick me up, so I can hear all about her date, and she can tell me all about her weekend. It's been years since I've been this excited for a Monday. Maybe I'm sick.

When Kayla pulls up to my house, I run out to meet her, for once ignoring my rumpled appearance. So, what if my clothes have wrinkles? It's high school, not Milan fashion week.

"You're smiling," Kayla observes cautiously. "Did your plan to take over the world finally work or something?" She laughs then speeds out of my driveway.

"Just had a good weekend. That's all," I say. Then I tell her all about it. About driving Isaiah's car and being really bad at games and nearly (but not quite) shrieking at *The Blair Witch Project*. I tell her about the next day when Isaiah decided to take Thomas and me for burgers at the diner by our house instead of eating leftovers like we normally do on Saturdays. I tell her about how much fun I had, and when I can finally say no more, I just keep smiling.

"Sounds like you had a nice date, then," Kayla gibes.

"Hey, now," I act offended. "But, speaking of dates, how was yours? Are you the future Mrs. Cameron Mathis?"

I know this is the only reason she even mentioned the word *date—Kayla's* manipulative like that. And judging by the smile she's trying to conceal, it must have gone very well.

"It was wonderful, Cade," she says as if she's auditioning to be Broadway's next Cinderella. "Dinner was delicious. We went to that new steakhouse that just opened up. He apparently knows the owner; we didn't even have to wait when we got there. Our table was already ready for us! Then we went to the movies. The movie was horribly boring. We left halfway through and went to walk around the park."

She seems so blissful, talking about her date. She has that new-relationship glow, the one she gets every time she starts dating a new guy she's been chasing for a while. She looks happy.

And beautiful. Another telltale sign that her date went well is that she's wearing makeup. Kayla's naturally pretty; she always has been. But when she's in a relationship, she's a knockout. She fixes her hair every morning, does her makeup, and wears nice clothes. I've always wondered why she didn't do this when she was trying to attract a boyfriend, but she always says that she has too much respect for herself to try to get a date based on her looks.

I get that, I guess. I mean, I'm not getting a date anytime soon based on my looks, so that's nothing I've ever had to worry about.

"So, are you guys an official couple?" I ask, already knowing the answer. The car wouldn't smell like Clinique Happy if she were still single.

"We are," she grins widely. "I wanted to call you and tell you everything yesterday, but I didn't want to disrupt your amazing weekend with Isaiah." I can hear disdain in her voice. "I didn't even know you two hung out, except at school."

I should have expected her to be mad, I guess, but it somehow still takes me by surprise. I honestly don't know why she's upset or why she has the right to be upset. I definitely wasn't a part of her weekend planning. And I was supposed to be.

"We don't," I shrug, knowing that I'm being passive-aggressive. "I mean, we didn't. That was the first time." *I'm allowed to have other friends*, I think, but I don't say. That would be bad.

"You were busy this weekend. Why's it matter that I hung out with Isaiah?" I feel like we're talking in circles and getting nowhere.

"I had a date. I thought you'd be happy for me, Cade. I thought you'd care." Her voice has reached a pitch that could shatter glass. When she's mad, her voice always gets higher, not louder.

"I thought you were my best friend. I thought you were supposed to be happy for me," she shrills.

I feel something inside me snap. I want to punch something. I want to bail out of her car and find a new way to school.

"Yeah? Well, I thought I was your best friend, too. But if I were, I wouldn't have been bumped for your date. You didn't even consider me, did you?" I notice that we are parked in Kayla's parking spot at school for the first time.

I've never snapped at Kayla like this before. I've never actually let her know she's hurt me before. It's never been worth it to me to be lonely before. Because, until recently, if I didn't have Kayla, I'd have nobody. It makes me wonder what the fear of loneliness has stopped people from doing.

"Screw your best day ever," I spit, throwing open my door and heading into school alone.

The halls are already cramped and crowded, booming with Monday morning chatter. Today, unlike most days, I don't even stop by my locker before going to the art room.

I'm glad to find Mr. Camplin already in his classroom when I get there. I need to paint. I need to do something to avoid punching a solid cinder block wall. I don't want to tell Mr. Camplin that I can't afford paint, so I just tell him I don't have any.

When I finally get to a canvas, I let my body do what it wants. Before I realize it, I've filled the canvas with varying shades of orange and red, like flames licking up the canvas.

It's not long before I feel a presence hovering over my shoulder. When I turn my head, I see Mr. Camplin surveying my work. He has that gleam in his eye that he gets just before he challenges his students.

"This is very interesting, Cade," he says, surveying. "But where are you going with this?"

"Where am I going with what?"

"With your art," he nods to the canvas. "Your art always has direction. I'm curious to see where this one will leave."

As I regard my own work, I understand what he means. Everything I create always has a focus. It may not have a deep meaning, but there's always a focus. But does my art *have* to go anywhere? Artists paint things solid colors all the time, lately, and pass it off as "art." They slap on ridiculous, nonsense names like *Blue Largo* and sell them from high prices.

But even as I ponder this, I can already see the direction this painting is taking. I can see where I want to overlay the silhouettes of people dancing through the flames.

When I set to work, Mr. Camplin returns to his desk to finish getting ready for the day. Another presence takes up residence behind me as I begin adding black-brown human figures to my canvas.

"Very tribal-looking," Isaiah's low voice says from behind me. "It's interesting. I've never seen you paint before; I don't think. Not on your own, I mean."

It's true. I've never painted on my own before—not without an assignment to guide me. It's not my favorite medium, and it's expensive. I can't afford paints just for fun. I'm technically stealing school resources, but I know Mr. Camplin won't mind.

"Yeah, I'm trying something new," I shrug, adding the final touches to what I can do for the moment. This is why I hate paint. You can't do everything you want all at once. It takes time to create the things you see in your head. With pencil, I can work straight through, if I want.

"Hey, my mom wanted to know if you could come over this afternoon. I showed her a picture of your drawing of Thomas. I, uh, hope you don't mind." He looks sheepish. "Anyway, she wants to meet with you. She thinks some of her former clients might be interested in your work."

I feel a mixture of betrayal, and confusion, and excitement rise in me. Betrayal because he showed somebody my art without my consent. Confusion because I can't imagine his mom having ever worked in a setting where she would have had clients. And excitement because if these people genuinely are interested in buying my work, I could finally afford the supplies I need to create the art I've always dreamed of.

I don't know how long I've been staring at him with my mouth half open until I say something.

"I, well, that. Uh. Yes? Yes. I sure. Can. Can over. I can." I'm not making even a little bit of sense, so I take a deep breath and try again. "If you don't mind being my ride, I'd love to meet with her."

And, just like that, my mood has turned completely around. Though I'm still angry at Kayla, I'm not seething. I can compartmentalize.

By the end of class, I'm already counting down the hours until this special meeting with Mrs. Rosenthal. Riverside isn't a big city by any means; it's nothing compared to Seattle or New York, where artists can make a good living. But there are plenty of rich people with old money. Maybe they'd be willing to support a near-starving artist.

On my way out of the classroom, I stop by my portfolio and rifle through the works I've collected. I make sure not to grab my best works; I'm selfishly saving them for the upcoming State Art Show. So, none of my favorite pieces can be sold.

Once I've collected a fistful of drawings, Isaiah and I make our way to our second-hour classes. Kayla doesn't meet us in the hallway. I wouldn't have expected her to because of her new relationship status. But after our fight this morning, she definitely won't be joining us anytime soon. And she won't have to *pretend* to ignore me in chemistry or at lunch.

And by lunch, my predictions have come true. Kayla has not so much as breathed in my direction. Her blue eyes have not even accidentally fallen on me. And I feel sick. I hate fighting with anybody. I'm incredibly non-confrontational, sometimes to my detriment. I just hate arguing. It makes me feel like I've done something wrong, even when I haven't.

When Isaiah sits down beside me at our table, I haven't touched my pizza.

"You okay?" He asks, an eyebrow arched in concern.

I shrug in acknowledgment, but I'm not totally sure. I don't want Kayla mad at me, but I'm not ready to end our fight. Sometimes I deserve to stay angry. This is one of those times.

"What's going on?" He asks through a mouthful of food. I'm glad to know *his* appetite is just fine.

I shake my head but decide to tell him anyway.

"Kayla and I are fighting," I explain. And without meaning to, I all but fall apart, opening up about all of my frustrations with Kayla. I tell him about how we fought over my spending time with him and how I've been mad at her for some time.

And as I talk, it's like I'm literally venting. Like someone has popped a hole in me, and I'm letting out all the pressure built up in me. When the steam in me is all gone, I feel all the better for it. Maybe I should talk things out more often.

"I'm sorry I caused an issue between you two," Isaiah sounds genuinely hurt.

"What? No!" I try to backpedal. "No. Kayla's the issue, not you. She just can't stand that I have somebody new to spend time with. Like I'm supposed to wait for her to come crawling back every time things go sour."

"Your language changes so much when you're mad at her." Isaiah is quiet in his observation as if afraid I'm going to turn my anger towards him. "You're so disdainful. Not that your feelings aren't valid, but maybe you don't see the whole picture because you're a part of that whole picture."

Isaiah fiddles idly with his napkin while I wait for something to qualify his statement. For a moment, he says nothing, only leans forward and takes a drink from his straw. He's done this since I met him; he doesn't pick up his soda can. Instead, he leans forward and sucks on the straw while the can is on the table. This is made even more comical by his towering height. He looks like Quasimodo trying to drink like that.

"It's just that sometimes you talk about what Kayla does to you but think about what she does to herself." He looks uncomfortable like he regrets saying every word that comes out of his mouth. "She's seventeen and can't find her identity alone, so she finds her identity in her boyfriends. She spends her time seeking the approval of guys to feel as if she's earned her own approval."

I blink hard and glance at Kayla, whose body language says Cameron has just made a joke she doesn't even find a little funny, so she's laughing twice as hard to appease him. I've never considered this idea before, but it makes sense, I guess.

"And through all the boyfriend changes, you're her stability. You're the guy who always approves of her." Isaiah shrugs, and I know that he's all talked out now.

That's the thing about Isaiah. For the most part, he says exactly what needs to be said, and then he's done. No more.

Is that the reason Kayla expects me never to change? Is that why she was so upset that I was unavailable for her to call this past weekend? *It's a dumb reason*, I think. *But it's a reason, at least.*

I'm not entirely sure that I am ready to forgive Kayla yet, despite Isaiah's pressing. I'm sad for her, but that doesn't mean she can be a jerk to me. Does she really hate who she is so much that she relies on others to define who she is?

The bell rings before I can ponder this anymore. I shove as much of my pizza into my mouth as I can, wash it down with a carton of milk, and rush to class.

I have trouble concentrating on my afternoon classes. Between the excitement of meeting with Isaiah's mom about possibly selling my artwork and Isaiah's observations about Kayla bouncing around in my head, to say I'm distracted is an understatement. I can hardly manage to speak when my government teacher calls on me.

When the final bell comes, I'm grateful that this signals the end of my anticipation rather than the end of school. I collect my things quickly and begin to make my way through the hallways, activating my superpower to disappear in the sea of teenagers.

When Kayla passes me, I'm so excited about my meeting with Isaiah's mom that I forget we're fighting.

"Kayla!" I call into the crowd, sticking my hand up to wave at her. Apparently, my superpower is working exceptionally well because she doesn't acknowledge me.

Or, for the first time in our friendship, she has blatantly ignored me. We have never ignored each other. That's a kind of unwritten rule among best friends, I thought. Because even though we're fighting, reaching out like that could mean something important. This time it means something important.

"Kayla!" I try again, louder, more forcefully. I still get no response. Actually, no response would have been better than what actually happens.

"It must suck to be so poor that you have to ride the bus to school every day," Kayla says to the person she's walking with, the slightest curl of a sneer at the corner of her mouth. She casts one last glance toward me before walking past me. The stake through the heart. She has gone too far. She had no right to say that; I can't help that I'm poor. *I can't help that I'm poor.* This thought echoes through my head.

By the time I get to Isaiah's locker, I'm furious. I've never been so mad. I thought this morning was the angriest I've ever been. But that was mere annoyance compared to the fiery feeling I feel now.

It's not until Isaiah looks at me, horrified, that I'm aware of the tears on my face. I'm not crying, not really. I'm just so mad that my emotions are materializing into tears. Red-eyed, fury-inspired tears.

"I'm fine," I hold my hand up to stop him from asking the obvious. "I'll tell you about it in the car. I'll wait for you in the parking lot."

Once I'm out of the building, and away from the scrutiny of my classmates' eyes, I let my shoulders drop. I let the full impact of what Kayla said hit me. And I want to cry because I feel violated. But I don't. I didn't cry when my dad left, and I won't cry now. I will not show weakness, and I will not weep.

I hear Isaiah's car unlock, and I look up to see him walking across the lawn between the parking lot and the school. I climb into his passenger seat and breathe in deep.

Count to ten, I tell myself. And I do. I'm not sure it helps, so I do it a second, a third, and a fourth time. By the fifth time, Isaiah has made it into the car and puts a large cardboard tube in my lap. My drawings. I had completely forgotten to grab them, even after I made sure to pack them up this morning.

"I won't ask if you don't want to talk about it," Isaiah says kindly, starting his car and putting it into drive. I consider saying nothing, but I feel that Isaiah deserves an explanation.

"I'm sorry," I say, at last, staring at the road ahead. "Kayla just-" I don't know what to say. Maybe I deserved it for my *screw your best day, ever* comment. But nobody deserves to be made fun of for their lot in life. *Nobody.*

"She just said something to really hurt me. I got so mad that I actually, literally saw red. I guess it's not really a big deal, but to me, at the moment, it was."

We sit in silence for the rest of the ride to Isaiah's house. The closer we get to his mansion, the more nervous I become. My thoughts race with images of their massive study—cavernous—and Isaiah's mom sitting on her studded leather throne of an armchair. Maybe she's not a monster or some great ruler, but this certainly felt like preparing to enter the belly of the beast.

When we pull up to the circle drive in front of Isaiah's house, I can feel myself blanch. I don't know how to market my art; I barely know how to make it. It practically makes itself.

"Dude, calm down. It's just my mom," Isaiah chuckles. "It's not like you're going to court or anything."

I breathe deeply—trying to steel myself—as I follow Isaiah. This time, he doesn't lead me to the dark, wood-walled library but the kitchen. The tiled walls are so white I'm nearly dazzled. Floor-to-ceiling windows let in so much sunlight I might as well be standing outside. Everything in the room is all robin's egg blue, and lemon yellow, and crisp white. It's all so bright. As if the room were inspired by Isaiah's smile. Or maybe it's the other way around. It would be impossible for even me to disappear in this warm, welcoming room.

Isaiah's mom is sitting at the counter, cutting the stems off flowers and arranging them in a vase. She's wearing an oversized button-down shirt and looks like she belongs in The Hamptons, not Texas. It's far too hot here to dress for gardening like that.

"Cade Swanson!" She exclaims when she looks up. She smiles a practiced party hostess smile at me and stands to give me an uncomfortable, stiff-armed hug. A handshake would have sufficed.

"I'm so glad you came to meet with me. I hope you brought some artwork for me to look at. But before we talk business, can I get you anything? Isaiah told me how your mom had cookies and milk waiting on you when you got home." She's now talking so fast that my head spins. "That's just so quaint; I love it. I was never a natural homemaker like that."

That's obvious from her arrangement of roses and carnations. And something about the way she says *quaint* unsettles me, but I ignore it. As she's talking, she pulls a jug of milk from a stainless-steel refrigerator as big as my bedroom. She retrieves a bag of chocolate chip cookies from the pantry, and though they are the name brand, they're nothing like my mom's made-with-love-and-the-good-vanilla cookies.

I politely accept what she offers, but I'm too nervous to eat. All this meeting business has had my stomach in knots all day.

"I brought some of my drawings," I tell her after an uncomfortable silence. "I don't really know where to go from here."

"Isaiah, sweetie, do you mind leaving me and Cade alone to talk business?" Mrs. Rosenthal asks.

I feel terror rise in my stomach, all the way up to my throat.

"No," I can hear the panic in my own voice. "No, he can stay."

I'm sure I sound desperate. But I'm not sitting through this alone. I'm already not good at talking to adults, much less ones I really want to impress. I try to beg him with my eyes to stay. He does.

Slowly, I begin to unroll the drawings I stored in the cardboard tube. I lay them out neatly in front of myself. Sometimes it's nice to see my old works laid out like this. To remember when I created these works. Each drawing has a story and memories attached to it.

If somebody buys my art, will they figure out its story? Will they care to figure it out?

"These are very good," Mrs. Rosenthal says in a voice that seems like she should be stroking her chin. "None of them are as good as the one Isaiah showed me, but these are very good."

She speaks in a deep alto voice with an affected accent, the kind of accent rich people on sit-coms have.

"These two, yes." She's speaking in sentence fragments; nothing she's saying makes very much sense. "Oh, yes. David would love this one, for sure."

She touches each drawing as if trying to read their auras or something. Her eyes are glistening like a mad man's. When she finally regains her composure, she looks at me with an eerily calm face. Her lips make a perfect line across her face, not smiling or frowning. She sits across from me, a strange, distant look in her eye.

"I'd like to act as your agent." She says in a very business-like voice. "I can negotiate the sale of your art and things of that nature. Maybe I can even get you a show at my friend Martin's gallery. He owns the gallery downtown."

I'm nearly stammering before she finishes speaking.

"I've never done anything like that. I'm not even good enough for that. The gallery downtown? Do you really think?"

I'm almost completing my sentences. Almost. It's all coming out so fast and jumbled that even I can't really understand what I'm saying.

"Nonsense," Mrs. Rosenthal says, shaking her head. "You're plenty talented. I can't make you any promises on an entire show, but I can definitely get you some space in the gallery. Martin owes me a favor."

My own space in a gallery? I wouldn't even know what to do with my own space. My body is practically vibrating with energy and anticipation. What 18-year-old gets his own space in a professional, high-end gallery?

My reflecting is interrupted by the thud of a notebook. Mrs. Rosenthal opens the cover to reveal pages of checks, those large ones like businesses use.

"Here's what I'm willing to offer," she says in a business-like tone. "I believe in you. I believe in young talent. I'm prepared to pay you one thousand five hundred dollars for the artwork you've brought today."

I hate when people are pretentious enough to say it like that. Why not just say fifteen-hundred dollars, like every average human being? Wait. $1500? For my drawings? One is literally just a bowl of fruit.

"I won't make any profit," she continues. "I intend to sell these pieces for

$200 and these for $150." She points to drawings as she speaks.

"I just want to work as a middleman for you. Gain you some exposure. My son says you're his best friend, and I'll do anything to help his friends become successful. Teach a man to fish and all that."

It's only now that I realize my mouth is open. I'm so stunned by all this that I have forgotten how to speak. First, I never realized that Isaiah considered me his best friend. But, also, there is a check sitting in front of me for $1500, and it has my name on it. I can cash this check today and buy the watercolor pencils I want. I can buy paints. I can buy the supplies to make the art I've always wanted to make.

"If you have any other pieces to sell, please do not hesitate to bring them to me. In this city, there is no shortage of art patrons and supporters."

A finality in her voice tells me our meeting is over. I look to Isaiah, still shell-shocked by the check and the reeling feeling that I may have gallery space. After a moment of total silence, Isaiah nods toward the door to signal that it's time to go.

"Okay," he says breathily. "I'm going to run Cade home."

"Thank you, Mrs. Rosenthal," I finally find the words to say. "Thank you so much for your help. For everything."

Isaiah all but pushes me out of the door before I can become a babbling wreck.

By the time I get into Isaiah's car, I'm clutching the check tightly, holding it in front of my face. I'm staring at it like I'm Charlie Bucket, and it's my golden ticket. Mrs. Rosenthal has given me the keys to my own chocolate factory, the keys to my own future.

Chapter Five

When Isaiah drops me off at my house, I'm loaded down not only with my school stuff but also with all of the art supplies I have ever wanted. I have so many bags Isaiah has to help me carry them in.

Ideas are already swimming around my head. I want to lock myself in my room and work all night, but I know I will have to take care of Thomas and help him with his homework. But maybe I will be able to fit some creativity in around that.

"I was getting worried. You're home late," Mom says as I come in.

I didn't notice how late I was; I was so caught up in my new business ventures. Thomas is already at the kitchen counter, his homework folder open and spelling words waiting to be practiced.

"I tried to call your cell phone, but it does nobody any good when it's left in your bedroom while you're at school." This is the closest thing to a lecture I've ever gotten from my mom. It's half-joking, but I know she's serious. I cut it awfully close, and she'll need to leave soon for her shift at the Megamart.

Her eyes widen when she sees all the bags and canvases. She sets her jaw, trying to save face, but I've seen the anger. Or was it shock? She'll wait for Isaiah to leave, then I'll likely get an actual lecture. Unless I beat her to the punch in explaining where all of this came from. So, I see Isaiah out and try to do just that.

"Cade, where did all of this stuff come from?" She asks, keeping her voice level, but I hear the strain. Why is she so freaked out?

"I sold some art," I can't control the smile on my face. "Isaiah's mom had some friends who wanted to buy my art."

So, I tell her about my afternoon and my meeting with Mrs. Rosenthal. And the check. And the trip to the art supply store. And the watercolor pencils. And the new pencils and paints and charcoals and pastels.

But despite my excitement, Mom does not look impressed.

"You sold your art?" She sounds angry. "What about your art show?"

"I didn't sell all of my drawings. I saved the best of them for the show." I shake my head, still confused by the anger in her voice.

"But what will happen to you if the school finds out? What if you're disqualified from being able to be considered for awards?"

Why would I be disqualified?

"I made $1500 today, Mom. And I can work from here and take care of Thomas like you need me to. This is ideal for everybody. Why aren't you happy for me?" I hear myself sounding like a poorly-scripted teen movie, but I don't care. I finally understand that whiny tone that bottle-blond protagonists get in movies like that. Because it really sucks that I've done something so amazing, and my mom can't even be happy for me.

"I've got to get to work. I don't have time to discuss this with you. I'm already late because I was waiting for you." The worry lines on her face are deeper than I've ever seen them. As she flies out the door, I say the only thing that comes to mind.

"Don't take it out on me that you're late."

I just want to scream. I want to punch something. Why does everybody want to push me over the edge today?

Thomas starts to ramble about his day, and I try to listen, but I'm too absorbed in the art floating around my head. Something about seeing red inspires me.

"Come tell me about it in my room," I usher Thomas as I sit down at the easel in my bedroom. "You want to draw, too?" I offer him some paper and colored pencils before I set to work on my own painting.

I allow myself to fall into the trance that overtakes me when I sit down to my art. As if by magic, my hands start to work, painting on their own. As Thomas keeps talking about his day, my canvas starts to fill with grays and blacks, shadows in a dark room. The shape of a face emerges from the shadows, and well before I add any details, I can see where blue eyes and a round nose are going to appear.

I can see this picture in my head. And for the first time, it's coming out exactly as I intend it to. I didn't have to sketch it first. I didn't have to plan meticulously. I just had to do it.

By the time I'm ready for a break, it's 6:30, my stomach is growling, and Thomas has retreated to his room to work on homework. I leave my easel—my butt sore from sitting for so long—and survey the kitchen for something for dinner. Nothing looks good. You can only eat blue box macaroni so many times before it makes you want to barf.

"Hey, Thomas!"

Thomas comes running like a puppy, and I can't tell if he's excited about anything in particular or just because I'm showing him attention.

"We don't have any food I feel like eating. What do you think about ordering out? Would you prefer pizza or Chinese?"

Thomas's eyes grow as big as saucers. It's an extremely rare occasion that we eat out, so moments like this are magical for him. He looks like this is the most difficult question anyone has ever asked him. Finally, though, his eyes sparkle brighter, and his lips open into a toothy grin.

"Can we get cinnamon sticks? I can pay for those." He reaches into his pocket and withdraws a wad of crumpled dollar bills and some quarters. Instinctively, I ruffle his hair and laugh.

"Hang on to your money, kid. Tonight's on me. I can even swing cinnamon sticks." I pick up my phone to search for the number. "Where'd you get all that money, anyway?"

"I sold mom's cookies. My friends paid me a dollar for a cookie. We're out of cookies, but I have twelve dollars now." He shrugs, trying to play it off, but I can tell he's embarrassed to admit this.

"What do you need twelve dollars for, buddy?" I crouch to ask him this. He's always more responsive if I'm on his level. "You know you can ask me when you need money. I've always got some stuck back in case you need it."

Thomas won't meet my gaze now. Instead, he stares at his feet, bouncing lightly on his heels.

"It's not for me," he shakes his head. "I heard you ask mom for art stuff, so I wanted to help. But then you came home with all of that stuff, so I thought maybe I could keep it."

I think he says I'm sorry, but it's too distorted by a chest-rattling sob for me to be sure. Before I can even realize what's happening, Thomas is all but a puddle, tears streaming freely down his face.

"Hey. Hey. It's okay, buddy," I grab his arm gently. "Why the tears? I'm not mad. It's so nice of you to think of me."

It's times like this I have to fight my anger at my mom and father. They should be here to take care of Thomas. They're the parents; I'm not equipped to deal with tears, or night terrors, or bed-wetting. Brothers aren't supposed to do that.

"Listen, I'm not mad, but promise me you won't do that anymore. You know Mom and I will take care of you." He falls into my shoulder, and I can feel snot and tears soak my shoulder. I don't know what else to do, so I just wrap my arms around him and pat his back. I feel like that's how Mom would handle this.

"Tell you what. Mom's birthday is coming up. Hold onto your money, and we can buy her something pretty together." Thomas nods his tiny head against my shoulder, then sniffs that wet sniff that comes at the end of a hard cry.

"Now, I'm going to order the pizza. Extra anchovies on your half?" I smirk, picking up my phone again. Thomas's noises of disgust and loud objections tell me he's feeling better.

Thirty minutes later, a ring of the doorbell announces the arrival of our pizza. Thomas looks at the door as if it's a giant turkey leg or something, and I'm afraid he's going to leap at the delivery person as soon as I open the door.

I nearly jump when I open the door to see Cameron Mathis standing on the other side. What's he doing delivering my pizza? Is this some kind of cosmic joke?

We stand in awkward silence, shifting our weight from foot to foot. The street light nearby buzzes overhead, and dogs bark from the neighbors' house. We're playing a game of conversational chicken, and neither of us is willing to cave first.

Finally, Cameron takes a deep breath.

"This yours?" He asks.

I nod slowly. I'm suddenly more aware of myself than I've ever been. Standing on my front porch with paint peeling off the railings and solid-gold Cameron with his mouth agape.

"Uh, yeah," I finally say, reaching out for my pizza.

We stand for another long minute, and I can tell he's taking in everything around me. I don't want his pity. I don't want him here. I want a do-over.

"You're Kayla's best friend, and we've never said even two words to each other," he says after another long silence. "Isn't that weird?"

"I'm not much of a talker," I shrug. I'm trying to activate my superpower, but it's harder when I'm the only person out here. There's nobody to blend in with.

"It'd be cool if we got to know each other. I don't know a lot of people here yet, and Kayla says we'd probably be friends," he's rocking on his heels. He may be more awkward than I am, which is saying a lot.

"Alright, cool," I finally manage. The silence between us would be deafening if not for the constant buzzing of the streetlight.

Cameron finally exhales a tight breath and smiles.

"Alright, cool," he repeats. "I've got more deliveries to make. I'll see you tomorrow."

When he finally drives away, I feel myself let out my own slow breath. I'm not sure how to feel after my conversation with Cameron. I would text Kayla, except we're fighting.

I would text Isaiah, except I don't know if we're close enough for my random musings. I guess I'm left to my own devices.

I hardly make it back into the house before Thomas is attacking me for pizza.

"Chill out, Thomas," I laugh. "You're like a rabid animal."

We do everything Mom advises us not to. We eat pizza straight out of the box while watching a movie on TV. We share a 2-liter of Pepsi, drinking straight from the bottle. It's like our own little party.

I always hope that when Thomas is grown, he'll look back on nights like this one and think of them fondly. I hope he'll see that I tried to give him the whole world even when we had nothing.

When Mom gets home, Thomas is sleeping, freshly over a night terror. I'm sitting in my room, adding details to my painting, to my blue-eyed face in the dark.

The door to my room squeaks open, and my mom's tired smile appears.

"How was work?" My standard greeting, but I'm genuinely curious. Sometimes she has stories about her crazy employees. They're always entertaining; Mom has always been a great storyteller.

"Long," she sighs and takes a seat on the corner of my bed. For a moment, I think she will apologize for our fight earlier. She takes a deep breath but gets distracted when she sees my painting.

"That's really good, Cade," she smiles, studying it closely. "It looks so familiar." She furrows her brow in concentration.

"Is that Sinéad O'Connor?" She stifles a laugh behind her hand. "I think I owned that album."

And I realize she's right. My painting *does* look like Sinéad O'Connor's album cover. My face burns with embarrassment. I can feel the heat of blush rushing up my face.

"We need to talk about this afternoon," Mom says, a lopsided grimace on her face. "I'm sorry we fought."

I'm shocked to hear my mom say this, but I'm unsure why. She's apologized to me before. But this time, she seemed so convicted about herself. She seemed so genuine in her protests.

"I'm not sorry for the things I said, but I'm sorry we fought." She sighs again. "I know that you're 18. And I know you've been grown for a long time. But selling your art is a big decision. I wish you'd have consulted me." She doesn't say *but you didn't even have your phone with you*, but I know she's thinking it.

"Your art is personal. It comes from a personal place. And the idea that someone will own your memories, your emotions, it's just strange to me."

I breathe to say something, but Mom holds her hand up to stop me. She's rehearsed what she wants to say to me.

"But I also want you to be careful. Your art show seems like a big deal to you. Sometimes students are disqualified from things like this if they start to accept money for their work. I just want you to have the best opportunities possible. If you think that comes from selling your art, then fine. But really think about it. As long as you're happy—and you know, not doing anything illegal—then I support you."

I have the opportunity to say something, but I don't have anything to say. How can I? Mom has said it all. So, I just shrug, my throat tight with tears that won't fall. Why am I so emotional lately?

When Mom stands up, she kisses the top of my head.

"You and Sinéad have a nice night. Sleep well," she chuckles on her way out of my room.

Mom's right, I guess. I should consider the art show. Will I be disqualified? Mr. Camplin never mentioned anything about selling our work. Surely, he'd have mentioned something so big.

I'm still in a haze, considering this when my phone rings. What lunatic is calling me at 11:00 at night? The screen displays Kayla's picture. I consider not answering it but change my mind.

"Hello?" Why is she even calling me?

"I'm sorry," she says. Her voice is flat, and I'm not sure how to take it.

"I didn't realize things were so bad for you, or I wouldn't have called you poor today. That was bitchy of me."

I'm not entirely sure what she's talking about, and I tell her as much.

"My dad bought one of your drawings today. He didn't realize it was yours, but I remembered when you drew it. He said you're an up-and-comer, and he paid $150 for it."

I think I hear a sob in her throat before she continues.

"I didn't know you were selling your art."

A flood of emotions hits me. Never, *never* has Kayla apologized to me. And my art sold. Already? I just relinquished it to Mrs. Rosenthal this afternoon, and already one of my pieces has sold. Should I feel elated? I do feel elated.

"He bought my art?" I hope I don't sound as confused as I feel. Why would Kayla's dad buy my art? He doesn't have an artistic or discerning bone in his body. Was Mrs. Rosenthal that good at marketing? Or did Kayla's dad feel some guilt-filled need to support me? Did he actually know it was my work?

"I have an agent," I finally say. I know it will only be to the detriment of this conversation to tell her that agent is Isaiah's mom. I don't tell her that.

"She gave me an advance and told me she thought she could get me gallery space. Things haven't gotten that bad, Kayla," I comfort her. "I just found a way to help out around the house and still stay at home with Thomas."

Silence passes between us for a moment. I'm not sure that this apology is enough to fix what Kayla broke between us, and I can tell she's not sure, either. We inhale in tandem, waiting for the other to make the next move. The eternal chess match that is mine and Kayla's friendship.

I decide to make the next move. My hands are shaky, and I feel sick. But I have to say what needs to be said.

"You really hurt me today," I say softly. "You know how ashamed I am of the life I live."

"I'm sorry," Kayla sniffles. She's about to say more, but I cut her off. I can't let that be it. Sorry only goes so far.

"I would never attack your insecurities like that. *Never.*" My voice is low and stead. "It's not my fault that I'm poor. And you don't understand what it's like. You've always been given everything you've ever wanted. Always."

I breathe deep. I don't want to lecture her. But she needs to hear this.

"If you ever, ever talk about me like that again, I will cut you out of every aspect of my life. I don't have room in my life for that negativity."

This is the meanest thing I have ever said to anybody. But it's true. And it's something I need to say. I need for Kayla to realize that she hurt me in an unacceptable way.

"I know. I know that's off-limits. I don't know why I did that." She's sniffling hard, trying not to choke on her tears. "It was bitchy," she concedes.

Another silence passes between us. This time it's Kayla who breaks it.

"So, an agent, huh?" I can hear a smile in her voice. "And gallery space. It's what you've always dreamed of."

I nod stupidly like she can see me.

"It's late, Cade," she says with a yawn.

I glance at the clock beside my bed. 11:50 glows red back at me. It is late.

"I'll pick you up in the morning. Breakfast tacos to celebrate your newfound celebrity status."

We chuckle and say our goodbyes, and I'm finally left alone in the dark—just me and Sinéad O'Connor.

When Kayla picks me up, things between us are awkward and stilted. It's like we're on stage and don't know what to do with our hands. So, instead, we revel in our breakfast taco and classic rock station I decided to set the radio to.

Is something still broken between us?

"So, this agent," Kayla turns down Hotel California to talk. Shame. I love Hotel California. "How'd you find her?"

I try to think of an answer that is both honest and keeps Isaiah out of this argument. That wouldn't help this whole patching-things-up thing we're doing. And I really want to patch things up.

"A kid in my art class," I shrug, trying to be nonchalant. "He told her about my work, so she asked to see it."

"And she loved it because she has a brain," Kayla prompts, wanting more of the story.

"And she loved it," I nod. "She gave me a $1500 advance. And said she knows the owner of the gallery downtown—"

"You love that gallery!"

"I know." This back-and-forth is comfortable. This is the way we usually converse.

"My space will be in that gallery." I'm smiling uncontrollably now. This is how I'd expected my conversation to go with my mom. "If she can get it."

I'm trying to stay realistic and not get my hopes too high. She promised to try. She never promised to deliver. And that's okay. Her trying is more than anybody has ever done for me.

"This is all so cool. You're going to be famous! And that'll make me your posse!"

"I think artists have entourages."

We laugh genuine laughs and enjoy ourselves. I don't know how long this peace will last, but I'm going to enjoy it while it does. When we get to Kayla's spot in the school lot, she hesitates. I realize she's still gun shy from yesterday. I was mean. I was needlessly mean.

"I'm sorry," I say, quiet because I'm not really sure how to say it. "I shouldn't have said that yesterday."

And I don't know where to go from here. Wishing me a good day every day is one of Kayla's favorite things to do. And I took that away from her yesterday. I should remember not to fight pain with more pain.

"Well," she says, a smile crossing her face. "Here's to your best day ever, Cade Swanson."

And with that, things are back to normal, however unusual our normal might be.

Chapter Six

It's amazing how easily days slip into weeks, and before I have even realized it, September has given way to Halloween. Halloween is my favorite holiday. Kayla and I always get together to carve pumpkins and watch scary movies and make Thomas's costume. On the rare occasion that Kayla is single, she and I even take Thomas trick-or-treating at the downtown Halloween festival.

"And all the colors," I hear myself telling Isaiah at lunch. "The oranges and browns and blacks and golds. That's my preferred palette."

He laughs and nods his head. "Yeah, I've noticed."

"What's that supposed to mean?"

"Your tribal painting a few weeks ago," he ticks off on his fingers as he talks. "The pastels piece you turned in to Mr. Camplin, that autumn tree piece you brought to my mom yesterday. You have a thing for the colors of fall."

I guess he has a point. I do an awful lot with the colors of fall, with the colors of fire. I've always been drawn to fire.

"Speaking of that tree piece," Isaiah says through a mouthful of chicken nugget. "It's sold. Mom says she has an $800 check for you. Your art has sold like crazy lately. You must have a nice college fund built up already?"

I do. But, more importantly, I have enough to buy a car. My own car. I won't have to rely on anyone else for transportation anymore. I won't have to depend on Kayla and Isaiah for rides to and from school. Mom won't have to worry while she's gone. I could even go to a school football game if I wanted to. Okay, let's not be ridiculous, now.

Of course, I'll never be able to afford a car like Isaiah's. Or even Kayla's, for that matter. But all I need is four wheels and an engine—just something to get me from point A to point B.

"Whatcha thinking about?" Isaiah looks perplexed, following my gaze.

"Oh, sorry, I must have zoned out." I shake my head. The ideas of $800 and a car are still sweet aftertastes in my mind.

"That ugly tree brought $800?" I laugh. It really was hideous. I didn't like it when I finished it, but I took it to Mrs. Rosenthal, anyway. I figured she'd slap a price on it that would cover the cost of the materials and framing. I can't even imagine having $800 sitting around to be able to buy some ugly painting with.

"Oh, thank God," Isaiah exhales, a goofy smile consuming his face. "Mom and I thought it was ugly, too. But you brought it with those really good drawings, so we thought we just didn't get it." He laughs so hard tears stream down his face. And I join him because it really is funny.

"For future reference," I say once I've caught my breath. "Very few of my works are that personal to me. Feel free always to tell me what you think."

The clatter of a tray on our table brings us both out of our shared world. It is so easy to forget other people exist when Isaiah and I are together, even in the noisy cafeteria.

"Hey," Cameron says as he sits in the empty chair across from me.

"Oh, uh, hey," I try to sound casual. This is the first time we have spoken since the pizza delivery incident weeks ago. Kayla hasn't mentioned anything about Cameron yet, so I can only assume he still hasn't told her about that entire awkward meeting.

"Do you know Isaiah?" I ask, trying to remember my manners.

"Yeah, we've got calculus together," Isaiah smiles, nodding in greeting to Cameron.

"I had a question for you guys," Cameron says, his voice uneasy, just like the night he delivered my pizza. "Kayla and I are going to see that new psychothriller on Friday. I wondered if you guys would want to come along, too. Like a double date or whatever."

Isaiah and I both sit bolt upright on our round, uncomfortable cafeteria stools. An uncomfortable chuckle catches in my throat. I cast an uncomfortable glance at Isaiah. Everything is just *so* uncomfortable.

"Um, did you talk to Kayla before talking to us?" I ask, trying to be delicate. I can feel the heat of blush exploding up my neck, to my cheeks, and spreading all the way to the tips of my ears.

"Now, sweetie," Isaiah says with an entirely straight face. How did he recover so quickly? "I'm sure she won't mind."

I'm vibrating from embarrassment. And Isaiah is only making it worse.

"So, you guys will come?" Cameron looks legitimately excited. Kayla's boyfriends never want to hang out with me. I'm genuinely perplexed by this entire conversation.

"Um," I finally gain control over myself again. "I'll have to check with my mom—"

"I'll only go if Cade's goes. I'm not about to be the third wheel on your date." Isaiah interrupts me.

"And, for the record," I revel in this back-and-forth. It's familiar, like with Kayla. "We're just friends." It feels like I have a mouthful of cotton when I say this.

"Why do you have to say it like that?" Isaiah mocks anger. "I'm a damn catch, Cade Swanson. You'd be lucky to date me."

I shrink in my seat and feel my ears light up again. People around us are starting to look and laugh. And my superpower is failing me. Miserably.

Cameron and Isaiah erupt into laughter as I pray for the sky to cave in around me.

"I'm sorry," Cameron says once he catches his breath. "I didn't mean to offend you guys if I did. But seriously. If you guys are free, I want you to come hang out with us. I want to get to know Kayla's friends."

He makes it very hard for me to hate him. Why is he being so nice? What's he playing at?

Isaiah elbows me like he can read my mind.

"I'm game, but only if Cade's mom says he can go. I refuse to be third-wheeled." Isaiah reiterates.

"Yeah, I'm in. I'll ask my mom, but it shouldn't be a problem." She's always telling me I need more friends, anyway. And maybe it wouldn't be the worst thing on Earth to get to know Kayla's boyfriend—especially if this one is so different from her usual duds. And he certainly does seem to be different from her usual duds.

The bell rings at long last, and I slip into the hallways, comfortably disappearing into the flow of chattering high schoolers. Conversations around me range from the inane chatter of who's going to whose party, to things of deeper value, like whether or not Thor counts as a Disney Princess.

I enjoy listening to chatter; it's soothing, and it inspires me. The thing about chatter is that it's just so human. It's part of the human experience. It's how we get to know each other.

As an artist, I'm always inspired by chatter, and I try to weave that into my work. I want my art—the real stuff, not ugly trees—to be authentic and raw and kind of human. I want to use idle chatter as a medium. I want to create work that speaks to people.

Thomas Kinkade made beautiful paintings, but nothing that ever spoke to me. I want to be a less creepy Frieda Kahlo, a more technical Clementine Hunter. I just want to create something that people *get*.

Before I can slip into my next class, I'm dragged from my daydreaming by Señora LeBlanc, my Spanish teacher. Her round face is always warm with a smile, and her deep-set brown eyes sparkle, even on dull, cloudy days. If she weren't so kind, I would find an excuse to ignore her gentle call.

"Hey, Cade," she says, almost inaudible over the roar of the hallway.

I step into her room, the bright colors of *Día de Los Muertos* washing over me. I didn't realize how close we are to Halloween already. Where has this school year gone?

"Yes, Señora?" I smile, adjusting my backpack on my shoulders.

"*El Día de Los Muertos* is coming up, and I was wondering if you would make some artwork for my classroom." Her smile is so sweet; it's almost saccharine. But I can't stop looking at it. She's what Disney princesses grow up to look like.

"I'd pay you, of course," she adds quickly. "It's just that you're kind of becoming a local celebrity, and I thought it would be nice to have something of yours to hang on the walls in here. Something to encourage future students to follow their dreams like you did."

I can't even bear the thought of charging one of my favorite teachers for art. Especially because she lives on a teacher's salary.

"I'd love to create something for you," I smile, the gears in my head already turning. I've been curious to use ash and soot in my art for a while. This will give me the perfect opportunity to experiment.

"But, please don't worry about paying me." I smile a bit uncomfortably. Students are starting to enter the room, and I want to turn unnoticeable again.

"Well, that wouldn't be right, Cade," she smiles her disarming smile. "My brother-in-law just paid quite a bit for that lovely tree you painted. It's hanging in his office right now. He's a psychologist, you know."

My eyes nearly bug out of my head when she says this. It's hard for me to wrap my head around the idea that anybody bought that ugly painting. It's even weirder to imagine my teacher's relative buying that ugly painting.

When the tardy bell rings, Señora LeBlanc looks surprised. Before I can argue with her again, she ushers me out of the door with a tardy pass to my next class.

By the end of the day, I have already completely envisioned Señora LeBlanc's piece and several other more macabre pieces I want to make if my ash-to-watercolor technique works as planned. My hands are itching to create, begging me to ignore physics and start drawing, sketching, anything. Sometimes the need to create is so strong I can't ignore it. I have to block out all else and allow my hands to work. Sometimes, it's like they work independently of my brain.

Which is why I've gone from an A student to failing physics in the past month. Since Isaiah's mom became my agent, my work has sold like crazy. And I've been creating more than ever. It's like someone turned on the tap, and everything keeps pouring out. But what happens when the fount runs dry? What if once the spring stops flowing, it doesn't start again?

This is the question that haunts me. This is the reason I allow my hands and heart to lead me. Because if I peak in high school, I'm going to make sure I enjoy the ride. I'm going to make sure to chase my dreams until the trail ends.

The bell rings, and I look down to my notebook to see a page covered in droves of birds. A scenic farmhouse landscape, covered in crows, sprawls before me in the crumpled pages of my physics notebook. I'm intrigued by my own imagination and what it chose to create while I zoned out. I wonder how this will translate to canvas. I wonder what medium I can use to bring this scene to life. And I wonder whose phone is ringing as my classmates begin to file out of the door.

And then I realize it's mine. That's my phone that's ringing. But who is calling me? School has only just ended, so it's not Isaiah, Kayla, or my mom. I dig my phone out of my pocket and accept the call, a number I don't know displaying on the screen.

"This is Cade," I answer my usual, regrettably informal greeting.

"Mr. Swanson," a man with a very proper accent greets me. "This is Martin Kimball. I own and operate Kimball Art, the gallery on Front Street. Are you familiar with it?"

Am I familiar? I'm more than familiar! I've visited that gallery once a month for years. I have gone to revel in the amazing things other artists have created. I've soaked in new techniques and seen what people are buying. I've drawn inspiration and built hope at Kimball Art.

Though my body is shaking and I want to scream with excitement, I try to play it cool.

"Yes, sir," I try to keep my voice level. "I've visited it a few times." And by a few, I mean several hundred. But he doesn't have to know that.

"Great," He sounds very passive. "The reason I'm calling today is because of your impressive collection of work. Betty Rosenthal sent me your portfolio, and I must say I am quite impressed by the things you've accomplished at such a young age. We have hosted many artists at this gallery, but my staff has never been so impressed by somebody so young."

I'm trying not to squeak or squeal. I want to shout *wahoo!* But, instead, I'm standing in the middle of the hallway, looking like a Taylor Swift fan at a meet-and-greet. And she just looked at me.

"Betty asked if we had any gallery space available, but we had something a little different in mind." He continues, his voice the formal, auditory equivalent of a black tie and tuxedo. "We would like to offer you a premiere at our gallery. We would like to offer you a full show at Kimball Art."

I nearly throw up when he says this. I nearly faint. I nearly do so many things that I nearly forget to respond.

"Mr. Swanson, are you still there?"

"Yes," I say too excitedly. "Yes, I'm here. And I gladly accept your invitation," I'm stammering now. "When? I need to get to work. When would you like me?" My head begins to swim with possibilities. If I have my own premiere, my own show, I'm going to have to work harder than ever before.

"Would you be able to have something together by mid-November? We could schedule a November 16 opening."

November 16. That gives me less than a month to get an entire show together. I can be ready if I use some of my pre-existing best works and only make a few more. So, I nod several times before I realize he can't see me.

"Yes, sir," I smile, my knees weak. "Yes, sir. November 16th is perfect. Thank you so much. Thank you."

"Fantastic," he says dryly. "I will arrange everything with Betty. Congratulations, Mr. Swanson. And thank you for choosing Kimball Art for your premiere. I foresee this to be the beginning of a beautiful partnership."

My phone beeps to indicate the end of the call, and I'm left standing stunned in the hallways. How long have I even been on the phone? It seems like it took hours, but the halls are still full and bustling, so it couldn't have been very long.

Over the sea of teenagers, Isaiah stands like a beacon. I find myself running to him, a broad smile on my face. And suddenly, I realize I must look like Thomas, running so giddily. So, I laugh as I make it to Isaiah and try not to talk a million miles a minute.

"She did it, Is!"

"Did you just call me *Eyes*?" He laughs at my excitement.

"Yeah, it's your new nickname, I guess." I laugh, looking up into his eyes. "Your mom got me my gallery space. Not just gallery space. She got me an entire show. My own opening!"

I know I'm rambling; my mouth is working on autopilot. Overwhelming joy bubbles up in me, and I throw my arms around Isaiah.

"I've got an opening at Kimball Art!"

Isaiah looks shocked but hugs me back. He laughs a hearty laugh that makes my ears ring.

"I'm so proud of you! Congratulations!" He pries me off of him. "But don't give my mom so much credit. All she did was make a call. It was your talent that did it. Don't sell yourself short."

I'm on Cloud Nine. Nothing can bring me down. Not even Kayla, strolling over and looking angry.

"Why the celebration?" She asks shortly, pointedly. I can tell she's angry that I didn't celebrate with her first. Honestly, I just saw Isaiah before I saw anyone else.

"My—" Isaiah starts to answer, but I cut him off.

"I got gallery space!" I tell her. "Not just gallery space; an entire show. My own opening!"

Even through her annoyance, Kayla's eyes light up. She celebrates my victory by jumping up and down and shrieking. Then she pulls Isaiah and me into a tight hug.

"That's amazing, Cade. You're amazing." She smiles broadly. "I don't know why I'm hugging you, Isaiah. Just go with it."

She lets us go and steps back.

"Okay. This weekend we have to celebrate—my treat. Anywhere you want to go. I have a date with Cameron, so I'll have to rearrange that, but this is so much more important."

She's as giddy as I am, and it's so refreshing after our ups and downs this school year. Is she really willing to reschedule a date for me? Is this the same Kayla I've known the past four years?

"Actually, Cameron invited us out with you guys this weekend, and I was thinking we would go."

As I think about it, today has been a totally bizarre day. I'm almost afraid of what will happen from this point on. What crazy things could possibly be left in store for me?

"What?" Kayla looks even more excited. "Cade Swanson, are you sick? You want to spend time with my boyfriend? This *is* a special day!"

And it is.

To avoid any extra drama, I ask Kayla to drive me home; I'd rather be riding with Isaiah. I'd rather be celebrating with Isaiah. He's quickly become my first call, and not just because his mom is my agent. He just *gets* me.

"I can't believe you're getting your own opening. Cade, that's amazing!" Kayla has been talking nonstop since we left the school. She started by filling me in on her day, then moved on to everything I told her.

"My best friend wants to hang out with my boyfriend, and he's getting his own art show. Let's go get ice cream to celebrate."

That's how I know Kayla is in an unusually good mood. Her family is all about organic and healthy and eating very few animal by-products. They aren't quite vegans, but they're awfully close. For her to suggest, ice cream is the rarest of occasions.

"I'd love to," I say, a sad note in my voice. "But I have to get home. Mom has to get to work."

I consider for a moment before continuing.

"But come over tonight!" And then I say something that surprises even me. "Invite Cameron; it'll be fun."

"He—" I almost say *already knows where I live,* but I don't. It still feels weird. "He just can't make fun of my house." I recover. But I know he won't; he's already seen it.

Kayla's eyes light up so brightly I'm afraid she's going to explode. And for the first time in a long time, things are right between us.

When I get home, I can hardly contain my excitement. It's obvious to my mom when I come into the kitchen.

"You look like you're about to spill over," Mom laughs as I come running inside. "What's up, sweetie?"

"Can Kayla and Cameron come over tonight?" I ask nearly breathlessly.

"You and Kayla are on better terms lately," Mom muses as she considers what I've just asked. "And you're inviting her boyfriend?"

She raises her eyebrows at me as she ties her hair up into a ponytail. I can see her pondering what this might mean. Mom knows how rocky things have been between us this semester. And that I've never asked one of her boyfriends over.

"Tell you what," Mom smiles. "If you guys promise to study for physics, they can come over."

She crosses her arms and quirks a brow. She's got this subtle way of letting me know that she knows what's going on in my life without coming right out and yelling at me for my grades. This way is more effective, anyway, I think. There are few things I hate worse than disappointing my mom.

"We will," I hug her in appreciation. I can't control myself. I want to hug everything. Hell, I'd even hug my father if we were here. Okay, maybe I wouldn't hug him, but I wouldn't punch him if he were here, and that's nearly the same thing.

"I have the best news," I finally spill. "Mom, I got a call from Kimball Art today."

"That's the gallery downtown that you love so much?" Mom asks as she inspects the fridge to make sure Thomas and I have something to eat for dinner tonight. "What do they want? Are they offering you a job or something?"

"Yes, ma'am. That's the place," I'm smiling goofily. "Mom, are you listening?"

She's busy pulling and pushing things around in the refrigerator. I'm not sure what she's messing with; it's not like we have much food in there. Or anywhere, for that matter. It's too close to her payday for us to have much left.

"I'm listening," her tone is less than attentive.

"They offered me gallery space," I'm nearly bubbling over.

"That's nice," Mom says. Her voice is full of consternation. She's realizing that we don't have anything to eat tonight, and she doesn't have any money to leave us.

"Mom," I say, my patience growing thin. "I'll take care of dinner tonight. Kayla and Cameron are coming over. We'll just order pizza or something."

I touch her shoulder, and it brings her back to our conversation.

"Did you say gallery space?" Mom asks, her eyes brightening. "You're going to hang in Kimball Art?"

A broad smile crosses her face as she realizes exactly what I'm saying. She hugs me tightly.

"I'm so proud of you, baby," she says into my hair. She's holding me unusually tight. I don't mind; I just let her.

"You're so grown up," she says softly. "I don't know when this happened. You should still be sitting at the counter with Crayola watercolors."

My mom loves watercolor. My grandfather painted in watercolor, so I think watercolor reminds her of him. When I was little, she used to sit me at the table with a brush and a cup of water, and a stack of watercolor paper and let me do whatever I wanted. Mom was actually pretty skilled with Crayola paints. She was great at florals.

Personally, watercolor is not my favorite medium. It's hard to control. And you constantly have to think about light source and shadows and where your lights and darks are. In graphite, if I forget this, I can always erase back to the white of the paper. But with watercolor, when it's gone, it's gone. Watercolors flow and have their own mind; I like to be in control. People are like watercolors; maybe that's why I keep to myself.

"It's not just gallery space," I continue, trying to pace the news so as not to overwhelm myself. "It's an entire show. I have an entire show, Mom."

I can feel tears catch in my throat. I've literally never been this excited in my entire life. I've never been this happy. I'm actually so happy that I'm crying. I didn't think that was possible before now.

"Cade, that's amazing," I can hear tears in her voice. She is so happy she's crying.

"What does the mother of a prominent artist wear to an art show?" Mom laughs into my hair, still holding me tight. She breathes in deep.

"We'll find you something beautiful," I smile. I don't mind that she's still hugging me. I can't remember the last time I let my mom just hug me like this.

I tell her the entire story. I tell her about the phone call and trying not to sound like an idiot and totally acting like an idiot. I can't stop talking about Mrs. Rosenthal and singing her praises. But mom just stops me and parrots what Isaiah said earlier. I did this on my own.

The door bangs open as Thomas runs in, perpetually on a faster setting than I can keep up with. He blurs past me to throw his arms around Mom and begins sputtering about his day. The house is full of light, and smiles, and sunshine. It's been a long time since we've all seen this many smiles and this much sunshine. The cynic or pessimist in me is waiting for the other shoe to drop.

Chapter Seven

When Kayla and Cameron arrive at my house, we order the largest Chinese food order I have ever placed. I feel bad for the delivery person who has to carry all the food we ordered, but at least my fridge will be overflowing with those little square boxes when Kayla and Cameron leave. Thomas looks delighted that we have ordered so much food. He can't wait to dig into the mounds of food he's already claimed for himself.

As I promised Mom, we spend a little over an hour studying physics as we dig through orange chicken, and Lo Mein, and fried wontons. Things are stilted at first, like Cameron and I aren't sure how to act toward each other. I guess we don't know how to act toward each other.

Cameron is messier than I expected. He spills food on his notes and in his textbook. He's like a ravenous animal; if this were a cartoon, there'd be stains and smears on the wall from the food flying everywhere but into his mouth. Kayla laughs her flirtatious laugh, the one that's an obvious put-on. She can't seem to stop staring at us. She turns her head from me to Cameron and back again. I watch her sigh as if she's the happiest she's ever been.

"This is nice, isn't it?" She smiles as we work another ridiculous problem about throwing somebody off a building. Physics problems are violent.

"What d'ya mean?" Cameron asks with a mouthful of egg roll. He really is like a rabid animal.

In this light, though, I can see exactly what Kayla sees in him. He's funny, but he doesn't try to be. He's got a nice smile, and his eyes look at you every time you talk like you're the most important person at the moment. I can see the appeal of Cameron Mathis.

"My two favorite guys in one room, talking about throwing Physics Bob off a building, eating Chinese food," Kayla smiles broadly. "People don't get many days like this."

She's oddly introspective. Kayla doesn't often reflect on the rightness of life. She's usually just concerned with how things aren't going in her favor. I'm surprised at her contented smile.

When we've finished our homework, I send Thomas to his room to read while Kayla, Cameron, and I watch a movie. I feel bad for Thomas a little. He's used to having me as his steadfast companion every night. Thomas doesn't need anybody except for me. At least that's what Mom says. But I'm afraid Thomas doesn't have any friends. I'm afraid I'm Thomas's only friend.

And I feel worse for him when I consider how often I ignore him for my friends or my work. And lately, I've been doing a lot of working and a lot of ignoring Thomas. I'm distracted by this thought for a moment, and when I look over, Kayla is snuggling in closer to Cameron. He wraps his arm idly around her as we watch the movie.

I realize I'm the third wheel. And I wish Isaiah were here. He'd make things less awkward. Because with Cameron's arm draped around Kayla, I don't even know what to say or how to say it. My throat tightens up. It's like I'm afraid I'll disturb their moment.

They're whispering something I can't make out, and jealousy builds in me. I'm not usually jealous. Not anymore, at least. I used to get jealous, but at some point, it started manifesting as irritation instead.

I'm jealous because that's how Kayla and I used to be. We used to sit close and whisper to each other through movies. Kayla would make up fake dialogue, and I'd respond. Or she'd comment on somebody's ugly clothes, and I'd laugh. Or I'd tell her a funny joke that popped into my head that was too urgent not to tell.

I'm not jealous of Cameron. I don't want to date Kayla. *I don't.* I have to reassure myself of this so many times that I'm afraid that maybe I do.

I look at Kayla, nestled against Cameron, and consider this. Maybe I *do* want to date Kayla. Is that why I get so mad when I'm blown off for the guys she's dating? It would make sense, I think. *We* would make sense. I know everything about her. I'm her first call.

First calls are important. A first call is the first person you call when something big happens in your life. Kayla *always* calls me first when she has news. I'm always the one celebrating with her.

Her family loves me. My mom loves her. We would make a good fit.

Do I want to date Kayla?

"What the heck, dude?" Cameron asks me, looking over Kayla at me.

Shit, I think. Did I say something awkward out loud? Did I ask that out loud?

"You weren't going to tell me that you're going to have an art show?"

Kayla must have told him while I was zoned out.

"That's really awesome!" Cameron gives me a thumbs up from across the room. "I mean, I think it is. It sounds awesome. I'm not really sure what that means if I'm being real with you."

"It is," Kayla hits him playfully. "It means that people our parents' age are having to deal with their broken dreams of football stardom, or whatever, and Cade's actually getting to live out his dream at 18 years old."

I don't exactly see it that way. But Kayla thinks my dream is to be an artist.

My dream isn't to be an artist. My dream is to get the hell out of this place and live far away and be able to eat at fancy restaurants, and come home to a house without holes in the floor.

My dream is to move to a big city, somewhere like New York City, and live in a high-rise apartment. My dream is to pay bills on time and that my kids never come home with the electricity off. My dream is to be a better father than my father ever was. But I don't tell Kayla that because she won't get it.

"That's really awesome, man." Cameron smiles, and I know he's being genuine.

I just nod my head in appreciation because I don't know what else to do or say.

Again, I wish Isaiah were here. He never finds me awkward. I'm always awkward. There's a reason I hide in the hallways.

I catch myself looking at Kayla again once Cameron and Kayla's attention is back on the movie. Do I want to date her? It *would* make sense.

When the movie ends, Kayla and Cameron stand up to leave. I'm surprised at how happy I feel, at how comfortable I feel. I didn't expect things to go so smoothly. Even the awkward parts were nowhere near as bad as I expected. If this is any indication for this weekend, the four of us will have fun.

Maybe I was quick to judge Cameron. I'll never tell Kayla that.

I reach my hand out to shake Cameron's, but he pulls me into a hug. I laugh, surprised. When Kayla hugs me, it's awkward. I can't shake the question that's been haunting me all night. *Do I want to date Kayla?*

I don't know why I keep asking myself that. It's not even an option. We've had plenty of opportunities, and neither of us has ever made a move. And even if she were considering it, she's with Cameron. And I don't get in the middle of things like that.

I send Cameron and Kayla off and help Thomas get ready for bed. It's past his bedtime, which almost guarantees I'll have to deal with night terrors tonight. Sometimes I think it's almost worth it, though. Thomas likes to stay up past his bedtime and talk to me.

"Bub," Thomas says softly, peering at me from his bed as I come in to see him. "I'm glad Kayla came over."

He smiles a sweet smile as I sit next to his bed. I run my hand through his hair.

"Yeah? Why's that?"

He closes his eyes and breathes in. Thomas lives for my attention.

"You're happy when Kayla's here." Thomas is oddly perceptive that way. He's very attuned to the subtle changes in my mood.

"Have I not been happy lately?" I ask playfully.

"You kinda haven't," he says candidly. "I mean, you have. But it's different when Kayla's here."

And I wonder for the millionth time if I do want to date Kayla. And I also wonder when that started to matter. I've made it to 18 without a girlfriend.

Why start worrying about that now? There are so many other things I could focus on.

Thomas and I talk about his day and the things that he wants to do. He tells me that he wants to be a nurse when he grows up, which is a new advancement. And a strange, kind of jarring change from astronaut farmer, which has been his life's ambition for as long as I can remember.

"Braxton's dad is a nurse," Thomas explains. "I didn't know boys were nurses. But Braxton's dad says it's cool for boys to be nurses. And he gets to poke people with needles and stuff."

I laugh. Thomas always makes me laugh. Of course, Thomas wants to poke people with needles.

"Did you know that there's a job where people play with bugs and dead people?" Thomas asks, nestling into his pillow, his eyes drooping.

"I did know that," I stroke a hand through his hair. "Do you know what it's called?"

"I think Dr. Owings said she was a 'flalensic insectologist?'" Thomas looks puzzled.

"Close," I hold back a laugh. "She's a forensic entomologist." It must have been career day at Thomas's school.

I think about career day when I was Thomas's age. My father came and talked about being an accountant. I remember thinking, even then, how boring his job sounded. Even in the first grade, I knew that his was a job I had no interest in. One of my classmate's moms talked to us about being a graphic designer. I had been so enthralled with the idea of designing posters and promotional artwork that I came home that day and begged for my first art supplies.

"Bub?" Thomas asks, his voice drowsy with near-sleep. "Did you always want to be an artist?"

"I did," I acknowledge for the first time. "I didn't know it, but I did."

Once Thomas is asleep, I return to my room and my art. I should do homework, but I don't. I can't focus on homework anymore. I have an art show. I'm taking steps to my future. I'm going to get the hell out of this dead-end town. The thought energizes me.

I look at my growing stash of art supplies. I don't even know what I want to use. So, I don't decide. I let my hands pick and create instead. I scoop up a set of pens and begin drawing. I let myself zone out and fall into the gentle trance of stippling.

I let my mind wander in the comfort and monotony of thousands of tiny dots. I think about Kayla. I think about Kayla with Cameron. I think about how this relationship is different and how I don't know what that means for me.

I think about Isaiah and his mom. I think about my mom. I think about Thomas. I do all the thinking I usually deny myself because I am in my element here, under lamplight, surrounded by millions of dots. I am home.

I look up for the first time when my mom appears in my doorway. After staring at all the stippled dots I've made, my mom's face seems oddly bright and overlaid with stipples, like something from a comic book.

"That's pretty," Mom appears in the doorway, smiling her smile that makes my room seem too small and dark. She crosses her arms and leans against my door frame, and I know she's exhausted.

"Thanks," I shrug. I haven't even really looked at it yet. I have no idea what I've been stippling or for how long. "How was work?"

"Peachy O's and Porn came back," Mom laughs halfheartedly. She leans her head against the door frame, and I feel my heart break for her a little. I wish she would push herself so hard.

Mom has had a recurring customer over the past year whom I have dubbed Peachy O's and Porn. Each week he comes into Megamart to peruse the new releases of adult magazines and buys one along with a bag of peach ring candy.

"You know, Mom," I say slyly. "He's probably single. Maybe you should ask him out."

"I'd rather stab myself in the eye," she laughs casually. "I think he doesn't bathe."

I laugh harder at this. I love my late-night conversations with my mom. They're the perfect way to end the day.

"Can I see what you're working on?" She moves over to stand behind me without waiting for an answer.

"I can't tell what it is, but it's a cool effect," she says, her voice thick with concentration.

I don't tell her it's going to be her. For some reason, it embarrasses me to admit that I'm making a larger-than-life portrait of my mother. And I'm afraid for her to see the wrinkles that are forming. Looking into art is like looking into a mirror but amplified. We can ignore blemishes when we think we're the only one who sees them.

"You're so talented," Mom pats my shoulder. "I'm so proud of you."

She kisses my forehead, and I feel embarrassed. I don't think talent is something to be proud of because it's not something I picked. It's not something to hold over people's heads, and it's not something that makes anybody better than anybody else.

I don't tell her any of this because she won't get it. Instead, I just smile.

"Don't stay up too late," she finally says before turning and leaving my room.

I don't listen, though. I stay up through the night and work until my wrists, and fingers, and elbows hurt. I stipple until my pens run out of ink, and when I finally look up, I see my room for every bit as dim and dingy as it is.

I can't contain my yawns as I click off my lamp and climb into bed. As soon as my head hits the pillow, my alarm goes off, and it's tomorrow.

"No," I moan, trying my best to ignore the shrill shrieks of alarm. "No. I just laid down."

Reluctantly, I get up and shower. As I get dressed, I hear Thomas's early-morning singing drift in from his room, and I find myself irrationally angry. How can he always be so damned perky?

I cast a glance over at my stippled paper, millions of tiny dots joining together to make half of my mother's face. It will take me several more hours to complete, and in my exhausted state, that seems daunting. But I want this to be a gift for her.

A horn blows in my driveway, and I'm surprised that Kayla is here so early. And I'm confused that she's honking her horn. She knows my mom is asleep.

"Thomas," I call quietly, reaching for my backpack. "Promise me you'll get on the bus safely."

I know he will. Thomas is the most responsible kid on earth. I hate that Thomas has had to become the most responsible kid on earth.

When I open the door, I'm surprised to see Isaiah's Audi, where I expect to see Kayla's sedan.

"Good morning, sunshine," Isaiah calls out of his open window as I approach the car.

"What are you doing here?"

"I'm picking you up for school," he says like it's the most obvious thing on earth. Of course, it's the most obvious thing on earth.

"I mean, why?" I slide into the passenger seat next to him. His smile is dazzling, and his clothes are pristine, and I feel as dim and dingy as my bedroom in comparison.

"I can't pick my best friend up for school, so he doesn't have to ride the disgusting bus?" Isaiah's smile brightens, and I feel myself succumb to a rare smile. It's nice to be Isaiah's best friend.

"Well," I pause for a moment thinking of the appropriate word. "Thanks?"

He just laughs and shoves a bag of donuts into my hand.

To avoid saying anything else awkward, I shove a donut in my mouth, and it practically melts there. It's buttery and warm and covered in sticky, melted sugar. It's the most delicious thing. I haven't had a donut in so long, I had forgotten how amazing they are. I have to stifle a guttural moan that threatens to escape because of my celebrating taste buds.

"Thank you for breakfast," I finally mutter.

Isaiah just smiles and cranks up the music. He gets me on a spiritual level. No talking until I'm good and awake. And after not sleeping last night, I won't be awake for a long time.

I shoot Kayla a quick text telling her she doesn't need to pick me up, and I hope she doesn't get mad about it. I don't explain why. Sometimes it's easier not to.

As we near school, Isaiah turns the radio down.

"Hey, Cade?" He sounds terrified. "Can I ask you something?"

"You just did," I answer jokingly.

He hits me with a flat glare, and I know he's being serious.

"Yeah, Is, what's up?" I concede. He's serious, which is beyond bizarre.

"I'm just kinda worried about you," he finally says, gripping the steering wheel tightly. "I know your grades are dropping, and I'm worried about that."

"That's not a question," I answer flatly, oddly self-conscious.

"Cade," he says pointedly. "I'm serious. Please let me help you. I'm no genius, but I'm doing a lot better than you."

I shrug, considering this. It's true. He is doing better than I am. But how can I let Isaiah help me in class? His family is already doing so much for me. I can't become their charity case. I'm nobody's charity case.

"Fine," I give in. "But only until the gallery opening. I'm having trouble concentrating lately."

It hurts to admit because I want to seem invulnerable. My entire high school identity has been found in my invulnerability. I've worked too hard to look like I don't care about anything for people to discover that I actually care a lot.

"Besides," Isaiah adds as if he has to get the last word. "Mr. Camplin won't let you enter the art competition at the end of the year if you fail."

And he has a point. Even in my exhaustion, I know he's right. One thing about Isaiah Rosenthal, he is always right.

Chapter Eight

"Mr. Swanson," Mr. Camplin signals me over to his desk as my classmates begin working on their projects. He's assigned us all very complicated color mixing exercises, and I'm irritated he's interrupted my work; this is where I need the most work. I've worked exclusively in graphite for so long that I don't know how to mix colors. I understand color theory. I understand the concepts behind it all. But I don't have the practice logged that my classmates do.

"Yes, sir?" I ask as I approach his desk. He looks angry. I don't know what I've done to make him angry, but it's been an awful week, so I'm not surprised that somebody's mad at me.

"Is there something you need to tell me?" He asks severely.

I can't think of anything I need to tell him, and I say as much. What does he expect me to say? I hate when adults resort to this kind of questioning. Just cut the crap and tell me what you want from me.

"I got a call from the newspaper," he says as if this will prompt me into a confession of some kind. When it doesn't, he continues.

"Are you having an exhibition at Kimball Art?" He looks at me with narrowed eyes.

"Oh," I hang my head sheepishly. "Yes, sir. I am."

I don't know why I didn't tell him. I was embarrassed, I guess. I didn't want him to think I was bragging.

"That's amazing news, Cade," his glare melts to delight. "You should be proud. Martin Kimball doesn't accept just every hack who submits a piece."

"How many pieces are you exhibiting?" Mr. Camplin's eyes are bright as he asks. He's living vicariously through me, and I don't mind. He's taught me so much about art; he deserves this.

"As many as it takes to fill the gallery," I shrug. I'm not entirely sure how much work I still have left.

"Fill the gallery?" He raises an eyebrow at me suspiciously. "Are you telling me that Kimball Art is giving you a full show?"

I nod self-consciously.

"Would you come, please?" I ask sheepishly. "I'm really nervous about it all."

It's the first time I've admitted this to anybody. And not just about the show, but about anything. I'm not the kind of person who gets nervous. But I'm also not the kind of person to get attention. I revel in my superpower. I revel in the fact that I can become unnoticeable.

"You'll be great," Mr. Camplin hits me with that supportive smile that he has mastered. "I'll be there."

I sit back down at my easel, canvas sprawling before me. I love a blank canvas. It means possibility. It means a world of imagination. Already, I'm seeing exactly what I want to paint, following Mr. Camplin's color-mixing guidelines.

"Oh, Cade," Mr. Camplin says quietly over my shoulder. "I think you need an extra challenge."

Isaiah eyes me from his own easel, already in his own color mixing. He knows Mr. Camplin is changing the game, making it harder on me.

"You're a big fan of photorealism," he comments, smiling. "I think you should try something abstract for this."

Abstract? I can't do abstract. I don't even see the point of abstract.

"But photorealism is harder?" I try to ask, hoping to sway his decision.

"Just trust me," he answers. "Sometimes, we all need to stretch ourselves a little."

So, I trust him and uneasily put brush to canvas.

"Let's talk about how unfair it is to have to be your friend," Isaiah laughs as we exit Mr. Camplin's room at the end of class. "Us mere mortals have to sit down and plan what we're doing. You, however, just look at the canvas, shrug, and start to paint a masterpiece."

I shrug him off. It's really not that great. I tell him as much. It's just smears of colors across a canvas. Each color means something to me, but I don't tell him that. I don't want him to know that the smear of blue that runs across the edge is him. It's weird to admit.

"Not that great?" Isaiah laughs in disbelief. "You're like Cézanne, and it comes so naturally to you. No wonder you sell so many of your works."

I don't argue with him because I'm irritable and exhausted, and I'll sound like a jerk. I just let him compliment me, even if it makes me feel uncomfortable.

"Hey, I didn't even ask," the brightness of his smile radiates down the hallway and reflects off blue, peeling lockers. The hallway is gravitating toward his height and smile, everybody waving him a good morning greeting.

"How was your evening with Kayla and Cameron?" His eyes are only on me, despite his gathering fan club. "As awkward as you expected?"

"No," I shake my head. "It was nice. I actually kind of like Cameron."

"Everybody look out," Isaiah laughs a hearty laugh. "The world is going to end, and Cade Swanson actually likes somebody."

I punch him playfully.

"How do you do it?" I ask, surveying the hallway, alive with Isaiah's enthusiasm.

"Do what?"

"Your fan club," I gesture to our classmates, all vying for Isaiah's attention. But his attention is totally on me. How does he deal with so much attention? How does he give so much attention?

He just laughs and shrugs. He's used to this.

"Everybody wants to be your friend," I comment as he continues greeting our classmates. "Why do you talk to me?"

The doubt in my voice sounds forced and flat, and instead of making a joke, it sounds like I'm seeking attention.

"Charity work," Isaiah jokes. "I'm working off some community service hours."

I laugh, but it sounds just as forced. I don't function well on no sleep. I'm not going to survive the day.

"Do you think your mom would let you stay over on Friday?" Isaiah asks kind of awkwardly. "It'd be nice to hang out."

He shrugs, a failed attempt at nonchalance.

"That should be fine," I nod, deciding not to question his sudden awkwardness. "As long as I'm back home before she has to go to work on Saturday."

I almost forgot about our Friday night plans with Cameron and Kayla. Dinner and a psychothriller are just what I need to get my mind off the upcoming art opening and school and everything else stressing me out.

When I get to my next class, I fall asleep nearly immediately on the back row. I miss the review for tomorrow's test, but I feel slightly less grumpy and disoriented. I can't wait for this day to end. It feels like it's never going to end.

Cameron is already at our table when I get to lunch. Why is he at our table? I'm not ready to be buddies yet. I don't want to have to entertain anybody today. I just want to sit in total silence, and blink slowly, and maybe eat a nacho or something. Kayla promptly takes her place next to Cameron. Isaiah takes his usual seat, and I'm left to slide into the seat next to Isaiah.

"Um," I survey Cameron and Kayla closely. "Hey, guys. What's going on?"

This is uncharted territory. Kayla never brings her boyfriends to sit with me. But this isn't even that. Cameron chose to sit beside us. I wasn't even sure what world I was in anymore.

"Not much," Cameron smiles, a mouth half-full of nachos.

"Don't be disgusting," Kayla mutters, glancing at him sideways.

"Sorry," he laughs, clearly unapologetically.

"Cameron felt like changing it up today," Kayla answers, answering the question I didn't ask. "So, we decided to sit with you."

I don't know how to respond, so I don't. Because what I really want to tell them is to leave. I enjoy this time with Isaiah. I enjoy sitting and sometimes talking and sometimes not. But when Kayla's around, I feel like I have to entertain her.

"I'll email you my notes," Cameron says once he's finished chewing. "You fell asleep in chemistry again."

"What do you mean *again*?" Isaiah turns to look at me. "Christ, Cade, is this why you're flunking?"

I feel my cheeks turn red. I don't want to talk about myself. I want to turn on my superpower. I want to be unnoticeable and send the attention to anybody else. I don't want to talk about my failing grades. I just want to sit in my room with my headphones and angry music and pencils. I want to go home.

"It doesn't happen often," I sigh, shaking my head. I shove disgusting nachos in my mouth so I don't have to talk anymore. But that doesn't work on my friends. They're all eyeing me as if I'm withholding the secrets of the universe. I'm not. I just don't like school. I'm allowed to not like school.

"Oh, go to hell," I mutter to all of them. I grab my tray, throw it in the trash, uneaten food and all, and make my way to Mr. Camplin's room.

When I get there, he has a class of freshmen, Art 1 students working diligently on some kind of baby project. Protractors and rulers tell me it's probably a study in perspective. I don't miss those days.

"Is everything okay?" Mr. Camplin asks, meeting me by his door.

"Yeah. Can I stay in here for the rest of lunch?" I don't want to tell him what's going on; I know he'll be disappointed in me. I don't know why I care, but I do.

"That's fine," Mr. Camplin nods, and I'm thankful he understands. "You can help me make sure everybody's getting one-point perspective."

I make myself useful, floating around the room like Mr. Camplin. I lean over shoulders and offer his students help.

"Sometimes it helps me to actually put a dot where my vanishing point is," I say, pointing to where it should be on the page. "That way, you always get the angle right."

This isn't true, though. Not entirely. This is how I taught Isaiah to do perspective. Perspective's always made sense to me. I don't need dots on paper and rulers to get it. Sometimes that makes me a bad teacher.

Sometimes, a concept comes so naturally to me that I couldn't even think of a way to explain the process. It just *is*.

"Thanks," the girl smiles at me, eyelids closing slowly over big green eyes. "That makes a lot more sense."

I'm positive Mr. Camplin has told her the same thing, but I just nod and walk to help somebody else.

When the bell rings, I'm feeling much better and a little foolish for how I reacted at lunch. But really. My grades are none of their business. What gives any of them the right to say anything about them?

I duck into the hallway and blend into the flow of the crowd, hoping my friends don't see me.

"You can't avoid me that easily," Isaiah laughs, falling in step alongside me. "I'm sorry if I crossed a line."

How is it so easy for him to apologize? It's pulling teeth with Kayla.

I shake my head because I don't know what to say and because I'm afraid that whatever I say will be mean. I *am* mean. I really shouldn't have friends.

"I'm worried about you, okay," Isaiah says in his seldom-serious tone. "The bags under your eyes are so big, you could be a vigilante superhero and not need a mask."

"Exactly how long have you been working on the phrasing of that?" I laugh, but it sounds bitter because I'm bitter. Because I want to be home and in my bed. Or at my desk, stippling. Or literally anywhere but in this school in this town.

"Cade, stop it," he says desperately. "We're worried about you."

We're. He said we.

"Who's we?" I narrow my eyes at him, stopping in the middle of the hallway.

"Me and Kayla," he looks sheepish now. Nine feet of embarrassed bean pole in the middle of the hallway.

"Wow, okay. I didn't realize you guys were meeting about me behind my back." I shake my head and start walking away. But one of Isaiah's strides is equal to three of mine, so I don't get very far.

"Cade, stop," he demands this time. "We're worried. You should be glad your friends care. People go through this life without having people who care. So, get the hell over yourself."

This makes me stop. Isaiah is the gentlest person I've ever met. I've never heard him talk like this. He's always level-headed. He's always calm.

"I'm sorry," I shake my head, angry at myself for apologizing but angrier at myself for upsetting Isaiah. "I'm just tired. I'm a dick when I'm tired."

"You're a dick all the time," Isaiah laughs, not maliciously.

"Wow, thanks," I laugh. But I know what he means. I'm incredibly difficult to be friends with.

"Now, you wanna stop being a punk?" Isaiah asks as we approach my next class.

I don't want to stop being a punk. I want to be angry and sulk for days. Or at least until I sleep again. But I won't be sleeping tonight. I've got an art show in a month. I've got so much to get done. I've got to finish stippling my mom. I've got to finish my graphite piece of Thomas. I've got to figure out what I'm going to paint. I got to stop worrying about everything I've got to do.

"Do you still want me to come over this weekend, even though I'm a dick?" I ask. I'm not ready to acknowledge the punk question yet.

"Of course," he laughs. "Things are going to be okay, Cade. But you've got to take better care of yourself, okay?"

I nod and enter the classroom and then immediately fall asleep.

Chapter Nine

By the time Friday finally arrives, I'm operating on so little sleep I'm slightly delirious. My art has slipped easily out of photo-realism and into some kind of surrealism I didn't know I had in me. As I stare at the acrylic snake-headed angel I'd made overnight, I wonder if Salvador Dali was actually just permanently sleep-deprived. It would make a lot more sense.

"Oh, you're already up," Mom smiles as she pokes her head into my room.

"Cade," She eyes me suspiciously. "That's interesting. But please tell me you slept last night?"

I nod because it's not totally a lie. I slept for about forty minutes while I let the underpainting dry. But she knows me well enough to know when I'm hiding something from her.

"That's it," she says in her rarely-used mom voice. "You need a break from art. You've become obsessed."

She's a mixture of incredulous and angry, and I'm not sure which emotion is winning. I'm afraid to ask which one is winning. Instead, I hang my head in shame. Because she's right. I'm being ridiculous. But I can't stop. It consumes me. How can I explain to her that finally being able to afford to create has opened the floodgates of creativity? If I tell her that, will she even care?

"Go to Isaiah's this weekend. Sleep in until 2:00," she smiles kindly. "Come home and watch your brother. Eat junk food, and don't you dare touch a canvas, do you hear me?"

I laugh. If this is my mom's version of grounding, I can list twenty of my classmates who'd happily trade punishments with me.

"If I hear of you falling asleep in class today, you'll be in actual trouble," she warns, shoving a large cup of coffee in my direction.

I nod and gulp down my coffee.

"Can I get this in a vat?" I'm going to need it.

When school is finally over, I collapse into Isaiah's car and feel my eyelids droop. I've survived the day. Thanks to Cameron and Kayla's insistence on my passing, I even made a solid B on a Chemistry test.

Isaiah takes me to my house to grab a change of clothes for the weekend. He walks into my living room and turns in a complete circle, soaking in all of the work I've done this week.

"Cade," he says breathily, lifting the covering on some of my pieces. "This is amazing. You must have a whole show already."

He observes the stippled portrait of my mother closely, his eyes sparkling in awe. He regards a large painting of a lion and crosses his arms, impressed.

"Can we not talk about art today?" I ask. I'm taking my mother's demand to heart: no art for the weekend. I need a break. My brain needs to rest, and art is a strain.

I hurry to replace the coverings on my work. I don't want Mom to see what I've been working on until the opening.

"Uh, sure," Isaiah shrugs and follows me into my room.

Hurriedly, I shove clothes into a bag. The Calvin Klein shirt Isaiah gave me weeks ago is hanging in my closet, tags still on it, and I notice it, embarrassed. I hope he hasn't noticed it. It's the nicest thing I've ever owned, and I haven't had the occasion to wear it yet.

As quickly as I can, I throw things in my bag and try to slip back out of my house before Isaiah has the chance to question me about anything else.

I hear the front door open, and Mom comes in, singing in her beautiful alto voice, filling the house with warmth. I stop in my tracks, hearing her gentle version of "A Dream is a Wish Your Heart Makes." I smile, thinking of my mom as she was when I was a kid. She had been Cinderella, living a dream. And something tugs at my heart, and I feel guilty and angry at my father. My default setting.

"Cade, have you got a second?" She calls from the kitchen, and I hear the ruffling of plastic bags.

I walk into the kitchen, Isaiah in tow, smiling goofily as we pass my display of art in the living room again.

"Isaiah, it's so good to see you," Mom smiles broadly, and again I'm stuck in the warring splendor of their smiles.

"You, too, Ms. Swanson," he nods to her, his manners and class outshining even his smile.

"Please, it's Teresa," she smiles, holding a long plastic bag beside her.

"Mom, what is that?" I ask, breaking up the meeting of the mutual admiration society in my kitchen.

"I got my dress for your opening," she lifts the bottom of the bag, and a beautiful, flowing black dress appears. I don't know how my mom could afford something so beautiful, but I know better than to ask her in front of Isaiah.

"That's beautiful, Ms. Swanson," Isaiah smiles, insistent on being proper.

"It really is, Mom." I feel excitement bubble up in me. Mom was so resistant to my selling my art I almost have whiplash from her sudden show of support. But I don't question it.

"Do you think this is fancy enough for an art opening?" She replaces the plastic covering and drapes the bag over the back of one of the chairs.

"You're going to be the most beautiful work of art there," I say, and I mean it. My mom deserves the opportunity to dress up and do her makeup and fix her hair again. She deserves so much more.

"I doubt that," she laughs. "I saw your drawing of Thomas. It's so good."

"It's one of my favorites," Isaiah interjects.

"Speaking of your brother, why don't you two go before he gets home," Mom suggests, looking at her watch. "He'll tie Isaiah down like in Gulliver's Travels if he gets the chance."

Isaiah guffaws at the idea, but I know Mom is right. Thomas adores Isaiah and looks for any opportunity to spend time with him.

So, I kiss my mom on the cheek, load up Isaiah's car, and head to his mansion.

It doesn't matter how many times I've been to his house; it still seems overbearing and cavernous and uninviting. Everything is too clean and too tidy, and in exactly the same place it was the last time I was there. Everything sits in perfect right angles and faces large windows and seems like it should smell of disinfectant. It doesn't smell of disinfectant. But it seems like it should.

"Cade, it's so nice to see you," Mrs. Rosenthal greets us as we cross through the foyer and into the giant living room. My entire house could fit inside the living room.

"It's good to see you, too, Mrs. Rosenthal," I smile politely, acutely aware that my cowlick is standing up in front and my shirt is a dingy, used-to-be-white color. I'm also acutely aware of how she's eyeing me, with a nearly imperceptible twitch of her lip, as if I reek of poor.

"Come with me," she motions for me to follow. She doesn't wait for a response; she spins on a heel and marches toward the wood-paneled library. She points to a big, empty space above a polished mantle when we enter the library.

"I'd like to hang something of yours here," she turns to me. "I want something big here. A painting of my house, perhaps?"

What is it with rich people wanting paintings of things they already own?

"I think I could do that," I nod, adding it to my mental to-do list. It's already longer than I'm ever going to be able to finish, I'm afraid, but I'm going to try. I won't ever turn down an opportunity to make money.

"You may go play with my son, now," she dismisses me like I'm the hired help. I feel a wave of anger sweep over me, but I swallow it down. She's the reason I'm successful, after all.

Isaiah leads me to the guest room next to his room when I get to the second floor. He opens the door to reveal an even less inviting room than the rest of the house. There is a massive bed that looks as if nobody has ever slept in it. The carpet scrunches beneath my feet like it's never been walked on. Nothing about this room says it has ever seen any company. And something about that unsettles me. What's the point of having a big house if you don't open it to people?

"This is your room," Isaiah smiles. "Mom insists you sleep here. But if you'd rather set up a sleeping bag in my room, I could arrange that."

I smile. He knows me all too well.

We spend the afternoon playing video games, shooting things mindlessly in mock war scenarios. We talk about school; we talk about life and our plans for our futures. I can feel my body start to unspool, layers of weeks' worth of stress falling off me in chunks. If laughter is the best medicine, I'm afraid I'm going to overdose. I didn't realize how much I needed an afternoon like this. It makes me wonder when my mom will ever get a day like this again.

"You worry about a lot of things," Isaiah says, suddenly very serious.

"What do you mean?"

"You get this look in your eyes," he gesticulates with big hands, his fingers flailing nearly comically. "Sometimes we're talking, and all of a sudden, you go rigid, and you look into the middle distance or something, and I know you're worried about something."

He shrugs, his deep voice gravelly with a hint of worry.

"I've got a lot to worry about, I guess," I shrug in response. We do our best communication through shrugs.

"I know," he cracks his knuckles nervously. "I just wish I could help you stop worrying. I can't even imagine everything you have to worry about."

And I know what he's saying. He's not saying he wants me to explain what I'm worried about. He just has never had to worry about the things I've had to. He's never come home to his electricity having been shut off. He's never taken public transportation anywhere.

That's something I like about Isaiah, though. The differences between us don't bother him. He just accepts that I come with my baggage, and he comes with his.

"I was just thinking about my mom," I finally explain. "I was thinking about how sad she must be. She doesn't have friends to spend time with. Or if she does, she doesn't have time to spend with them."

He nods knowingly.

"You have a certain look when you're thinking about your mom," he smiles, his eyes sparkling.

That's something else I like about Isaiah. He's perceptive. He notices things and may not ever comment on them. But he always notices. In fact, the list of things I don't like about Isaiah is much shorter than the list of things I like. It's no wonder everybody who meets him loves him.

Golden sunlight slants through Isaiah's window, and the sky is turning a royal purple when I look up.

"I guess it's about time to head to the theater," I nod to the window. "Don't want to keep Cameron and Kayla waiting."

Isaiah insists on paying for my ticket when we get to the theater, even though I have my own money now. I don't argue too much. I know he won't even miss $10 for a movie ticket. Should I feel bad for having that thought? I don't. But I do insist on buying his popcorn.

We meet Kayla and Cameron outside of the auditorium showing our movie. The marquee over the doorway reads *Three Blind Dice*.

"It's about a Las Vegas detective," Cameron is explaining to Kayla when we find them. "He loses his vision in a car accident, but he apparently thinks it wasn't an accident. He thinks he was targeted by a crime boss. So, he starts to investigate his own case. Half the movie is just a black screen with flashes of lights and vague shapes."

"Sounds scary," Kayla says in her flirty voice. "But if you hold my hand, I should be okay."

I make a gagging noise under my breath. Isaiah elbows me, but he's chuckling, too.

We're the first people in the theatre and manage to nab the best four seats in the theater. People crowd in around us. I spot our classmates around the auditorium. Everybody spots us; I'm sitting next to the Jolly Green Giant. Everybody smiles and waves at all of us. They even greet me. I wish they wouldn't.

"Hey, Isaiah," a sweet voice calls from across the auditorium. Keiko Tanaka waves, smiling broadly.

"Looks like someone has an admirer," Cameron says softly, laughing good-naturedly.

"She's had a thing for Isaiah since freshman year," Kayla explains casually.

"I don't know why he's never asked her out. She's cute."

"I'm just not feeling it," Isaiah shrugs.

The lights darken, and I know Isaiah is grateful for the end of the conversation.

Almost as soon as the room darkens, I notice a shift in Cameron and Kayla's posture. I can see Kayla's hand intertwined with Cameron's in the screen's glow. He draws little circles on the back of her hand with his fingertip.

I want that. I want my hand intertwined. I want to draw little circles on smooth skin. I want it so badly I can't even focus on the previews.

Isaiah leans over to me, bending awkwardly to whisper in my ear.

"You okay?"

Why is he always so concerned about me? I feel bad that he pays such attention to me.

"I'm fine," I smile. I turn my attention to the movie, but I'm constantly aware of Kayla's proximity to Cameron, the smell of Isaiah's cologne, and the sounds of popcorn-munching behind me. My senses are on overload. The music is loud. The detective on screen is running, climbing into his car.

The action on the screen is intense. He revs his car, speeds through an intersection. Suddenly the screen is lit up, bright white, and airbags deploy at the camera. The screen goes black.

In the flashes of light, I see Isaiah glance at me. I see Kayla and Cameron intertwined. I feel myself relax and go rigid at the same time. What the hell is wrong with me?

The rest of the night is peppered with flashes of light, gunshots, shouts, sirens. Chains. The protagonist is handcuffed, I guess?

After the movie is over, my nerves are shot. Something about sitting in the dark with only my ears to guide me sets me on edge. Cameron and Kayla invite us for dinner with them afterward.

"That'd be nice," I say as nonchalantly as possible. Something in me wants proximity to Kayla and Cameron. I want to observe this relationship. Maybe it's because I've never seen any of Kayla's relationships up close.

Perhaps it's because I've never seen any relationship up close.

So, we head out to a dimly lit restaurant known in our town for its delicious, cheap Italian food and the misspelled sign that hangs outside. The bright red lights of the RESTURANT sign outside illuminates Kayla's and Isaiah's faces as they slip into the booth, sitting by the window.

"That movie, man," Cameron said over a basket of warm, baked bread. "It was intense."

This launches us into a long conversation about the movie. It was thrilling. It messed with my brain. I hope I don't have nightmares about it.

We fall into a comfortable conversation. The entire time, I'm aware of the distance between Kayla and me, between Isaiah and me, between Cameron and Kayla. I'm aware of how some part of Cameron is always touching some part of Kayla. I'm aware, but I don't know why.

When our food comes, conversation lulls as we dive face-first into piles of pasta. The place is dark and grimy, and our corner booth is comfortable. The company is friendly, and I feel peaceful for the first time in weeks.

I breathe in deep and memorize the smell of happiness. It smells like Kayla's perfume, and warm bread and mozzarella, and Isaiah's cologne. It sounds like chatter, and the squeaking of pleather seats, and the clatter of forks on half-empty plates. I memorize every aspect of this moment and see it forming as a work of art in my mind. I see it in ink and watercolor. I see the glow of happiness. I feel a glow. I sigh amidst the conversation and settle into this brief bubble of joy I've escaped to.

"We're about to close," the waitress tells us irritably. Have two hours really passed? I hadn't even realized.

We collect our things and say our goodbyes. I hug Kayla, and I hug Cameron. It's as if the four of us have always been together. As if Isaiah and Kayla have always been my best friends, and Cameron has always been there. Why had I judged him so harshly?

When Isaiah and I return to his house, he fumbles in his pocket for his keys.

"This was fun," he smiles, digging in his pockets.

It was. I nod, reflecting on the night. I can feel that I'm smiling like a fool.

And then Isaiah kisses me.

Chapter Ten

For half a second, my internal monologue stops. My eyes are open, and his are closed. I feel myself grow rigid, and then relax, then grow rigid again. His eyes are closed, his body is shaking, and the hands he places on my shoulders are tight and nervous.

I finally get my wits and pull back. Isaiah loses his balance. At some point during the kiss, he'd raise one leg, poised perfectly on the other. He quickly repositions himself and looks at me with big, apologetic eyes.

"What…" I try to ask, but I can't make sense of words. "Isaiah, what was that?"

Isaiah kissed me? What the hell? Isaiah kissed me?

"I'm sorry," he looks broken, and I want to pick up the pieces. But I don't want to get too close for fear he'll throw himself on me again.

"It's just," he stops to consider what he wants to say. "You looked so happy. And you're so damned cute when you're happy. You were smiling all goofy, and your eyes were sparkling. And it's so hard not to stare when your eyes are sparkling."

I don't know what to say. I don't want to say anything. I want to tell him to leave me alone, but I don't want to hurt his feelings.

"You just," he shakes his head. "I'm sorry. Do you hate me?"

I don't know what I feel, but I don't think I hate him.

"I need some time to process all this," I say to him as much as to myself. I don't know what I want. I don't know what I need. But I know that I cannot sleep in a sleeping bag on his floor tonight. Or ever again.

He nods and opens his door, and I brush past him. I make my way upstairs to my designated bedroom and shut the door behind me before he has the chance to speak to me.

While I brush my teeth, the memory of Isaiah's lips on mine keeps resurfacing, no matter how far back I try to push it. I don't want to think about it. I don't want to remember. I just need time to process.

Isaiah's lips pressed against mine.

Not for the first time, I wonder if I was any good. This was my first kiss, and I don't even know if it was good.

And it was with Isaiah.

When I leave the guest bathroom, I half expect Isaiah to be in my bedroom waiting to talk. But he's not. And I want to know what he's thinking.

I grab my phone and text Kayla. I need to talk to somebody.

Hey...

I text her.

I need to talk.

But she doesn't respond. I don't know what I was expecting. Kayla never answers when I need her.

Never mind.

I drop my phone on top of the dresser beside the bed and curl up, still clothed, and try to convince myself to sleep.

But I can't. My mind is filled with gunshots and kisses. With chains rattling and laughter. The good and the bad, sharing the same spaces in my brain, where they've always lived. I heave heavily and roll around in the bed several times. I can't get comfortable.

I know Isaiah is across the hall, and I want to talk to him. But I haven't forgiven him yet for kissing me. I haven't forgiven myself for kissing back. Or maybe for not kissing back. Did I kiss him back?

I squeeze my eyes shut, willing myself to sleep. After a week of staying up all night and falling asleep in class, you'd think this would be no trouble for me. But it's futile.

I pick my phone back up and stare at it.

As if on cue, it vibrates in my hand.

Are you awake?

It's Isaiah. I don't open it because I don't want him to know I've read it. I don't want him to think I'm ignoring him, even though I am. It's not his fault I'm ignoring him. He didn't do anything wrong.

I want to kiss him again, I think. But I also want to punch him. Why the hell did he do this? Things were fine the way they were.

He doesn't deserve this treatment, I finally decide.

Yes.

Can we talk?

No.

I understand.

I love that Isaiah has perfect grammar when he types. He's not like Kayla. He always uses complete sentences and punctuation.

I'm not mad, I type but erase. And type again. And erase again.

I don't know if I'm mad. I don't know what I feel. What I feel is kind of numb.

Yes. I finally send. *We need to talk.*

Isaiah raps lightly on my door, and I let him in. The air between us is charged with electricity and something else—something I can't define. Tension? Anger? Disappointment? I don't know, but I don't like it.

"You had no right," I tell Isaiah before he has the chance to speak. He sits on my bed, thinks better of it, and sits in an armchair across the room.

"I know," he hands his head in shame. I hate that he's ashamed. He shouldn't be ashamed. He can't help the way he feels.

"You can't help the way you feel," I shrug, sitting down on my bed. "It's just,"

I don't know what to say. It's just *something.*

"I know," he shakes his head. "You don't feel the same way."

I shake my head. It's not that. How do I make him see?

"I don't know how I feel," I sigh. "But that's not the problem."

He looks at me with hurting puppy dog eyes. I just want to pull him next to me, and hold him, and make the pain go away. But that wouldn't solve anything. That might make just everything worse and more confusing.

"You're my best friend," I say, like that explains everything, even though I know it explains nothing. "And I like that you're my best friend."

He shrugs, still not understanding.

"And I can't get caught up in things like *this*," I gesture vaguely, "with my best friend because what happens when it doesn't work out?"

Isaiah stands up and takes a step toward me before changing his mind and sitting down again.

"What do you mean when it doesn't work out?" Anger is added to the pain in his voice, and it only hurts me worse.

"We're 18, Isaiah," I'm incredulous. What does he think's going to happen? I'm just going to say yes, I love him, run into his arms and stay there forever?

"And?" He's obstinate now. He crosses his arms and eyes me suspiciously.

"What do you want from me?" I finally beg. "How can I make it better?"

I say this like an accusation. I don't mean it like an accusation, but it's coming out that way.

"I want you to choose happiness," he finally says, his voice dry, like he's swallowed sand. "And if I'm not your happiness, that's fine."

I don't know what he means. What does he mean by choose happiness? I'm plenty happy. I almost tell him this, but he shakes his head.

"I am happy," I say, but it catches in my throat. I try to force a smile, but I can tell it looks as forced as it feels.

For a long time, neither of us says anything. I just stare at him while he picks at his fingernails idly. I wish I knew what to say to him. I want to rewind and redo everything about this night. Why hadn't I seen this coming?

I feel anger building in me. I'm mad at Isaiah. He ruined it. He ruined us. He's the first friend I've made in years, and he ruined it by kissing me. Why did he kiss me? He ruined us.

"Look, can I just ask you something?" Isaiah finally asks, breaking the silence.

I nod, unsure of what he's going to ask. Unsure of what I'll say.

"Will you just," he shakes his head. "I don't know. Will you consider it? Consider if we made us into an *us*."

I do consider it. Before I agree to consider it further, he continues.

"And if you don't want that, then that's fine."

It's strange seeing Isaiah this way. He's always so happy and loving. He's always so supportive. But this demanding part of him is new. It reminds me how complex he is.

"If you don't want that, we can go right back to how we were. We can just go back to being Isaiah and Cade, two goofs who eat lunch together."

I nod, considering this. I don't think it's possible to go back, but that sounds nice. We fall back into silence for a minute.

"I need some time," I tell him again, I tell myself again.

"That's fine," he nods and stands to leave.

"Hey, Is?" I ask, and he smiles at his nickname.

"Yeah, Cade?"

"Was that," now I'm the one embarrassed. "Was that your first kiss?"

I don't know why I want to know this. I don't know why it matters to me. But I want to know.

"No," he shakes his head sheepishly. "Was it yours?"

I nod, looking down at my hands. "Was I any good?"

"The best," he smiles his bright smile. "A real natural. Good night, Cade."

I wish Isaiah a good night and change into my pajamas once he's gone. I slide into the giant bed, plusher and nicer than anything I've ever slept on. It's exactly as uncomfortable as I'd predicted.

I start to consider Isaiah and me as something beyond just Isaiah and me. What would that be like? Would it be strange? Would it be comfortable? What kind of future could we possibly have?

Kayla never texts me back, and I never fall asleep. When morning comes, I've done a lot of considering, a lot of thinking, a lot of fantasizing, and imagining, and wondering. And I've come to no conclusions. I don't know what I want.

What I want is to go home and sleep and pretend yesterday didn't happen. What I want is for things to be back to normal, but I know things won't be back to normal. Once you've kissed somebody, you can't go back to the way it was.

The sun peeks over the edge of my bedroom window before I decide it's a reasonable time to be up and moving. I shower and dress, and then slip into the hallway and pad quietly down to the giant library. The massive house is eerie with the lights off and everybody asleep.

I flip on a green parlor lamp and search for any book that sounds interesting. Nothing on these shelves looks even remotely interesting; it's all the stuff rich people have on their shelves. Books of photography by overrated photographers; research-heavy books about mindfulness. Nothing that people read for fun. I grab *The Tao of Pooh* with no intention of actually reading it and then plop down in one of the heavy leather chairs in the library. I've always wondered what it would be like to live in a mansion, but if they're all as uninviting as this one, I think I'll pass.

I hear feet pad behind me on the carpet, and I turn, expecting to see Isaiah. Instead, I'm met by the face of Mrs. Rosenthal.

"You're up early," she comments as she sits in the armchair beside me.

"Yes, ma'am," I nod. "I always have trouble sleeping in strange beds."

I suddenly consider my words. I hope she doesn't think I mean the bed is strange. Just that it's unfamiliar.

"I understand," she smiles. "I don't often stay in hotels for that reason."

She eyes me for a moment before donning that serious face that means she's about to talk business.

"Cade, I think we should talk," she says, quirking a brow. I don't like her tone; something in it tells me I'm not going to like this conversation.

"Yes, ma'am?" I try to stay calm, but my heart is already racing. Those words always lead to something terrible.

"I saw you and my son last night on the front porch," she says, maintaining a cold, calculated stare.

Jesus Christ. This? I had just managed to stop thinking about it.

"Yes, ma'am," I've decided, apparently, that I'm just going to use the same response with different inflections for the duration of this conversation. It seems safer.

"I've had my suspicions for some time about him," Mrs. Rosenthal says, conversationally. The thing about people like Mrs. Rosenthal is that they're calculated, and everything she says leads into something else. She's spinning a web. I nod; I don't say anything.

"You, however," she nods to me. "You, I did not suspect one bit."

"I'm sorry, ma'am," I feel cornered. "You didn't suspect what?"

"Don't play dumb," she says, her voice saccharine sweet, her eyes filled with fire. "Here's what you need to know about The Rosenthal Family, Mr. Swanson."

I don't like the way she says my name. There's something venomous in it. There's something dangerous.

"We are a long and proud family," Mrs. Rosenthal begins, and I can already tell where this is going. "The Rosenthals were one of the first families in Riverside. My husband's family at one time owned all the land along the bank of the river from the northernmost boundary of the city limits to the city center."

I settle in for a long lecture about class and wealth. Two things Mrs. Rosenthal clearly thinks I don't have.

"It will come as no surprise to you, then, that we have certain expectations within this family," she's formal. She's speaking to me as if I'm the hired help. I hate when she speaks like this. It's like she's keeping a clear line between herself and filth like me.

"Yes, ma'am," I decide to keep my head level, even though I want to tell her exactly what I think of her and her expectations.

"You're a very talented artist, Cade," she says in an almost pitying tone. "But talent can only take you so far. I'm afraid you and my son come from very different worlds. I won't tell him who he can be friends with, by any means, but I don't think it's best for you to see him anymore. I will continue to act as your agent through your show at Kimball Art. But after that, you will need to seek new representation, I'm afraid."

I feel my cheeks warm, but I say nothing. I work on keeping myself stable.

"Yes, ma'am," I answer. I stand and thank her, now acting as if I'm the hired help, and return to my room. I gather my stuff and punch a number on my phone.

"Mom, can you come pick me up?"

And this is the last time I hope to see any of the Rosenthal family.

I'm quiet for the ride home, but when we get home, I fall apart. Kayla won't answer her phone, and I don't know why I'm surprised. I can't call Isaiah. I hate Isaiah. I hate everything he stands for.

"Oh, baby," Mom says, pulling me into her arms. "I'm so sorry."

She strokes my head, and I fight tears. I don't want her to see me cry over something so stupid. I don't want her to say *I told you so*. But she did tell me so. She told me not to go into business with Mrs. Rosenthal. Not in those words. But I knew it.

"That woman is heartless," Mom says, and it's the first time I've ever heard her speak against anybody. My mother is usually so proper and kind.

"I'm sick of her ruining lives. She has no right." And now I know Mom is talking about something I don't understand.

I look at her with questioning eyes. She breathes, holds in a breath, and lets it out slowly.

"I didn't want ever to have to tell you this," Mom says, a severe look in her eye. "But I think it's important for you to know now. Betty Rosenthal is the reason your father and I divorced."

Chapter Eleven

Mom sits me down in a chair in the kitchen, and as she starts to talk, my phone starts to ring. The screen says Isaiah, so I ignore the call. I ignore the call all five times he calls in rapid succession. Ignoring him is like a knife in the gut, but talking to him would be worse. I can't face that now. Maybe ever.

"Don't hate Isaiah," Mom says with a sad smile. "He's sweet, despite his raising."

"Everything's so complicated," I exhale.

"That's how life is," Mom says gently. Then she launches into her story.

Betty Rosenthal, née Fitzgerald, grew up with my parents. They went to high school together, and Betty was a living terror to my mother the entire time my parents dated. For a brief period during their senior year, my parents broke up. Betty Fitzgerald tried to convince my father to date her during that time.

"Apparently, Swanson men are just irresistible to the whole Rosenthal family," my mom chuckles softly, running a hand through my hair.

Betty made nasty comments about my mother all through high school. My father, it would seem, was born into a wealthy family and was upwardly mobile, whereas my mom was part of a large, working-class family; her parents immigrated from Colombia. Betty convinced my father for a long time that my mother was not good enough for him, and he deserved better. And that was when she intended to make her move.

"What does any of this have to do with your divorce?" I ask as my phone vibrates for the billionth time. I ignore it again. I'm never talking to Isaiah again.

"I'm getting there," Mom sits down across the table from me.

She tells me about marrying my father and their few good years of joy before the fighting started.

"Then, he started getting angry at me. All the time, angry," she says, her eyes watering with tears.

Mom starts to tell me about how she used to try to do things to make him happy, but nothing worked. And then she found the letters. Not emails. Old school letters. Shoved in a drawer.

"I wasn't snooping, I promise," Mom says, defending herself. I don't care if she snooped.

"But when I found them, they were all from Betty Fitzgerald. The postmarks were well after all of us had been married, but she had addressed each one from B. Fitzgerald and used a PO Box as her return address."

Mom explains how she became consumed, reading letter after letter. Each more intense than the rest in their professions of love and growing disgust of Mom.

I feel sick to my stomach. I've spent so much time with Mrs. Rosenthal lately. I've rubbed her face in my friendship with Isaiah. How could I do that? How could she let me do that?

"When your father left me," she says, her voice barely above a whisper as she relived her pain. "He told me Betty had been right all these years. I didn't understand him or his lifestyle. He needed to be on his own."

"And then he sold us," I respond. It's supposed to be a joke, but I know it's not as soon as I say it. Mom crumples.

"Baby, that's not it," she shakes her head, but she can't say much. She knows it's true. He bargained with her to never had to see us again.

"I'm sorry I talked so much about her," I stand up and hug Mom. "I didn't realize how hard it was for you. And that I brought him over here."

Mom just shakes her head, smiling.

"No," she runs her hand through my hair again. "No. Isaiah's kind. And maybe Betty's been helping you out of guilt, but she has been helping you. I wouldn't trade everything that's happened for anything."

The doorbell rings then, and Thomas comes running out in his pajamas. "Mom, that's Isaiah. I know it is," I sigh. "Please tell him to go away."

"You shouldn't punish him," Mom's eyes are pleading. "It's not his fault he fell in love with you. And it's not his fault his mother hates you."

Something makes me think Mom is talking about her own situation as much as she is mine.

"Mom, please, send him away."

She nods, and I know that she understands. I can't face him today. I can't face him ever. I won't face him ever.

Before Thomas can get the door unlocked, Mom meets him there and sends Thomas back in the kitchen to sit with me.

"Good morning, Ms. Swanson; I'm sorry it's early," Isaiah's voice makes me ache. He sounds so sad. So sad. "Is Cade available? I need to talk to him."

"Oh, Isaiah, good morning," my mom says in her perfect hostess voice. "I'm sorry, but Cade's not feeling well."

"Are you sick, Bub?" Thomas asks me, and I shush him quickly.

"I'm sorry, now's just not a good time," Mom says more sternly. "But I can give him a message."

I hear Isaiah breathe in deeply and exhale slowly.

"My mom did something awful to him, Ms. Swanson. I just want him to know I'm sorry. She doesn't speak for me. Can you tell him that? Please?"

"I'll tell him," Mom says kindly.

I hear the slow scuffle of Isaiah's giant feet as he walks slowly back to his car.

"Isaiah," Mom calls behind him. I hear him shuffle back to the door, and Mom says something I can't make out. Maybe she's telling him never to come back. That'd be nice.

"I'm calling in today," Mom says with a loving smile.

"You don't have to do that," I shake my head. "I'm okay."

I don't know if I'm okay, but people deal with much worse stuff than I'm dealing with, so I know I'll survive.

"We're fine, Cade," she says in exasperation. "And what's the point of having the world's best kids if I don't get to spend time with them?"

As stupid as it sounds, I'm excited to spend the day with my mom. She's the best listener. She's the best everything.

Before I can argue more, she picks up her cell phone and dials a number.

"Hey, Peter," she says in her businesslike voice. "It's Teresa. Listen, I'm having some troubles at home today. Do you want to take my shift tonight? I know your wife's birthday is coming up, and you were looking for some extra hours."

She hangs up with a smile and looks from me to Thomas and back again. "Who wants pancakes?"

Something about my mom is different. She's drifting around the kitchen, a big smile on her face as she mixes together ingredients for the most delicious pancakes in the world. She mixes together cinnamon and sugar and turns on the electric griddle.

The smell of sizzling butter is enough to relax me despite the awful morning I've had. Mom turns on the radio, tuning into an oldies station. She smiles broadly as "The Loco-Motion" booms through the speakers, Little Eva's voice joining the chorus of sizzling and clattering in the kitchen.

Mom joins the song, and Thomas dances an adorable little dance in his pajamas. Mom grabs his hands and twists with him as the pancakes firm up on the griddle.

"Come dance with us, Bub," Thomas calls with delight.

"I'm okay," I say passively from my chair. I'm having fun watching them.

But Mom doesn't take that as an answer. She reaches out her arm, wraps her fingers around my wrists, and pulls me into a circle with them, singing loudly.

And here I am, eighteen years old, dancing in the kitchen, singing "The Loco-Motion" with my mom and my baby brother. I throw my head back and laugh hard when the song is over. I'm exhausted. I'm angry. I'm upset. But in this moment, I feel so happy.

"I have something to tell you two," Mom says as she puts a plate of pancakes on the table.

"I'm going to have more time to spend with you guys," she smiles as she pulls a bottle of syrup out of the fridge. Something in this is unsettling.

"Really?!" Thomas exclaims through a mouthful of pancake, unable to wait even for syrup.

"Today was my last shift at Megamart, in fact," she sits down. "So, I guess yesterday was my last day at Megamart."

"Mom, did you lose your job?" I sit upright. She looks younger than she has in ages. Why is she so calm?

She nods her head a little sheepishly.

"I didn't want to worry you until I found something else," she's smiling, so I assume she's already found something else.

"What did you find?" I ask her, unable to eat my pancakes until my fears have been put to rest.

Mom's face lights up, unable to contain her excitement.

"I told my boss at Golden Acres about it and asked if there were any other jobs I could do for extra hours until I figured something out. But she told me she had a secret to tell me."

I hate when Mom tells stories like this. Just tell me the conclusion. Are we going to starve or not? When I don't prod further, Mom continues anyway.

"You know Oak Hollow, that big complex that they just finished building next to your school?" She looks at me intently. "My boss was just hired as the director there. She said she was planning on asking me to move with her and be the activities director for her there."

I smile contentedly. As long as Mom has a job that makes her happy, I'm happy, I guess. I'll find a way to pick up any slack with my art. And then I feel the knife in my gut again. Mrs. Rosenthal fired me.

"I haven't told you the best news yet," Mom is glowing, and I'm finding it hard not to be excited for her, even though I don't know what the news is.

"It comes with a raise. A big one," she's practically foaming at the mouth from excitement. "I'll be making almost twice what I made at Megamart and Golden Acres combined."

I feel the world's largest boulder lift from my shoulders, and I sit up straighter. My mom is going to be working fewer hours and making more money? How is that even possible? The cynic in me keeps waiting for the other shoe to drop. What's the trade-off going to be?

"That's really awesome," I say more for her benefit than mine.

The mood at breakfast is so different than it has been in years. My mom seems lighthearted and happy. She's smiling so brightly that I feel wrapped in the warmth of it. Her worry lines are practically receding in front of me, and even though her hair is peppered with silver, she seems much younger today than she has in years.

I even catch myself smiling a truly joyful smile. I've had a sucky morning, but Mom's and Thomas's moods are so light that I can't help myself. I want to sing "The Loco-Motion" with them again. I want to stand up and dance around and laugh because laughter is the best medicine.

"I think we should celebrate," Thomas smiles broadly, giggling.

"Oh?" Mom stands up and kisses the top of his head. "How do you propose we celebrate?"

"How about ice cream and the zoo?" He giggles uncontrollably, his face scrunching.

"Yeah?" Mom tickles him. "You think the zoo and ice cream would be nice? I think we could do that."

I feel my eyes grow heavy; my week of not sleeping is catching up with me.

"I don't think I'm up to the zoo today, Bub," I blink hard.

"Cade's had a long week," Mom explains. "What if you and I go to the park and let Bub sleep for a while."

I'm grateful for Mom and her intuition as I climb into my bed and fall quickly into sleep, but not a restful one. I can't stop thinking about Kayla, and Isaiah, and art, and Mrs. Rosenthal. Mrs. Rosenthal with red horns. Mrs. Rosenthal, seven-stories-tall as I'm dressed in rags, painting a larger-than-life reproduction of their mansion. Isaiah, meek and puny, compared to his gargantuan mother, is just at the edges of my vision, locked in an iron cage. I want to save him, but his mother won't let me move until I'm finished with the painting. All Mrs. Rosenthal has given me to work with is tiny brushes, and I feel like I will never finish this piece. It seems to grow exponentially every time I look away.

My mom appears, dressed in white, brandishing a long sword. She looks like a middle-aged Guinevere, proud and regal. Her hair is done up in intricate braids, and she steps with the most delicate grace. I can't imagine how she's going to beat the lumbering Mrs. Rosenthal.

My mom holds her glowing sword to the sky and begins to sing a gentle, lilting melody. The song spreads through the air like static, sending chills down my spine. Mrs. Rosenthal crashes to the ground at my mother's song, leaving an impression in the ground like a crime-scene chalk outline. The canvas shrinks to the size of a gravestone. In cemetery script, it reads, "Here lies Grendel. May peace be restored to our realm."

When I wake up, I'm disoriented. The sun's bright rays pass through my window and filter in like the magic that charged my dream. I look at my cell phone to see the time, but it's dead. I don't know if I've slept for an hour or a day, but I feel better. I have a pressing headache from a week's worth of not sleeping, but in the immediate time, I feel better.

I plug my phone in to charge and make my way to the kitchen to dig into leftover pancakes. I feel hungover, or what I imagine a hangover feels like, as I sit down with my stack of carbs and a giant cup of coffee. I watch syrup cascade over my short stack and wonder if I've been doing everything wrong. Maybe I should have been focusing on school and not art. Maybe I should have been doing everything differently.

I wouldn't have ended up here at the bottom of a syrup bottle if I'd done things differently.

My phone rings in the distance. It's Kayla's ringtone. Convenient for her to try to call me now that I'm not in a state of emergency. I roll my eyes and ignore it. I'll call her back when I feel like it. But that's not now.

The front door opens, and I hear Thomas come skipping in.

"You're up?" Mom sounds surprised. She sits down next to me at the table.

"Yes, ma'am," I nod. She puts an arm around my shoulder as if to channel her energy into mine.

"Are you ready for the zoo, Bub?" Thomas's voice is always so full of energy. How does he do it?

"Let me finish eating, and I will be," I smile. I can't bear to show Thomas my lousy mood. I try hard not ever to show him anything but positivity. I don't want Thomas growing up bitter like me.

"You don't have to do with us," Mom says soothingly. "We're all entitled to days off, Cade."

"You never take one," I say pointedly. I'm aware my exhaustion and mood are making me rude, and I try to swallow it down.

"I'm taking a whole week off," she says comfortingly and not angrily.

"You deserve it," I smile. "Congratulations, Mom. I can't say it enough."

I agree to go to the zoo with them; I'll take any escape I can get.

I have to keep reminding myself that the things I'm dealing with aren't really that big a deal. People go through worse things every day. I've been through worse things. But this all still feels really big. I'll feel better after I get more sleep, I think.

The zoo is busier than I expected on an overcast day in October. The animals are more active, too.

Thomas giggles at ring-tailed lemurs as they race about their island. He claps his hands as macaws squawk loudly. He jumps up and down in excitement at the otters splashing around their enclosures.

When we get to the tiger exhibit, he's more excited than I've seen him in his entire life. He couldn't be more energized if he'd taken caffeine in an IV. His eyes light up, and he rushes to the window, practically shoving people out of the way.

The tigress takes notice of Thomas and approaches the window slowly. When Thomas realizes he's being noticed, he walks along the glass. The tigress follows him with her eyes before stalking steadily along beside him. It's terrifying and exhilarating watching this game of play and chase. Thomas has no idea that the glass is the only thing keeping him alive. I'm not sure the cat does, either.

"Do you have any paper and a pen?" I ask my mom excitedly. I want to capture this moment. I want to capture in broken lines and weird shading, not my photo-realism that's become so comfortable and natural to me.

Mom digs around in her tiny purse and pulls out a chewed-up pencil and a small spiral-bound notebook. I capture Thomas's little form running back and forth in messy, sketchy lines. I capture the tigress, lumbering, much larger in my sketch, stalking him. I picture it in colors I'd never use. I picture it as something completely different than anything I'd typically pursue. But it's there, etched in my mind.

"I envy you," Mom smiles at my sketches, broken up by blue and red notebook paper lines. "I could never do what you do."

"You could," I shrug. I've seen my mom draw; she's not bad. She's not a refined artist, but she doesn't practice.

"Never like you," she shakes her head smiling, watching Thomas from a distance.

"That's okay," I smile, sketching the crowds of people gathering around Thomas. Two little boys join him, running along the edge of the glass. "I can't paint like Degas or Cezanne or Monet or Van Gogh. I think if we could recreate the art we enjoy looking at, we'd stop enjoying it as much."

"I wish I had your outlook on things," Mom smiles even more broadly, that smile that draws everybody in. "I want to be you when I grow up."

We both chuckle. I want to be her. I want to be the type of person who does whatever it takes to support my family. I want to grow up to be somebody my children look up to.

"I want to be Thomas," I say instead, nodding at him as he runs back and forth.

"Thomas, sweetie, let's go. There are other animals we haven't seen yet." Mom calls.

I enjoy the gentle breeze and the smell, and the sights. I feel myself unwind, even in my exhaustion. I almost forget about the events of this morning. Almost.

"I think I owe Isaiah an apology," I tell Mom in the dark of the reptile and amphibian house.

"Take some time," Mom says, watching Thomas staring intently at poison dart frogs. "Be angry. Be upset. Be hurt. We need those things, Cade."

I smile for the millionth time today.

"Everybody thinks we're supposed to just get over our feelings," Mom says introspectively. "But that's not how it works. You have permission to feel bad. Your feelings are valid."

I know Mom knows this from experience. I wonder if these are the things she wishes somebody had told her when she was going through her divorce. I wonder if these are the things she told herself during her divorce.

"Take some time to hurt," she reiterates.

I nod quietly. Isaiah needs some time, too.

When Thomas has finally marveled and reveled over every animal in the zoo, we finally make our way to the zoo's exit. The sun hangs low and tinges of indigo and purple start to kiss the sky.

"It's practically dinner time," Mom observes as we make our way to her car. "What would you say to going to Cantina Del Sol and then getting ice cream?"

Cantina Del Sol is my favorite restaurant in the entire world. I feel like a little kid. Mom made pancakes this morning and is taking us to dinner tonight.

"Mom?" I ask before I catch myself. "How are we affording this?"

I know there's the promise of money. But the promise of having money is not the same as actually having money.

"We're fine, Cade," is the only answer I receive.

Chapter Twelve

When I get home, content and full of Mexican food and ice cream, Thomas is chattering excitedly about how nice today has been. And I can't help but agree. I can't imagine a better day than hanging out with my mom and brother. I didn't realize how much I needed this until I had it.

"This has been nice," I hear myself say before realizing it. "It's exactly what I needed."

Mom laughs and runs her fingers through my hair again in that protective way she has my entire life.

"Are you going to go paint?" Mom asks, offering me the notepad I'd sketched in at the zoo.

"You said no art this weekend," I remind her, going to my bedroom to change into pajamas. I want to watch a movie with my family and enjoy this rare bonding moment.

When I get to my room, my phone has 133 notifications. Kayla has spent the day calling and texting me. I have forty calls and ten voicemails. I have 83 text messages. I almost laugh at how desperately she tried to contact me. But the cynical part of me wonders if she wanted to call to check on me or if she needed my help with something.

I listen to the voicemails and immediately regret that cynic in me. Kayla's voicemails are frantic with worry. I was cryptic in my texts last night, and now she's worried. She even came to my house while we were gone. I feel guilty; I had no idea she'd actually react that way.

I send her a text message to help her calm down.

Hey, I'm okay. It's been a weird day. I'll call you tomorrow.

"Oh, you're already ready for bed," Mom comments as I come back into the living room. She and Thomas are sitting on the couch, Thomas telling her excitedly what movies he'd like to watch.

"I just put on PJs," I say, sitting next to Thomas on the sunken-in couch. "Why, what's up?"

Mom stops for a second to consider what she's going to say. Then she says it anyway.

"Thomas and I decided we wanted to learn how to paint," she says carefully. "And we wondered if you'd teach us something tonight. But we want to watercolor."

I roll my eyes.

"You know how to watercolor," I chuckle. More importantly, I hate it.

"It's been a long time," she sighs playfully. "And Thomas doesn't. Come on; you're just being greedy now. Right, Thomas? He doesn't want to share his secrets with us."

Thomas looks at me with his wet, puppy dog eyes, and I give in immediately. I'm positive they planned this.

"Fine, but we have to go buy paints. I don't have any watercolors," I grab my phone and wallet from my dresser. "The art store closes in 45 minutes; we've got to go."

When we get to the art store, I make a mad dash to the paint section. There are so many to choose from. There are kids' sets, and students' sets, and hobbyists' sets, and professional sets. There are masses of brushes. Brushes made from squirrel hair, and sable hair, and, synthetic squirrel hair. I can't even begin to understand why there are so many brushes.

"This is why I prefer graphite," I gesture to the masses of things before me.

Mom rolls her eyes and grabs a set of kids' paints and a set of student paints. I reach for a metal tin full of professional paints, my bulging wallet weighing down my pocket with anticipation.

"I cannot believe you came to the art store in your pajamas," Mom says as she grabs a stack of watercolor paper and heads toward the counter to pay. I follow suit, grabbing a pack of professional-grade paper.

We stand in line behind a man in tailored jeans, a button-down dress shirt and a blazer. He's dressed to the nines with a fistful of expensive brushes in hand. Twice, he eyes my mother and me, and at first, I think it's because he's interested in my mom. The third time he glances at us, however, it becomes evident that he's judging me and my pajamas.

"Can I help you, sir?" I demand before I catch myself. Suddenly I wish I could go unnoticeable again.

"I just couldn't help noticing how you're dressed," he sneers in a want-to-be posh accent. "I can't believe your mother would let you leave the house like that."

He turns a cold eye to my mother and smiles before he continues.

"Not much control over your teenagers, I presume?"

My mom opens her mouth, thinks twice about it and shuts it again.

I, however, don't think twice.

"Guess your mom never taught you any manners, either," I say loudly and pointedly. Sometimes it just feels good to fight. And with a total stranger, it's even better.

"How about you don't open your mouth to my mom ever again," I clench my fists tightly.

"Cade, it's okay," Mom shakes her head. "People need to watch the way they treat others."

The passivity in my mother's voice makes it seem as if she's correcting me, and for a moment, I'm angry. And then I realize just how brilliant she is.

"How are you doing, Mr. Kimball?" The cashier asks as he approaches the check stand.

"Oh, God," I mutter under my breath.

Mom looks at me with confusion until a slow realization spreads over her face.

"What, Bub?" Thomas, the king of tact, asks loudly.

"Nothing," I whisper to Thomas, hoping to deflect all attention. Maybe I can go unnoticeable. I definitely don't want Martin Kimball to realize that not only am I the unkempt, pajama-clad urchin from the art store but that I am also the artist he's just dedicated his gallery to in a month.

"This, Cade," Mom says quietly as Martin Kimball pays for his supplies. "Is why I tell you always to mind your manners. It's because you don't know when you'll piss off the wrong person." She smiles good-heartedly, but I know she means it.

When Martin Kimball leaves, casting a final glance over his shoulder at us, I feel myself breathe for the first time. Thank God he's gone.

I refuse to let Mom pay for my expensive art supplies, even when she insists. The girl at the counter smiles knowingly.

"He doesn't let his boyfriend pay for anything, either," she says good-naturedly, and it's like a shot to the gut.

"I'm sorry?" Mom asks, quirking a brow.

"She means Isaiah," I shake my head, wishing I could melt into a puddle of embarrassment. "He always offers to buy my art supplies when we come here."

Mom nods knowingly. She doesn't argue with the girl because it would make things harder on me.

"I guess that's what I get for raising independent kids, right?" She asks the checkout girl instead.

Mom looks at me intently when we get into the car, studying me like it's the first time she's seen me.

"I guess I never realized how close you and Isaiah have gotten," she says like things are finally making sense to her. I don't know what makes sense to her now that hadn't before. "I'm sorry everything's so complicated."

I don't say anything because I don't know what to say. I just want to go home and paint. I want to bury my head in my work and not come up for air until college.

When we get home, I set Mom, Thomas, and myself up with our paints, cups of water, and a handful of brushes apiece.

In typical Thomas fashion, he makes the world's biggest mess, paint covering every square inch of his entire workspace. Mom, however, is cautious and intentional with her paint as she blocks out a rose. She watercolors like a pro; why doesn't she paint more often? While they busy themselves with their own projects, I begin to sketch out a larger version of Thomas running happily alongside a tiger.

In my imagining, the glass is gone, and the tigress is protecting Thomas, not stalking him. My lines are sketchy and imprecise as I transfer the image in my head to the paper. Usually, I would clean this up to make the lines precise and perfect. I'd erase until they were almost invisible and would be hidden underneath the paint.

But I don't. I throw caution to the artistic wind and let the paint lead the way.

Before long, Thomas has abandoned his stick figure, brown and murky from paints mixing on the page in bizarre ways. Mom is working steadily on her rose, delicately painting shadows on the rose in a way that stuns me. Her work is more precise than even anything I do. Her rose looks realistic. It looks like you could pluck it off the page. Why did she ever stop painting?

I look at my own painting, taking a step back to view it from a distance.

The tiger, blue and green and proud, stands protectively over a diminutive Thomas, brave and fragile. I don't know how much time has passed, and it's clear Mom has no idea either. We might have been working for hours.

I step away from my painting to find Thomas. He's asleep on the couch with the remote in his hand. I pluck it gently from him and carry him to his bed. When I tuck him into his bed, he stirs and opens one eye.

"Bub?" his voice is dry after sleeping open-mouthed in the living room.

"Yeah, Thomas?"

"We're so lucky," he says, a smile crossing his face. "Some kids don't have a mom like ours."

"Nobody has a mom like ours," I whisper, covering him up. "We are lucky."

When I turn, Mom is standing in the doorway, her eyes wet. I'm suddenly embarrassed that she heard our conversation. Something about being eighteen and still thinking my mom is the best makes me uncomfortable. Kayla always fights with her mom, and Isaiah barely speaks to his. Granted, that's probably because she's a monster. But that's neither here nor there.

And then I think about how disappointed in me my mom would be if she knew I thought that about Mrs. Rosenthal, even if it's true. Because Mom believes in kindness and goodness. I'm not sure those things even exist.

"How did I get so lucky?" Mom asks, crossing her arms and surveying me when I leave Thomas's room. "I have the two best boys in the world."

"You've got one, at least," I shrug, nodding toward Thomas. "I can't speak much for me."

Mom just smiles at me with that beaming smile that accentuates the wrinkles around her eyes and makes me feel washed out in comparison.

When I get back to the kitchen where we've been painting, Mom's done with her rose. It looks amazing. It looks professional. How does she do it?

"Why didn't you tell me you could paint like this?" I demand playfully, pointing at the rose still taped down to the table to prevent the page from curling.

"I didn't know I still could," Mom says seriously. "Your father wasn't big on me painting. He said it took too much of my time. I think he was a little jealous, too. He was always very competitive."

This is the first negative thing I've ever heard her say about my father. She believes in kindness and goodness.

"Do you think about him a lot?" I ask. I don't know why I ask.

"No," she shakes her head. "I used to. I used to wonder what I did wrong. I used to wonder how I could have fixed it. I thought that if he'd just come back, I could do it all right things next time."

She holds a deep breath.

"I don't want you to hate your father, Cade," she says for the zillionth time in my life. "But he was bad for me."

I nod, not saying anything. I can tell she needs to talk, and I don't want to do anything to remind her that I'm her son and not her friend.

"Sometimes it's hard to see when you're in an abusive relationship," she finally says, sitting down in the chair and busying herself in taking the tape off her rose. "Because sometimes you can't see the marks."

She looks at me, and I don't know what to say. So, I say nothing. It's one of my strong suits.

"He was a good dad to you, though," she smiles at me. "He was so proud of you. And in those times when he was showing you off to everybody and saying, 'you see this boy? He's going to be somebody great one day.' In those times, I loved him more than I thought possible."

I see her fight a tear. This is a happy day; I wish she wouldn't cry.

"Because we had this beautiful son that he was so proud of," she wipes away the tear as it rolls down her cheek. "Do you remember that?"

I do remember that. I feel nostalgia well up in me. I forgot about all the times that Dad used to cart me around to show me off to his work associates. He'd hold up the drawings I'd made and show them off to his coworkers. He'd say, "my boy made this." And I'd smile wide and proud. Because my dad was the greatest.

"I don't want to remember that," I say stubbornly. And there I am again, eighteen years old and bitter. Always bitter. Always angry.

"You look so much like him when you smile," she says gently, ignoring my petulance. "He was so handsome when he smiled."

I try not to smile, but I do. I shouldn't want my mom to call me handsome; I'm far too old to need that kind of approval. But something about my mom saying this reminds me of Isaiah. He says my eyes sparkle when I smile. I feel my cheeks warm. And then anger. And then pain. Because everything sucks, and everything is complicated.

"Did you love him?" I ask. I don't know why I ask. I don't want her to dwell on this painful memory.

"I did," Mom nods slowly. "Love's a complex thing, Cade."

She thinks for a moment before continuing.

"Sometimes you love somebody, but they can't love you back the same way," she surveys her rose and smiles like something unspooling inside her. "And it's not their fault. Just like it's not your fault you love them."

I don't really understand what she's saying. I mean, I know what all those words mean when put together in the same sentence. But I don't understand.

"I loved your father," she clarifies. "And he thought he loved me, I think."

I nod now, understanding. She's absolving him of hurting her.

"I'm lucky, though," she says, running her hand through my hair for the zillionth time in my life. "Because at least I came out of it with you two."

I nod again. Then look at her rose another time. In this moment, there's nobody I'd rather be like in the entire world.

"Cade, I've been thinking about something," she says gently, clearly stepping lightly in how she says it. "I think you should invite your father to your gallery opening. He probably won't come. But he should know it's happening, at least."

"I'll think about it," I say in the way Mom always does, which actually means no. It seems more diplomatic that way.

"Please do," she says softly. "It's been four years. Maybe he's different now."

I'm positive he's not different. But not arguing with her makes it easier for everybody. I make my way to my bed, fall face-first into my mattress, and sleep better than I have in a month.

Chapter Thirteen

"What happened?" Kayla asks when I let her in my house Sunday afternoon. I've been avoiding contact with the outside world for as long as possible. But with Kayla here, I realize that I need her more than I ever have before.

"Isaiah kissed me," I say bluntly without looking at her. I'm expecting her to say she told me so. Because she did tell me so. She pegged that Isaiah liked me the first time he spent the weekend with us. I should have seen it.

But she doesn't say she told me so. She just hugs me. She doesn't know what to say. And I don't know how to respond.

"What's got you so upset?" Kayla smiles. "Was it a bad kiss?"

She's trying to break the tension, but in a way that also gives her the juicy details.

"I don't think so," I shrug. I lead her into the living room, and we sit on the couch. "He's my friend, Kayla."

She looks at me with the same confused look that Isaiah did when I said this.

"What on earth does that mean?"

I shrug. It makes less sense now that I'm saying it to Kayla. It's a weak argument.

"And even if I liked him like that, his Mom hates me."

I recount the weekend to Kayla. I tell her everything that happened from the time we parted from her and Cameron until the moment she appeared on my doorstep. I tell her about the awful conversation with Mrs. Rosenthal. I tell her about how I felt backed into a corner and how she told me I wasn't good enough for Isaiah.

"That's awful," Kayla shakes her head. She's angry. "I'm so sorry, Cade."

She swallows hard like she's physically swallowing down anger. But the anger wins.

"What a bitch," she finally says, exasperated. "I'm sorry. But you're not good enough for them? She should feel lucky you even deigned to step foot in her presence."

Before I know it, Kayla is pacing around the living room, all but shouting.

"You're the kindest, most caring person I know, and she doesn't think you're good enough?" She's venting. But it's flattering to hear her talk like this. Kayla usually only talks about herself.

"You work so hard, and you're so talented. You're a local celebrity. Everybody loves your art. You have an art show coming up." She's sorting through all the reasons I'm a rock star in her eyes, and, surprisingly, it makes me feel better. Even if I do hate the attention.

"She's jealous, Cade," she finally concludes. "She's jealous of you and your life. She can't paint. She can't create. Since she can't, all she does is destroy. She sees how beautiful you are and wants to destroy that beauty. You can't let her. What a bitch."

Kayla reaches for her keys.

"Come on," she instructs me as she heads toward the door. "I'm going to tell Mrs. Rosenthal exactly what I think of her."

I stop her before she gets to the door. That would only end in disaster. She'd probably have us arrested for trespassing or something. She'd probably have her butler have us arrested for trespassing.

"Kayla, stop," I hear Isaiah's voice echo in my head as I command Kayla. I wonder if she's as angry as I was when Isaiah spoke to me like that. "Anger only makes everything worse. And this is all so complicated, already."

"Fine," Kayla concedes, sitting back down on our sunken-in sofa. "I'm just pissed."

"I'm pissed, too," I shrug with my arms crossed.

"Not pissed enough," Kayla laughs a little bit.

I'm grateful that Kayla doesn't ask me if I like Isaiah. In fact, Kayla drops the conversation altogether. Instead, she opens her backpack and pulls out her notes from school.

"We've got to get you caught up in class," she says calmly. "No best friend of mine is going to fail classes. Not if I can help it."

We dive headfirst into everything I've ignored in classes. Surprisingly, I'm not distracted by the need to paint, and I start to worry if I'm already losing my inspiration. Have I already run the tap dry?

By the time Kayla leaves, I'm feeling confident again. I feel like I can handle anything Monday has to throw at me. As usual, though, I'm wrong. I'm as ready for what Monday brings as I am for Armageddon.

When I wake up, my head throbs, and my vision's blurry. I can't breathe through my nose, and my throat feels raw like I've swallowed sandpaper and glass shards.

Great. A cold is exactly what I need right now. Perfect.

Mom drives me to school for the first time in four years, and it's kind of nice. I've missed starting my morning with her. And I also feel a little childish, enjoying my mother's company so much. Shouldn't I hate her or something? That's how the movies make it seem, at least.

When I get to art, I look for Isaiah, but he's nowhere to be seen. I feel a stab of pain in my gut. I miss him. It's been three days, and I miss him. How ridiculous is that?

Mr. Camplin gives us our assignments, and I get to work, burying myself in my work. It's familiar. It's safe. I can disappear in my work and forget everything that's going on.

The door opens sometime into our work, and I feel Isaiah's presence enter the room. I refuse to look at him, though. I can't make things worse for him. I can't make things worse for me.

This all sucks so much.

"Cade?" Mr. Camplin summons me to his desk after giving Isaiah instructions for the day. I feel nauseated as I cross the classroom to talk to Mr. Camplin. I always feel nauseated when a teacher calls me. I always fear I've done something wrong.

"Yes, sir?" I say, muffled in my own ears. I hate being sick.

"Is everything okay?" he asks, concerned. I hate when Mr. Camplin is concerned. It makes me feel guilty.

I also hate that he's so attentive that he knows when something's wrong with his students. Teachers aren't supposed to care that much.

"Yes, sir," I nod because I don't feel like going into details. But he doesn't accept it. He rarely does.

"Take a seat," he points to the chair beside his desk. "Tell me what's on your mind."

I take a seat, but I don't tell him.

And then I do. Not everything; I don't tell him any actual details. It protects me, and it protects Isaiah. Isaiah's story is not mine to tell.

"I'm just dealing with a lot," I say guardedly. "Just teenage relationship stuff."

I shake my head to show him how meaningless I know it all is. Adults have real problems. I have this.

"There aren't many problems harder to deal with than relationships," Mr. Camplin says kindly. "There's a lot at stake."

I feel myself relax. I feel validated in my emotions.

"Don't let it get you so down," Mr. Camplin smiles. "You're an artist and a teenager. You feel things in a much heavier way than most people. And that's okay. That's probably one of the things that attracts the relationship-problem-causer to you."

I have to work hard not to make eye contact with Isaiah. I have to strain not to look at him. I want to look at him. Is it true?

I still don't even know if I like him.

I still don't know anything.

"Thank you, sir," I say, not making eye contact. I'm still embarrassed that there was something noticeably wrong with me. And for the first time in four years, I miss my father. He used to give me advice like this. Mom is right; he was a really good dad when he was around.

"If you ever need to talk, I'm here," Mr. Camplin smiles his comforting, fatherly smile, and I wonder why Mr. and Mrs. Camplin don't have kids. He'd be a really good dad.

I take a seat back at my desk and look at the charcoal portrait in front of me. I'm as comfortable in charcoal as I am in graphite. I feel myself slip into my relaxed Zen of drawing, and shadowing, and shading. I allow my hands to go to work while my brain zones out. I do my best thinking while I'm drawing. I do my best reflection when my hands are busy.

The bell pulls me from my thoughts. I look at my charcoal and see what I've been working on. It was supposed to be a self-portrait; my reference photo sits beside me, with my face scrunched and my cheeks puffed out. However, the charcoal in front of me is Isaiah, sad and reflective across the room. I feel my cheeks warm with embarrassment, and I quickly cover it with newspaper and stow it in my slot at the back of Mr. Camplin's room. I don't want to have to explain to Mr. Camplin, but I also don't want to have to restart this project.

Lunch is quiet without Isaiah around. I don't know where he is, but he didn't show up at our usual table. Cameron and Kayla are laughing loudly, telling jokes, and I laugh along so they won't worry about me. But I just feel sad. I don't know why I haven't bounced back yet. I always recover from these things quickly; I don't understand why this is any different.

"I'm so glad you and Isaiah came out with us on Friday," Cameron says a while into lunch. I don't know if he'd been talking to me before now, but I'm only just paying attention to him. "Speaking of Isaiah, where is he?"

Kayla winces noticeably and whispers something in Cameron's ear. I don't hear what she says, but he blushes and changes the subject quickly. Not for the first time, I'm thankful for Kayla. And I remember why she's my best friend. She has my back, for the most part.

In the rest of my classes, I'm the best I've been in a long time. I answer questions out loud and even pass a physics test. I've brought my grade securely to a C. It's not great, but it's passing. It'll have to do for now.

Before I meet Kayla at her car, I swing by Mr. Camplin's room and ask to take my charcoal home to finish working on it. He doesn't generally let us, but I have a suspicion he's put 2 and 2 together and figured out what's going on in my life.

"Sure. Just make sure you bring it back before class tomorrow so that I can critique it," he smiles. He studies me for a moment.

"Things are going to be okay," he smiles. "You've got art to help you cope with everything. Look at all the greats. They all coped with their problems through art."

"Didn't Van Gogh cut off his ear?" I ask, half-joking.

"Yeah," Mr. Camplin winces playfully. "Don't be like him."

I wish him a good afternoon, grab my giant charcoal drawing, and meet Kayla at her car.

"Is that a giant drawing of Isaiah's face?" Kayla asks as I shove it into the back seat as surreptitiously as possible.

"I don't want to talk about it," I say flatly. I'm hungry.

I convince Kayla to take me to Whacky Reggae, a disgusting little hole-in-the-wall near our school where our classmates collect in droves. Whacky Reggae is a Jamaican/Korean/Taco infusion restaurant where you can basically get jerk-and-curried-anything on a tortilla. It's so dimly lit inside, you can have just to trust that the waiter has actually brought you what you ordered when you bite in. But the food is amazing, and the atmosphere is great.

I pay for our food and sit down at a table near some of the people we go to school with. I don't really know them and don't really care to. But they're talking about a party this coming weekend, and I'm intrigued. I've never been to a party.

I mean, I've been to birthday parties. Who hasn't? But this isn't a birthday party. There won't be any cakes or cartoon character banners. This is a real party with people and loud music and all the things that I typically avoid.

"We should go," I tell Kayla, nodding to the gaggle of girls.

"I don't think we're invited," Kayla mutters. She's never been to a party either, surprisingly.

"So? We can still go," I feel very confident in myself.

I walk to the group of girls and invite myself to sit.

"Hey, question," I say, noticing they're confused looks but not caring. "Does Bryce still live on Greenwood Road?"

One of the girls scrunches her face and laughs.

"You're thinking of Brice Cooper," she giggles. "He lives near Greenwood.

We're talking about Bryce Johnston. He lives on Boulevard Drive."

"Thanks," I say, standing. "I'll see y'all on Friday."

I sit down next to Kayla, content in my victory. I got us invited to a party.

"How will we know which house is his, genius?" Kayla asks as our food is delivered.

"The one with all the people, Einstein," I fire back, taking a bite out of my jerk chicken taco. I've never been to a party, but I'm ready for anything right now.

"My parents won't let me go to a party," Kayla says uneasily.

"Then tell them you're hanging out with Cameron and me," I say. I wonder if Cameron is working on Friday. I wonder if Cameron ever told Kayla that he works. I wonder how long I'm going to have to keep this secret.

"Maybe I can crash at Cameron's house," I suggest. "That could be fun."

"I don't know," Kayla says, still unsure. "I don't think we're really party people."

"We could be," I shrug. "We don't know what kind of people we are, kiddo."

She says nothing and finishes her taco. I don't know if I've convinced her yet. That's okay. I can go without her. I've spent half this semester without her. What's one more night?

Chapter Fourteen

"Mom said to give you this," Isaiah says, shoving an envelope in my hand on Friday.

It's the first time we've spoken in nearly a week, but he doesn't even give me time to thank him before he leaves. Not much of a conversation, but it's something, at least.

I open the envelope and peek inside at the check. I'm floored by the amount on the check. It's the biggest check I've received yet. On its own, it's almost enough to buy a car. Added to the money I've saved, I'll be able to buy anything within reason. It feels nice having options.

Inside the envelope, Mrs. Rosenthal has also slipped a handwritten note.

Mr. Swanson, your work continues to impress me. I'm sorry that our partnership has had to come to such an end, but I have no doubt of your continued success. Your gallery show will be highly successful. I've already assembled a strong guest list of art supporters in our community. If you have any new work to send, please send it as soon as possible. I will not accept submissions after next Friday. It has been a pleasure working with you, and I do hope you will not harbor any resentment toward my son because of the termination of our partnership. Wishing you all the best, B. Rosenthal.

My blood turns to fire, and my vision goes red. I wouldn't send that woman a used tissue, much less another completed artwork. I feel myself unspool and turn to look at Isaiah. I want to talk to him. But I can't stand him. I can't stand his family. I can't stand to be in the same room as him. He may be embarrassed, but at least he has his pride. I don't even get to keep that. Betty Rosenthal has taken it all from me. Because I'm poor.

I take comfort in the fact that I'm going to my first party tonight. Maybe I'll even buy a car and drive myself. I've made plans to stay at Cameron's house. He and Kayla have reluctantly agreed to attend the party with me. Neither of them is interested, but Kayla is taking pity on me after my head-on collision with the Rosenthal family. I appreciate the effort. Especially considering the pints of ice cream and teen dramas I've endured during her head-on collisions.

I try to make eye contact with Isaiah, and I feel that now-familiar empty spot in me grow wider. Is it always going to be this way? Have I lost my best friend forever?

"I'm buying a car after school," I tell Kayla and Cameron at lunch. I haven't asked my mom to go. And I haven't done any research or preparations. But I've said it, so now it's true.

"What kind?" Cameron asks, more interested in the possible car purchase than in the party I've been discussing until now.

"I don't know. Whatever I can afford," I shrug. Whatever I can get insured for? Whatever I can get my grubby little hands on.

I dream of a sports car. I dream of walking out of school every day and sliding into something fast and loud with an engine that rumbles. I dream of finding a back road and opening it up, driving as fast as possible.

I think of Isaiah's Audi and sigh. I'll never get to sit in that again. I think I may miss the car as much as I miss him. No. That's not true. But I do miss riding in that beautiful piece of art.

"You have enough money for a car?" Kayla perks as she realizes what I'm saying.

Instead of answering her, I slide the check from Isaiah's mother to her. She opens the envelope cautiously, then looks at me open-mouthed. Her face flashes a series of emotions from surprise to shock to anger to betrayal. It all happens so quickly I feel like I've got whiplash.

Oh, God, I think. *Oh, God. I never told her about Mrs. Rosenthal.*

"Nice of her to send you a, what's that called when you get fired?" Kayla snaps her fingers, trying to remember. "A severance check."

"Kayla," I say, trying to keep my voice level.

"Why didn't you tell me Isaiah's mom was your agent?" She asks angrily. I swear her eyes flash red for a minute.

"Because I knew you'd react like this," I say, apparently throwing caution to the wind. I'm so tired of being so guarded around her. "It happened when you were mad at me for spending so much time with Isaiah."

"So?" She says as if this doesn't matter or shouldn't matter. But with Kayla, it always matters. Timing is everything.

"Don't do this, Kayla," I sigh. "Don't get pissed because there was something in my life you didn't know about."

This makes her even angrier. I can't say anything right. I don't understand. How is she always so hot and cold?

"Don't do, what, Brutus?" Kayla glares. "I'm not allowed to be angry that you hide things from me?"

"Don't get all Shakespeare on me," I spit. I'm pissed.

"Hey, you got one right," she crosses her arms. "Maybe you won't fail twelfth grade after all."

Cameron's eyes flare wide, but he continues to eat in silence. He apparently knows better than to step in front of the moving train that is Angry Kayla. I'm not smart enough, however. Instead, I just keep going.

"I can't do this anymore, Kayla," I shake my head. "I can't deal with you when you're like this. And I shouldn't have to."

I pick up my tray, throw it, food and all, in the trash can and stomp my way to the front office.

"I feel sick," I tell the receptionist. "I need to call my mom."

When Mom comes to get me, she looks concerned. Not because she thinks I'm sick; she knows me better than that. But because she knows that I don't cut class and I've never asked to be picked up from school before. School was my escape from my house that I hate and the neighborhood that I hate.

"What's wrong, sweetie?" Mom asks once I get in her car.

"I'm just having a bad week," I sigh. "And Kayla's being awful. And I want to buy a car."

It all comes out jumbled, and I realize, for the hundredth time lately, how childish I sound.

"I know," she sighs. "About the car, I mean. I know. I've been trying to figure out how to afford you one. But I just can't right now, Cade. I'm sorry."

I hold in a breath and let it out slowly. Mostly because I'm a mess.

"Mom, it's okay," I say. "I have the money for it."

I explain about my savings and how that has been the goal for my art money from the very beginning.

"How much money do you have saved up?" She asks suspiciously.

I do some quick math in my head. Carry a one. Add in the check that's in my backpack.

"About $12,000?" I estimate. I don't tell her the exact amount is $12,163.14. I don't want her to think I've obsessed over it. And then my head reels. I made a third of what my mother makes in a year in just a few months. I've made more money than I have saved, but I've had to buy new supplies and stuff.

"Christ, Cade," Mom says, looking at me with shock. "You've made that much money from your art? I didn't realize Betty Rosenthal had that kind of power."

"Apparently," I shrug.

"I'll make you a deal," Mom says, after a moment's consideration. "If you can find a car, I will cover your insurance."

So, off we go on an adventure. I can't believe Mom is okay with taking me out of school to shop for a car. It's not like her.

Mom takes me home to get my money, and we devise a plan of attack. We pull up to a small dealership with a gravel lot and a salesman in a nice business suit. He smiles a charming smile at us and extends his hand to my mom.

"Good morning," he shakes her hand firmly, never breaking eye contact with her. "I'm Chuck Charleston."

He's younger than I'd expect somebody named Chuck Charleston to be, and he has blond hair and brown eyes. I can tell his smile alone sells the bulk of his cars and probably gets him a lot of dates. The way he eyes my mom makes me think he's expecting to do both in this sale. I laugh a little to myself. It'll be fun watching my mom reject this guy.

"How can I help you today?" He asks, extending his hand to me after he's greeted my mom. He's got a firm handshake that sends electricity through me. He must be very good at his job.

"My son is looking for his first car," Mom smiles, surveying the lot around us.

"There's no way you're old enough to have a son who can drive," Chuck Charleston says, adding extra *umph* to his smile. He is laying it on thick.

"What kind of car are you looking for?" Chuck Charleston asks me, speaking to me like an adult. It takes me by surprise. I just expect adults to think of me as a kid.

"Really anything that drives," I shrug. "I mean, ideally, I want a car with as few miles as possible. And my dream would be a sports car. But I don't have a ton of money, so I'm basically just looking for the best I can get within reason."

He scratches his chin, impressed. I'm sure he spends much of his day listening to ridiculous demands within meager price constraints. I imagine it's like watching those home-buying shows on TV when people want 4-story mansions on a shoestring budget.

"I think I might have something you're interested in," He leads us to the lot of cars. The first vehicle he leads me to is an SUV. It's nice enough with leather seats and too many miles to make it worth buying. But it's a start.

The next vehicle he leads me to is a turquoise pickup truck that is every bit as ugly as it sounds. It sits low to the ground and looks like it would bottom out if I put anything too heavy in the bed, which is kind of counterintuitive to the idea of a pickup truck. I try to hide my disgust for this truck. After all, I did just say I only needed something with four wheels.

"Not your thing?" Chuck Charleston asks, noting my reaction.

"Not really," I shake my head. "But it does have fewer miles and is in my price range."

Chuck nods knowingly before leading me further into the lot. We round the corner of the building. There are fewer cars here than the front lot, but most of them look a lot nicer than the others.

"I knew you wouldn't want any of those," he says, leading me toward the back corner.

And suddenly, it comes into view. *My car*, I think. It's right there, waiting for me. Begging me to drive it home.

"We just got it," he says. "I mean, it just came in this morning."

He runs his hand over the sleek frame of an early 2000s model Ford Mustang. It's bright yellow with a big black stripe down the center. Something about it tells me I'll never be able to afford it. It's beautiful. I catch myself nearly drooling.

I look inside the window to see black leather seats. The steering wheel is black and yellow, and the dash has bright yellow accents. My mother will think it's tacky when she sees it. But I'm in love.

"Automatic, 8-cylinder," Chuck Charleston begins rattling off the car's specs. But I know all these things. "Rear-wheel drive. Remote entry."

"Well, that's certainly bright," Mom says as she catches up to us. "It looks like the type of car you'd kill to have."

I nod as Mom approaches.

"Would you like to take it for a drive?" Chuck Charleston asks.

"How many miles are on this?" Mom asks dubiously. "How can a car like this fit in my son's price range?"

"It's got 90,000 miles on it," Chuck Charleston concedes. "It's been well cared for. We gave the engine a once-over when we took it in. As long as it's taken care of regularly, this car will last another 150,000 miles or more."

I know that Chuck Charleston is right. Cars are like people; the better you maintain them, the longer they last.

I agree to a test drive, and we all pile into the car. Chuck Charleston, being a gentleman, climbs into the backseat behind my mom. I slide in and look around for a long time at the interior. The center console is almost glaringly yellow. The seats have stains and wear and tear. This was obviously a well-loved car.

"What year did you say this is?" Mom asks, still the voice of reason.

"2006," Chuck Charleston answers as I crank the key, and the car roars to life.

As soon as I hit the highway, I know that this is the car for me. It handles like a dream. I feel like I'm one with the road. I weave through traffic without a single problem, and by the time we make it back to the dealership, I'm ready to sign my life and every penny I have away to this beautiful machine. It will be mine.

"Sports cars are expensive on insurance, especially for boys," Mom muses, and I can feel myself start to fall. She made a deal with me. I'm paying for it; she's supposed to cover insurance.

I don't say anything. I don't argue. Mom is helping me out by covering insurance, so I have to play by her rules. Sometimes I really hate being responsible.

When we get back to the lot, Chuck Charleston lets Mom and me talk it out while he hovers awkwardly at a distance.

"I really want this car, Mom," I say, trying not to sound like the bratty teenager I know I sound like. "It's beautiful."

"I know you do, Cade," she says. "I just need you to play along for a minute."

She smiles slyly. Mom has a plan, and she's not telling me. I don't say anything; I've learned not to question my mother by now. She's always right.

She marches over to Chuck Charleston and smiles broadly. I hear her explaining why we can't take the sports car, and I put on my best dejected face. She gesticulates wildly as she talks insurance, and depreciation, and anything else she can think of. Chuck Charleston's smile falters for the first time, and I realize we've won. And Mom has somehow negotiated the price down by $1,000. She's amazing.

I've never felt more powerful than I do sitting in the driver seat of Roxy, my bright yellow Mustang. I roll the windows down, let the wind whip through my hair, and take the long way home. When I get home, Mom already has lunch ready. I throw my arms around her and thank her for helping me buy my car. And for the first time in a long time, things are looking up for all of us.

And I'm going to my first party tonight.

Chapter Fifteen

I pull up to the party, feeling powerful for the first time in my life. My car is old. The seats are stained. But it's mine. I feel giddy. I feel energized. Electricity and adrenaline surge through me. Tonight, I am unstoppable.

I park my car in the line of cars lining Boulevard Drive. I take a few steps and click the lock button on my key ring to hear my own car's honk. I can't shake the smile from my face. There's a pep in my step that has never been there before.

I follow the booming of bass, in awe of the neighborhood around me. Every house is massive, with high fences and neatly manicured lawns. This neighborhood is much nicer and more exclusive than Kayla's but not as imposing as Isaiah's side of town.

Sometimes I can almost pretend I'm not different than my classmates. Then I see where they live, and I remember I am.

The door to Bryce Johnston's house is open, and people are mingling inside, iconic red cups of mysterious liquids in their hands. I take a breath, steel myself, and enter the already loud and thriving party.

People are everywhere. Wrapped around each other on the couch and in the corner. Guys are yelling in another corner, arguing about sports. Girls are giggling, red-faced and already tipsy. I think some people are trying to dance, but it doesn't look like any dance I know. The smell of smoke wafts in from somewhere nearby, and I don't know enough to know if it's cigarettes or weed or something entirely different.

"Cade Swanson!" A shrill voice calls from across the living room. Before I know it, I'm getting dive-tackle-hugged by Nicole Bannister, a girl in my art class. I didn't expect ever to see her at a party.

"I didn't know you were gonna be here!" Apparently, Nicole didn't expect to see me at one, either. "Let me get you a drink!"

She disappears into another room, the kitchen, I suspect, and returns with one of those telltale red cups everybody's holding. The contents smell like rubbing alcohol and gasoline and don't taste any better. I sip it cautiously. Everybody around me seems to enjoy whatever is in this cup, so I try to follow suit.

"Are you here alone?" Nicole asks loudly over the roar of the music. This isn't accusatory or pointed; she's just asking.

"Yeah," I shrug. There I go again, always shrugging.

"Come hang out with us!" She waves me over to a group of girls I've probably seen before but never met.

They all wear dark-framed glasses and have their hair pulled into tight braids. They're all wearing sweaters and jeans, and if I were to see them in a criminal lineup, I wouldn't notice a big enough difference between them to identify any one of them. And I have the trained eyes of an artist.

"Have you met my friend Cade?" Nicole asks, introducing me to her friends. I'm grateful when they all say no; it means I haven't just avoided them.

"This is Cade Swanson," Nicole says formally. "He's the most talented artist in the entire world." I shrug, then blush, and then shake my head. I don't know how to take a compliment, for sure.

I chat with Nicole's friends for a while, all sunshine and bubbles and giggles. One of them leans in close every time she talks to me, and it takes me too long to realize that she's flirting with me. It takes me even longer to realize that I like it.

The more I sip this gasoline-alcohol concoction, the more I like it. And I like being here. And I like Nicole and her friends. And I like this loud music. And I like not being around Kayla or Isaiah. I like having the opportunity to be just me. I like the bubbles in my head, and I start to giggle.

I look up to Nicole, but she's not there. A second later, she blurs into place, and I giggle harder.

"Sorry," I say, trying but failing to control my laughter. "My eyes fotused slow."

"Fotused?" Nicole giggles, red-cheeked from the magic that is in our cups.

And then we fall into simultaneous and uproarious laughter. And I laugh harder because somewhere, my brain has accessed the word uproarious. I wasn't even aware that I knew that word until my brain accessed it.

Nicole's friends stare at me hard for a moment, then smile knowingly.

"Is this your first time drinking?" One of them giggles. I think maybe her name was Mona. But I might have just assumed that because she reminds me of the Mona Lisa for some reason.

"No," I shake my head furiously. "Yes."

Nicole and I giggle harder.

"Maybe you should take a break after this one," Mona says kindly. I agree that she's probably right. I haven't even been here twenty minutes yet.

"Come on," Nicole says excitedly, grabbing me by the hand. "Let's go talk to people."

I've never met somebody so excitable and happy. Is this her default setting, or is this the product of whatever it is we're drinking?

Nicole drags me around to meet what feels like a million people. She's sure I've met them all before, but she and I don't really run in the same circles. I don't know any of these people.

"Everybody, this is Cade Swanson," Nicole says, kind of. It comes out more like *Kay Swansish*. And we both giggle obnoxiously.

"This is Toni," she points to a girl with heavy eye makeup.

"This is Larkin," she motions to a boy clad in plaid. I giggle as I rhyme clad in plaid in my head.

"And I'm Dylan," a guy with thick, wavy hair and smoldering eyes extends his hand.

"Is that with an *i* or a *y*?" I ask. He looks at me funny like nobody's ever asked this before.

"A *y*," he finally answers, smiling, my hand still shaking his.

"Figures," I keep my hand tight around his.

"What does that mean?" He doesn't break his grip either, and I'm not entirely sure what's happening now.

"Guys who spell it with a *y* are always cuter," I giggle. Then I feel myself go bright red. What the hell did I say? Damn it. I didn't mean to say that.

"Yeah?" He asks.

I expect him to break his hold on my hand and walk away, but he doesn't. Instead, he moves closer than me and leans into me.

"I've never met a Cade that wasn't hot," his lips graze my ear as he whispers this.

It sends shivers down my spine, and suddenly my head is ever foggier than before. I don't know if it's the drink or Dylan, but I'm feeling the most intense euphoria I've ever felt. I lean my head closer to his, unsure what to do next. I don't know the steps to this dance. The only other person I've ever kissed was Isaiah, but I want to kiss Dylan. I don't even know him,

What if Isaiah finds out?

"I need another drink," I say, finally letting go of Dylan's hand and taking a step back. I need to get Isaiah out of my head. I don't want to think of him tonight. Not when I have Dylan standing here in front of me, in fitted jeans and a sweater that hugs his body.

I feel Dylan on my heels as I head to the room where Nicole got my drink. I was right; it is the kitchen. I look at three nearly empty bowls of foul-smelling liquid. They seem to dance in front of me for a moment, and I don't remember what color I had before.

"Do you know what I was drinking?" I turn to Dylan, smiling goofily at me with his sultry eyes. Can eyes be sultry? I don't even know. He's hot, okay?

"The red one," he points to the emptiest of the bowls.

"How do you know?" I ask, mockingly suspicious. I hope it sounds mocking. Am I flirting? This is complicated as hell.

"You've got some on your lips," he leans in close and presses his lips against mine as if to indicate where.

I drop my plastic cup to the floor and let my hands drape over his shoulders. I let Dylan lead; I'm not resistant like I was to Isaiah. There he is in my head again. Can't I have this one moment without him bugging me?

Dylan pushes me against the counter, pressing against my mouth hard.

I don't know what to do with my hands. My eyes shoot open, wide when Dylan knows exactly what to do with his hands. I want to push him away, but I want to keep kissing him, and I don't know what I want more. This is something unlike anything I've ever experienced, and no amount of teen-movie watching could prepare me for this.

"Not in here," I finally whisper around his mouth. I don't want people to see his hands all over me. I don't want anybody to know I'm interested in Dylan. Or in anybody for that matter. I feel ashamed and dirty.

"We can, uh, go upstairs, I guess," he sounds disappointed.

I nod, retrieve my cup from the floor, fill it up, and follow him up the stairs. I down it, trying to get Isaiah out of my head, where he currently occupies every non-clouded space I have. The stairs rock underneath me, and I hold onto the banister for support. Then I laugh hard. Tonight started with me getting support from a Bannister and now I'm being supported by a banister.

I sit on the stairs and laugh so hard my head hurts. Dylan turns around to help me up.

"You coming, Cade?" He asks in that deep, rough voice. He's like the opposite of Isaiah. He's like the anti-Isaiah. He's shorter than me and muscular and confident and aggressive and assertive. He helps me up, takes me by the hand, and leads me into an empty bedroom.

He turns on a lamp, and a bright pink unicorn chandelier gleams in the low light. Everything in this room is pink, and as Dylan starts kissing me again, I feel oddly self-conscious. I'm making out in the room of a little kid. Dylan is taking my shirt off in the room of a little kid. I'm taking his shirt off in the room of a little kid.

I'm kissing his neck in the pink unicorn room of a little kid.

And suddenly, I'm not. I can't take this. I keep thinking how I'd feel if somebody had sex in Thomas's room, and I can't do this anymore.

"Is everything okay?" Dylan asks more sweetly than I expected he could.

I just nod, embarrassed and shy and awkward. How does anybody do this? What the hell am I doing? I don't even know Dylan, and I've just had my hands over his entire body.

I feel sick to my stomach. I feel embarrassed, and exposed, and vulnerable.

"I'm sorry," I say and try to kiss him again. He leans naturally back into it. He's so good at this. I don't care that he's a complete stranger. His mouth pressed against mine is the best thing I've ever felt. I think. Come to think of it, I can't feel my lips.

His big hands start to run over my back again. The unicorn chandelier sparkles in the corner of my eye, and I feel sick all over again.

And then I barf. Everywhere. On the pink comforter and the pink rug, and the leg of Dylan's pants. I wipe my face with my shirt and stand up. I can feel tears streaming down my face as Dylan makes disgusted noises. I try to run out of the door but miss and hit my head on the door frame. I see stars for just a second before finally angling for the door and leaving.

I see Bryce Johnston in the hallway as I try to trudge my way to the stairs.

"Cade Swanson, my man," he holds his hand up for a high five. "Welcome to the club. Hooking up at one of my parties is like initiation, dude."

I don't high-five him.

"I just barfed in your sister's bedroom, I'm sorry," is all I can manage to say.

"It's cool, man," Bryce chuckles good-naturedly. "The maid will clean it up tomorrow. She's gotten red puke out of everything here."

The maid? I don't even have time to consider what it must be like to have a maid because I have to run. The tears are flowing freely, and I'm not sure how many more times I need to puke. I snake my way through the crowded living room, shirt still in hand, face tear-soaked and disgusting with vomit. I make my way to my car and throw myself into the driver's seat.

I press my head against my steering wheel and breathe deeply. I can't drive home. Not like this. I can't believe I did this. What the hell is wrong with me?

I can't call my mom. I'm the responsible son. I can't let her know I got drunk when I told her I was just going out with some friends. I can't believe I lied to her. I can't stop crying. I can't do anything right. I can't do anything at all.

I lean out of my car and barf into a pristinely manicured yard. I wipe my face with my shirt again and do the only thing I can think to do. I pick up my phone and look at the screen for a minute. The light hurts my eyes, and the apps dance around the screen as I try to find my contacts list. I finally find the name I'm looking for and press it hard. I lean my head against the steering wheel as it rings. When a deep voice answers, I feel relief for the first time in a week.

"Isaiah," I say weakly into the phone. "I'm so stupid, and I'm drunk and," I don't know how desperate I sound.

"I'm at Bryce Johnston's house. Can you come pick me up?"

I hang up, lean out of my car, throw up one more time, and wait for my knight in shining Audi to come to rescue me.

Isaiah's headlights pull into view fifteen minutes later, and I've only just pulled myself together. I haven't barfed in a while, but that's mostly because there was nothing else in my stomach to empty. My eyes are so puffy that it's hard to see. I sniffle pathetically as Isaiah approaches my car.

"Are you okay?" Isaiah catches me as I fall out of my car to hug him.

I wrap my arms around his slender frame and hang on for dear life. I shake my head yes, then no. I don't know if I'm okay.

"I'm an idiot," I say in response. It's the only thing that makes sense to say at this point.

"I know," he laughs, and I'm not upset. He's right. He has every right to call me an idiot.

"I can't go home," I shake my head. "I can't let my mom see me like this. I can't drive yet. I'm so stupid."

And I'm crying again. Why the hell am I crying? Is this what drunk people do? Why would anybody ever want to get drunk?

"Shhh," Isaiah says softly, sweetly. Why does he even care about me? I don't deserve that. "Everything's going to be okay. It's only 9:30. Let's go get something to eat and some water and see how you're feeling then."

I climb into Isaiah's Audi. The world around me feels rocky and unstable. I feel shaky and unstable. Something in me feels unsettled and sick, but not in the I-need-to-barf-again way. Something bubbles in me, and I can't stop the words that are coming.

"I kissed a guy named Dylan," I tell him. And I'm crying again. "But I couldn't stop thinking about you when I did it."

Isaiah doesn't say anything. His grip on the steering wheel becomes so tightly that his knuckles turn white. I cry harder and can't stop it, which is unusual for me. I'm not somebody who cries. Not when I'm sad, at least. I tear up when I'm angry. And when I'm excited. But crying is different than tearing up.

"Isaiah," I let out of a puff of air and try to pull myself together. "I screwed up. I'm so sorry."

I need a friend right now, but I don't have any. Nicole Bannister might be the best I've got. And that's not saying much.

"We all screw up," he says gently, even though his hands are tight. "We all make mistakes."

The speech he gives me is something a father would give to a son; it's the speech of somebody mature and with life experiences. It's not the speech of an 18-year-old screw-up who got drunk at his first party and puked in a unicorn room. It's not the speech of somebody like me. Isaiah is better than me in every way.

"Everybody makes them," he says, turning onto the highway. "It's how we deal with them that matters, Cade."

I sink further into my seat and fall into the comfort of being with Isaiah again. It may be rocky. It may feel like he's driving me in circles. I may feel like the biggest jerk on the planet. But I'm with Isaiah, and he makes everything okay.

"So, you kissed another guy," he says passively. "And you got drunk at a party. You clearly feel bad about one of those things."

"I feel bad about it all," I tell Isaiah. "I don't just mean the party."

I put a hand on his arm; it feels safest.

"I feel bad about how I treated you. I feel bad about how I reacted."

He doesn't say anything. He keeps his eyes on the road. He sets his jaw and grips his steering wheel more tightly.

"I don't know what it's like to be happy," I finally sigh. "But you make me happier than I've ever been."

I see Isaiah relax when I say this. He takes one hand from the steering wheel and laces his fingers between mine. I'm surprised by how soft his hands are. His fingers are long and slender, unsurprisingly. His thumb lightly rubs the back of my hand.

"You make me happy, too, Cade." And for the first time in what seems a lifetime, his million-watt, blinding smile fills his Audi. "I just hate that you had to be drunk to tell me how you feel."

I wince. I want to tell him that's not fair, but I don't want to cause any more trouble.

"I don't like being drunk," I admit. I know that anything I was feeling is wearing off. And this feeling is much worse. I still feel like I need to throw up, but there's nothing left in me to wretch.

"Why'd you do it?" Isaiah asks with a current of anger in his voice, but his thumb still caresses the back of my hand. It sends chills up my back. His touch is so sweet.

"I didn't mean to," I confess, embarrassed. "Nicole Bannister gave me a drink, and it was disgusting. But I kept drinking it, I guess, to fit in."

"When have you ever tried to fit in?" Isaiah laughs so hard it hurts my head. My head is killing me. *Please stop.* I beg, mentally. *Stop that right now.*

"I guess tonight," I laugh a labored laugh because it is funny. Our laughter dies out, and we sit in silence for a while. When we pull into an IHOP parking lot, I don't want to let Isaiah's hand go, even just to get out of the car.

"We have a lot to talk about, don't we?" I ask as we walk inside. Isaiah just nods solemnly.

So, we talk. And eat pancakes. And laugh. And eat more pancakes. And talk some more. And I feel more like myself than I have in days.

"I have to find a way to tell my mom," I sigh. Relationships are complicated. The one word that describes my entire life.

"I have to find a way to tell *my* mom," Isaiah laughs nervously.

By 10:30, I'm sober again. I've gulped down what must be a gallon of water and eaten more pancakes than any one human being should be allowed to. Since my shirt smells like vomit, I'm wearing Isaiah's jacket, and we're standing by my car. I'm right back where I started and nowhere near where I started.

Isaiah is hesitant, awkward, not sure if he wants to kiss me. I don't know why I know this, but I do. It's instinctual. Finally, he leans in to kiss me, but I pull away.

"Don't," I say cautiously. He looks hurt. He looks like he's afraid I'm being crazy all over again.

"No," I shake my head. "It's just that I've puked so much tonight, and I kissed Dylan."

"Stop," he says sternly. "Let's not mention that anymore. I'm trying to forget it."

"And I don't want this to be the way you remember our first kiss."

"But it's not our first kiss," Isaiah winks.

"Let's not talk about the last one," I raise my eyebrows as if threatening him. "Please. In fact, let's not talk about tonight, either. Let's just pretend we have some kind of fairy tale story."

I can imagine in twenty years telling somebody the story of how Isaiah and I started dating.

Well, he kissed me, but I didn't like it because I was scared. And then his mom said I wasn't rich enough for him. So, I ran away. And then we didn't talk. And then I almost screwed a total stranger in a unicorn room, but I threw up, so Isaiah saved me. And then I wouldn't kiss him because I tasted like booze and barf. And now we're here.

Yeah. That'd make for one hell of a story.

"I think ours is pretty fairy tale," Isaiah smiles and kisses my cheek. Already we talk like an old couple. Is it always this way when you start dating your best friend?

When I get home, Mom is waiting up for me. My watch reads 10:59, and I have made it home just in time for curfew.

"Did you have a good night?" She asks, unsuspicious that anything is different. I think.

"I did," I smile. It ended well, at least.

"How's Isaiah?" She asks, quirking a brow.

"He's fine," I smile goofily. "Wait. How did you know I saw Isaiah?"

"You're wearing his jacket," she nods to me. "Got cold?"

Shit.

This is not good.

"I got something on my shirt," I look for the easiest half-truth. "And he loaned me his jacket."

"Anything you want to tell me?" she crosses her arms slyly. My mother is too smart. I don't want to tell her anything. I want to revel in this one night of complicated simplicity. My best friend is my boyfriend. That's simple, right?

"I guess I'd better," I concede. I consider how to pick my words carefully. I don't know if Mom suspects I was at a party. I don't know if I smell like booze. I don't know what she knows and what she doesn't.

"Isaiah and I made up," I say slowly. My voice is oddly raw. I feel more vulnerable and exposed than I did with Dylan.

I force the memory of Dylan out of my head. Do we ever recover from our stupid mistakes?

"And we're together, now," I feel myself shaking. I feel tears form in my eyes. Why is this so hard to say? Shouldn't I want to celebrate with my mom? It would be so much different if I'd started dating Kayla. It would be easier if I'd started dating Kayla.

"He's a great guy," Mom smiles easily. Her smile is as warm as always and as comfortable as always, and I feel relieved.

"But we need to establish some rules, now," she motions toward the couch, expecting me to sit. I do.

"No more sleeping over," she says. "That goes either way. He can't spend the night here, and you can't spend the night there."

"I don't think Betty Rosenthal will let me on her property even if I wanted to," I laugh bitterly.

"Your father always said we'd make a rule that girlfriends wouldn't be over if neither of us was home," she sighs. "But I trust you, and I'm not putting that rule into place until or unless you give me a reason not to trust you. Don't break my trust."

I feel myself relax. She doesn't know about the party. I'm safe.

"And you need to tell Betty that you guys are together," she sounds almost angry. She sounds like she is betraying herself, defying her own beliefs. "I don't like her. And I don't like the way she spoke to you. But I'm also a mother, and I would feel so hurt if you lied to me and dated Isaiah, or anybody, behind my back."

"Yes, ma'am," I nod. I don't say anything because moms have a way of finding secrets in the things you say.

"Aren't you upset?" I finally ask, a well inside of me breaking as tears run down my face.

"Upset about what?" Mom sits beside me, concern flashing across her face.

"That I'm," I can't find the words. I don't know what to say. Everything is embarrassing. Everything hurts. I know the exact words, and I know exactly what to say. And that hurts more.

"That I'm gay, Mom," I say angrily and sadly, and I don't know what other emotions.

She pulls me into her shoulder and rocks me gently. She strokes my hair and lets me cry for a long time before she says anything.

"I don't care who you love, baby," she whispers when I've finally pulled myself together. "I told you as long as you're happy and not doing anything illegal, I support you."

"The first time you brought Isaiah over here, you looked at him with such admiration," she shakes her head, lost in memory. "I knew it then. It was like the sun shone from his face. And you know what I said to myself?"

"No, what?" I look at her, wiping my eyes.

"I thought how nice it was to see you smiling," she brushes her fingers through my hair. "I thought 'Cade has somebody in his life who makes him laugh.' And I would give anything in the world to see you laugh the way you laugh when you're with Isaiah."

I can't help my smile. It's bigger than I think I've ever smiled before. I wonder if it looks like my mom's. Did I inherit her smile?

"All parents want is to see their kids happy and successful," she continues. "And you're both of those things. What more could I want?"

I lay my head on Mom's shoulder again and cry the last few tears that come. I feel so complete. It's like I've found something that's been missing in me all along. Is this what I needed? Is it Isaiah? Is it this conversation with Mom? Is it something else entirely?

"Now," Mom says, her voice cautious. "Not everybody else is going to be so supportive of you two. People won't understand. And as much as I'd like to protect you from that, I can't. This world is full of hate, Cade. This world is full of people who think they know what's best for you, what you should be doing, and who you should date or marry. And they're mean. And they're loud. And full of hate. And you just have to ignore it, Cade. You have to show kindness, even when it sucks. You have to keep your head up and be true to yourself. Because that's how you make a difference. Don't sink to their level. Don't fight hate with hate."

I nod slowly. I know what she means. But before, it never felt real to me. It never felt like it affected me. But it does. And it will. And as long as Isaiah and I are Isaiah and I, we will face hate. I know that. I don't want to admit it.

"I love you, Mom," I say, hugging her tightly. I don't think she'll ever understand how much better she's made me feel.

"I love you, too, sweetie. Always. No matter what," she kisses the top of my head.

"Can Isaiah come over tomorrow?" I ask. I want to spend all the time I can with him to make up for the time we've spent apart.

"Oh, absolutely not," Mom smiles a knowing smile. "You're grounded, sweetie, for at least three weeks."

I look at her, confused.

"You smell like puke, and you look like hell. I know the aftermath of a party when I see it." She laughs an evil little laugh. "I was young once, too. Now, I'll be taking your keys. You might have bought your car, but I pay the insurance."

She beats my argument before I even make it. Because my mom knows everything. I slink to my room, change into my pajamas and try to sleep, trying to ignore my splitting headache. I will never do something so stupid again.

Chapter Sixteen

When I wake up on Monday, I feel odd. I'm filled with butterflies and dread. I'm nervous. I'm excited. I feel sick. I'm the happiest I've ever been, which scares me. My happiness doesn't usually last very long; I try not to worry about what will come along to ruin it.

I'm nervous about school. How are people going to react to Isaiah and me? What are people going to think about Dylan and me? What am I going to tell Kayla?

I wonder why everybody has to know. I'm wondering why anybody needs to know.

But when I get to school, Isaiah takes my hand as if it's the most natural thing on Earth. He laces his fingers between mine, and I relax. Things will be okay. As long as Isaiah is at my side, things will be okay.

"Good morning, sunshine," he greets me as we walk to my locker. "Sucks you're grounded."

It does suck I'm grounded. I want to see him. I want to spend all of my time with him. I want to ride in his car and listen to sappy love songs, and paint pictures of the sunset.

I want to barf because I want to do all of those things.

Today, my superpower isn't working. Everybody sees me and smiles or greets me or nods in acknowledgment. But they all see me. And I don't know if I like it. But I like this feeling of Isaiah beside me, towering over me, smiling at me like a goofball. I like his presence nearby.

When we get to art, I dread talking to Nicole Bannister. I dread facing the events of Friday night. I dread somebody asking about Dylan. I dread explaining anything in front of Isaiah. He already knows everything that happened, but I don't want him to relive that as much as I don't want to have to relive it. I can't believe I was so stupid.

"Cade," Nicole greets me as we enter the art room. "You disappeared on Friday."

She sounds concerned but also suspicious. She raises an eyebrow slyly at me.

"Did you have fun with Dylan?" She nudges me with her elbow, ignoring Isaiah standing beside me.

"If you count puking everywhere fun, then yes, we had a freaking blast," I say as flatly as possible. I already want to curl up and die. I already miss my superpower. Why aren't I unnoticeable?

"Not my definition," Isaiah shakes his head, his voice light and good-natured. He's always good-natured.

"But we managed to turn the night around after that," Isaiah winks at me, but I know it's for Nicole's sake. Nicole returns the wink and takes a seat at her desk.

I'm more grateful for Isaiah than I was before. Will he always come to my rescue? I hope so.

"Thank you," I whisper to him as we find our seats comfortably next to each other, the way it has been all year. The way it should be forever. I slip into this comfortable life, and my art reflects that comfort. The colors I use are bright, all greens and blues and yellows. I've never used these colors before, maybe ever. I surprise even myself with the spring scene that is unfolding before me in pastel. I didn't know I had this in me. I thought I was like Dali, with everything muted and dark. But somewhere in me, there has been a Thomas Cole waiting to break free.

"Very nice, Cade," Mr. Camplin smiles as he passes by. "This is unusual for you. I'm glad to see you're challenging yourself."

I hear a few of my classmates mimic Mr. Camplin under their breath.

"Very nice, Cade," Nicole says in a high-pitched voice, and I'm not sure if it's playful or angry.

"How are things going with your end-of-the-year portfolio?" Mr.

Camplin stares angrily at the mockers as he asks.

"I haven't even had time to think about it," I answer honestly, not looking up from my pastels. I'm covered in chalk, and I'm sure I look ridiculous.

"Are you serious?" Mr. Camplin says skeptically. "You can bet your competition has been working on thumbnails and value sketches and figuring out how to create a unified portfolio for months now."

I nod. I know he's right. But I don't have to do those things. Art is in me. I'm doing just fine without all of that. I don't say this to him because I know it sounds bratty, and my mother did not raise me to be a brat.

"You can't rely on your talent forever, Cade," he says simply before walking away to help some of my classmates.

"Who pissed in his cheerios?" I ask Isaiah under my breath.

He just shakes his head and shrugs.

When we get to lunch, Kayla beats Isaiah and Cameron to our table. I don't remind her that we're not talking. I'm trying to avoid any drama with her. I'm trying to find a way to tell her about this weekend. I'm trying to figure out how to explain everything that needs explaining.

"We need to talk," Kayla says quietly, almost inaudibly over the Howler screams that always fill the cafeteria. I just nod.

Kayla leads me outside of the glass doors to the cafeteria. The sound immediately dampens when the doors shut. We stand awkwardly for a minute, staring each other down. I can't tell if my eyes are as angry as hers are, but she looks like she'll lunge and kill me at any moment.

"You went to the party anyway?" She demands.

I just nod. Kayla, like my mom, is good at using my words against me, so I say nothing.

"Heard you got wasted," she says even more angrily.

"I didn't mean to," I shake my head, unsure how to explain this. "I didn't realize I'd had too much until it was too late."

I want to tell her I didn't enjoy it, but I don't know if that would help, so I don't.

"What an idiot," she spits.

Again, I just nod. I am an idiot.

"Anything else you think you should tell me?" She demands, crossing her arms accusingly.

"I don't know," I bite back. "Just so you'll have something else to attack me for? What's the point, Kayla?"

She looks offended and incredulous.

"I never attack you," she says quietly, fire burning in her eyes.

"Sure," I roll my eyes. "You don't like it when I spend time with Isaiah, so you yell at me. You don't like that his mom was my agent, so you yelled at me. If anything happens in my life that you didn't plan, you yell at me. It's ridiculous."

I sigh, and Kayla rolls her eyes. We're having this awkward standoff that has become the norm for us. What's happened to us? When did she start hating me so much? Why did she start hating me so much?

"I know about Dylan," she hisses finally. I feel my blood run cold.

"Who?" I try to play it cool, even though it's clear she knows what she's talking about.

"Don't," Kayla holds up a finger. "He's in my English class, dumb ass. You think he's not telling everybody he can find about how you guys hooked up?"

I feel my blood turn colder. Sweat forms on my forehead, and I feel my knees go weak.

"He's what?" I shove my shaking hands in my pockets. I want to throw up. I want to cry.

"Everybody, Cade," she sounds concerned now. "I didn't even know—"

She stops short of saying something, but I don't know what. She breathes in and collects herself.

"I didn't even know you were like *that*," she emphasizes like she's avoiding saying something awful. Like she's avoiding saying herpes or Hitler.

"That I'm like what?" I demand. I want her to say it. If it's a dirty word to her, I'm going to make her say it first. She doesn't get to decide I'm dirty.

"You know," she's suddenly walking on eggshells. "That you're like that. You know, like that you'd kiss another boy."

"Gay?" I ask, raising an eyebrow. "Say it, Kayla. Tell me you didn't know

I'm gay."

She shakes her head. Tears stream down her perfectly made-up face. Why is she crying? What right does she have?

"No," she shakes her head harder.

"For the record, Dylan and I didn't do anything more than kiss," I say gently. "But we probably would have if I hadn't started puking."

"Cade," she says weakly. "Stop." She starts to cry like I'm somehow hurting her with this confession.

This is what my mom meant, isn't it? This is what my mother wanted me about. That some people wouldn't understand me or support me. I just didn't expect it to be Kayla. Instead of trying to make her feel better, though, I feel myself twisting the knife that I've obviously dug into her.

"I ran out. I called Isaiah, and he picked me up. I bet Dylan didn't tell you that part, did he?" I cross my arms. "I wanted to call you, but you always yell at me, and I couldn't deal with that."

I want her to know that I don't feel safe calling her with my problems anymore. I want her to know I'm wary of her.

"So, you called him," she resigns, understanding.

"I called him," I nod. "I called my boyfriend. Just like you would do if you were in trouble."

Kayla's eyes grow wide when I say this. She shakes her head harder and backs up against the wall. Why is she so dramatic?

"Your boyfriend?" She finally says. She's crying harder.

"Yes," I nod. "I was going to tell you today. But not like this. And then you came at me like that. Attacked me like that, like you have some authority over my life. You don't."

I know I should stop talking now, but I can't. I'm so angry.

"I don't try to control you like that, Kayla," I say while she's standing there crying. "And it's not fair that you do that to me."

Before she can respond, I open the door and return to our table. Isaiah and Cameron are sitting there, laughing loudly. They get along so well. I wish Kayla and I still did.

"Congratulations, dude!" Cameron stands up and claps my back as I get to the table. I can tell I'm red-faced and angry, but I quickly melt into pleasant comfort around Cameron. Is there any way I can keep him and get rid of Kayla?

"I'm guessing Isaiah told you?" I raise an eyebrow, first at Cameron, then at Isaiah.

"He did," he laughs. "And I totally called that."

"You did," I concede happily.

I hesitate and bite my bottom lip. I don't want to ruin this moment. But Kayla is my best friend, and she needs some comfort.

"Cameron," I say cautiously. "Kayla's outside crying, and it's my fault. Could you maybe go check on her for me?"

Cameron dutifully stands and nods.

"Uh-oh," Isaiah raises his eyebrows at me in curiosity.

"Let's just say Kayla's not nearly as excited for us as Cameron is," I sigh heavily.

Isaiah grabs my hand and squeezes it. He doesn't say anything, but I know what he's thinking. This is going to be complicated.

"Anything worth doing is hard," he says finally. I just nod uncomfortably. I don't like fighting with Kayla, but lately, all we seem to do is fight. I miss her, but I can't deal with her dramatics anymore. It's all become so toxic."I've got a lot on my plate," I sigh after realizing I've been staring into space. "The school art show. Always fighting with Kayla. The gallery showing. I don't know how I can deal with everything. And did I mention Dylan is apparently telling everybody he and I slept together?"

I feel Isaiah's hand tense around mine. He sits up straighter than before.

"Where is he?" He asks calmly, a strange gleam in his eye.

"I don't know. Why?" I'm suddenly nervous. Maybe I should have told Isaiah.

"I'll take care of that troll," he says calmly.

"No," I tell him sternly. "No. I'll deal with him."

And I will. My own way. If I ever see him again.

I will make sure to see him again.

I track Dylan down after my last class and smile broadly at him.

"Dylan," I exclaim excitedly and wrap my arms around him in the middle of the hallway.

He smiles back, just as broadly, nodding at some of his friends in a territorial way. He's proving that I'm his property; he's explaining to them that he owns me now.

"Listen, about Friday," I say sweetly, looking at him with big doe eyes. "I had a lot of fun."

I'm speaking more loudly than I should, and I can see his friends leaning in to hear what I have to say. They're exchanging looks and giving Dylan nods of approval.

"But twelve seconds is hardly a record," I wink. "I wouldn't do all that bragging if I were you."

I kiss him delicately on the cheek and walk away as his friends begin to mock him. They're loud and obnoxious, and I feel satisfied and vindicated. It's like walking away from an explosion in an action film; if I look back, I'll stop being the badass I just became.

Chapter Seventeen

Three weeks pass more smoothly than I expected it would, and we're all settling back into our new collective existence by the end. Mom loves her new job, and I love not having to pretend to be Thomas's dad. I haven't slept as much as I should have, but I've finished my full show. My entire house smells like spray paint from the finishes I've used to protect my graphite pieces.

Hulking frames lie ready for assembly around my house, and sheets of clear acrylic of every size create an obstacle course in the living room. I know Mom and Thomas are frustrated with it all, but neither of them says anything about it.

It's kind of embarrassing to have my art lying around the house. Some of it is so personal; I don't want my family to see it until the show. I keep half of my show under a sheet that I don't let Thomas or my mom or even Isaiah see.

I stand in my living room and review my show. I feel like I've been framing, and sealing, and painting, and drawing for a lifetime. I feel like every day of my life has led to this moment when my art hangs on a wall for the wealthy to see. For my mom to see. For me to see.

I've been thinking about how to arrange my show. How things should flow. How to hang which paintings.

I start with the centerpiece first. The highlight of my show is going to be the stippled piece of my mom. In it, she looks happy. Her eyes shine with the joy that my mother has always had. I can't imagine making anything else the centerpiece, the shining glory of my show. I secretly hope it doesn't sell so I can keep it forever.

"Are you ready?" Isaiah asks as he slides into my bedroom. I don't know how long he's been here; I've been lost in my own world imagining my show.

"It's really happening, Is," I whisper in excitement. "I'm really getting my own show."

"You deserve it," he says sweetly. I want to kiss him, but I don't. I have a strict rule against kissing Isaiah at my house.

"I don't," I shake my head. "Nobody deserves anything. But I'm grateful for this opportunity."

"Sometimes you're such an old man," he laughs. "Now, where do we begin?"

He's surveying my room, trying to decide how we're going to haul everything for the show. I smile and start handing him things to load in his car.

"It's going to take us a year to get it all set up," he jokes as he carries things to his open trunk.

"Imagine what it's going to be like when you help us move next week," I smile. "You'll be glad we moved all of this stuff."

I try not to be too excited at the prospect of moving, but I can't help it. We're going to be living closer to school. We'll be in a neighborhood that doesn't embarrass me. We won't have a giant hole in our floor. I'll have an art space that's not the cramped corner of my tiny bedroom. I can't imagine how things can possibly get any better.

"I don't remember signing up to be your personal servant and strong arm," he winks.

"That ship sailed when you started eating lunch with me," I laugh and carry one portfolio of sketches out to my Mustang. *My Mustang.* That will never get old.

Carefully, I arrange everything. It takes my car, Isaiah's car, and my mom's minivan to take everything we need.

"You boys with your toys," Mom nods at our sports cars. "Those are all fun and games until you have to haul something. Then it's the mom van to the rescue."

When we arrive at Kimball Art, I give myself the once-over before entering. The last time I saw Martin Kimball had not gone well, and I need to make a much better second impression. No wrinkles, hair styled, shoes tied, portfolio under my arm. I look like the professional artist I'm pretending to be. I can do this.

I breathe in deep and hold it for a few seconds. My palms sweat, and my knees feel weak. This is really happening. Despite everything in my life always going wrong, this is happening.

When I open the door to Kimball Art, its familiar oaky smell fills my nostrils. It smells like art and class and money. It smells like success. And now my art will get to smell like this.

"Mr. Swanson, right on time," Betty Rosenthal smiles her genuinely fake smile as I enter, arms loaded.

It's the first time I've seen her since that night at Isaiah's house. Isaiah and I have been dating for three weeks, and we haven't told his mom yet. We will. Tomorrow. Once the show is open and people have seen my work, and she doesn't have the power to stop it. After that, we'll tell her. I'm sure she'll figure it out, though, once I've hung the portraits I made of Isaiah. One in charcoal I accidentally started in class. I finished it because it's beautiful and because he's beautiful, even sad. The second charcoal Isaiah is smiling, his brilliant smile hard to ignore. I'm afraid I'll never be able to capture its magic in my art, even if I tried. Janet Fish couldn't even capture his smile.

"This is Cade Swanson?" Martin Kimball raises an eyebrow at me. He's trying to place where he knows me. "You look very familiar."

"Yes, sir," I extend my hand to shake his. "I'm Cade Swanson. You've probably seen me around. I visit your gallery every time there's a new showing."

It's not a lie. But I'm positive it's not the event he had in mind.

"I'm sure that's where I've seen you," Mr. Kimball shakes my hand dumbly before showing me around the gallery.

"I hope you'll find this space suitable for your show," he gestures to the open showroom, hooks adorning the walls awaiting my art. I feel jittery with excitement. I still can't believe this is happening to me.

"Yes, sir," I nod, wide-eyed. "It's more than suitable. I can't thank you enough for this opportunity."

"I'll leave you to set everything up," Martin Kimball says stiffly. "If you need anything, I'll be in the back, finalizing arrangements with Betty."

Isaiah, Mom, Thomas, and I create a very efficient assembly line, matting and framing all of my pieces. It takes hours to get everything arranged exactly as I want it. We hang and rehang pieces. I stand back and stare. I walk around the space. I try to get a feel for what patrons will see when they enter for the first time. We mix and match. I direct and redirect and direct again where things should go.

"There's something missing," Mom points out, looking around. "You've left several big gaps."

"Yes," I nod. "That's because I've got some things you three aren't allowed to see."

Mom and Isaiah exchange glances but say nothing.

When I'm finally content with the way everything is arranged, we begin placing information plaques beside each piece. The title of each piece gleams, along with a description of the materials and the work itself.

"There's so much here," Isaiah spins around, looking at everything around him. "I don't know how you did it."

"You should see the pile of stuff he has at home that's 'not good enough,'" Mom mutters.

"His words, not mine," she adds defensively when Isaiah looks at her.

"It's my favorite thing, Is," I say gently. "It's what I've always wanted to do."

"I know," he smiles proudly at me. "And you did it."

I shake my head. I can't take credit for this show. His mom did it. She did everything for me. My success is dependent solely upon her.

"No," Isaiah says firmly. "Stop that. She didn't do this for you." He gestures to the back room, and we both know he means his mom.

"You did this," he says seriously. It's always exhilarating and terrifying when Isaiah gets firm.

"She has even less talent than me. She didn't draw a single piece that's here. Don't give her any credit," He takes my hands to show how much he means this. "You deserve every amount of praise you get tomorrow. And always."

"You listen to that boy," Mom says softly, and I suddenly remember she's in the room with us.

"Ms. Swanson," Isaiah smiles to my mom as if he's just remembered she's there, too. "Would it be okay if I take Cade out tonight? I think he deserves a fancy dinner before his big day."

"I think he does, too," Mom nods, smiling at both of us. "Have him back at a reasonable time."

When Mom and Thomas leave, it's just Isaiah and me in a beautiful room, with nobody and nothing around us except for my art. The bright lights shine down on realistic flowers and faces. All around me, people smile and wink. They're people I love, and places I love, and things I love.

"What are you calling it?" Isaiah surveys the room as I put the giant sleeping Thomas in a frame.

"Adoration," I smile.

I haven't let anybody in on any details of my show. I don't want anybody to have any clue what's in it before they arrive. I want it to be a secret. I like the idea of secrets, of being a secret. There's something exhilarating in being unknowable.

"I like it," he smiles, helping me hang Thomas's portrait.

I step back and survey things. Everything looks amazing, and I'm overwhelmed with joy. My eyes drift to a portrait of Kayla and Cameron, and there goes my happiness. I haven't talked to Kayla in three weeks. I doubt she'll be at my show. I deflate. She's my best friend; I want her here to support me.

"Don't do this to yourself, Cade," Isaiah says sweetly. "She'll come around. Or she won't. And if she doesn't, then your friendship was one-sided."

I should take comfort in this, but it just upsets me further. Instead, I shake my head and get to work, framing my large stippled piece of my mom. She hangs at the head of the room, her smile demanding the attention it deserves.

"It's amazing how you capture people," Isaiah smiles at me. "I'm jealous of your gift."

I cringe at the word gift. I've spent hours and hours practicing the things I do. I used to sit with magazines sprawled around me, copying details of actors and actresses and models. I used to check out book after book from the library and sit in my room for hours. Gift isn't quite the word I'd use for it. But I don't argue with him; he wouldn't understand.

"You're better than me in every way," I smile. "Now, you have to leave. You're not allowed to see what I've got left to hang. I'll meet you outside."

When I finish hanging the portraits of Isaiah, I stand back and admire everything. I breathe in deep. I hold it in. I try to memorize everything about this moment. It's my dream come true. It's everything I've wanted in my life. I'm 18 years old, and my dreams have come true.

"It all looks wonderful, Mr. Swanson," Martin Kimball says as he appears from the back room. "You are going to be the talk of the town for a very long time."

I feel color rush to my cheeks. I can't even imagine what that means; I can't imagine what that will be like. I can't imagine what it will be like to meet the people who want to buy my art.

For a moment, I get lost in my imagination as I try to picture it all. Men in suits and women in dresses milling about, examining my art, and sipping champagne from long-stemmed glasses. The string quartet Mrs. Rosenthal has hired will sit in the corner, playing classical selections as guests shake my hand. I'll be there in the first suit I've ever owned, wearing the Calvin Klein that Isaiah gave me months ago, smiling and greeting guests, accepting business cards and congratulations.

I sigh and feel the goofy smile that's on my face. I don't care. It can linger as long as it wants.

"Before you go, we need to discuss the pricing of these pieces," Mr. Kimball nods to my collection. "Keep in mind we keep fifty percent of everything sold."

I laugh a loud, barking laugh. I don't mean to; it just happens. Fifty percent? That's ridiculous.

"Excuse me," I say as if my laugh had been an intense cough.

"That's standard, then?" I ask, trying to play it cool.

When Mr. Kimball nods, I try not to get angry. This is the tradeoff. I get art in the public eye of wealthy patrons, and Martin Kimball takes his cut. Mrs. Rosenthal was more than kind to me to not keep a cut of my art sales herself.

"Well, then, let's work out some prices," I smile and guide him through my show.

When everything is squared away, I make my way to the parking lot where Isaiah is leaning casually against my car, a lazy smile on his face. I'll never get enough of that smile.

"That took longer than I expected," he says good-naturedly. Always good-naturedly.

"I had to put a price on creativity," I say flatly

He just sticks his hands in his pockets, raises his eyebrows, and whistles a low, long whistle.

"Well, I've got a table ready for us at Havana," he says casually, checking his watch. "Let's get out of here."

Electricity charges through me. Havana is the fanciest restaurant in town. My father used to take my mom there on their anniversary. Havana nights were the nights Mom would break out her Chanel No. 5. I can hardly believe I'm having my own date night at Havana. I look down at my clothes and feel inadequate.

"I'm not dressed for Havana," I sigh. I'll never be dressed for Havana. Not for a long time. Because even with my mom's increase in pay, I'll never ask her for new clothes. I'm too proud for that.

"You look fine," he smiles and pulls me close. "We'll walk in, and everybody will drop their forks, and they'll all say, 'who's that hot guy with that awkward, tall goof?' and I'll have to stare them down with my most intimidating and territorial stare. And I'll have to cover your eyes, so you don't see somebody better."

There's nobody better than Isaiah. He's the best I've ever met. I don't say this because I don't like to be sappy. At least, not out loud.

"Pretty sure that won't happen," I laugh into his chest because that's where my face hits. "But I like the sound of that."

"What, the hot guy part?" Isaiah pulls away to look at me.

"No, the awkward, tall goof," I wink. "I think I'll call you that from now on.

"I think let's just stick to Is," he laughs and then opens the door for me to climb into his car.

"It'll be a sacrifice," I overdramatize. "But I suppose I can make it for you."

When we get to Havana, I try to act as civilized as possible. The maître d'hôtel seats us at a table with white linens and crystal drinkware. The plates are arranged with silverware on all sides, and I feel completely inadequate. I don't understand this life. Why do there need to be so many utensils? I didn't realize people could complicate eating. Eating is simple when you're poor.

Isaiah doesn't look uncomfortable in the slightest; he must be used to this lavish lifestyle. Of course, he's used to this lavish lifestyle. He and I will always be different that way.

The server fills our glasses with water and offers us menus. For the first time in my life, I feel pampered. But I can't help but notice the distinct differences between Isaiah and me. He observes the menu as if he were ordering a combo meal at a fast-food restaurant. I try to look as calm, but then I see the prices. I feel my eyes widen. Everything is expensive. And everything is á la carte. I've never been to a restaurant that didn't have combo meals. I wish I were exaggerating, but I'm not.

I scan the menu for the cheapest foods. I can't let Isaiah pay these prices for me; it's wasteful. Maybe I'll just order a bowl of soup and a side salad. That seems reasonable.

"What are you ordering?" I ask slyly. I'll make sure to undercut him. It will make me feel better about the expense.

"Nope," he shakes his head. "I'm not telling you."

I raise an eyebrow at him, and he smiles knowingly.

"Order what you want, don't make this about the cost," he puts his hand on mine. "We're celebrating. Let me celebrate you."

I feel myself blush because I'm genuinely embarrassed. I wonder if our relationship is destined to be one-sided. Will it be all give on his part and all take on mine? I can't live like that.

"Stop it," Isaiah says softly. "We're celebrating. You can paint me something if you insist. We'll call it even."

I smile. I love that he reads my mind. I love that he wants to celebrate me.

"Thank you," I finally concede. "For everything. For believing in me. And for seeing me when I'm invisible."

"Don't get sappy on me," he says lightly. "That's not the Cade Swanson I know."

Dinner is wonderful. The atmosphere is beautiful. The company is handsome. The night is perfect. Mom is waiting up for me when I get home, and I tell her everything.

She smiles her bright smile.

"It's so nice to see you happy," she says. "Now, go get some sleep. Tomorrow's a big day."

Chapter Eighteen

I enter Kimball Art at 5:00 the next evening, and I'm blown away by how amazing things look. Mrs. Rosenthal has truly outdone herself. There is a bartender in a white tux shirt and black vest. The musicians are setting up in a corner, dressed elegantly with glistening instruments. Men and women in black and white are carting in plates of snacks. No. This is a fancy event. Hors d'oeuvres. They're bringing in plates of hors d'oeuvres.

"This all looks amazing," I tell Mrs. Rosenthal, hoping she could genuinely see how grateful I am. "It's all better than I imagined."

She smiles contentedly and superiorly. She smirks contemptuously as if to imply that, of course, I've never imagined something so lavish. How could I?

"Those are beautiful pieces you've done of my son," she says instead. "It's cheating, of course, to make an offer before the show has even started, but I've arranged with Martin to buy them."

I smile and thank her, thinking how uncomfortable it will be for Isaiah to have hand-drawn portraits of himself hanging around his house. I can't imagine how uncomfortable I would be in that situation. But I can't argue. I priced them unreasonably high to deter people from making an offer. Instead, Betty Rosenthal will be writing a big check to her son's boyfriend. I choke down a laugh when I think about it.

"I can't thank you enough for all of your help," I tell her, and I genuinely mean it. She may be awful. She may have broken up my parents' marriage. She may have told me in no uncertain terms that I am not good enough to be in her son's life. She may be a pretty awful human being. But I will never be able to thank her enough. She's given me my start. She's turned my life around.

"I'm sorry our partnership is ending tonight," she says in a dutiful way that implies she's not sorry at all. It's that false humility rich people develop. They're taught to say things like that. It's their form of charity. Emulate empathy to look like you care.

I want to say something snide back, but my mother taught me better. Sometimes I really hate that my mom is so good at raising me. Sometimes I wish I could ignore her voice in my head.

Isaiah arrives, dressed to the nines. He looks impressive in his custom-tailored suit. He's so tall and goofy and handsome. I want to rush to him and wrap my arms around him, old-movie style, but don't because of his mom. We have got to tell her tonight. We have got to clear the air.

"You're early!" I exclaim instead. "I'm so glad you're here!"

And I'm not lying. My stomach is in knots. In the weeks leading up to this, I've given newspaper interviews, spoken on the radio, and wrote a guest post on the city's website in the Arts & Entertainment section. I spoke on the school news and had my picture taken for announcements.

Tonight, I'll shake the hands of lawyers, and doctors, and business executives. I'll greet society wives and smile even—when they talk about things I don't understand. I'll have to be charming and graceful, two things I'm not. I can't imagine doing it without Isaiah by my side. I'm so glad he's by my side.

The door opens again, and my heart stops. Is it 6:00 already? Is the show starting?

My mom enters next, looking like her old self, like the 50's movie starlet I remember from my childhood. Her long hair is curled, and she's dressed in a flowing black dress like she's attending the Oscars and not my art show. She's wearing dark red lipstick; it's a shade most women can't get away with. And she smells like Chanel No. 5.

I breathe in her scent and feel a smile spread broadly across my face. It smells like innocence and childhood and hiding under the sheets until my parents came home. It smells like smiles and chocolate chip cookies and bedtime stories. It smells like red lips on my forehead after she kissed me goodnight. It smells like heaven.

"You look beautiful," I do rush to her and hug her. Mom hugs are always acceptable; they give strength.

"So do you," she smiles, and her bright smile is amplified by her dress, and her makeup, and the atmosphere. "My son is all grown up."

I don't let her in the main gallery. I don't want her to see my centerpiece until the show starts. She'll have to be surprised just like everybody else.

We stand for a minute, Isaiah, me, and our moms, in complete silence. You could cut the awkwardness with a knife. It's palpable.

"People will be arriving soon," Mrs. Rosenthal says softly.

The string quartet starts tuning; the twang of strings slipping into the desired pitch is the only sound.

"Mr. Swanson," Martin Kimball calls as he enters to room. "Who is this beautiful young lady with you. I didn't know you had a sister."

I restrain the desire to roll my eyes. This is another thing rich people do. Overly exaggerate compliments, so people think you're charming. I see my mom's face and know that nobody fools her. For most of her adult life, she walked among the elite. She knew exactly what he was doing.

"It's nice to meet you; I'm Teresa Swanson," my Mom offers Mr. Kimball her hand. He takes it limply as if holding a dead fish. I smile as Mom forces him to take her hand in a genuine grip and shake her hand firmly.

"It's a pleasure to meet you as well," Martin Kimball stares at her as if he's meeting the Queen. "I'm Martin Kimball."

Mom lavishes Mr. Kimball with thanks and praise for welcoming my art into his gallery. I'm mesmerized at how easily mom slips back into society and society talk. She's an old pro at it. She hates it, I can tell by the plastered-on smile. But she's good at it.

Martin Kimball looks like the stars glitter in my mother's name, and I smirk. He's probably never met somebody as beautiful as my mom. He hasn't. I can guarantee it.

Mr. Kimball leaves us after a moment longer, and mom returns to me, smiling broadly.

"Is that my new daddy?" I laugh harder than appropriate.

"I will kill you, Cade Swanson," she whispers through her teeth. "Don't think I won't."

When the door opens again, I nearly jump out of my skin. I find myself wishing the show was already over. I'm tired of these nerves and this sick feeling in my stomach. This is not an experience an introvert like me will enjoy; I can already tell.

When I look at the door, though, I'm surprised to see Kayla in a blue dress and Cameron in a dress shirt and tie. My head reels. I didn't expect her here. We haven't talked in three weeks. I haven't even seen her outside of class. If I'm skilled at becoming unnoticeable in the hallways, Kayla has mastered the art of invisibility.

"You came!" I shout much more loudly than I mean to and run to throw my arms around Kayla. Her presence is a comfort I didn't know I needed until I had it.

"Of course, I did," she hugs me back. "I wouldn't miss my best friend's show. We're fighting, but you're still my best friend."

If there were a sentence that could best summarize my friendship with Kayla, that was it. We're fighting, but you're still my best friend.

And this is the way Kayla makes up. She doesn't apologize. She doesn't admit wrong or defeat. Sometimes she doesn't even acknowledge that we're fighting. She just one day stops being mad at me and is the most supportive person I've ever met.

I'm so grateful that today she has decided to make amends. I need her support to get through the night.

"I'm so glad you're here," I say. And I can't wait for her to see the charcoal piece I've done of her and Cameron. I had considered not hanging it in this show, but I knew I'd regret it if I hadn't. I'm glad I had that forethought.

Finally, the bell tolls 6:00, and guests begin to enter the foyer. We've staged this as a holding area. Guests will mingle, and sip champagne, and eat stuffed mushroom caps, and chat about the weather and the stocks, and tell jokes about X-rays. They'll mill about and browse the first phase of the show, simple sketches I've hung about—some acrylic and watercolor pieces that are beautiful but not my typical style. I want the holding area to make them wonder why they've even come to the show. I want them to be shocked when they enter the main exhibition.

People begin to trickle in twos and threes. Every time the door opens, I feel a new wave of panic rise up in me.

I smile happily and extend my hand and greet them all. Women are dressed in beautiful dresses, and men are in suits and ties. Everybody seems excited to meet me. My head starts to spin from the attention. I've spent the past four years trying to be totally unnoticeable; now, I'm the center of attention. It's more than I know how to deal with.

The door opens, and I prepare my uncomfortable smile to meet more people. Instead, I see Mr. Camplin in a navy-blue suit, his wife at his arm in pearls and curls. They look beautiful together. They look happy together.

"I'm so glad you're here," I tell him as he comes in. We stand awkwardly for a moment; I want to hug him, but I don't know if we're close enough for that. We're definitely too close for a handshake. Finally, I decide to hug him. He's stiff and awkward but hugs me back before introducing me to his wife.

"Cade, this is my wife," he gestures toward her awkwardly. He's more awkward than I am. It's like he's never left his classroom. Maybe he hasn't.

"It's nice to meet you," she extends her hand and shakes it firmly. "My husband has told me so much about you."

For the first time, I wonder if teachers talk about their students at home. I wonder what they say about me.

"I can't wait to see your show," she continues. "I've heard all about your talents. I can't want to see them for myself."

With Mr. Camplin and Kayla and Isaiah and my mom here, I feel unstoppable. I have a support system. I have people who are rooting for me, even if nobody else is. I don't need anything else. I don't need anybody else.

I wish Thomas were here; he'd be having so much fun. He'd be asking me so many questions. I'm glad Thomas isn't here.

As the night ticks on, more and more people fill the foyer of Kimball Art.

Some of my classmates appear, wearing smiles of support and their nicest clothes. Some of Mom's co-workers from Megamart and Golden Acres are here, too. Some of my teachers are here. I didn't know I had so much support.

It's getting hot and stuffy in this foyer. I want to open the doors to the main gallery, but it's not time yet. I'm impatient, and so are my guests. I want to open the doors wide and let everybody see what's been consuming me. I want to show off all the things I've done. I want to tell the world, "here I am." But I can't. Not yet. I must be patient.

"All these people are here to see you," Isaiah says into my ear. I turn to see him, and he's beaming. "Not that I had any doubts."

"I did," I smile and let my fingers graze his hand.

Kayla catches my eye, and I jerk away self-consciously. I don't want to start anything today. I just want to enjoy one night that's about me. Isaiah noticeably deflates but doesn't say anything.

"Look at my mom," I smile, nodding in her direction.

She's working the room like this is her event. She's smiling broadly, and laughing demurely, and behaving all the ways a society lady seems to. She greets women with gentle smiles and offers firm handshakes to men.

"She's amazing," I shake my head, smiling. I wish I had an ounce of her grace.

"It runs in the family," Isaiah whispers. Why is he so sweet?

As if on cue, the string quartet begins playing Europe's The Final Countdown. It's the cue that it is time for my main show to open. I feel anticipation rise up in me. It makes me nauseated. It makes me exhilarated.

"May I have your attention, please," Martin Kimball calls from the wooden doors of the main gallery when the quartet plays its final note. "It is my immense pleasure, in partnership with Betty Rosenthal, to introduce you to the newest young talent of the art world."

Polite applause answers as Mr. Kimball motions for me to join him.

"We are proud to introduce everybody to Cade Swanson," he smiles once I've made my way to where he stands. "And though this is the first time many of you have heard his name, I guarantee it won't be the last."

I feel my cheeks go red. I try to smile politely and accept the attention as my mom would, but this is not natural to me at all. I'd be much more comfortable in rumpled jeans. I'd be more comfortable at my drafting table.

"And now, without further ado, I present Mr. Swanson's world premier and his show, Adoration."

With that, the docents open the gallery doors, and even my eyes widen in amazement. The gallery glistens with shiny frames and new glass. The air smells of oak and perfumes. The foyer thins out as people make their way into the gallery.

Almost immediately, I hear impressed murmurs and whispers of praise. I feel pride grow in my chest as people point and discuss my art under their breath.

"Excuse me, sir," Mom sidles up to me. "Will you escort me through this show?"

I smile and offer her my arm.

"It would be my pleasure."

"Sinéad, it's so nice of you to join us," Mom smiles at me as we pass the painting I made what seems like a lifetime ago.

We wander through the gallery, and I stop to tell Mom about the various pieces we pass. Patrons stop me every few steps to congratulate me and to compliment me. They tell me how impressed they are by my work. Businesspeople slip me cards and ask me to call them to arrange meetings about things I don't understand. I smile and thank them and shake their hands. I notice Martin Kimball accepting checks and writing receipts.

"People are buying your art," Mom says, impressed as we pass more of my art.

We pass Cameron and Kayla stopped at the charcoal, featuring them laughing at the lunch table. Beside them, an older couple is looking from the portrait to Cameron and Kayla and back again.

"So lifelike," I hear the woman say quietly, and I see my mom glow with pride.

"He's the best artist you'll ever meet," Kayla smiles broadly.

"It helps that he had such a good-looking couple to draw," the older gentleman says kindly.

Kayla glows with pride, and Cameron blushes, hanging his head.

"Cade!" Kayla waves me over excitedly. Mom and I join the group gathered around my picture.

"This is my Uncle Albert and my Aunt Marjorie," she introduces. "They love your work."

I smile and thank them. My entire night has been a blur of smiles and thanks. I shake their hands, and accept their praise, and introduce them to my mom. I step back and smile as they overwhelm her with compliments. I can't stop smiling. My cheeks hurt. And for the first time in my life, I don't want to be unnoticeable.

"It was so nice to meet you," Mom ends the conversation with Kayla's family. "But there's still so much of this show I haven't seen. Cade has kept it all under wraps at home."

I lead her to the finished graphite picture of Thomas, asleep in bed. It took me forever, but I finally got the folds in the sheets right, the peaceful look on his face. The moonlight glints in his hair, and even in black and white, everything looks beautiful and serene.

"I'd forgotten how beautiful this is," Mom breathes quietly.

"I really hope it doesn't sell," I tell mom, regret filling my stomach. "I should never have listed it."

Mom leans in and reads the plaque closely.

"There's a $5,000 price tag on this," Mom says suspiciously. "I doubt anybody's going to pay that for a picture of your brother asleep. Even if it is amazing."

I smile and hope she's right.

"This is amazing, Cade," she says for the billionth time as we meander through the exhibition. I stop every few steps and accept praise and congratulations from the attendees. I'm feeling more comfortable in my suit and Calvin Klein, surrounded by men and women in their finest clothes. I could get used to this life. Isaiah must be used to this life.

I look up and see Isaiah staring at one of the portraits of himself. It's the one I did when he was sad. Seeing his glowing eyes next to her hand-drawn likeness is bizarre. I'm used to working from reference photos; I'm used to seeing the things I draw for hours on end, so I'm not shocked when things turn out exactly right.

This portrait of Isaiah, however, was done from memory. It strikes me as somehow strange that I was able to do all of that without a reference. How have I never noticed how much time I've spent noticing the curves of his face, the sharp angle of his jaw, the gentle jut of his chin?

"Go see Isaiah," Mom smiles. "I'll be right here. You can take me through the rest of the show later."

I smile in thanks and walk to him.

"I look weird in this one," he says, nodding to his charcoal doppelganger. "I don't make this face."

I take his hand gently.

"You have," I nod gently. "Just once. And it was my fault."

His smile is distracting. His honey-and-amber eyes search my face for a second, and I forget we're at my art opening. For just a moment, we're two very well-dressed teenagers standing in a beautiful room surrounded by art and engulfed by the music of a string quartet. I squeeze his hand more tightly in mine, afraid it'll slip away if I don't, afraid he'll slip away if I don't.

"There's another one of you around the corner," I nod my head in the general direction of the smiling Isaiah. "Did you see it?"

"Not yet," he smiles. "I was so caught off-guard by this one. You're amazing, Cade."

Something in his voice tells me he's not talking about the art, but I thank him for it anyway.

"Anybody can do it," I shrug. "It's just about values." It's the same thing Mr. Camplin always says. If you know where your darks and lights are, the rest comes on its own.

"I don't mean the art," Isaiah laughs his deep, resounding, infectious laugh. "I mean you. You're living your dreams. Everybody here wants to know you. Everybody here wants to be your friend."

I laugh at the childishness of it all. Everybody wants to be my friend. In elementary school, that was how success was measured.

"You're doing the thing you've always wanted to do, and I don't just mean making art," Isaiah touches the little red SOLD sign that hangs below the artwork details. "You're successful. You're escaping the things you wanted to escape."

I feel myself blush and look to the floor. I can't be mushy like this. Not here. Not where I might cry in front of every important person in the city. The mayor is here. The press is here. I can't cry.

"Thank you, Is," I kiss him delicately on the cheek. "I'm going to take my mom on the rest of the tour. And then I'm all yours."

I lead Mom through the rest of the exhibition until we get to the pièce de résistance. There is a crowd gathered around, talking quietly about the piece. Mr. Camplin, I can see, is leading the discussion. A few of my classmates listen intently as he points to different sections. Some college students look as if they're hanging on his every word, and I wonder if they're art majors at one of the nearby colleges.

"And here's the artist himself," Mr. Camplin smiles and motions for me to come.

Mr. Camplin introduces me to the students around him, all former students of his who are attending various schools in the area. It's a mix of artists of different abilities and media and interests, and at this moment, they're all enamored with my work. They shake my hand excitedly, and offer critiques, and smiles, and words of encouragement.

"Oh my God," one of them says when she sees my mom. "It looks just like her."

My mom smiles, confused.

"What does?" Mom asks me.

"This is the centerpiece of my show," I say softly. I'm suddenly embarrassed. In the dark, in my bedroom, with nobody around, the stippled piece of my Mom didn't seem strange. But now that other people are looking at it, I'm self-conscious of being the 18-year-old who spent hours making portraits of his mother.

On the information plaque, I've titled the piece Quiet Strength. I've listed the price at $7,500, another attempt at keeping it from selling. I want to keep it for myself. But I won't turn down the money if there's an offer.

When the crowd parts, my mom's eyes are immediately drawn to the portrait while mine go straight to the bright red 'sold' sign. Somebody already bought this portrait? Who? Why? Who wants a picture of my mom hanging in their living room?

"Oh, Cade," Mom says breathlessly. "It's amazing. I… I don't even know what to say."

I feel myself blush. As we stand there, people start to surround us. Everybody has been eyeing the picture from a distance. But with Mom, the subject, standing beside it, everybody is suddenly intrigued. It's like meeting the Mona Lisa in person.

"Mr. Swanson, your work is tremendous," a tall, slender woman reaches her hand out to me.

"My name is Cynthia Reid," she says as we shake hands. "I'm the dean of the College of Fine Arts at Magnolia State University.

She hands me a business card.

"I hope you'll consider applying to MSU," she smiles first to me and then my mom. "You'd be an asset to our program. I'm sure I could even find a little scholarship if you're interested."

I feel myself beaming broadly. A little scholarship is nothing the sneeze at but winning the state art show comes with a full ride to any art school in the state. That's an opportunity I can't afford to pass up.

"I know you're busy tonight," she gestures around her to indicate the show. "But give me a call sometime soon so we can discuss your prospects. I'd love to have you in our program."

Mom hugs me tightly, despite the important elites around us. A flash goes off, and a newspaper reporter has snapped a shot of Mom hugging me in front of the portrait I made of her.

"Who do you think bought this?" Mom asks as we turn back to her portrait. I've been wondering the same thing, myself.

"Yes, ma'am," I hear a deep, distantly familiar voice behind me.

I notice a tall, handsome, dark-haired man talking to the newspaper reporter. I stare for longer than I should, trying to catch a glimpse of his face.

"What led you to buy this particular piece?" The news reporter asks the tall, suit-clad man.

"Cade has always been talented," the man answers, his voice stinging the back of my memories. "When I saw this beautiful picture of his mother, I knew I had to have it. My son knows beauty when he sees it, and this is an amazing homage to that beauty."

I feel my heart stop. A noise catches in my throat. My hands clench. The room blurs. I have to save face. I have to keep it together.

I feel Isaiah approach me and slip his hand into mine. As his fingers tighten around mine, the man turns slowly to smile at me, and I see, for the first time in four years, the face of my father, of the man who abandoned me.

Without knowing what I'm doing, I run. The room is too hot. The lights are too bright. I need fresh air. I need to go somewhere. I need to be anywhere but here.

I shove the glass doors open and tumble into the night. What the hell is he doing here?

Chapter Nineteen

The night air is cool against my warm face. The breeze carries with it promise and anger. I want to scream. I can't scream. There's a media team inside that would love to run a headline about my demise.

Local Artist Has Breakdown in Alley

I can't let him win. I can't give him any power over me. He hasn't had power over me in four years. He hasn't even seen me in four years.

I can't breathe. I can't think. I don't know where I am. When I left the art gallery, I went running, but I have no idea where I've wound up. I look around me, but I don't recognize any of the buildings. I look at the skyline as if that will help me. But I'm hopelessly lost. Where am I?

Shit.

Shit.

I spin 180 degrees and try to get my bearings. I have no idea. I'm going to miss my own show. I'm going to get murdered in this alley. At least my art would sell. Van Gogh didn't sell until after his death. Artists are always romanticized after their deaths.

I start to breathe hard and heavy. I can't catch my breath. I can't see straight. Where am I? Why is he here? This was supposed to be the night that things went well for me. Even Kayla was being nice. Why the hell did he have to ruin it?

I try to slow my breathing, but I can't. Breathe in. Hold it. Breathe out slowly. In. Out. In. Out.

It's not working.

I feel tears pool in my eyes, and I lean against the side of a building.

I don't know what I'm doing anymore. I want to just crumple up here and let the world pass by.

A loud click-clack sound echoes down the alley as I focus on my breathing. I hear muffled voices, and I freeze. I've got nowhere to hide. I really am going to die in this alleyway. I've watched enough true crime shows to know that this is how it ends. I bend at the waist and bury my face in my hands. I throw my weight into my heels and slam the small of my back into the wall.

"Cade?" I hear Kayla's voice call. The click-clacking gets louder and faster until I can feel her hovering beside me.

"Guys!" She calls down the echoing, brick alley. "He's over here!"

I look up at her, knowing exactly how much of a wreck I must look. I must look awful. I feel awful.

"Cade, are you okay?" Kayla asks gently as clunky footsteps close in on us.

I try to speak, but I can't. I'm gasping too hard. I shake my head yes and then no. I don't know if I'm okay.

The sky's supposed to open me up and swallow me whole right now, right? Shouldn't the earth crack and buildings crumble around me? Isn't this the part of the movie where I realize I have supernatural powers and destroy my high school or something?

"What happened in there?" She asks, pulling me into a tight hug. She's taller than me in her heels, and somehow that's comforting. I feel tiny, and delicate, and broken. I feel pocket-sized. I keep shrinking. Every time Kayla looks at me, I get smaller.

I try to tell her, but it doesn't come out.

"Breathe, sweetie," she says softly. "Breathe in and hold it."

I do as she says. I do as she does. Something about doing it in synchronicity with somebody else helps. I breathe in. I count to ten. I exhale.

When I finally calm down, I see Cameron and Isaiah there, too. Their looks of worry mirror Kayla's. They look almost rehearsed.

I want to fling myself into Isaiah's arms, but I'm afraid I'll fall if I let go of Kayla. Kayla is holding me up. Kayla is holding the world up. For the first time in months, Kayla is keeping the sky from caving in around me. Around us.

"What happened?" Kayla tries again. Isaiah doesn't say anything.

"I'm a time bomb," I say by way of explanation. "And all of you are getting caught in my explosion."

Cameron laughs uncomfortably but tries to cover it as a cough.

"You're not a time bomb," Kayla says gently. This is the kindest she's been in a long time. Why is she being so nice?

"He's here," I finally spit out. I want to elaborate on the time bomb statement, but they won't get it. They won't get how I always feel one day away from an explosion. They won't understand that I want to spare them when I finally detonate.

"Who's here?" Kayla rubs my back gently.

"My father."

I hear three surprised gasps. They are all as blindsided as I was.

"Why?" Kayla asks angrily, defensively. "He's been gone for, what, four years? And now that you're successful, he's back?"

She's articulating all the things that have been in my head. She's saying all the things I want to say, all the things I want to hear.

"What an asshat," Kayla sighs.

I feel a smile creep across my face.

"Your mother would die if she heard you speak so unladylike."

She brushes her hand in the air as if to show how little she cares.

"How did he know about this?" I all but spit.

Now I'm venting. Now I'm ranting. Did Mom invite him? She wouldn't dare do it behind my back. She leaves those decisions up to me.

I bet it was Betty Rosenthal. She is constantly trying to ruin my life. She is out to get me. I want to tell Isaiah that I hate his mother. I want to say to him that I hate everything she stands for. But how can I without hurting him? It would kill me if he said something like that about my mom. Not that my mom is anything like Betty Rosenthal.

I shake my head and wipe my face with the back of my wrist.

"I don't know," I shake my head. "Maybe he was invited by Martin Kimball. Maybe Martin didn't know he was my father. Maybe he just invited local business people. Or maybe he didn't realize that I hate my father."

"You say 'father' every time," Isaiah says softly. "Every time. You never say 'dad.'"

I want to roll my eyes at Isaiah. I never want to roll my eyes at Isaiah.

"I didn't realize you hated him so much," he whispers.

Did Isaiah invite him? I can't bear to ask. I don't want to hate him. I want to continue in blissful ignorance.

Kayla, however, doesn't care.

"Did you invite him?" She demands. Her voice snarls like a lioness protecting her cub.

"No," he shakes his head violently. "I just… I didn't realize."

He looks hurt. He looks like he wants to hold me in his arms, but he doesn't.

"Listen," Cameron says, level-headed. "I know this sucks. But you've got to get back into your art show. The worst thing you can do is let him win."

I nod. He's right. This is what Kayla sees in him. He's friendly and intelligent. And he knows how to play this wretched game of life.

Kayla leads me in breathing one more time. Isaiah holds my hand for strength. Cameron gives me the pep talk of the century, and we make our way back to my opening.

As we walk back to Kimball Art, I feel myself sink into the calm familiarity of my friends. I am terrified to go back inside. I'm nervous about facing my dad again for the first time in four years. I don't know if my mom has seen him yet. I don't understand why any of this is happening. I'm angry. I want to punch something. But I keep my composure as best as I can.

Isaiah slips his hand naturally into mine as we walk. Our fingers fit together perfectly, aligning like the teeth of a zipper, like stitches, like sunflower petals. I draw strength from him.

"I'm sorry I'm a time bomb," I whisper as we walk. "I'm sorry you have to be caught in my explosions."

Isaiah looks at me, those all-knowing honey eyes seeing straight through to my soul. I feel exposed under his gaze.

"If you explode," he says, not arguing. "I will be the happiest casualty."

I squeeze his hand. Is he in this for the long haul? Is there a long haul? Are all high school relationships doomed for failure? My parents' was.

"You ready?" Cameron asks as he puts his hand on the handle to open it for us.

When it swings open, my Mom's eyes meet mine immediately.

"Cade," she rushes to me. She doesn't say anything else; she's trying to maintain our composure. "I was wondering where you had gone."

"I just needed some fresh air," I tell her. Translation: I was having a panic attack in an alleyway.

"I didn't expect there to be so many people here," I continue. Translation: I didn't expect Cole Swanson to be here.

"There are a lot of people here," she agrees, nodding her head. Translation: I had no idea either.

"Mr. Swanson?" A woman with a needlessly large camera smiles, interrupting Mom and me. "Do you mind if I get a picture of you with your parents for the paper?"

She starts rambling about standing in front of the portrait of my mom, but the pounding of my heart in my ears soon drowns her out.

"I don't think it's fair for us to share his spotlight," Mom says delicately, and I'm more grateful for her than ever before. "This is his night, and besides, without Cade's younger brother, no family photo is complete."

I come unspooled. Every tight place in me loosens before I even realized they were tight. Mom is brilliant. She's the best at everything.

"Well, that sounds fine, too," the girl says, obviously dejected but relentless in her quest for a photograph of me.

As I approach the portrait of my mom, I see my father standing in a corner, hobnobbing with other businesspeople. Where Mom seems elegant and commands a room with her grace, Cole Swanson controls a room with is assertiveness and a firm grip. He holds everybody's gaze with a strong smile and a warm laugh. His laugh roars through the room, echoing in a way that makes everybody want to join in the joke. He's charming, and people practically elbow other people on their paths to his circle.

Once the photographer has taken a plethora of photos and taken a few statements from me, Betty Rosenthal waves me over to my father's circle.

I don't want to go there. I don't want to join his group. I focus all my energy on opening the ground beneath them and watching the earth swallow them whole. When it doesn't, I realize that I have no way to escape. I resign myself to talking to the two most vile people on the planet, standing in charge of a group of vile groupies.

"Cade," Cole Swanson roars, clapping me on my back as if we've been best buds my entire life. As if we watch football together on the weekends. As if he knows anything about me.

"This is my boy," he says proudly, oozing charm and venom out of every pore, out of every word. If I were to paint his portrait, he'd be green. Toxic and noxious. He'd be the odor that hangs over a landfill. He'd be the mushroom cloud of a nuclear explosion.

"You must get your talents from your father," a shriveled old man adjusts his glasses as he observes me.

"Not really," I shake my head innocently. "My old man doesn't really have any talents."

I force a laugh after this, and my father's mindless friends laugh along. They think this deprecation is a game between my father and me. It's not.

"Unless you count running," I smile. Dad ran track in high school. But that's not what I mean, and he knows it.

I watch his smile crumple at the edges. He's never been undermined in front of his posse before, I can tell. He doesn't know how to react to this. If he loses face, he'll have to deal with the public humiliation of admitting defeat. If he keeps smiling, he's just welcoming himself to more torture from me.

I feel giddy inside. I want to keep attacking him. I want to embarrass him. I want to destroy him the way he destroyed my family. I want to humiliate him and let the world know how awful he is.

But in doing so, I'll ruin my show. I can't give myself the pleasure of destroying him without destroying me. Like all families, unfortunately, my father and I are inexorably linked. If I detonate his time bomb, I will detonate myself, too.

"I've seen the pictures you've done of your best friends and your mom and brother," one of my father's minions starts. "But I don't see any portraits of your father."

He says this like he meant to ask a question but directs it into an observation at the last second. It's like he verbally erased the forming question mark and replaced it with a period.

"Well, you know what they say," I smile. "Not everything that glitters is gold. My old man just didn't make the cut."

They laugh harder than I expected. It's like this is some game of societal chess, and I've somehow just declared checkmate. But I don't know how. I don't understand why these people think I'm funny.

"He's just charming, isn't he?" Another posse member asks. "He obviously takes after his father."

"I don't know," my father's voice bubbles with a frustration I recognize even after four years. "It seems he's got a lot of his mother in him."

I smile at this comment, and a sense of superiority overwhelms me. I'd much rather be compared to Mom than to my father.

"I'd love to stay and chat," I smile coolly. "But I have to go see some other guests."

I nod noncommittally to nobody in particular.

"Mrs. Rosenthal, thank you for everything," I smile kindly, genuinely meaning it. "All of this was your brainchild, and you deserve more praise than I can ever give."

Mrs. Rosenthal smiles graciously but quirks an eyebrow at me suspiciously. She's aware of how badly I hate her, how deep my disdain for her runs.

"Seriously," I smile easily. "I could not have done any of this without you and without that amazing son of yours."

I see Isaiah out of the corner of my eye. His face glows bright red, and he ducks away to avoid anybody seeing. It's like we have our own secret code. His Mom has no idea he's my boyfriend. Nobody except for Kayla,

Cameron, and my mom has any idea. Isaiah is my secret. It gives me a rush. It gives me a buzz.

"Well, yes, I suppose he does deserve some praise," Betty Rosenthal acknowledges.

The night wears on after I leave my father's group. I try to avoid him at all costs. I try to avoid Betty Rosenthal at all costs. I try to avoid anybody. I'm wearing out. All these people are exhausting me.

"Cade," Mr. Camplin calls me over once I've circulated the room a few times.

"Yes, sir?"

"This is the point in the evening when most artists give a speech. They introduce their work formally. They offer their gratitude to the people attending. They mention upcoming projects. Those kinds of things." He places his hand on my shoulder and looks me straight in the eyes.

"Cade, I'm so proud of you," he smiles so deeply, his eyes squint, and wrinkles appear at the corners. "You've worked so hard for this night. You work hard for everything. You're an amazing artist, Cade. You deserve this night."

I almost cry. It's one thing for my mom to tell me how proud she is of me. She's my mom; she has to. But Mr. Camplin doesn't have to say anything nice. His compliments are always honest.

At his suggestion, I stand beside the focal point of my show: that stippled piece of my mom. I smile, drawing strength from her likeness so nearby. I look around the room for a second to acknowledge all the gathered people. There's no reason that so many people should be here looking at my art. There's no reason that I should be hanging in a gallery. There's no reason any of this is happening.

"I want to thank all of you for attending tonight," I scan the room. I can't see my mom. I can't see my father. I don't see Isaiah or Kayla, either. I try to ignore it; maybe I just glanced over them. There are a lot of people here.

"Tonight, as I passed by everybody, I heard so many kind words, and I cannot tell you just how thankful I am for your support."

The crowd applauds politely.

I take a moment to tell everybody about some of the more significant pieces in my show. I intentionally ignore the portraits of Isaiah. How can I describe him without outing myself to a room full of strangers? I consciously don't talk about the picture of Kayla and Cameron, either. I feel like it's only fair to Isaiah.

I talk about Thomas and his inspiration in my daily life. I talk about my supportive mom. My father's lackeys wait with bated breath as they wait to hear what I say about him. I say nothing.

I explain how the show will be up for a month before the sold pieces will be taken down. Everything remaining will be relegated to a smaller space for two more weeks. And what is left will go back to my house. As I scan the room, I see that everything in the main exhibition has sold already—everything except the picture of Thomas.

"Before I started my speech tonight, my art teacher told me something interesting." I smile and nod to Mr. Camplin. He's beaming at me, his wife on his arm, proud to show him off as hers. They're a beautiful couple. I hope they're always this happy together. Forever.

"He told me I deserve this night because I work hard," I smile and shake my head. "But the truth is I don't deserve tonight more than anybody else does. There are artists working as hard as me every day whose work may never hang in a show."

I laugh, thinking of Mr. Camplin's class.

"Rumor has it that Van Gogh only sold one work in his lifetime, and he worked way harder than I ever have." Mr. Camplin laughs a surprised laugh. Maybe it's the first time he's ever gotten to observe that his students actually listen to him.

I finally spot Isaiah and Kayla in the crowd, standing beside Cameron, whispering energetically. Kayla is smiling a forced smile, but Isaiah's not even trying. Are they fighting? Did Kayla say something insensitive? It wouldn't surprise me. I try to save face and keep talking.

"That said," I continue. "I am more grateful for tonight than words can express. First, I'd like to thank my agent, Mrs. Betty Rosenthal."

I clap in a way that is directed toward her. The audience applauds her politely. She glows with pride, puffing out her chest as if she'd discovered art, not just me.

"I also would like to thank Mr. Martin Kimball for opening his beautiful gallery to my work. And for opening his doors to let us spend this evening together. Being an artist isn't like being a musician; we don't always get to see people appreciate the fruits of our labor."

I clap for Martin Kimball, who takes an elaborate bow as if he were hosting the first viewing of Starry Night and not the work of a high school student.

"And finally, I need to show my unending appreciation to Mr. Camplin. Without his support and encouragement, I would have given up ages ago. But he taught me perseverance. He taught me the value of values and the unimportance of colors. There's no reason somebody as talented as he is should be teaching high school art at Riverside High School, but I am so glad he is."

And I smile with glowing pride as the crowd gives Mr. Camplin genuine, thunderous applause. They clap like he's an Academy Award-winning actor, not like he's a high school art teacher.

And that, I think, is something somebody deserves. Because nobody works harder than Mr. Camplin.

Once the applause has died down, I thank the audience for attending and make my way to Isaiah, Kayla, and Cameron. I want to know what they were arguing about. Before I can take Isaiah's hand, Kayla throws her arms around me.

"Have I told you how proud I am of you?" She asks emphatically.

"What's going on?" I'm suspicious.

"I can't be proud of my best friend?" She sounds hurt.

"I saw you guys fighting," I say flatly, looking from Kayla to Isaiah. Somebody owes me an explanation.

"We'll talk about it later," Kayla says quietly. She looks dejected. Whatever this is, Isaiah must have won.

I decide to ignore them; I'm on too big of a high from tonight. I'm also too busy avoiding my father.

Speaking of which, where is he? I search the room once more and finally see my mom. She's at the edge of the crowd looking flushed and scratching her neck uneasily. I make my way to her, stopping to shake hands and accept congratulations as I move. She looks different. She doesn't look like the woman in my stippled centerpiece anymore. What's changed about her?

"Is it time to go yet?" I mutter. I'm through being nice. There are too many people here. The best thing about my art is that it's a solitary practice. I sit for hours all alone with nothing but my thoughts and audiobooks to keep me company. Audiobooks are a recent addition. Isaiah begged me to use them to complete my reading assignments for English while working. And I can't resist when his eyes go all watery and adorable.

"Almost," Mom says wistfully. There's something in her eye, a sparkle I haven't noticed before. What's going on with her?

"Mom," I smile knowingly. "Did you meet a guy here?"

She waves me off as if it's the most absurd question she's ever been asked.

"You should go see your father off," she says with a knowing look. She knows if she doesn't instruct to do this, I won't.

I find him near the door, slipping into a wool coat much too heavy for November in Texas. He's glowing with pride and something else. Something I can't place.

"Mom told me to tell you bye," I sigh as he notices me. I want to tell him good riddance, instead.

"I'm so glad I was able to come," he smiles, but I can't tell if he's being sincere, if he's being kind. Right now, all it seems he's being is a nuisance. "You've always been talented; I've always been so proud of you."

"I don't want to do this here," I say quietly, fighting back the stinging of tears. I don't want to fight with my father at my art show. I don't want to see my father at my art show.

"Do what?" He asks. "I can't tell my son I'm proud of him?"

"I don't know," I say before I realize what I'm saying. "You'll have to ask your son when you have one."

His façade drops for just a second, and I see I've hurt him.

Good, I think. He can feel what it's like to be abandoned and unwanted.

"I deserve that," he says. "But maybe we can have a fresh start one day. When you're ready."

I'm not ready, and I won't ever be. But I don't tell him this. Because this is my art show, and I have the upper hand here.

Before I know what he's doing, he wraps his arms around me and hugs me gently. For only a second. For only a moment. And then he leaves, leaving me smelling of a mix of expensive cologne and Chanel No. 5.

Chanel No. 5.

Like my mom.

Chanel No. 5 on my father's business suit.

And for a second time tonight, my father lights the fuse I always feel inside of me. But it's my mother who handed him the match.

Chapter Twenty

"Can we go get something to eat?" I ask Kayla, Cameron, and Isaiah when I get back from sending my father away. "I need to drown the memory of tonight in syrup and scrambled eggs."

"You know, then," Kayla hangs her head. "We hoped you wouldn't find out."

Cameron looks from me to Kayla and back again. He squints like he's trying to decipher some kind of secret code. He blinks hard, opens his mouth, but then shuts it again.

"Yeah," I nod. "Her perfume's all over him."

"I wanted to tell you," Kayla shakes her head, then cuts a pointed glare at Isaiah. "But somebody thought we should wait."

"I just didn't want to ruin your night," Isaiah wilts. He looks like he's not sure what the right decision was. I can't tell him there wasn't a right decision in this.

"Wait," Cameron makes a face like he's doing complex mathematics. "How did you know he knew?"

Kayla laughs uneasily.

"You know how some girls eat a lot of ice cream when they're upset?" She smiles. "Cade eats waffles when he's upset."

Cameron nods slowly as if this is still some kind of complicated word puzzle.

"And he's upset because?" He asks, guarded.

"Because he knows about his mom and dad," Kayla answers impatiently.

I don't want to talk about it, so I don't. I want to curl up against Isaiah and let this night pass us by. And every night from now until we're old enough to run away together. I'd be happy to take on the world, just me and Isaiah. I can't wait to take on the world, just me and Isaiah.

"I have to finish saying goodbye to everybody," I sigh at last. "Will you guys wait for me?"

They agree, and I make my way to the dissipating crowd. I'm all smiles and appreciation as people depart. I thank Betty Rosenthal profusely. I thank Martin Kimball even more.

"No thanks needed, Mr. Swanson," Martin smiles broadly, shaking my hand. "Your entire show sold out tonight. You are probably the wealthiest teenager in town tonight."

I feel my heart drop. My entire show? Everything? Including the picture of Thomas?

For the millionth time tonight, I try not to cry. I knew I shouldn't have listed it. I let greed get the best of me. Mom warned me about this, didn't she? The day Betty Rosenthal became my agent. Mom warned me that my art was personal.

I was going to save that picture for my portfolio for the state art show. What have I done?

"I will have your check sometime later this week," Mr. Kimball is saying. I don't know if he's said anything else; I zoned out. I hope not.

"Thank you," I pull myself together. I want to ask him who bought the picture of Thomas, but I decide against it. I don't want to know. I need to let it go.

When Martin Kimball walks away, I allow myself to lean against one of the walls to support myself. I feel empty inside. I feel broken. I should feel excited; this should be the greatest night of my life.

I start doing the math in my head. Between just the pieces of Mom and Thomas, I've made $10,000. With everything else added together, I've more than made back everything I paid for my Mustang; I've got a nest egg for college. I try to take comfort in this, but it's hard. I really love that picture of Thomas.

When the last guests have left, the only people left are my mother, Kayla,

Isaiah, Cameron, Martin Kimball, Betty Rosenthal, and me. I survey the room around me and want to laugh. This is the most broken, motley crew I have ever seen. We're beyond irreparable.

"How about a celebratory dinner?" My mother asks my friends. "On me. This is a special night."

"Maybe another day," I hold back the venom that threatens to shoot out at her. "We're going to hang out."

I see her face fall. The sparkle in her eye dulls a little bit. I almost feel remorseful. Almost.

"Oh, I see," she smiles, trying to look unfazed. "Like a double date."

Isaiah and I both stiffen when she says this. Betty Rosenthal is hardly out of earshot, and we're dreading telling her we're together. We're only going to as a favor to my mother.

"Could you freaking not?" I spit. "For real, mother? We're just hanging out."

"I'm sorry," she holds her hands up defensively as if she hasn't done anything wrong. "I need to get home to Thomas, anyway."

When Mom leaves, I send Kayla and Cameron ahead to get a table for us at Wafflez 'N More.

"Mrs. Rosenthal?" I approach her slowly. "I want to thank you. Really. For everything."

It makes me sick to say this. Because I also want to tell her that she's the vilest, most disgusting person I've ever met. I also want to tell her how much I hate her. But that wouldn't be fair. I wouldn't be here tonight if it weren't for Betty Rosenthal.

"Before we officially cut ties, I have something for you." I smile.

Isaiah enters the room with a large canvas. I've painted her house, just as she requested to hang above her mantle. I know this in no way repays her for the effort she put into my career, but I hope it at least buys a small part of her favor.

"Before we part ways," Mrs. Rosenthal smiles, accepting her gift without a word of thanks. "We should talk about how you disrespected your father today."

I shake my head, immediately seeing red. I hate Betty Rosenthal, and I always, always will.

"You had no right to invite him," I snarl before I even process what I'm doing. "He was not welcome here tonight. He's not welcome anywhere near me."

I nearly turn to leave, but I catch a second wind. I'm not finished with the things I want to say to her.

"And I'll talk to whoever I want however I want. You're my *former* agent, not my mother," I spit former at her like it's a curse.

She looks taken aback. She's one melodramatic gasp away from asking who I think I am.

"I know you're in the business of ruining lives," I continue. "But you have no authority over mine. You don't get to tell me how to treat my father. You don't get to tell me how to treat your son."

Isaiah's eyes open wide.

"Cade," he whispers. "Calm down. She didn't know."

"Didn't know what?" Betty Rosenthal asks calmly. Her motherly tone pisses me off.

"She knew," I tell Isaiah quietly. "She's the reason."

The room grows cold. The room grows still. For just a moment, I can feel the rotation of the earth beneath my feet.

I don't say she's the reason he left. It's not fair to Isaiah. He needs to hear it from his mother, not from me.

"My father walked out on us four years ago," I stare Betty in the eye, and for once, I don't feel like crying. "And we've gotten along perfectly well without him. It wasn't your place to invite him back tonight."

A slow realization crosses her face, and I know that Betty understands what I'm saying. She knows I know she's the reason for my parents' divorce. She knows I know about their secret relationship. I see the ghosts of her past surface, as well.

"Have a good night, Mr. Swanson," she says, business-like and stern. "Isaiah, be home by midnight."

She takes her picture, turns on a heel, and exits the room.

"You can't talk to my mom like that, Cade," Isaiah says shortly. "I don't care if you hate her; she's still my mom."

I hang my head, but I don't feel shame. I feel victorious.

When Isaiah and I meet Kayla and Cameron Wafflez 'N More, we're grossly overdressed. Isaiah hasn't spoken to me since we left the art gallery. I don't push him to. He'll come around when he's ready. I've earned his anger, but I'm not sorry for what I said.

"I thought y'all had abandoned us," Cameron laughs as we take a seat. "I figured you guys had snuck off."

Isaiah, Kayla, and I all look at him with horrified, confused looks.

"What?" He laughs. "You're both dressed up, and Cade's having the night of his life. I figured—I don't know—it was like prom or something."

The table grows icily quiet at Cameron's joke. He really does have a penchant for saying the wrong things at perfect times.

"I'm not sleeping with you after prom," Kayla says flatly, honestly.

"I didn't mean that," Cameron blushes, sinking in his seat.

"I'm not sleeping with anybody," Isaiah rolls his eyes, irritated.

"Why don't we just order some waffles and not talk for a minute," I suggest.

The table is uncomfortably silent for a long time. We place our orders, but aside from that, say nothing. Time ticks by more slowly than I imagined possible. Isaiah, Cameron, and Kayla are all sulky.

"Okay, this sucks," Cameron finally breaks the silence. "This is Cade's big night, and we're all being jerks."

"I can't believe you put that image in my head," Kayla snaps almost before Cameron's finished.

"What image?" I ask pointedly.

"I don't want to think about you two together," Kayla shakes her head, disgusted. "It's already hard being here with you two on this awkward double date. I don't want to think about you two kissing."

And there's that knife in my back again. I didn't realize Kayla had room for a knife so big in her clutch. The more she talks, the more she twists it.

"Well, we do," Isaiah says flatly, his eyes narrowed at her. "And we're pretty good at it, too."

I hide a snicker. Isaiah's never this catty.

"Kayla, that's really out of line," Cameron says quietly. He regards her as if she's brand-new like he's never seen her before. "You should apologize."

But Kayla doesn't because Kayla never does. Because Kayla's never wrong. It's the entire world that's wrong.

"I think you should take me home, now," she says tiredly. "Good night, Cade. I'm proud of you. Good night, Isaiah."

She says the last half like an afterthought like she had been planning to ignore his presence completely.

The door swings shut behind them the moment the food arrives. I don't care; I'm so hungry and stressed that I'll eat their portions.

"For what it's worth, honey," the waitress says as she places the food in front of me. "I think you two make an adorable couple." She winks at Isaiah and me and leaves us to eat in buttery, syrupy, uncomfortable silence.

"I thought you were exaggerating," Isaiah says quietly, halfway through his waffle.

I look at him with a confused look. I've been taken captive by my third waffle.

"She's awful," Isaiah shakes his head. "She's awful to you. It's no wonder you're always so sad. She beats you down."

I sigh and feel my shoulders slump.

"Sometimes," I shrug, at last, swallowing a bite of flaky, golden heaven. "But, like in the alley today, she really helped me out. She's a good friend."

Isaiah stares down at his waffle for a long while before looking back up at me. He breathes in deeply. He's deciding whether he wants to say something or not. He's considered it 30,000 times before he finally says it.

"That's called being a decent human being, Cade, not a good friend."

The table between us feels 400 feet wide. Because I know he's right. But I'm not ready to admit it. Because Kayla has been my best friend since I needed a friend the most. She was always there for me when I needed people the most. When I tell him this, he shakes his head.

"Your father showed up for the first time in four years tonight. Your mom kissed him. You lost your temper with my mom," he sighs. "I'd argue that tonight is one of those times you'd need your best friend."

I want to argue with him, but I don't. Because he's right. And because I want to argue just to argue, not because I disagree.

So, I order another waffle instead.

We load back into my car; the silence is so thick around us it's turned green and putrid. It smells like anger and something else, something uncomfortable and embarrassed.

"Cade?" Isaiah finally asks in the dark. I can't see him, but I know his eyes are soft and broken. Why do I break him? Why do I hurt him?

"I need to know if it's always going to be this way," he asks softly, and I immediately know what he means.

"No," I shake my head. I put my hand on his knee and rub it with my thumb. "It won't. I'm sorry. One day, we'll be out of here. And we can be just us. Just you and me."

I smile, staring at the highway ahead of me. It's 11:30 at night and practically empty. The lights stretch on for miles. And after that, the night is dark and open. The air is cool and fresh and smells like autumn.

"Let's do it," I say excitedly. "Let's just keep driving. We'll drive somewhere where nobody knows us and start over."

The more I think about it, the more excited I get. We'll just leave. We'll put Isaiah's mom behind us. We'll put my parents behind us. We'll leave Kayla and be gone before the sun comes up. Nobody will ever find us.

"We can't," Isaiah shakes his head, but I hear a smile in his voice. My car is practically alight with his laugh.

"It'd kill my mom," he says through his smile. "My brother and sister already did that to her."

I want to tell him that I can understand why they did. But I don't. Because that would be mean, and I've been mean enough tonight.

"And besides," he laughs a giant laugh. "Thomas would be upset if he never saw me again."

I shrug. He's right. I didn't even think about Thomas. Sweet, little Thomas. Now, I have to stick around as long as possible to protect him from both of my parents. Both of them. They're going to destroy our family again.

They're going to destroy him again.

"They're going to break Thomas's heart," I say, feeling my good feeling deflate. We can't run away. I'll never be able to leave.

"My father's not going to stay," I shake my head. "He's a runner. He ran in high school. He ran in college. And he ran from my family."

Isaiah squeezes his hand around mine. He gives me all the strength he has left.

"Maybe it'll be different this time," Isaiah says weakly. "Or maybe it's not what we thought."

This reminds me of his fight with Kayla. What were they fighting about? I ask Isaiah, and I hear a shrug in his voice.

"She thought we should interrupt your speech to tell you what we saw," he explains. "But I convinced her to wait."

I thank him. I wouldn't have wanted to be interrupted with that. I was already uncomfortable enough.

"She told me that I don't know you like she does," he sounds injured. "And she's got a point."

Suddenly his smile is gone, and the car seems darker. She doesn't, though, and I tell him as much.

"She's known me longer," I rub my thumb on his knee again. "That doesn't mean she knows me better."

And besides, I tell him mentally. I pick you every time.

We ride silently for a while longer before I take him back to his car. I don't want him to get out.

"It's not too late to run away," I remind him half-heartedly.

His golden smile fills the car again. I'm swallowed in its warmth and light. I pull it tight around me, like a towel fresh out of the dryer. I want to paint hundreds and thousands of pictures of his smile, just to have it to look at any time I need it.

"One day," he sighs. "One day, we can run away together. Like Bonnie and Clyde."

"Butch Cassidy and the Sundance Kid," I smile.

"Raymond Fernandez and Martha Beck," Isaiah laughs.

"Why can we only come up with outlaws?" I giggle. Yes. Giggle.

Isaiah leans over and kisses me gently before leaving my car.

"Talk to your mom," he says. "Nicely. Respectfully."

He raises his eyebrows in warning before he shuts the door. I watch his car pull away before I decide to drive home. I suddenly feel more alone than I ever have. Tonight, it's just me and Thomas against the world. Not even my mother is on my side anymore.

When I get home, Mom is waiting on the couch. She's taken off her makeup and is in sweatpants and a t-shirt. Her eyes are red like she's been crying, and she looks forty years older than she did three hours ago.

"Glad you're home," she says gently. "Take a seat. We need to talk."

"Got that right," I sit uncomfortably, ready to take off these dress clothes and go to bed.

"I think you owe me an apology," she says, level-headedly. I knew this was what she was expecting. But it's not coming.

"I'm sorry," I say against my will. And I mean it.

"But you owe me an apology, too," I say before she can say anything else. "Or at least an explanation."

She considers me for a moment, then sighs.

"I didn't mean for it to happen this way," she shakes her head. "I didn't know he was going to be there."

"And you were so overcome by shock that you freaking made out with him at my art show?" I'm fuming. The fuse is burning again. The time bomb is ticking.

"It's not like I planned it," Mom says level-headedly. I want her to yell at me. I've spent all night wanting to fight with somebody. And nobody's biting.

"He abandoned you, Mom," I say her name the same way she says mine when I've done something stupid. "He left us. He cheated on you."

"I'm not proud of it, Cade," she says, still even. "I've loved him since we were kids."

She sighs and brushes a stray hair from her face.

"You don't get it now, but you will," she shakes her head. "It's a stupid thing. It won't happen again."

Chapter Twenty-One

Mom lied.

That wasn't the last time.

Neither was the next time.

And now, it's Christmas, and my father is officially back in my life.

Well, that's not totally fair. Now it's Christmastime, and my father is back in my mother and Thomas's life.

Whenever I hear his tires pull into the driveway, I lock myself away in the spare bedroom of our new house. Mom has let me convert it into an art studio, and it's currently covered in unfinished pieces of art. There are shelves with unfinished graphite and charcoal pieces along the walls. Colored pencils roll around on the drafting table every time I shut the door. Paints hang in a caddy over the door, and canvases are shoved haphazardly into every square inch of usable space.

Today, however, when Cole Swanson pulls into the driveway, I'm not up to deal with him. I'm not even going to stay in the house while he comes over to play dad. I throw my field-sketching things in a bag and try to head out the back door before he comes in.

"Where you going, Cade?" He calls cheerfully from the front door.

Damn it. I wasn't quick enough.

"To hang out with Isaiah," I call passively. I promised my mother I won't fight with him. It's almost Christmas.

"Daddy!" Thomas yells, coming running downstairs at the sound of our father's voice. He launches himself into Cole Swanson's arms the way he used to greet me.

I feel a stab of pain—jealousy?—as Thomas wraps his arms around our father's neck. It was so easy for Thomas to accept Cole's triumphant, fanfare-filled return in our lives. It breaks my heart. Because he's going to break Thomas's heart, and there's nothing I can do about it.

"You sure do spend a lot of time with Isaiah," my father muses, as if he's welcome to make observations about my life.

"You sure do spend a lot of time here," I mutter as I reach for the door.

"I didn't hear you," he yells back.

"That was the point," I sigh and shut the door behind me.

When I get to our driveway, a bright yellow Porsche is parked so close to my Mustang I'm not sure I'm going to be able to back out.

"For the love of everything green," I sigh. "Are you kidding me?"

I throw my stuff in my car and begin to examine the situation. I can get out of this.

"I thought maybe you could stick around with the family tonight," Cole says from the porch, watching me.

"Funny," I spit back. "I said the same thing to you in eighth grade."

He winces but doesn't say anything.

"I like your car," he smiles, trying to find some kind of common ground. "Seems like you're just like your old man. I love fast cars, too."

"Gee, Pop," I say in my best Beaver Cleaver voice. "Just what I've always wanted to hear. Can you let me out?"

He just stands there for a minute. Christmas music drifts through the air from a neighbor's house. My new neighborhood is oddly quiet. There aren't any dogs barking or street lights buzzing. Except for us, everybody drives brand new cars. All the houses here look the same, and all the people in them look the same. I'm almost homesick for that hole-ridden rent house.

"I told you to stay in tonight," he says a little more firmly.

"No," I shake my head, opening the driver-side door of Roxy, my Mustang. "You said you thought I could. But I'm not."

I get in my car and start it up.

And for the next four excruciatingly long minutes, I reverse my car for millimeters at a time, then pull forward for millimeters, until I successfully navigate my way around his car. All the while, Cole Swanson watches me from the front porch, a grimace on his face. If it wouldn't also damage Roxy, I'd cut too close and destroy his paint job.

"I'm nothing like you," I tell my rearview mirror as I pull away, his reflection growing smaller and smaller until he's gone.

When I pull up to Rosenthal Manor, Isaiah is already waiting on the front steps for me. He's also got a bag of art supplies, even though he doesn't enjoy sketching the way I do. He is willing to do anything to spend time with me.

"Well, aren't you a tall drink of water," I roll down the window to call out as I pull up. I've donned my best Clint Eastwood accent; I've failed miserably.

"You always go for the height," he laughs as he folds himself into the front seat of my car. I try not to laugh every time he squeezes into Roxy. He has to lean the seat back to avoid hitting his head. His knees practically meet his chin.

"It's what I like the most," I chuckle, my mood instantly lightened by his presence.

"Not my bright eyes or my cock-eyed smile?" He laughs in that deep voice that rattles my windows.

"How would I know?" I shrug. "I've never seen them. I don't have binoculars."

He shoves my shoulder playfully as we pull away and head downtown.

Today we're urban sketching; we're going around the city to sketch buildings, and parks, and things. I think we'll find a café to share a scone and a museum to visit. We'll walk around hand-in-hand without the fear of running into anybody who knows us. We'll walk around hand-in-hand without the fear of seeing Betty Rosenthal or Cole Swanson. Because nobody ever comes downtown. All the social parts of the city have moved uptown.

The open road stretches out before us, and I think of running away once more. We've turned it into a game. Now when we go on car rides, Isaiah and I plan our new lives.

"I'll start," I say, turning the music down. "We'll go to Schenectady."

"Why there?" Isaiah guffaws.

"Because you never say it right. So even if somebody tracked us down, you wouldn't be able to tell them where we are," I tease. "And I'll get my cosmetology license and dye my hair green. I'll legally change my name to Vyper Sting. Vyper. With a y."

"Too obvious," Isaiah laughs.

"And I'll work to put you through school," I glance over at his smiling face. "You'll major in engineering and minor in film studies."

"Oh yeah?" He laughs. "And what's my name going to be?"

"Spyder Sting," I wink. "Also with a y."

"So, people will think we're brothers," he interjects. "With matching names like that? They're going to think we're some kind of weirdo spinster brothers with hippie parents."

"Can men be spinsters?" I ask.

"I think we can be anything we want to be," Isaiah smirks.

"Then why can't we be eccentrics who changed our names to match?" I give him a playful side-eye.

"Fair enough," Isaiah concedes. "But your plan's not going to work."

"And just why not?" I demand.

"Because we're already running away to Disney World," he said. "And I'm going to wear the Chewbacca suit. And you're going to be one of those caricature artists. And I'll come home every day, my hand cramping from a long day of signing autograph books, to a house full of my own private caricature sketches of me in various states of Chewbacca undress."

I feel myself blush at this idea.

"I can't draw you like that!" I argue. This is part of the game. We always argue as to why the other plan won't work.

"And just why not?" He mimics me.

"Because if your hand is cramping from all those Chewy autographs, imagine how mine will feel after I've spent all day drawing giant noses and long necks and massive lips."

"We'll just have to find somewhere else, then," he chuckles a deep chuckle.

When we arrive downtown, the sky hangs high overhead. My first order of business is to collect my last check from Martin Kimball. The last of my watercolor pieces sold, and Mr. Kimball has offered me a permanent space in his gallery to display and sell new pieces.

"Oh, Mr. Swanson," Martin smiles as he hands me the final cut of my sold pieces. "We're doing an exhibition in January I hope you'll be a part of."

"Tell me more," I smile, intrigued.

"It's going to be called *PRIDE in the Urban Jungle*," he smiles. "I thought maybe you could come up with something to contribute."

"Keep going," I quirk an eyebrow.

"We've asked a collective of artists to submit pieces. All of the art will be auctioned off, and the proceeds will be donated to New Hope, an organization that helps homeless and at-risk LGBT+ youth. You may even know some of the people who would benefit."

I nod slowly, trying to take everything in.

"And you want me in the show?" I'm incredulous. I'm honored.

"Your art is really sought after right now," he concedes. "It'd be great to have in the show."

Isaiah nudges me with his elbow, and I remember he's with me for the first time.

"He'll do it," Isaiah smiles.

I nod. I will do it. I've already got a piece forming in my mind that would be perfect for it. And I'll have all of Christmas break to finish it.

"You two have a nice time," Martin smiles. "It's a good night for a date."

"It's not—" I almost argue, but I stop. "We're just sketching today."

It's nice to tell someone we're on a date. It's nice to acknowledge it without a scowl or a sneer from Kayla or hide it from Betty Rosenthal.

I hate that I thought of her because I immediately feel guilty. We still haven't told her we're dating, despite my mom asking. It makes me uncomfortable, but I'm following Isaiah's lead. He knows her better than me.

"What will you do when your mom keeps trying to set you up with society girls?" I ask, testing the waters to see if he's ready to tell her.

"I'll keep saying no," he smiles. "And one day, she'll just realize that you and I are together."

"So, we've decided on not telling her?" I ask. "I mean, I'm fine with it. I was going to do it because my mother asked me to. But she's been making *such* great choices lately."

We both sigh as we walk. Neither of us reaches for our sketchbooks.

"My mom's smart," he says after a long silence. "She'll figure it out."

I suspect she already has; she certainly knew he was interested in me the night we first kissed.

"I don't feel like sketching," I sigh, looking at the world around me. Downtown suddenly looks gray and dreary and dirty, hardly worth sketching.

"I never feel like sketching," he laughs, shifting his backpack to the other shoulder.

So instead, we walk the streets, enjoying the cool breeze, shivering in the shadows. We bask in the daylight and let the cares of the world wash away as we enjoy the company of each other.

Kayla's not talking to me. I'm not talking to my mother. Thomas ignores me whenever Cole's around. I spend my entire waking life in my studio, lately, trying to get things together for the state art show. I want to win so badly it hurts. A full scholarship to art school hangs within my grasp. I have to win it. I have to get as far away from here as possible. Especially now that Mom can take care of Thomas without me.

"You're doing a lot of thinking today," Isaiah muses as we walk. "Everything okay?"

I nod and wipe my face. When did I start crying? God. I'm being ridiculous.

"I'm fine," I smile. "I'm just stressed about the art show."

"The Urban Jungle thing? You don't have to do it." He squeezes my hand gently. I feel his strength flow into me. There's something about his quiet strength that I envy and desire. I thirst for it.

"No," I laugh. "I've already figured out what I'm doing for that. It's the school art show."

Isaiah laughs.

He shakes his head. "I will never, ever understand what's going on inside that giant, cute head of yours."

We turn into the museum. It smells old and dusty and rich with history. The people inside are milling about, reading different plaques. People speak in hushed tones and discuss ancient civilizations under their breath. I love museum people. They're quiet and ignore other people. They're all there to look into the past; they all let the present pass them by.

"Look," Isaiah nods to a group of friends around our age. They're all dressed in bizarre clothes and have multi-colored hair. A few have eyebrow piercings, and one has a septum ring. They're beautiful. I want to be them.

All of them are in their own sketchbooks, all shabby and well-loved. As they sketch, they hardly look at their books. They're drawing practically blindly, spending time staring at the statues and making purposeful marks on their sketchpads.

When they dip their sketchbooks down, I see their different takes on the same sculptures. Some of their drawings are very precise perfectly proportioned. They've drawn S-shaped guidelines to pose their figures. They're sketching out head shapes to make sure their statues are five heads tall. They're being as meticulous as you can be while sketching.

Others have defaulted to a cartoon style of drawing. Their statues stand in awkward shapes and are angular and disproportionate. But they're intentional and amazingly crafted. They look like something from an old cartoon, like the early days of Walt Disney.

One of the artists has decided upon a cubist impression of the statue. She's turned it on its side, squished it flat, and turned all of its dimensions two-dimensional. It's lovely. It's nothing I could ever do. It's everything I wish I could do.

"I think he's waving at you," Isaiah says, breaking me out of my hypnotic state. "Do you know him?"

I look up to see one of the artists, the tall one with green hair, signaling me over. I shake my head. I had no idea who he was. Slowly, Isaiah and I approach the group.

"Cade, right?" The green-haired realist asks, smiling. "I'm Thad."

Thad? I raise my eyebrows at Isaiah. How does he know who I am?

"We were at your show," he nods to indicate his friends around him. "It was amazing. Really."

"Really inspiring," Cubist Girl offers from under her mane of platinum hair. "I wish I could draw like you."

"Why?" I laugh and point to her sketchbook. "When you can draw like that?"

"It's the fate of artists," Septum Piercing says dramatically. "To always want what we can't have."

"I'm pretty sure that's just human nature," Isaiah laughs uncomfortably."Ah, the tall, cute one speaks," Cubist giggles, flushing.

"Why do you always get to be the cute one?" I wink, bumping Isaiah with my shoulder.

"This is Isaiah," I say by way of introduction. "My boyfriend"

I blush. It still feels weird to say. Isaiah seems like so much more than my boyfriend. Boyfriend seems so fleeting, like one day Isaiah won't be there anymore. Isaiah's my best friend and my confidante. And he's got my back every time. Should I have introduced him as my knight in shining armor?

"Called it," Thad laughs, looking around at his friends.

"Called what?" I ask, looking awkwardly to Isaiah. I don't know that I like where this is going.

"I have a sixth sense for this stuff," Thad puffs his chest out proudly. "I usually know when somebody's gay."

Why is my sexuality any of his concern?

"It was a lucky guess," Septum Piercing laughs. "Besides, you said *you* were his type."

He emphasizes this as if Thad had been scoping me out. Thad's definitely not my type. I don't have a type. My type is Isaiah.

"Well, everybody's entitled to be wrong once in a while," I shrug. Is this as uncomfortable for them as it is for me?

"I'm Cathy," Cubist Girl offers her hand. "You've met Thad."

I learn that Josiah is Septum Ring. Pink Hair is Ramón. I forget the names of the rest of the posse as quickly as I hear them. I'm overwhelmed. This is too many people. I had hoped to attend the museum unnoticed. I wanted to be unnoticeable. I thought the museum was a place where Isaiah and I could escape and be us. I thought here, surely, we could be that unbridled, unrestrained kind of us we want to be.

"Do y'all want to hang out or something?" Thad asks, closing his sketchbook and eyeing us.

"Thad, they're on a date," Cathy rolls her eyes. "Leave them alone. You can pick his brain about art later."

We all share a laugh. Isaiah and I are more grateful for Cathy than she'll ever realize. Few things sound less fun than hanging out with a group of total strangers.

"Well, listen" Thad smiles at us uncomfortably. "We take a life-drawing class at the Arts Council every other Monday. If you're interested, you should join us. We'd love to talk art with you."

"I'll think about it," I smile and nod. Now that does sound like fun.

"You can even bring Tall, Dark, and Handsome, if you'd like," Josiah winks at us.

He's right there, I almost say, annoyed. He can hear you.

Instead, I laugh, take Isaiah's hand, and drag him away behind me.

I've never moved so quickly to get away from a group of people before. Not even Betty Rosenthal. Not even Cole Swanson.

"I don't want to go to a life sketching class," Isaiah admits, eyes growing as we meander through the museum.

"I know, baby," I laugh comfortingly.

Isaiah doesn't love art the way I love art. He appreciates art. He loves my art. He enjoys looking at it and learning about it. But for him, art is a hobby, something he does to destress. He doesn't require it. It doesn't pour out of him as it does me. And that's okay.

We walk silently through the museum until my phone starts to ring. It's my mother. I don't want to talk to her. We haven't spoken in nearly a month. At least, nothing more than the pleasantries of good morning, how are you?

"Hello?" I ask.

"You need to come home," she says evenly, her voice wrought with anger. "Your dad would like to spend time with you."

"No, thank you," I say passively. "Not interested."

"Who is it?" Isaiah mouths to me. I roll my eyes in response. He nods knowingly.

"I didn't give you an option," my mother sounds angrier than I've ever heard her.

"That's okay," I try to sound as positive as possible. "I'm still not interested. I'll be home this evening. Sooner if you kick him out."

"Cade Allen Swanson, you are being unreasonable." I can count on one hand how many times my mother has used my full name since I was 8. Twice have been this year. Both times have been in relation to my father.

"No," I shake my head, trying my hardest to remain calm. "You're being unreasonable. I don't have to spend time with somebody who walked out on me. I refuse to spend time with somebody who walked out on me. You shouldn't want that, either. I know I can't change your mind, though, so you should respect that you can't change mine."

I want to hang up on her, but that will make things worse. I want to scream at her, but that definitely won't fix things. So instead, I'm stuck in this awkward limbo of this phone conversation where neither of us is yelling, and neither of us will hang up.

I picture my mother on the other end of the phone with the face of a viper, ready to strike if she sees me. I see Cole behind her, snake-charming pipe in hand. If I were to draw this moment, this is how they'd be.

"Cade, it's Christmas," she sighs into the phone, and I feel my heart shatter. It's not quite Christmas, but I don't correct her.

"I can't," I say after a long pause. "I can't do this. You may have forgiven him, but I haven't. And I won't. I would consider it if he asked for it."

"He wants things to be different," she sighs. I can hear the wrinkles in her forehead. I can hear the gray in her hair.

"He doesn't," I grab Isaiah's hand for strength. This is the hardest conversation I've ever had. "If he wanted it to be different, he'd have apologized to Thomas and me. If he wanted change, he'd ask for forgiveness.

He hasn't, and he won't because he doesn't."

"Cade," she's pleading now. "Give us a chance. Give our family a chance. This is what we've wanted for so long."

No, I almost say. This is what you wanted. I never wanted him back.

"I've got to go," I sigh. "I'm at the museum, and people are staring at me."

I hang up, trying to swallow down the sick feeling in my stomach. I hate fighting with my mother. I hate hating her. I don't mind hating Cole.

"I just can't trust him," I tell Isaiah.

There's a chasm between us that feels like an ocean. He still doesn't know his mom and my dad had an affair. I can't tell him. But the secret separates us; it leaves us worlds apart. How can I keep this secret from him? How can I tell him? Both options will kill us. I just have to decide if I want it to happen slowly or quickly. Secrets are slow-acting poison but telling this secret would be a gunshot to the heart. Which is better?

For the millionth time, I feel bad. Isaiah is caught in my explosion. He's always taking the shrapnel of my life. Any time there's an explosion, he's in the line of fire.

"Stop it," he smiles and pulls me close to him, closer than we've ever been in public. My face falls instinctively into his chest, and I breathe in the scent of his cologne. I melt into him and let him hold me as close as possible.

"Don't worry about me. I knew what I was getting into," he whispers, holding me so tightly I think we may become one person. "I'm all in. Through all the worst moments of the Cade Swanson saga."

"But why?" I ask, taken aback. How does he always know what I'm thinking?

"Because you are art," he whispers. "And there has to be dark to emphasize the light. And your light is too beautiful to let the dark get in the way."

I love when he talks art to me.

"We'll move to Austin," he whispers, his chin on top of my head. "We'll buy a bungalow in the arts district. You'll work full time as an artist, and I'll be a high school history teacher. The house will always be a wreck, covered in paint and graphite. We'll have a yellow lab who fetches Frisbees, and he'll be our entire world. We'll have friends over for dinner parties, and you'll burn the lasagna, but your cheesecake will make up for it. And Thomas will have a room at our house to run away whenever he needs it."

I smile so broadly it tickles Isaiah. I breathe in his scent and let him hold me tight as we stand in the rotation of the earth. And I don't care who sees or what they think. If they're not jealous, they're wrong.

Chapter Twenty-Two

I don't know how I'm going to make it through this week without Isaiah. His family left for Colorado the Monday before Christmas, and I'm stuck at home with Thomas, my mother, and Cole Swanson.

I am more grateful than I'm willing to admit that my mother makes Cole go home every night. She hasn't let him sleep over since they've started trying to work things out. I don't believe for a moment that my father actually wants to work things out. I don't believe for a moment he's able to remain faithful to my mother. But as my mother has told me countless times, that's not an opinion for a child to have.

I'm not a child; I want to argue. *Sometimes it's like I'm the only adult in this house.*

But I know better. I don't want to incur the wrath of my mother.

So, to deal with the inconvenience, I've adjusted my sleeping schedule. I go to bed at 3:00 every afternoon and sleep through the majority of my father's after-work visits. I wake up at midnight and go into my art studio. The lights are so bright that it's easy to trick myself into thinking I'm working in the middle of the day.

I've always worked better in the middle of the night, anyway.

Of course, my going to sleep doesn't actually stop Cole from waking me up and expecting me to spend time with him. I don't. He's stopped arguing with me.

"He'll come around when he's ready," my mother always says under her breath when she thinks I can't hear. "There's no denying he's your son, what with his devotion to that grudge."

And they both laugh like kids. Like Isaiah laughs when I say something stupid. Like Cameron used to laugh whenever Kayla made an off-hand joke.

They're so stupid. Behaving like children. They have children. They should think about them.

My mother slips into my room on Christmas Eve to wake me from my Cole-avoiding slumber.

"When are you going to be done hating your father?" She asks gently as I wake up.

"I don't hate him," I mutter. "That takes too much energy. I just don't want him in my life."

"He wants to be in your life," she says softly. She's given up fighting with me. Part of me wants to believe she knows I'm justified in my hatred.

I sit up, exhausted. I know Mom wants me to come downstairs and be with the family. It is Christmas Eve. The house smells of fresh-baked cookies and homemade cider. And this is the first Christmas Eve since my parents' divorce that she is off to enjoy the day with us. I'm depriving her of the only thing she's wanted for years. And for the first time since my art show, I feel guilty about punishing her.

"Look," I say, my exhaustion creeping into my voice. "I don't want him in my life. He hasn't earned my respect or my trust."

She opens her mouth to say something, but I cut her off.

"But I will come downstairs. Not for his sake, but for yours and Thomas's." I shrug. "I won't let him alienate me from you two anymore."

Her smile fills my whole room. It overpowers my blackout curtains. It overpowers winter. It's the first drop of rain after a drought. It's the first bite of a warm donut. I laugh at the comparison. I've missed my mother's smile.

I resist the urge to hug her. I'm still mad at her. I'm still fighting with her.

"Can I ask a question since we're talking more than we have in a month?" She asks shakily.

"Sure," I concede. That doesn't mean I have to answer it.

"Why haven't you spent any of this break with Kayla?" She sounds like she's walking on eggshells. "You usually spend all of Christmas break with her."

I shrug. I don't really want to go into this. I really don't want to think about Kayla, maybe every again.

"She can't handle Isaiah and me together," I hang my head. "She basically told me I have to pick."

"And you picked Isaiah," Mom finishes, her voice sounding distant.

"I didn't, though," I shake my head. "I want them both. I shouldn't have to pick. She decided for me, though. By making me pick."

"And I think Cameron broke up with her over it," I sigh. I know Cameron broke up with her over it.

"Maybe you should call her," Mom says gently. "It's Christmas, and she's probably sad."

I promise her I will. But first, I need to shower and caffeinate. If I have to spend time with Cole, I'll need to be at my very best.

"Can I ask *you* a question, since we're talking for the first time in a month?" I echo her sentiment. She nods.

I take a deep breath and steady myself. I don't want this to seem accusatory, but I don't know how to ask this without it sounding any other way.

"How was it so easy for you to forgive Co—" I catch myself. "My father," I amend.

"He hurt you; he left you. He left us," I'm not trying to make this a fight. I just want to understand. What am I missing?

"Your father has a lot of apologizing to do," she admits after a deep sigh. "He has a lot of things to fix. I understand why you're frustrated."

A second of silence passes between us as she considers whether she can hug me, ruffle my hair. She decides against it.

"But forgiveness is something that is given, not something that is earned," she finally says. "You don't have to be angry on my behalf. I've been angry for a long time, Cade. I'm ready to feel something else for a while."

I look at my mom for the first time in a long time. I study her for the first time since my show at Kimball. She's changed, but I can't describe how. She's stronger, somehow, different and new.

Without saying anything else, Mom leaves me alone in my studio, still sorting through everything she's said.

"Bub, we're going to see Christmas lights!" Thomas shouts, bounding towards me when I come down the stairs, showered and irritated.

"Oh?" I ask, expecting him to jump into my arms. But he doesn't. He just stops and stands awkwardly close to me. I feel my heart crumble a little more. "That sounds like fun."

I'll always put on my best face for Thomas.

"Can I grab a cup of coffee before we get in the car?" I ask. This will be a long night, trapped in a minivan with my perfectly delirious family.

When we go to the cars, my mother bypasses her car and walks to Cole's Porsche.

No.

God no.

I cannot spend all night in his Porsche with him. The Porsche is beautiful. And I have wanted to sit in it since I first saw it. I have been dying to listen to the rumble of the engine from the inside. I've dreamed of running my hands over the beautiful leather seats and the pristine dashboard. I've imagined wrapping my hands around the heated, carbon fiber steering wheel. I've fantasized about taking her on the freeway, opening her up for all she's worth, and watching the world blur by me.

I have never imagined that my three-plus-one family would pack itself into that tiny 911 and snail our way through gated neighborhoods to see Christmas lights. I'd rather hang out with the art kids from the museum while simultaneously being lectured by Kayla about the morality of my relationship.

"Cade, you're tall," Mom calls as she opens the door. "You sit in the front. Thomas and I will hold down the back."

Shit.

I have to sit up front. With Cole.

I think about faking a stomach bug. Or an earache. Nobody can tell if you actually have an earache, right? Or maybe the flu. Can I fake the flu?

No, I'm not a good enough actor. And I'm an even worse liar.

I'm stuck.

Shit.

I'm not even tall. I'm hardly taller than my mother. I'm not like Isaiah, who barely fits in my car.

"You can sit up front," I try with futility. "You two should sit together."

But Mom knows me too well. And I know her too well. She's arranged it just like this. This is her attempt to make me get along with Cole. She's not as sly as she thinks.

"Sit up front," she smiles. "Maybe your dad will let you drive his car if you're lucky."

I almost ask who my dad is, but it's Christmas. This can be his gift. I'll keep my snarky comments to myself. Just this once.

I don't argue; I don't roll my eyes, but I want to. Instead, I reluctantly climb into the second-most beautiful car under God's bright sun.

"Isaiah's Audi is nicer," I tell myself under my breath, so I'm not hypnotized. This becomes my mantra. Just remember that Isaiah's R8 is the car dreams are made of. Just remember that I have driven something bigger and better.

This mantra lasts precisely 2.5 seconds. My father turns the car on, and it purrs to life. I feel myself melt. I become a puddle in the passenger seat. I feel my eyes widen in wonder and forget who I am for just a minute. Just long enough to glance at my father and see him smiling. Then I deflate.

I will not let him see me smile. He hasn't earned the right to see me smile. He hasn't earned the right to get to know me.

The car is silent except for the hum of the engine as we back out of the driveway. Occasionally, Thomas whispers something, or the soft click of the turn indicator breaks the silence. When we're on the freeway, my father turns on the radio, and a jazz arrangement of Jingle Bells kills the silence.

"We used to do this when you were little," my father's deep voice pulls me out of my dark musings. I try to think back to a single time we did this, but I only remember creeping around in Mom's rundown minivan with Thomas hungry and asleep in the backseat.

"Do you remember?" He asks when I don't say anything.

I shake my head.

"You used to beg your mother to let you sit in the front seat," he says, and I can hear a smile in his voice. When I look at him, I notice just how much I look like my father for the first time. I don't want to look like my father.

"We would drive slowly through all of the nicest neighborhoods, and you'd rate your favorite houses," he laughs. "You had your own rating system. What was it?"

I roll my eyes against my will. I'm grateful it's dark in the car so nobody can see it. I don't know what he's talking about.

"Wasn't it blue lights?" My mother offers from the backseat, and suddenly I'm a kid again.

It *was* blue lights. I catch myself smiling against my will. I don't want to be nostalgic. Tonight, I want to be irritable. But with the memory of the blue lights, I can't help it.

"What's that mean, Bub?" Thomas asks excitedly, and I can't help but answer.

"I used to think that the more blue lights a house had, the better it was," I chuckle, feeling myself sucked into my parents' nostalgia. "I'd give it a percent rating. A house might be 10% blue or 45% blue. And if it was more blue, I liked it more."

As my parents and I laugh, years wash away from us. It's like layers of grime are being peeled back and revealing these young, not yet calloused versions of ourselves. I don't like it. I don't want this to happen.

"If you saw a house that was more than 60% blue, you'd make me remember where it was. So, you could have a runoff of the bluest houses," Cole says this with such wonder; I allow myself a moment to remember what things were like when he was my Dad.

I allow myself a moment of silent reflection and recollection. I roll back the cover and blow the dust off the memories. The lights zip past us on the freeway, and I slip into childhood. The rumble of the engine, the heater blowing, and the soft music transport me to six years old.

I'm sitting in my family's old Volkswagen, staring out of the window, wide-eyed in wonder. Beside me are a pad of paper and a box of crayons. I've spent all evening sketching my favorite houses. Every house is a rectangle with a triangle roof. My top favorite houses are lined out beside me with their blue ratings. A white house with a brown roof is 50% blue. A gray house has a 62% blue rating. And the reigning champion of the night is a red brick house with a 75% blue rating.

"We have to go see this one again," I tell Dad and pass him my drawing of the brick house, covered in blue lights.

Dad pulls over to examine my drawing. He considers it carefully and then smiles at Mom. The car smells sweet like childhood should. My sweater swallows me whole in the front seat, and John Denver and the Muppets are singing "Twelve Days of Christmas." It's two days before Christmas, and the air crackles with electricity and magic. It's Christmastime. Anything can happen.

Dad turns the car around and drives us past the winning house for the third time that night. He stops and lets me press my face against the window to admire all the blue lights lining the sidewalk. The trees are strung with blue lights. There are blue, icicle-shaped lights hanging from the eaves.

The shrubs in front of the house sparkle with bright red, orange, pink, and white lights. But I don't care about them. The windows are all decorated with flickering candles. I don't care about them, either. It's the blue lights I'm enamored by.

"How did they know I love blue?" I ask with the enthusiasm of a child. I'm so much like Thomas at this age.

"I don't know, Bucko," Dad laughs.

Bucko. How did I forget he used to call me Bucko?

"I guess they just wanted to give you a present," he puts the car in park and lets me stare for as long as I want. For as long as it takes until I fall asleep with my face pressed against the glass.

"Bub, look at that!" Thomas's excitement rips me from my memories. I prepare to paste on a smile for him but find that I'm already smiling, bizarrely enough.

I look out the window to see a massive house decorated in bright lights. The yard is covered in lit reindeer, all in various stages of taking flight, a chubby red Santa in the sleigh behind them.

The trees are hung with giant, lit balls. The sidewalk is lined with red and white candy canes. The house seems to sparkle in the night. It's alight with the same magic Christmas had when I was little. Thomas is seeing the same magic I saw all those years ago.

"It's pretty, isn't it?" Mom asks, a broad smile in her voice.

"Very pretty. Right, Bub?" Thomas giggles.

"I don't know," I joke. "There's not enough blue for me.

It's only 10% blue.

I realize I don't recognize the neighborhood we're in. I don't even know how long we've been in the car. I try to look for anything that might hint at our location, but I don't recognize anything. Have we driven all the way into the city?

My father drives the car slowly through the neighborhood. As we creep along, the houses get older and bigger. We're in a wealthy part of the city I've never seen before. These are decorated in the most subtle, classy ways. They're all white lights and simple designs. Something about the simplicity draws me in. There's not a single blue light in sight, but I don't care. They're beautiful.

I can't stop the smile on my face. I'd forgotten what it was like to love Christmas. I'd forgotten what it was like to ride in a car and enjoy the Christmas lights. I'd forgotten what it was like to relax.

The car feels cavernous as we settle into a comfortable silence. For a moment, I allow myself to imagine we're actually a family again, and I finally get what Mom wants. This. This is what she wants. All of us together again, happy and content. This is why she was so willing to forgive my father for destroying our family. This happiness is powerful. This contentment is beautiful and wonderful. I'd do anything to keep this feeling.

I get it.

We drive around more, taking in all of the lights. Some houses are simply and beautifully decorated. Some houses are extravagantly decorated, depicting full scenes from Frosty the Snowman or Rudolph the Red-nosed Reindeer. Some of the houses we pass were decorated by professionals; some entire neighborhoods are all decorated identically. Some houses were decorated lovingly by the homeowners. They're all beautiful. They're all expressions of the families inside.

"Look at that," somebody says breathlessly. I'm surprised to realize that somebody was me.

We stop in front of a small house in a historic neighborhood. The house is decorated sparingly, a simple string of white lights running along the roof. In the front yard stands the most beautiful hand-carved nativity. Each piece was lovingly made, standing tall and proud and life-sized in the leaf-strewn lawn. The statue of Joseph stands every bit of six feet tall. Mary rests beside him, nearly the same size as my mom, staring down at the baby in the cradle.

How long did somebody spend on this beautiful work of art? How much love is in this? How much of the artist exists in these pieces? I'm in awe. I can't take my eyes away.

"They're beautiful," I say, my voice almost quivering.

Nobody says anything for a long time. The car idles for what seems forever. I realize I'm holding my breath like they're going to move. I wipe a tear from my face. When did that get there? Will my art ever move anyone to tears like that?

I feel Mom's hand on my shoulder. I reach up to grab her hand with mine and squeeze it. I don't know why I'm crying now. Is it the carvings? Is it the atmosphere? Have I finally cracked? I'm so tired of crying all the time. The car starts to creep away, and I pull myself together.

"I wish I'd brought my sketchbook," I smile, feeling six years old again. "And a box of crayons."

I hear Mom giggle behind me. Dad's hand reaches for my shoulder, hovers a moment, and returns to the gearshift. I'm glad he didn't touch me. I'm not sure I'm ready for that. Not yet.

"I've got one more place to show you before I take you home," he says quietly. He turns the radio up and drives us across the city to a small neighborhood nestled between two larger business districts. It's disorienting to see skyscrapers surrounding this tiny neighborhood. As we drive, I see perfectly-manicured lawns. The houses are small, nice, and sitting on identical plots.

I catch myself smiling as John Denver and The Muppets sing "Twelve Days of Christmas." I crack up as it progresses. I've always loved The Muppets; they've always made me laugh. They've always brought a smile to my face.

"Do you remember that year you made everybody Christmas cards?" Dad asks. He catches me off guard, and I forget that I'm busy hating him. It's the magic of those damned Muppets.

"I made everybody a different Muppet," I smile.

I still have the one I made for Thomas. He wasn't born yet. Mom was seven months pregnant, and I could not wait to have a little brother. I'd spent days making everybody Muppet Christmas cards. My dad had gotten Kermit, and my mom got Miss Piggy. I'd worked hardest on Thomas's Bunsen Honeydew card. I always imagined Thomas would be smart. He was going to be brilliant, so he deserved the smartest Muppet.

I'd spent days perfecting everybody's cards. But I held on to Thomas's and swore I'd give it to him when he got older. I didn't want him to ruin it whenever he came. For some reason or another, though, I never gave it to him, and it's been sitting in my art supplies since. The memory makes me smile more broadly.

"Where are you taking us?" Thomas asks. He's been chattering away with mom in the backseat, but I haven't been paying attention. I've been too introspective to listen to him. I feel selfish to admit this; I'm usually tuned into his needs.

"Well," Dad says carefully. "While your mom and I are figuring things out, I thought it'd be nice if you came and spent some time at my house. You guys both have rooms here. I've been working on getting them set up for you. It's just here at the end of the street."

We pull up to the end of the cul-de-sac. The lot is bigger than the others. It's an old house with decorative front windows and a giant tree in the front yard.

"Look, Bub," Thomas instructs, but I've already noticed, and I'm smiling in spite of myself.

It's 100% blue.

Chapter Twenty-Three

When we get home, I disappear upstairs to call Kayla. I'll use this good mood to propel our conversation. I'll use it as a guard from her bad attitude. Maybe it'll protect me. Maybe.

"Merry Christmas," Kayla sighs when she answers to phone.

I need more than this one good day to survive her melancholy.

"Merry Christmas!" I answer as joyfully as I can in response. I'm not going to let her sour mood bring me down.

"You sound happy," she sounds shocked.

"Surprisingly, I am," I say. We're on this rocky ground, again. We've been on this rocky ground so often this year, but it somehow still surprises me. I'm still unable to navigate it.

"Tell me what's so good," she sighs. "I need to hear something happy."

I consider how even to begin to tell her about the bizarre evening. It's like I'm in the Twilight Zone, and nothing I say will make sense.

"Wait," she interrupts me before I even begin. "It's not about Isaiah, is it?"

"No, it isn't about Isaiah," I roll my eyes. I almost point out the double standard in her statement; she always got angry when I didn't want to hear about her boyfriends. But I don't.

"Okay," she says like she's getting comfortable to hear a bedtime story. "Tell me."

"It might be the strangest story I've ever told you," I start. "So, hang on."

I tell her about everything. I tell her about Dad coming over every day since the show. I tell her about me avoiding him. I tell her about tonight and the lights and 100% blue.

"You're forgiving your dad over blue Christmas lights?" She asks. I can hear the doubt in her voice.

"I haven't forgiven him," I shake my head as if she can see it.

"You called him 'Dad,'" she points out.

I want to argue, but I don't. I didn't even realize that I had made the shift. I didn't do it consciously. It just kind of happened.

"I'm just saying," I pull my knees up to my chest and press myself against the headboard of my bed. "Maybe he's different. Maybe he really does want to be part of our lives, again."

And for some crazy reason, I actually mean it.

"But he doesn't," Kayla argues quietly. "I mean. Cade, somebody who actually loves his kids doesn't disappear for four years."

I shrug. She's got a point. This is the Kayla that I miss. This is the Kayla who lets me bounce ideas off her. This is the Kayla who tells me exactly what I need to hear, even when I don't want to listen to it. This Kayla is the one who has always been there for me.

"You're right," I finally sigh. "I don't want to hate him, Kayla."

I'm out of things to say. Because I don't want to hate him. I've never *wanted* to hate my father. But he disappeared. He left me. He destroyed us. He made me hate him.

"Then don't hate him" I hear a tired, lazy smile in her voice. "But that doesn't mean you have to accept him with open arms."

I wish Kayla were here. I miss her. And we work better in person than on the phone.

"Do you wanna come over?" I ask her. I know that it's 7:00 on Christmas Eve, but I want to see her.

"No," she sighs. I deflate.

"But you can come over here if you want," I hear the relief in her voice. She was hoping I'd call. She was expecting I'd make the first move. And it only took me a month and a half. I'm the absolute worst.

"I'll be there after we eat."

"Good," she giggles. "I haven't showered in two days. That'll give me time to clean up."

When I get to Kayla's house, I feel like an outsider. I haven't been to her house in more than six months. I haven't been here since we started our school-year-long fight. I don't even know what we're fighting about anymore. I don't want to be fighting anymore.

Kayla opens the door, hair still wet from her shower. Her sisters start giggling the minute they see me. This has been their default setting for the past two years. Both of them developed these odd crushes on me at some point and giggle uncontrollably whenever I'm around.

"Cade, come in!" Kayla's mom yells from the kitchen, where she's standing over a vegetable tray. Of course, she's at a vegetable tray. I don't think I've seen any of Kayla's family eat a real meal. "Can I get you anything from the kitchen?"

Kayla subtly shakes her head no.

"I'm okay, thanks!" I yell back.

Kayla leads me to her bedroom.

"You dodged a bullet. Mom made ravioli with textured vegetable protein instead of meat."

I make a gagging noise as I fall into the bright pink bean bag on Kayla's floor.

"It's been forever since I've been in here," I say, not thinking. I look around her room. It has gradually become less pink and more grown up in the past four years. Today, the only remnant of hot pink is the bean bag I'm in and the fuzzy rug on which it sits. Kayla curls up in her Papasan chair, and I feel like we're complete again. We're back where we're supposed to be.

"How's your break been?" I ask her lamely.

"I've had better," she shrugs. She looks sad, even through her smile. "I've been lonely."

Kayla's never this candid with me, and I don't know if she's trying to make me feel guilty or just confiding in me as her best friend. I know that her loneliness is, in part, my fault.

"You could have come over," I say, but it sounds pointed. It always sounds pointed.

"You're busy hating me all the time," she says. It's not accusatory; it's just a statement of fact.

"I don't hate you," I hope mine also sounds like a statement of fact.

She shrugs. It's like she's too tired to argue with me.

"I don't," I reemphasize. "I'm angry, and I'm hurt. But I don't hate you."

"Can we just not do this today?" Kayla begs. "I've been fighting all Christmas break."

I nod.

"I brought your Christmas present," I reach into my pocket and pull out a flipbook.

"You haven't made a flipbook in a long time," she smiles, her eyes sparkling.

She takes it from me and starts flipping through the book, my animations popping to life.

Before our eyes, Kayla and I appear. We're sitting in my car, and as she flips, it's apparent that we're speeding down the highway. Our smiles are broad, and our eyes are bright. The wind is whipping through Kayla's hair, tangling it around itself.

The scene zooms out, and the car speeds down the highway. The view continues to zoom out until we're microscopic until the moon can be seen circling the Earth until the Earth is orbiting the sun. Until the entire galaxy is spinning and expanding and pulsating.

The scene zooms out even more until the universe is just a white speck, a sparkle in a sea of black. Again, this sea grows smaller and smaller until it is a sparkle in an eye. Until it is a sparkle in Kayla's eye. Until Kayla is sitting in my car, exactly like the beginning.

"I love it," she whispers softly. Her eyes are sparkling, just like in my flipbook. "Thank you so much."

"I'm glad you like it," I smile. It took me forever.

"Why did you make this if we're fighting?" She sounds sheepish. I'm assuming she didn't get me a present, but I'm not bothered. I'd rather give gifts than get them.

"We're fighting," I agree. "That doesn't mean we've called it quits on our friendship. We're too far in at this point; I'm too old to train a new friend."

She laughs and then sighs. Neither of us is sure if we want to keep fighting or not. We both feel so strongly about our opinions. We both feel so confident that we're right in our beliefs.

"And it's okay that we believe different things," I offer. "If we agreed on everything, we wouldn't enjoy each other."

She smiles a weak smile. She knows I'm right, but she'll never say it.

"And, it's okay if we keep fighting," I smile. "But let's call a ceasefire until after New Year's."

Kayla smiles, throws her arms around me, and squeezes so hard I think my eyes might pop out.

"Since we're calling a truce," Kayla says seriously. "We need to talk about your father."

By the time we're through, we both feel like different people than when we started. It's like Christmas Eve is a chance for rebirth with everybody.

"You know what would make tonight better?" Kayla has a mischievous gleam in her eyes.

"These?" I pull a bag of mom's homemade Christmas cookies from my jacket pocket.

"Oh my god," Kayla giggles excitedly. "You have no idea how badly I hoped you'd bring these! I'll be right back!"

When Kayla returns, she's got two glasses of ice-cold vanilla almond milk. I resist the urge to fake gag again. Why don't her parents buy anything real?

"When we graduate," I laugh. "I'm going to buy you four hundred pounds of junk food."

Kayla and I erupt into laughter as we tear into the cookies. We enjoy the glow of good friends and good conversation. We talk about nothing and everything. We become the people we were before this year. We become the friends we've always been. Why can't it always be this way?

"It's late," I look at my phone and see it's already 10:00. "I've got to get home."

I wish I didn't have to leave. Something in me fears that when I walk out of Kayla's bedroom, we'll go back to being the same fighting friends we've been all school year. That tonight was one isolated night of happiness amidst a fading friendship. I'm not ready to lose Kayla yet.

When I get home, Dad's Porsche is still in the driveway. The lamp in the living room is still on, and the TV is flickering. The smell of chimney smoke hangs in the air from somewhere in my neighborhood. I wish it would snow; then, it would truly be a magical Christmas. But this is Texas. We never get snow at Christmas.

When I open the door, I find my parents on the couch. My dad has his hands inside my mom's shirt, and his lips are pressed against her neck. A moan stops in the back of her throat when they hear the door open.

"Oh my God," I can't shut my mouth. What the hell? What are you supposed to do when your parents are making out on the couch?

"Cade," Mom says, straightening her shirt and smoothing her hair nervously. "We didn't hear you pull up."

"Well, that's apparent," I roll my eyes. I am not prepared for my parents to be dating each other. "What would y'all have done if Thomas had caught you?"

Mom looks sheepish, but Dad doesn't look embarrassed at all.

"He'll have to figure things out at some point," he says in a tone that can only be described as chauvinistic.

"He's seven," I say flatly. "I don't think he's ready for that whole birds-and-bees talk."

"We would have stopped when we heard him on the stairs," Mom says evenly. She's panicking but trying to save face. That's what the Swansons are all about, isn't it? Saving face.

"Just like you heard me coming in?" I'm trying not to be accusatory, but it's difficult.

The room is weirdly quiet for a while. Dad looks pleased with himself. Mom looks embarrassed. I feel sick. I want to go back to my art studio. Or back to my bed. Either way, I don't want to be here, doing this.

"Isn't it time you go home?" I ask, nodding toward the front door. Dad has overstayed his welcome today, and I want to like him still tomorrow.

"It's late," Mom says. And for a moment, I think she agrees with me.

"I know," I nod. "I'm about to fall asleep standing here. I need to put out Thomas's Christmas presents and go to bed."

"You don't have to do that," Mom smiles. "I figured your father and I could do that, and he could spend the night here."

"No," I cross my arms. When did I become the parent?

"I always put out Thomas's presents. For four years, that's been my thing," I'm not even trying to hide my irritation or jealousy. I'm too tired, and the magic is wearing off.

"This year, I'm not working," Mom says. "And we thought it would be nice to do Christmas together again, this year."

Her eyes are saying more than her words. She wants Dad to stay. She wants to superglue this family back together as quickly as possible. She wants it to be smooth, and seamless, and effortless. But that's not how things work.

"That makes sense," I say before I can stop myself. "He gets to disappear for four years and waltz right in and play Santa again."

"Cade," Mom warns. But I've passed the point of redirection.

"I'm trying, Mom," I'm exasperated and exhausted. "But this is too much for me. I'm sorry."

"You need to calm down," Dad pipes in with his sternest father voice. I almost laugh.

"It's okay," Mom says quietly. "I can take care of this."

"No, Teresa," Dad says sternly. "He needs to remember to respect me; I'm his father."

It sounds so immature when he says it. He says it like he's reminding himself that he has authority over me. He has no authority over me.

"That's hilarious," I cackle. "I didn't ask for a daddy this Christmas. I'm not Little Orphan Annie. I was doing just fine without you. This isn't a Christmas miracle. Don't kid yourself."

I storm my way to my art room, pleased with myself in my teenage rage. I'm well aware that I'm behaving exactly how I always try not to. But enough is enough. I can cut my mom some slack trying to rekindle the flame with the man she loved. I can understand her wanting him to be in our lives again.

But I can't deal with this. I can't deal with him trying to walk in after four years and act like he's SuperDad for Thomas and my disciplinarian and authority figure. He lost that right the day he walked out.

When I get into my studio, I look around me. There are mostly-finished pieces of art covering every square inch of my room. I sit down for a moment, trying to calm my rage. I look at Thomas's Christmas present, a large, very detailed, very realistic watercolor of our day at the zoo. This is life as it really happened. Thomas is on one side of the gleaming glass; the tigress stalks patiently on the other. My heart aches when I see it. Tomorrow, we'll exchange gifts, and he will appreciate my gift to him. Then he'll look at whatever expensive crap my father buys him, and he'll immediately love it. And once more, I'll be knocked back into my place.

I look at my mom's present. It's somewhat of a self-portrait. I've drawn a very detailed version of my face in black charcoal on white paper, serious and intense. In white charcoal on black paper, I've created Thomas's face, smiling and jubilant. I wanted it to be like yin and yang. I want us to be opposite and complementary. I've tried to capture a perpetual hint of mischief in Thomas's eye. I've hoped to capture soft, loving eyes on my own likeness.

When it's apparent I won't be getting any work done on my art, I leave my studio and make my way to my bedroom. At the top of the staircase, I hear my parents whispering. Dad sounds angry; mom's apologetic. I stop and listen closely. It's like I'm ten years old, all over again.

"No," my dad says sternly. "He needs to learn some respect."

He sounds angrier than I anticipated.

"It's hard from him, Cole," Mom says. She sounds like she's defending me? Why?

"I don't care, Teresa." I picture him with his arms crossed and his chest puffed out. I can see him looking at her disdainfully. "Life is hard; he doesn't get to have a chip on his shoulder."

"He kind of does," Mom says softly. I see her small as a mouse, scared of my dad's gleaming fangs. "He's justified in his anger."

"I can't believe what I'm hearing," Dad says. He's gritting his teeth. He's a boiling pot whose lid is about to fly off.

"I'm not saying the way he spoke to you is acceptable," Mom's no longer a mouse. She's a fox. Her voice is soft and comforting; her tone is as if she agrees with my father. But her words still support me.

"Then what are you saying?" My father is softened, if only a bit.

"I'm saying that maybe we pushed him too hard, too quickly," Mom's victorious. She's a lioness in her own right.

"Thomas has had no problems adjusting," Dad says flippantly.

"Thomas never has trouble adjusting," Mom half-laughs. "He's the easiest kid that way."

She's got a point. Thomas has always been able to go with the flow.

"Cade is different, though," Mom's voice has returned to the original hushed volume. It's becoming difficult to understand them.

"Cade deals with things at a different pace; he feels things a lot more intensely than most people," I almost feel offended, but she says it with such love. "It's what makes his art so beautiful."

Suddenly, my eavesdropping feels more invasive than it had before. Suddenly, it's not like I'm listening to a conversation about me, but I'm listening to an intimate discussion between my parents. Guilty, I open my door, slip into bed, and give way to the weight of sleep.

"Bub!" A delighted Thomas screams from my doorway as soon as I shut my eyes.

I moan and look at the alarm clock. Eight hours have passed, but I'm positive I've only slept ten minutes. I've got a pounding headache, and the last thing I really want is for Thomas to be screaming from my doorway.

"Bub, come see!" Thomas waits impatiently for me at the door. "Bub, come on!"

I drag myself out of bed and walk down the stairs. I see Thomas as a blur, bounding from step to step faster than I can comprehend. I slug my way behind him. I cannot keep up with him this morning.

"Bub, look!" He's more excited than I've ever seen him. His voice is liable to wake the neighbors, it's so loud.

When I enter the living room, I'm surprised. The living room is covered in gifts. There are wrapped presents from one end of the room to the other.

I can't even begin to process everything I'm seeing. We've never had this many gifts in our house at once. It kind of makes me sick. He's evolved to trying to buy our affection.

Thomas has a stack of presents practically as tall as he is. I know just by looking at them that my painting will pale in comparison. I know that Thomas will thank me, but he'll spend all day playing with the iPad or PlayStation or whatever is in that stack that will keep his attention. I know that Dad will cross his arms, pleased with himself for bribing Thomas into loving him. I know that I will be angry with both of my parents.

My own stack is nothing to sneeze at, and I'm conflicted. On the one hand, I want to open them all and see what expensive crap he's bought me. I want to take stock and see what I can sell to fund my art, or my education, or maintenance on my car. I want to see what things he's thought will buy my heart. On the other hand, I want to ignore them out of protest. I cannot be bought. I want him to understand that buying me presents and buying my art aren't going to absolve him of his wrongdoing.

"You know Mom doesn't like us to open our presents until she's up," I tell Thomas quietly. He looks disappointed but nods.

"You boys go ahead," Dad's deep voice comes from behind me, startling me. He's in pajama pants and a tank top. For a moment, I'm taken aback by how fit my dad is; I guess I don't expect dads to be athletic, I don't know. I'm shocked that he's here, but I shouldn't be. I am shocked that he's in pajamas, though. Mom made it seem like a snap decision to let him stay over last night. The evidence would indicate otherwise.

"No," I put my hand on Thomas's should before he can tear into his presents. "We'll wait for Mom."

"It's okay," Dad looks like he's about to grow a second head and devour me whole. "Let her sleep in."

"We will," Thomas smiles. "We can wait to open our presents until she wakes up."

I smile at my victory. I haven't totally lost Thomas yet. He's anxious to open his presents, but not enough to violate our tradition.

"You don't have to keep making things so difficult," Dad says softly to me.

I'm not sure if he sounds defeated or irritated, so I say nothing back. One of us has to be the mature one, but I really want to tell him that he started it.

"Let's go get breakfast ready," I tell Thomas. His eyes light up.

This is another of our traditions. Thomas and I have made Mom breakfast on Christmas morning every year since Dad left. Thomas always insists on making Mom cinnamon French toast with eggs and bacon. He always cuts the bread into hearts or Christmas trees or some other cute shape and calls it done. He's never participated in the actual cooking.

"I'll take care of things," Dad says, joining us in the kitchen.

"No, it's okay," I try to sound as pleasant as possible. "This is our tradition."

I see his face drop, and for the first time, I think I've actually hurt my Dad. It kind of upsets me, and I don't expect it. I've been taking little digs at him for days now, but something about one of them finally connecting feels wrong. Vengeance isn't really my thing.

"Cade, can I talk to you in the living room?" Dad asks as Thomas starts cutting pieces of bread with large cookie cutters. It looks like he's decided on snowmen and is cutting stacks of circles of bread.

I follow my Dad into the living room. It's like there's no room for us among all the gifts. It's like there's no room for my thoughts among the gifts. They're big, and they're pressing, and they represent so much more than Christmas presents. I don't know if they're apologies or if they're something insidious. I'm afraid they're beautifully wrapped rattlesnakes.

"When will I get to stop apologizing to you?" He asks. He sounds tired. Have I actually worn him down?

"When will you start?" I promised Mom I wouldn't fight with my father. But he's cornered me.

"I've been trying," he throws his hands up.

"No, Dad," I say, trying to hold my anger in. "You haven't. Can we please not do this today? It's Christmas. For Mom's sake, can we please just pretend like we get along?"

"We used to be close," Dad says as a last-ditch effort. "Can we go back to that?"

I don't answer. I'm trying hard to keep my promise to my mom. I'm not going to fight with him. Not today. It's Christmas.

Instead, I go into the kitchen to help Thomas prepare breakfast. I notice he's set out enough food for all of us, including our father. I'm glad Thomas is more thoughtful than I am. I wouldn't have made any breakfast for him.

"Can I at least do something to help?" Dad says, sounding more like Thomas than like a parent.

"You can help me set the table," Thomas's smile is infectious, and I feel myself give way to it. I'm glad he's here as a buffer. It's impossible to be upset when Thomas is around. My family doesn't deserve Thomas. We're not good enough to have somebody as sweet as him.

"Yeah," Dad says in a voice that sounds a lot like mine when I speak to Thomas. "I think I can handle that."

While Thomas and Dad busy themselves setting the table, I get to work at the stove. I scramble eggs and fry bacon and cook French toast. I make the bacon too crispy and the eggs too dry. I'm always burning or almost-burning food. I catch a smile spreading across my face, broader and brighter than I expected this morning.

"We'll move to Austin," I tell myself as I plate breakfast. "Isaiah will be a teacher. I'll burn the lasagna, but the cheesecake will make up for it."

Mom emerges from her bedroom as I put all the food on the table.

"It smells delicious," she says by way of a greeting.

When she gets to the table, she blinks and looks from Dad to me to Thomas and back to me again.

"You guys look happy," she sounds almost surprised.

And I guess we do. But not for the reasons she's thinking. I can't wipe the foolish smile from my face as I think about Isaiah and me and getting away from all this. Thomas can't wipe the smile from his face because he's always smiling. My father can't wipe the smile from his face, but God knows why. He's probably picturing himself kicking puppies or something.

After we eat, Mom leads us into the living room. She's excited to watch us open our gifts. Thomas is excited to open his. I'm ambivalent. I can't shake the image of beautifully-wrapped rattlesnakes. It feels like opening these lavish gifts from my father would be betraying myself.

CHAPTER TWENTY-THREE

"I need to run upstairs," I tell Mom. "I left your presents upstairs."

I run up to my studio and grab Thomas's and Mom's presents. Something in me feels endlessly guilty that I don't have a gift for my father. I open and shut the door to my studio four times before I decide to dig through my completed works to see if there's anything I can give him to appease my own guilty conscience. I hate myself for this.

I sort through stacks of paper until I find a small pastel. It's kind of generic, just depicting a waterfall in a forest somewhere. He doesn't have to know I didn't make him anything. It'll ease my guilt, and I won't have put out any extra effort. It's a win-win, right?

When I come back down, my family is waiting patiently. I figured Thomas would have torn into his presents already, but he'd decided to wait for me. I feel my heartthrob. I haven't lost him yet. He's still mine. Dad hasn't won yet.

"I didn't wrap them or anything," I tell my family. "But here are your presents."

I give Dad his, first. He looks at it for a long time, unsure what to say. He looks at it like a parent whose kid just gave him an ugly stick-figure drawing for the refrigerator. He looks like his next response is the make-or-break moment of our relationship.

"It's beautiful," he says. And for some crazy reason, I believe he means it. "Thank you, Cade."

I feel oddly satisfied. It's gratifying to have your dad's approval, even if you don't like your father, guess. I can't stop the smile that spreads across my face as I thank him.

I give Thomas his watercolor painting. In the picture, he's as gleeful as he is in real life. I revel in this brief moment of superiority when my gift exceeds all else. He looks like I've given him the keys to the world. He looks like he's never been given anything so beautiful.

"Thank you, Bub!" He hugs me tight before dashing off to his room to put it safely away.

"And this is for you," I give Mom her yin and yang portraits of Thomas and me. Her eyes fill up with tears as she looks at them.

"Oh, Cade," she smiles so broadly the room is washed out from her brightness. "They're beautiful. These are amazing. Maybe your best work yet."

I curl up in the warmth of her smile. I'm born anew when she hugs me. For just a moment, I'm 3-years-old and want nothing more than my mom to hold me forever. Things have gotten so complicated lately; I miss times like this. I miss my mom ruffling my hair and our late-night chats. I miss the mom I had before we moved and before Cole came back, and before things got so oddly complicated.

When Thomas comes down, Mom instructs us to open our gifts. I watch as Thomas opens his presents and it was just as I expected. Dad has gone out of his way to buy our affections. Thomas has a new TV for his bedroom and a brand-new tablet wrapped in beautiful packages. There's a small laptop and an e-reader. So much technology. So many useless things that a seven year old doesn't need. Why didn't Mom tell him not to give Thomas those presents?

"Oh my god, oh my god," Thomas says as if it's one word. "These are awesome! Thank you, Daddy! Thank you, Momma!"

I cringe when Thomas says Daddy. It seems too familiar. It seems too intimate. Dad is mostly a stranger to Thomas.

"Cade, you're not going to open yours?" Mom encourages. She's pressed against Dad, his arm draped casually around her. It looks territorial, not loving. Or maybe I'm projecting. Is my hate so deep for my father that I can't imagine him doing anything kind?

My stack of presents is as extravagant as Thomas's but tailored to me. There's a new floor lamp for my easel, with a dock for a tablet. I don't have a tablet, though. At least, not until I open the next present and there's a brand-new, state-of-the-art drawing tablet. There are high-quality paints imported from Australia. There are canvases and real-hair brushes. The extravagance is too much. This is just *stuff*. These aren't gifts. This is hush money.

I've never known Christmas to be so unfulfilling.

I thank my parents all the same and feel guilty as I cart my new things to my art studio. Just because I didn't ask for this stuff doesn't mean I can't use it. As I arrange things, I decide that I won't sell any art using the materials my father gave me. I will donate it all to charities. I will use his hush money to make my *PRIDE in the Urban Jungle* piece. I'll put his bad decisions to good use.

Chapter Twenty-Four

"You're where?" Isaiah asks me as we talk on the phone. "I'm driving through a tunnel, but I could swear you said your dad's house."

"I am," I laugh into the receiver. "See what happens when you abandon me for Colorado? I do crazy things."

Isaiah laughs a hearty laugh. I've missed that laugh. I know we've only been apart a week, but it feels longer. I'm used to seeing Isaiah every day.

"Can I come over?" Isaiah asks. I don't see why he can't, so I give him the address.

When the doorbell rings, I leave my room for the first time since getting to my dad's house. Thomas and Dad are sitting on the couch, watching some bizarre show with a talking dog that plays viola.

"He lives," Dad laughs as I head for the door. I wonder why he didn't move when he heard the doorbell.

"It's Isaiah," I say as I open the door. "He came to hang out for a little bit."

Dad raises an eyebrow at me as I open the door, but I don't say anything.

"Your Christmas present is in my car," I tell him and lead him to my Mustang before inviting him in. Of course, this is all just a ruse. When we're at my car, I press him against my car and kiss him hard.

His lips are sweet. It's like I haven't kissed him in weeks. It's like I haven't kissed him in years. And just as quickly as it starts, I pull away.

"What's wrong?" He asks.

"Nothing," I shake my head. "I just don't know if his neighbors are home." He smiles, but his eyes darken.

"It's okay if people see," he pulls me close. His lips close on mine again.

"They'll all just be jealous."

I smile and want to believe it. But mostly, I don't want my dad to see. Something in me tells me he's not ready to know this. And we haven't fought in, like, nine hours. It's a record.

"I'm just," I sigh, shaking my head.

"I know," he smiles and takes my hand. "And it's okay. Whenever you're ready, I am."

I break his gaze because I'm blushing and because he's so sweet. I reach into my car and pull out the flipbook I've been working on for him. Flipbooks are my favorite. I wish I had time to do more, but they're so time-consuming. I put so much work into them; I reserve them only for the people I love most.

In this one, Isaiah stands, lumbering over me, comically taller than in real life. He bends down and lifts me up in his arms. My feet dangle playfully, and I turn my face towards him to kiss him. As our lips meet, a heart grows in front of our faces and fills up the entire view. Inside the heart is our future. I'm standing at an easel, and in front of me stands Isaiah, furry Chewbacca legs and tank top, posing for me. The view pans over to my easel, where instead of the Chewy/Isaiah hybrid, I've drawn the two of us cuddled up on the couch, watching a movie. The view pans to the TV and zooms in on the screen as the credits roll.

Isaiah and Cade: A Story of Love
Starring
Isaiah Rosenthal as himself
Cade Swanson as himself
They Live Happily Ever After

He looks at me with bright, wet eyes when he's finished flipping through the book. Isaiah's not one to cry, not like me. I'm surprised when a tear rolls down his cheek.

"Cade," he says breathlessly. "It's beautiful. It's way better than what I got you."

I use my thumb to wipe his face dry. I stand on my tiptoes to kiss his cheek, and—for just a moment—I don't care who sees.

"You shouldn't have gotten me anything," I say softly. "You know I don't like presents."

He smiles and takes my hand. He drags me to his car and reaches into the passenger seat. When he turns around, he has a small, pristinely wrapped box. When I open it, I see framed pictures of us; pictures I didn't even know were taken. We're so happy in them. In every picture, he is staring down at me like I'm the only person in the entire world. And I'm smiling so broadly I don't even recognize myself. One is from my gallery opening, we're both in nice suits, and I'm standing so close to him it looks like we're one person. Another is on the couch at our old house. We were watching a movie, and he'd made a lame joke. I'm in the middle of rolling my eyes. It's a chronology of our happiness. It's a collection of little moments that meant nothing and everything.

"How did you even…?" I ask in wonder.

"Your mom helped. And Cameron. And Thomas." He smiles, and I'm swallowed in its warmth, even on this chilly December day.

"Thomas kept a secret?" I ask, laughing. That is so unlike him. Then my face falls a bit.

"Have you talked to Cameron this break?" I've been worried about him, but calling him would feel too much like betraying Kayla, and I don't want to violate our treaty.

"Yeah," he smiles. "He's doing well. He seems sad. I think he really likes Kayla, but he can't get over how she talked to you."

"And you, too," I interject.

"I don't care about how people talk to me," he laughs, pulling me close. "I can take care of myself. You, however, are small and have to be protected."

I laugh and nestle my face into his chest for just a moment.

"We'd better go in before Dad starts to wonder," I nod towards the house. I sniff in one more deep sniff of his cologne.

"Why are you here?" He asks the question that's been killing him since he got here.

"Short version? My parents are reconciling, so while they work it out, we're forced to spend some time here," I roll my eyes.

"That's rough," he nods.

When we get into the house, Dad and Thomas haven't seemed to move from the couch.

"Hey, Dad," I call. "Isaiah's here."

He grunts in acknowledgment, still absorbed in this weird talking dog show.

"Is!" Thomas exclaims, practically jumping over the back of the couch to see him. He launches himself into Isaiah's arms. Isaiah holds him tight and swings him in the air. I feel my heart melt. There is no cuter sight than my beautiful, tall boy with my little brother. I wish I had a picture of this moment. I wish I could save every detail of this moment and draw it later.

"Isaiah, it's good to see you," Dad says, finally getting off the couch to acknowledge Isaiah's presence. His tone, however, does not indicate that it's good to see Isaiah.

"You too, Mr. Swanson," Isaiah returns my dad's firm handshake.

I notice my dad doesn't correct him or insist on Isaiah's calling him Cole. This is a show of power. Isaiah will always have the upper hand, though. He's actually nice.

We start to head to my room when Dad stops me. I let Isaiah go ahead of me.

"If you spend all of your time with him, people will start to assume you guys are dating or something," he warns me.

"Okay," I shrug and try to walk away.

"Cade," he says sternly, and I turn back around to avoid a scene. "Don't you care what people think?"

I force back a laugh. He knows nothing about me, and it's clear.

"No, Dad, I don't," I shake my head. And it's true. I just didn't realize that it is.

His eyes narrow as if he's trying to decide if I'm serious.

"You know what, Pops?" I ask. There it is. Pops. That's my word when I'm spitting venom.

"Never mind," I shake my head. "If you don't want Isaiah here, just tell me, and we'll go somewhere else."

I go to my room when he doesn't say anything else, where Isaiah is flipping through his flipbook again.

"I just don't understand how you can do things like this," he smiles when I walk in. He's laid back on my bed like it is the most comfortable place in the world. I want to crawl up next to him lay my head on his chest, but I am not prepared to deal with the homophobic wrath of Cole Swanson.

"Just takes work," I shrug. I never know what to say when people compliment me. "Tell me about Colorado."

Isaiah regales me with tales of family Christmas. It sounds so extravagant. His whole family, including his brother and sister, gathered at a family cabin. When he describes the house to me, however, *cabin* does not seem to describe the house in which they lived. It sounds extravagant. I imagine silver flatware and crystal drinking glasses. I imagine a sparkling chandelier and giant, fluffy beds.

"When you say cabin," I finally say, putting things together. "You mean ski lodge."

"I mean ski lodge," he blushes and laughs.

Sometimes I forget how different Isaiah's life is from mine. When we're here, alone in my bedroom, we're the same. But the door opens, and the world reappears, and he is from a completely different world from me.

I like it better in my bedroom where we're on level playing ground.

Isaiah and I talk about everything and nothing, and before I know it, the sun is about to set. I don't know where the day has gone. We talked through lunch and never noticed. I have no idea if Dad and Thomas are still home and, if they are, what they're doing. We've been laughing so much and enjoying each other's company so much that I've lost track of the world around me.

I've told Isaiah everything about the break. I've told him about making up with Kayla. I've told him about Dad's house and 100% blue. I've told him about the lavish gifts my father gave us. About drawing and painting and hiding away. I'm all talked out when Dad comes into my room.

"You hungry, Bucko?" He asks, Thomas's bright smile on his face. I've never realized how much Thomas favors our dad. "I thought we could go get some dinner."

"Yeah," I smile. "Can Isaiah come, too?"

It feels weird asking my father if Isaiah can eat with us. With Mom, there's never a question; it's always expected. Isaiah will always be welcome at our table. Isaiah will always have a plate set for him.

Dad hesitates for a minute before agreeing.

"I don't know how we'll all fit in my car," he shrugs. "But we can make it work."

"It's an impractical car for a family," I say before I can help it. It's true, though. It may be a beautiful piece of machinery, a mechanical work of art, but it is not meant for a family to cruise around in.

"Watch it," he warns sternly.

I roll my eyes.

Is this how it's always going to be?

I cast a glance to Isaiah, who shrugs. He doesn't know what to say or what to do. This will technically be the first time Isaiah and my father have spent any amount of time together, and Isaiah is already naturally inclined to hate my dad. But for some reason, I really want them to get along. Something crazy in me wants my dad to like Isaiah. Does everybody need their father's acceptance? Is that something built into us?

"I can take my car," I offer, but Dad shakes his head.

"No, I think we can all fit if you don't mind squeezing in the back with Thomas," he offers.

So, we all pile into my dad's ever-shrinking Porsche, four men in a sardine can. Isaiah's head rests against the ceiling, and he struggles to find the seatbelt. I'm reminded of the comically large Isaiah in my flipbook. Thomas laughs at Is's conundrum.

"So, tell me about yourself, Isaiah," Dad says in a more fatherly way than he's entitled.

"Well," Isaiah sounds much more confident than I ever do when I'm talked to this way. "My Dad is a contract lawyer. I think your firm works with his firm; he's Marcus Rosenthal."

Dad nods in slow acknowledgment. I notice his eyes in the rearview mirror as he loses face for just a moment. That in-control gleam dulls for a fraction of a second. I can't fight the smirk on my face. Dad's just made all the connections. Between Isaiah and his parents. Between himself and Isaiah's mom. Between Isaiah's friendship with my mom. I notice him cast a glance at me. Our eyes meet for a fraction of a second, and I can tell he knows I know everything.

"I should have seen the resemblance," is all he says. "You do look an awful lot like your dad."

Isaiah smiles uncomfortably, his bright smile dimming a few watts.

"And are you going to take over your dad's firm when you grow up?" Dad's feeling Isaiah out. He's trying to see if I'm friends with Isaiah strategically. He'll forgive our spending time together if it's an attempt to improve my own status. My father has always believed in being upwardly mobile.

"No, sir," Isaiah shakes his head. "I think I'd like to be a high school teacher."

"Well, that's no good," Dad laughs like he's understood a joke that we haven't. "Your parents have put you in a place to literally do anything you want to do when you grow up. Why would you want to spend it working so many hours and making so little money?"

"Money is not everything, Dad," I say flatly.

"Of course, it's not," Dad smiles. "But it certainly makes things a hell of a lot easier."

I wince. I wish he wouldn't talk like this in front of Thomas. I wish he wouldn't talk like this in front of Isaiah. I'm embarrassed, suddenly. I want to dig a hole and crawl into it.

Please don't let Dad scare Isaiah off, I pray silently.

"Where's your dad these days?" Dad asks casually. "He's always traveling, I'll bet."

"Yes, sir," Isaiah nods quietly. "He's in London this week."

"Wasn't he just in Paris?" I ask. "He must have more frequent flyer miles than he knows what to do with."

My dad lets out a hearty laugh. This time he really does know a punchline

I don't.

"Isaiah's family owns their own jet," he volunteers freely.

I blush and shrink down in my seat. I'm suddenly uncomfortable with my dad knowing my boyfriend's financial situation. I'm also suddenly very uncomfortable knowing my boyfriend's parents own a mansion, a ski lodge, three cars that cost more than my mom's house, and a private jet. It makes my head swim. It makes me feel sick.

What can I possibly offer to the boy who has everything?

The night goes better than I expect, surprisingly. Dad takes us to a swanky new Asian fusion restaurant that's all low-lit and neon colors. The chopsticks glow in blacklight, and all the tables are close to the ground with little cubes to sit on. Isaiah is as charming as ever and captivates my dad as the night goes on.

I feel a shift in the air as we chat. My dad relaxes, and I start to see a little bit of that man that my mom always described. He is charming. He's funny. He's oddly fatherly toward us. One of Dad's business associates approaches our table as we eat our dinner.

"Cole," he smiles. "This is a rather unusual business meeting."

He and my dad chuckle like this is the funniest joke anybody has ever told. Isaiah and I smile uncomfortably.

"Dan Schaeffer," Dad smiles, standing to shake his hand. "These are my boys."

He gestures to Thomas first.

"This is Thomas," he instructs Thomas to shake Dan's hand.

"And this is Cade," he offers me next. "Cade is a successful artist. You probably saw the write-up about him in the newspaper last month."

Dan studies me closely for a moment while he shakes my hand.

"Yes," he smiles. "I did. I thought you looked familiar. I didn't realize you were Cole's boy."

I resist the urge to say something mean. We're having a good night.

"I am," I shrug. What am I supposed to say?

"I'm not surprised," Dan smiles broadly. The edges of his eyes crinkle, and he looks like the nicest person I've ever met when they do. "Your dad was quite the artist in high school."

My eyes widen in utter shock. I had no idea. I try to play this off as best as I can.

"You went to high school with my dad?" I ask, trying not to ask about his art. He looks so much older than my dad.

"Yeah," he laughs. "Not all of us age as well as he did."

We both laugh, and suddenly I understand Dad's awkward laughs. They're expected. That's how adults interact. It's bizarre.

"Did you guys take art together?" I look from Dad to Dan.

"No," Dan laughs. "I wasn't good enough for all that. Your Dad won the school art show, did he tell you?"

"No, he didn't," I turn to my dad, trying to hide my shock.

I'd always assumed that I'd inherited my artistic ability from my mom. Her dad had been an artist; she was an accomplished artist in her own right. Nobody had ever told me my dad was an artist. Much less a good one.

"I think he only signed up for art to impress your mother," he laughs. "But then it turned out he was actually good."

"That's ancient history, Dan," my dad says jokingly.

For the first time, I remember Isaiah sitting there. And I immediately feel guilty.

"Oh, I'm sorry. Mr. Schaeffer," I gesture to Isaiah. "This is my boyfriend, Isaiah Rosenthal."

No. God, no. Please.

I try to shove the words back into my mouth.

I try to teleport.

I try to spontaneously combust.

I try to become another person, and change my name, and move to Bora Bora.

"Rosenthal, eh?" Dan Schaeffer, much to his credit, does not even seem shocked. "Marcus' boy?"

Isaiah smiles more brightly than I've ever seen him smile. The whole room is alive and charged in his smile. I am alive and charged in his smile. Everybody pales there against his bright smile. In this moment, commanding this room, he's the most beautiful thing in the entire world. Has my publicly calling him my boyfriend made this transformation?

I can feel Dad's eyes on me. They're angry and terrified. I don't want to look at him. I don't want to acknowledge what just happened. I want to pretend I said best friend.

And, then again, I don't. I don't want to be uncomfortable introducing him as my boyfriend. I don't want to be ashamed. I don't want to hide anymore. And I don't want to be scared of what Cole Swanson will think.

When Dan Schaeffer leaves, we all sit, exchanging glances. Thomas is happily munching away at his dinner, oblivious to the tension around him. Isaiah is smiling at me like a fool. Cole is glaring at me, and I can't discern his emotion. Is he mad?

"Cade, can we step outside for just a minute?" Dad says. My stomach drops. This will definitely not go over well.

"Yes, sir," I nod and exchange glances with Isaiah. He's still smiling like a fool.

We step outside. The night air is freezing. Our breaths hang angrily in the air, mixing with each other before vaporizing completely. Our eyes lock.

"Could you please give me a warning next time?" Cade says quietly.

"I didn't mean to," I shake my head. "I'm sorry."

And then I feel my head cock.

"What am I apologizing for?" I ask angrily. "I don't owe you an apology. This is my life, Dad."

"I know that, Bucko," Dad says. "I meant, could you warn me next time that I'm meeting the boyfriend."

The world stops spinning. The air grows still. I almost ask him to repeat himself. Maybe I've had a seizure. Maybe I've been sucked into an alternate dimension. Maybe I'm dying. Maybe I'm on a hidden camera show, and this isn't my dad, but some actor they've paid to be my dad.

"I'm just saying," he shrugs. "That I'd like to be informed of these things before my co-workers is all."

And then he hugs me. And I let him because I'm still in shock. And because I don't know what else to do. And I feel my shoulders relax. And I feel a tear fall down my face the millionth time this school year. And I feel myself hug him back.

And I feel like I finally have my dad back. And I don't know how I feel.

"I like Isaiah," he says when we finally part. "Your mother seems to like Isaiah, too. And Thomas definitely likes him."

I feel myself smile so broadly it almost hurts.

"I just wish you didn't feel like you have to hide things from me, is all," he says gently.

"Earlier, you told me I should be worried that the world would think Isaiah and I are a couple," I roll my eyes.

"That was before I realized you were a couple," Dad says by way of apology. "That doesn't make it any less shitty, does it?"

He winces, and I know he's genuinely sorry. And I wonder when I started being able to read my dad. And I wonder when he started being my dad again. And I wonder when he's going to hurt us all again.

"I'm sorry," Dad says at last. "I know it's hard for you, and I haven't made all this easy."

I'm in shock. This is the same man who was angry with me at Christmas? How many versions of Cole Swanson will I meet? How long will this one stay around?

"But I'm trying," he says softly. "And I hope that one day we can be close again. I'm not proud of the things I've done, Cade. I hope you won't always shut me out. But I'll understand if you do."

I feel myself wilt. And I don't know what to say. I don't know how to respond. I've never been asked forgiveness before. I don't know that I know how to give it. But I want to. I want to like my father. I want to love him the way that Thomas does, but I'm not ready yet.

I just nod without saying anything. I walk back into the warm restaurant and find Thomas laughing so hard he's crying. Isaiah has shoved neon green chopsticks in his mouth and is clapping like a walrus. I catch myself laughing at the ridiculousness of it all. And how beautiful Isaiah looks when he's making my baby brother laugh.

And I realize for the first time just how lucky I am.

Chapter Twenty-Five

"Can you come pick me up?" Isaiah says into the phone.

He's been crying. His voice sounds raw.

"Where are you?" I ask, grabbing my keys and making my way to my car. Before he can finish speaking, I'm speeding off to his house.

I can't get there fast enough. My brain is racing. Isaiah won't tell me what's wrong. The ten-minute drive from my house to his feels like several hours. When I pull up to his driveway, Isaiah is sitting on his porch, two gym bags beside him. He's crying harder than I imagined he could. It's a silent cry, and he heaves when he sees me. His skin is splotched and tear-stained. He looks awful.

"Isaiah?" I fly out of the car, almost forgetting to put it in park. "Isaiah, what's wrong?"

He shakes his head but says nothing. When he finally catches his breath, he stands, grabs his bags, and marches to my car.

"I have to get out of here," he throws his bags in my back seat, and I drive him to my house.

I don't know how to comfort him; I don't know what's happening. I put my hand on his knee. I squeeze gently and rub my thumb over the fabric of his jeans. I want to give him what little strength I have, but I don't know how.

When we finally get to my house, Isaiah takes a breath and speaks in a broken, ragged voice.

"It's my mom," he looks so small, suddenly. "She found out about us."

I feel my heart sink. I knew we should have told her.

"How?" I ask, but I already know the answer. It's my fault. I should have never told Dan Schaeffer.

"Dan Schaeffer told my dad he'd met us," Isaiah sobs. "And Dad told Mom."

I feel embarrassed. I feel angry. I feel betrayed.

"Is your dad mad?" I don't know why I'm asking this.

"No," Isaiah shakes his head. "No. Dad was. I don't know. Dad was cool with it."

We're sitting in my car in the driveway of my house. I don't know what to do. Do we get out? Do we stay here?

"But Mom told me she had already talked to you about this," he wipes his face. His hands are shaking.

"And then she told me to pack my bags and leave."

I feel my stomach sink. She did what? She kicked Isaiah out?

"She can't do that," I growl. I want to kill her.

"She can," Isaiah nods. "I'm 18. She took my car."

"It's okay," I say calmly. "You can stay with us."

When he's calmed down, I grab his bags and lead him inside.

"Isaiah, is that you?" Mom calls from the kitchen. When neither of us answers, she comes out to greet us.

"Just go up to my room," I tell Isaiah. "I'll be up to check on you in a little bit."

I set his bags down and walk with my mom back into the kitchen. Her hands shoot to her mouth in rage and shock when I tell her what happened. She looks the angriest I've seen her in a long time. She's grown very protective of Isaiah in the past few months.

"I can't believe that bitch," Mom says. It's only the second time I've heard her speak like this, and it shocks me all over again. "She's awful, Cade."

For a while, Mom and I sit in silence.

"Of course, he can stay here as long as he needs," Mom says softly. "I mean, we'll have to lay down some new rules, but I wouldn't dream of turning him out. I just can't believe her."

I don't know what to say or do. I know Isaiah needs to be alone right now, but I want to comfort him. I want to be his shining knight the way he's always been mine.

"It's all my fault," I whimper before I realize I've done it.

"What?" Mom looks sad and pulls me into her arms. "No, sweetie. Don't think that way. This is Betty Rosenthal's fault and nobody else's."

She strokes the back of my head gently.

"Parents who kick their children out are selfish," she whispers. "And they're awful parents. Don't you dare for a second let her make you believe you've done anything wrong."

I feel guilty, letting my mom comfort me. Isaiah's the one in need of comfort. I know Mom is right, but I can't help feeling like this would have been avoided if I'd kept my damned mouth shut.

"Should I go check on him?" I ask. I don't know how to handle this. I don't know how to deal with everything.

"Give him some time alone," Mom says gently. "He needs some time to process. He'll come down when he's ready."

Instead, I help Mom in the kitchen. It's the day before school starts back, and we have to get ready to get back in the swing of things. We clean the house and take down the Christmas tree. We prepare meals for the week. We do all the things that are a million times easier to do when Thomas is spending the day with Dad. I think about Dad and Mom while we work. I think about how surprisingly supportive they've been. I wish Isaiah had that. I can't imagine what he must be feeling right now. I want to cry for him, but I decide not to. Isaiah can have these tears; I'll be strong for the both of us.

"What's Isaiah's favorite dessert?" Mom asks when the house sparkles and smells like lemon cleaner.

Mom sets to work making a mile-high red velvet cake. Some people show love through acts of service. Some people show love through giving gifts. My mom shows love through baked goods. This cake says everything Mom wants to say. It says *welcome home*. It says I *love you*. It says *you are special, and important, and you matter*. For my mom, cake says a lot.

I want to thank her. I want to tell her she'll never understand how grateful

I am. I want to tell her that there isn't another mom in the world like her. But I don't know how to do it without crying. And I'm not going to cry. I'm saving that for Isaiah.

Mom and I work together to cook dinner. We hand make what seems hundreds of arepas for the first time since I was a kid. I smile as Mom hums a lullaby she sang when I was little. As we pat the arepas, I dig deep into my memory to find the words. Mom's voice drifts me back in time as she hums, and I'm Thomas's age again.

"Arrorró mi niño, arrorró mi sol," she sings in my memory. I'm in my tiny bed, bundled up in blankets with my stuffed Winnie the Pooh beside me. I feel my eyes get heavy, but I don't want to slip into sleep just yet. The best part is coming. But I can't remember what the best part is.

"Arrorró pedazo de mi corazón," she continues, stroking her fingers through my hair. A contented smile crosses my face as I fight the urge to sleep. I can't sleep, something special is coming. But I can't remember what that special thing is. It's like the file is corrupted in my head. My memory just isn't there anymore.

"Mom?" I ask. It bugs me that I can't remember. "What was the special thing that happened when you used to sing that to me?"

Mom stops making arepas to look at me. There are smudges of flour on her face and in her hair. I stifle a laugh.

"I don't know what you mean," she says after a moment of consideration.

"I don't know," I shrug. "I just remembered that I'd try hard not to go to sleep while you were singing to me because something special happened."

Before we can talk further, a sniffle and footsteps on the stairs announce Isaiah's presence.

"It smells amazing, Mrs. Swanson," he says half-heartedly. His eyes are dull. I hate when his eyes dull.

"I hope you enjoy it," Mom smiles. She pats a floured hand on Isaiah's hand. "Let me know if there's anything I can do for you."

There's a heavy feeling in the kitchen as we work. I try to stay light-hearted for Isaiah's sake, but I can't fight the feeling that I've ruined everything. I want to fix it. I want to call Betty Rosenthal and tell her she's awful and should feel lucky to have such an amazing son. I want to tell her that she should be ashamed of herself. I want to make her cry the way she's made Isaiah cry. I want to take his face in my hands and tell him how special and important he is.

But I don't.

I just watch him break. I watch him stay broken. I watch the pieces fall to the floor and feel my heart shatter for him. But what can I do?

"I can't stay here," Isaiah says after a long, uncomfortable silence.

"Of course, you can," Mom smiles. "You can stay here as long as you need."

For the millionth time, I realize just how wonderful my mom is and just how grateful I am for her.

"I appreciate it," he says. "And I will stay—if you don't mind—until I find something else. But I can't live with my boyfriend's family. Something tells me that won't make things better between my mom and me."

"I guess you're right," Mom says gently. "But you're welcome here as long as you need to stay, okay?"

She continues making her arepas, but I don't feel much like cooking anymore. I sit down beside Isaiah and take his hand in mine. We don't say anything. What is there to say?

"I'm so sorry," I finally say because nobody has ever taught me what to say in this situation. "This is all my fault."

Isaiah shakes his head, but he doesn't say anything. It makes me wonder if he thinks it's my fault, too. I didn't mean to ruin things. I squeeze his hand. I need to make him see I didn't mean to ruin things. I need him to understand. For my own selfish sake, I need him to understand.

For a long time, we just sit, breathing in synch as silent tears run down his face. I can't stop staring at him, this beautiful, broken boy, as he stares into the middle distance, unblinking. I wish I could tell him I know what he's going through, but he won't get it. He won't understand that it's true because I didn't when my dad abandoned me. And maybe I don't know what it's like, because eventually, inexplicably, he came back. And maybe Isaiah's mom will come back. This whole world is too complicated a place.

"If she's making you pick between her and me, you can pick her," I finally say. I feel my heart shatter when I do.

I see my mom stop in her tracks. She starts to cry, too. I don't know why.

"No," Isaiah shakes his head. He laces his fingers with mine and squeezes, taking my strength for himself. "She's not asking me to pick between you and her. She's asking me to pick between her and *me.*"

I stop breathing without realizing it. I hadn't thought of it like that.

Neither Mom nor I know what to say. I exchange a glance with her; she's still silently crying. I know that she would have excused herself from the room if she weren't cooking.

"Cade," Mom says softly. "I need to call your dad. Do you mind finishing up dinner?"

I know that she's going to warn him about everything and have him prepare Thomas for what's going on. I know she's excusing herself so that Isaiah and I can work through this together. I wish we didn't have to work through this. It's not fair. It's not fair to Isaiah. He deserves better. He deserves a family.

For so long, I'd wished to be rid of Betty Rosenthal and the ever-looming threat of her bigotry and pride. But I didn't mean for this to happen. I just didn't want to have to deal with her anymore.

I'm grateful that Mom hasn't said, "I told you so." Because she did tell me so, she told us when we first started dating: we needed to tell Betty Rosenthal. And then she and I started fighting. I never apologized for fighting with her. I never apologized for taking her for granted. Mom didn't kick me out or give up on me.

I try to focus on Isaiah again; today is about him. Today, he's suffering through his own problems. I can sort mine out later. I try to look into Isaiah's honey-colored eyes, but they're still staring at nothing. He's still broken.

"Would you like a glass of water?" I ask meekly.

When I was little, my dad offered me water when I was upset. I've never understood why, but it's always been my go-to offer for comfort. When Thomas is upset, I always offer him water. When I think about this, I have to fight back a laugh. It seems so ridiculous.

"No, thank you," Isaiah shakes his head.

"It's going to be okay," I kiss his cheek. "It won't seem like it now, but everything will be okay."

By the time Dad and Thomas return, Isaiah has moved from the kitchen table to the couch. He's now looking at every one of his fingernails as if considering the meaning of the universe. I can't stand to see him like this. If I've had this thought once today, I've had it a thousand times.

"Hey, Bucko," Dad says when he enters the house. "Hey, Isaiah."

Isaiah nods in acknowledgment but doesn't even turn his gaze toward him.

Dad must have explained what was going on very well because instead of running in to tackle Isaiah, as Thomas is wont to do, he sits down quietly beside him on the couch. In the single sweetest gesture I've seen in my entire life, Thomas sits with his body as close to Isaiah as possible and rests his head on Isaiah's arm. Instinctively, Isaiah lifts his arm and hugs Thomas close to his body without speaking. They sit still and silent for longer than I thought Thomas possibly could. My heart melts. Thomas didn't need any help; he knew the kind of comfort Isaiah needs without hesitation.

"How you holding up?" Dad asks me quietly. I didn't even realize he'd slipped up behind me.

"I'm fine," I raise an eyebrow. I'm not the one hurting.

"It's hard to see the ones we love go through so much pain," Dad says, answering my unasked question. "It takes its toll on us, too."

"I'm fine," I say again. Dad pats my shoulder and walks away to find Mom.

Dinner is quiet. The usual energy that has been bubbling at our table since Christmas is gone. Isaiah hardly touches his food. Thomas says nothing. Mom and Dad keep looking from Isaiah to each other. They're having a silent conversation, but I can't translate.

When it's time for dessert, nobody feels like having cake.

"That's okay," Mom smiles. "We'll eat it for breakfast."

When dinner's over, Isaiah and I go to my room. My parents keep Thomas downstairs. Against the rules and the advisement of my parents, I shut the door. Isaiah falls into my bed again and stares at the ceiling. His giant frame barely fits in my twin-sized bed, but he doesn't seem to mind today. I lie down next to him, squeezing myself into the spaces he doesn't fill, and lay my head on his chest. His long arm wraps around me, and he holds me tight.

"We'll run away," I tell him softly. "We'll move to California and live on the beach. We'll both be so tan nobody will recognize us."

"You're Colombian," he laughs, offbeat. "You'll tan way faster than me."

"We'll learn to surf, and we'll live off the land. We'll learn to grow our own food and make artisan butter and goat cheese."

The rise and fall of Isaiah's chest tell me he's laughing, and I feel all the better for it. I lace my fingers with his and stare at the wall. This is comfortable. We could do this. We could do this forever.

"Artisan butter?" He asks, and I know Isaiah is back. My Isaiah. He's still broken, but he's here.

"What?" I laugh. "People love that word. We could make everything artisan. Artisan cheese. Artisan art. Artisan sand."

"Artisan sand?" He's in genuine stitches now. "What about artisan sand art? You can make those little sand scenes and glue feathers on top."

I close my eyes and let the bounce of his chuckle comfort me.

"Is?" I roll onto my stomach so that I can look into his eyes. "I'm so sorry. About everything."

"It's really not your fault," he says, sobering.

"I know," I shrug. "I feel like it is, but I know it's not. That doesn't mean I'm not sorry that it happened to you. I wish I could fix it."

"Me too," he runs his free hand through my hair, and suddenly it seems like he's comforting me instead of the other way around.

"What am I going to do?" Isaiah asks in a way that makes me know he doesn't mean immediately. He means long-term. What is he going to do forever?

"You'll go to college," I say. "Same as me. You'll get your degree. You'll have thousands of dollars of student loan debt. You'll drive a crappy car. You'll be the most successful high school teacher who's ever lived. You'll write books and go on talk shows. You'll be successful despite your mother."

I run my thumb along the backside of his hand. He's smiling again, so I know I can go on.

"You'll move on to bigger and better things, and you'll forget about this city, and you'll forget about me, and you'll make a name for yourself that's better than any Rosenthal before you."

"No," he argues. "You'll be there, too. I'm your muse, you know. You can't make half the art you make without me."

It's kind of true. Isaiah has become ingrained in half of the art I've created since we became friends. Well before I fell for him, he was in my art. I just didn't realize it at the time.

We lie still for a moment longer before he sits up.

"Your mom will be mad if she catches us like that," he says, sitting up.

"I don't care," I shake my head, beckoning him to lie back down. I'm comfortable; I don't want to move.

"I do," he laughs. "She's letting me live here until I figure out what's going on."

"Until forever," I say back. I like the idea of Isaiah living here.

"Until I figure out my next step," he smiles. "If we live together, you'll just get bored with me. You'll kick me to the curb before January's through."

"I won't," I argue, pulling on his arm playfully.

"I know you won't," he laughs. "Because I can't live here."

I know he's right, but I don't want him to be.

"We could move out and move in together," I suggest, only half-joking.

"No," he laughs. "We're not ready for that."

And again, I know he's right. And again, I don't want him to be.

We walk back downstairs together. Mom and Dad are sitting on the couch, and Thomas is asleep on the armchair. How long have we been in my room doing nothing?

"Hey," Mom smiles her comforting smile. "How are you feeling?"

"Better," Isaiah nods. "Thank you. And thank you for letting me stay here. I promise not to be trouble."

"You could never be trouble," Mom smiles and runs her fingers through his hair like she does mine. "You're welcome to stay as long as you need.

You're welcome to stay through college."

Isaiah's smile slowly spreads throughout the house. I notice my dad get lost in it. And then he's lost in Mom's smile. And the whole place is absorbed in warmth again.

"Really, I can't thank you enough," Isaiah says again.

For a moment, they don't know what to say to each other.

"I talked to your mother," Mom says at last as if she's betraying herself by saying this. "I'm the last person she wanted to hear from, I know. But I wanted her to know you were safe. And I wanted her to know where to find you when she's ready."

Isaiah seems relieved. He seems to be grateful that his mother has been filled in. I don't understand this at all. If my mom had kicked me out, I'd want to go into hiding and make her suffer from worry.

"Do you think she'll ever be ready?" Isaiah asks. I see Mom's heart break. I see her recover and try to save face. It all happens so quickly, I hope Isaiah doesn't see it.

"I think so," Mom nods. "She'll come around."

I know Mom doesn't believe it when she says it, though. I don't believe it, either.

"When your dad gets back, everything will work out. I'm confident," Dad smiles. Oddly, he does believe it. I've never met Isaiah's dad. I don't know what I believe.

I let Isaiah have my room when it's time for bed, and I hide away in my art studio, intending to sleep on the little couch there. Instead, I stay up all night, working in a piece that I can't get out of my head. When morning comes, I step back and look at my creation for the first time.

In the shadows are rows of nondescript faces. In front of them are the recognizable faces of Betty Rosenthal and Kayla. In a shaft of light, on the opposite side, stand my family and Cameron amidst a sea of unrecognizable faces. Isaiah stands tall and proud in the middle, with a meek and small me beside him. The world stretches out in front of us, the earth cracked and broken. The sky is a swirl of green and gold and purple and orange. The shafts of light and shadow stretch out around us, leaving only a narrow path of the in-between where we stand. Our hands are clasped, and the energy of the painting makes it apparent that we're about to make a run for it.

And so begins the last semester of high school—me and Isaiah against the world, living in the In-Between.

Chapter Twenty-Six

Getting back into the flow of school is weird. Adding a new person into our morning routine has its challenges, but nobody says anything about it, for which I'm grateful. There is something fun and exciting about driving to school with Isaiah every day. There's something less fun and exciting about arriving at school at the same time as Kayla. She always glares us down. The ceasefire has ended, and we're back on opposite sides of enemy lines.

Cameron starts spending every lunch shift with us. It's nice to have him as a distraction from the weight of everything going on. He's got his own problems, and they're a welcome distraction from ours. As the days drag on, it's apparent that misery loves company. Even usually perky Isaiah turns into a storm cloud for the month of January. He deserves to.

"Do you need a job?" Cameron asks one day at lunch. "We're hiring. I could get you hired if you want."

Isaiah considers this for a moment.

"I don't have a car," he shrugs. "Mom took that away."

"I can take you to work," I offer. "Or you can borrow my car."

"Yeah, man," Cameron smiles. "Or I can pick you up and stuff. We'll work it out."

I don't deserve people like Isaiah, Cameron, or my mom in my life. I don't know what I've done to have them in my life. For a moment, despite all our general glums, we're all smiles and jokes again. Until I make eye contact with Kayla across the cafeteria.

"She can't stand to see you happy," Isaiah shakes his head, the first thing he's ever said against anybody the entire time I've known him. "Don't let her win, Cade."

I shake my head and start to defend her, but Cameron sighs and interrupts.

"No," he says. "It's kind of true. She doesn't like it when you're happy."

This is the first time Cameron's ever talked poorly of Kayla since their breakup. He looks like it hurts him to say—like this is betraying Kayla. And maybe it is. I'm surprised by how much it doesn't hurt when Cameron tells me. It's like a confirmation of something I'd always known.

"What do you mean?" I suddenly need to know more information.

"I mean," Cameron shakes his head. "It's not like she wants you unhappy, at least not that she's ever said. I just kind of realized that she wants you to be happy on her terms."

I try not to eye her suspiciously. I try to stay calm. But something in me snaps. I'm angry. I'm madder than I deserve to be. Why has it taken me this long to realize?

"She didn't even get me a Christmas present," I sigh. It's a ridiculous thing to say, but it's true. I hand drew her a flipbook. It took days. And she didn't even give me a card.

Even Cameron got me a Christmas present. Before I had even had the chance to give him the flipbook I'd made him, he presented me with a Christmas card and a gift card to the art store. It was nice and totally unexpected, and totally unnecessary.

"I'm sorry, dude," Cameron smiles kindly. I feel guilty all over again; Isaiah's the one dealing with actual problems. I have got to stop being so selfish.

"Would you guys wanna come hang out this weekend?" Cameron asks, and I'm surprised. I don't know why, but it shocks me that he wants to spend time with us as a couple.

"Sure," I nod, without even consulting Isaiah.

"That'd be great," he nods.

It will be nice to get out from underneath my parents and brother. It will be nice to spend time with Cameron again. Oddly, I've missed him. I hated him at the beginning of the year, and I feel bad for it. He was nothing like I expected. He's not stuck up or entitled or anything. He's nothing like I had anticipated.

And that is how our friendship evolves. Cameron turns out to be the nicest person I've ever met. He turns out to enjoy mine and Isaiah's company. His dad loves us, and his brothers are accepting and kind. The Mathis men are wonderful people. They're the kind of people I wish I'd been able to know my entire life. Cameron's dad welcomes us with open arms and a kind smile. He always cooks for us when we're over, and it's always delicious.

Isaiah and Cameron quickly bond while working together. Every night, I pick Isaiah up from work, and he smells of pepperoni and tomato sauce. He's full of stories of funny things Cameron said and did. His smile returns to normal the more time he spends with Cameron, and soon, it's like he's forgotten about his mom and everything that happened before he came to live with us. Before I've realized it, Cameron has filled the gap in my life that Kayla used to fill. And has become Isaiah's constant companion.

"Didn't realize you liked sloppy seconds," Kayla says one day in the cafeteria as I head to the lunch table with Isaiah and Cameron. I want to ignore her. I want to keep walking and pretend like she doesn't matter, but I stop against my better judgment.

"Can I help you?" I raise an eyebrow at her. My voice sounds bored and tired. I've given up fighting at all.

"You're done with me, so you're hanging out with my *ex*?" She says ex with such disdain. She says it like she can't believe she stooped so low as to date Cameron Mathis. She could do a lot worse than Cameron Mathis.

"He wants your boyfriend, you know," she says. When she says boyfriend, it seems like a curse word.

I laugh in her face. This is by far the most ridiculous conversation I've ever been part of.

"He's gay, Cade," she rolls her eyes like she's explaining something obvious. "He thinks you're not good enough for Isaiah. He practically told me so, himself. The night we broke up."

"Maybe that's how we like it, Kayla," I feel a devilish smile creep across my face. "Maybe the plan all along was to steal him from you so we could bring him into our secret, crazy sex cult. You know how I like a good sex cult."

Kayla flinches, and I turn on a heel, content with myself in my victory. I don't even feel bad that I've made her angry. I don't feel bad that I've engaged. Should I feel bad?

"That looked like fun," Isaiah rolls his eyes when I sit down. He and Cameron were laughing at a joke that neither one volunteers to clue me in on. "You look awfully proud of yourself."

"I am," I smile but don't expound.

And this is the beginning of the end, I think. This is how things are going to end with Kayla. With her sulking and hating me and me not caring. With her trying her hardest to undermine my joy. And me ignoring her.

I eat quietly and watch Isaiah and Cameron talk animatedly. For the first time in a long time, I feel unnoticeable again. No eyes are on me, not Isaiah's, not Cameron's. Nobody sees me but Kayla, across the room, looking smugger than she has any right to look. She eats alone, nobody around her, and somehow, she's in control.

"I think I'm going to move in with Cameron," Isaiah announces on the ride home that afternoon.

I nearly wreck.

"What?" I pull over to the side of the road. I'm not in the headspace to drive right now. "Why?"

"I told you I wasn't going to live with you guys permanently," Isaiah says as if this explains everything.

"I know," I feel betrayed, even though I shouldn't. "But it's been nice, you know?"

And it has been nice. Sometimes, when Mom and Dad go out on dates and Thomas goes to bed, Isaiah and I have the house to ourselves. We sit on the couch as close as humanly possible to each other. He sits on the couch in my studio while I paint and draw. I have his undivided attention at all times.

When he finishes showering, the bathroom that Thomas and I share smells like Isaiah, and I catch myself standing nearby just to breathe in his shampoo and deodorant. When he's at work, I climb into my bed and imagine his arms wrapped around me while I lie on the pillow he's been using.

"I don't want you to leave," I'm pitiful when I say this.

Isaiah laughs his hearty laugh that's too loud for my little car.

"It's not like I'm going away forever," his smile comforts me, but only a little. "I'm just going to move in with Cameron's family. I'm going to pay rent there. It'll be easier for me to carpool to work, and we can stop feeling like we're under your parents' supervision all the time."

"When will we see each other?" I ask. I'm being ridiculous, and I know it.

"We didn't always live together," he laughs again. "It'll be like before."

I'd nearly forgotten we haven't always shared space. I had almost forgotten there was a time before Isaiah. It's as if he's always been here.

"I guess," I sigh. I don't mean to be jealous of Cameron, but I am. Maybe Kayla got to me more than I realized.

When we get home, Mom and Thomas are already home. They're sitting at the kitchen table, working on Thomas's spelling words, and I catch myself smiling goofily. My little family always makes me smile. I actually wish Dad were here to make this picture perfect. Cade Swanson from a year ago would think Cade Swanson today had gone crazy. Maybe I have.

"Oh," Mom smiles. "Isaiah, your mom dropped some stuff off for you today."

Isaiah perks up noticeably. He's hoping it's a truce. He's hoping it's a sign for him to come home, at last. When he takes the lid off the box, however, he wilts. Tears run down his face almost immediately. When I look over his shoulder, I see it's a stack of all the art he's done for class. Poking out from the stack is the edge of a perfect attendance award. He starts to sort through the pile. There are honor roll certificates. Star Student awards. There are letters of recognition from teachers.

"Oh, no," Mom wilts, too. "I should have looked in it first. Oh, sweetie, I'm so, so sorry."

"Just stop," I tell her more sternly than I intend. "You didn't know, okay."

"She's awful," he weeps. "She's cutting me out of the family."

"No," I say quietly. "No, she's not. She's just trying to hurt you right now. She's trying to seem superior and powerful."

"No," Isaiah shakes his head. "She did this to my brother and sister. She cut them out, too. It took her four years to forgive them for leaving her. This Christmas was the first time I've seen them since they left."

I've never wished actual, physical pain on anybody before this moment. But I want Betty Rosenthal to suffer. I want her to hurt the way that she's hurting Isaiah. I want her to tumble down a staircase and break every bone on the way down. I want a piano to fall on her head.

"She'll come around," Mom says softly.

But it's no good. Isaiah is broken all over again. Just when I thought we had patched him up and glued him back together, he's in pieces again. I picture him as a vase, fissures and cracks running through him. No. Isaiah is strong; he will survive. He will rise up.

When he's at work, I set to work more on The In-Between. Isaiah and I stand hand-in-hand, staring into the future. Isaiah is covered in cracks and fissures, his skin pale as porcelain. I gild his cracks with gold, like Japanese pottery. He's beautiful, my Kintsukuroi boy.

I've determined to do a series of him, this Kintsukuroi boy, broken but repaired with gold, more beautiful and stronger than before. More interesting and determined. His scars sparkle, and he doesn't hide from them. Once Isaiah finishes repairing himself, he will be more beautiful than any Kintsukuroi boy I can imagine.

"That's beautiful," Mom says from behind me as I paint the last of Isaiah's gold-gilded scars. "I don't know how you come up with all of this."

She looks around my studio. It's chaotic, but it's mine. There are partially-finished paintings everywhere. There are half-completed drawings in stacks. Art supplies are floating around on every surface. I can tell she wants to talk about the mess, but she doesn't.

"I didn't hear you knock," I say, not pointedly.

"I didn't; sorry," Mom says softly. "I just wanted to come to check on you."

Are my parents really that worried about me? They've both been checking on me a lot lately. They've been more concerned for my mental health since

Isaiah moved in than they have been at any other point in my life. I almost laugh at the absurdity of it. Mom didn't worry about me whenever I was playing parent to Thomas. She didn't worry about me when I did most of the cooking and cleaning. Only now that she has time to worry.

"I'm okay," I smile, putting my paintbrush down and turning to look at her. "Why do you ask?"

"I'm just concerned," Mom crosses her arms and sits on the couch. "You've been pushing yourself hard for a long time. And now you're supporting Isaiah, too. It's a lot for an eighteen-year-old."

I nod. She's right. It is a lot. It's always been a lot. I know the bags under my eyes aren't secrets. I know I've been looking flabby and exhausted. But soon, I'll be out of here, and Isaiah and I can run away and start our new lives. I don't tell her this; I don't want to hurt her feelings.

"I'm okay," I repeat. "I'm tired all the time. But what teenager isn't, right?"

"You're always in here," Mom says quietly. "Sometimes, I'm afraid you're not sleeping at all."

"Sometimes I'm not," I laugh, off-handed. "I always regret it the next day."

"What I'm saying is you don't have to do all this," Mom says softly. "You don't have to work so hard. I know you're trying to win that art show for the scholarship. But we'll make college work without it. Your dad and I are your parents. We're supposed to make college work for you."

I hadn't considered Dad paying for my college. Even in our new, golden-gilded, fractured state, I haven't allowed myself to think of Dad as a provider for me. I've never considered letting him help me pay for college. I've never really relied on anybody else. I don't know how to, I'm afraid.

"Just take care of yourself," Mom says quietly. She kisses the top of my head. "If you're trying to win this art show for yourself, then work as hard as you want. But if you're trying to win it because you think it'll be easier on me, then don't. It's not worth killing yourself over."

I can't tell Mom that I am terrified of instability. I can't tell her that I'm scared she'll lose her job, that Dad will leave again, that Thomas will start having night terrors again, and I will have to pick up all the pieces again. I'm so tired of picking up pieces. I'm so tired of being the glue that holds things together. I'm running out of gold to gild all the fractures of everybody around me.

"Isaiah's moving out," I tell her after a minute. "He's going to move in with Cameron."

Mom looks oddly relieved. Has she been feeling the stress of having him living with us, too? I hoped it wouldn't be an imposition. Has everybody been feeling the same pressure?

"That'll be nice for him," Mom says, as supportive as possible. "I know he's got to feel so awkward living here with us. It'd be different if you guys were just friends."

I've never found it awkward. I've never found it weird. Why should it be uncomfortable for him?

"Can you imagine if you'd had to live with Betty Rosenthal for a month?" Mom must understand my confusion. "You'd feel weird about it, too. Even if you liked her."

She kisses my head and leaves me to my art. I can see my mother's gilding, too. And my father's. And Thomas's. We're all broken in different ways, aren't we? We're all just searching for someone who won't break us more.

Isaiah comes home late, full of smiles and glee. He and Cameron went out for dinner after their shift.

"He really helped cheer me up," Isaiah explains as we sit in my room. He's already stripped off his work shirt and is standing in a tank top and black shorts. He looks amazing like this. I can't stop smiling.

"I'm glad," I say passively. I'm glad somebody cheered him up, but I wish it had been me. Am I destined to always be on the sidelines?

I have got to stop feeling sorry for myself. Cameron is not trying to steal my boyfriend. I look to the collection of pictures Isaiah gave me for Christmas. Does he still look at me as lovingly after living with me for a month? Have I started to bore him?

I shake my head. I'm being absolutely ridiculous. I've let Kayla get in my head. She always knows how to get to me. She knows how to unsettle me.

I want to work on my Kintsukuroi Boy paintings, but I've hidden them from Isaiah. I don't want him to see them until they're finished.

"Are you okay?" Isaiah reaches his arms out for me to sit beside him on the bed. "You seem off."

"I've just had a weird day," I shake my head. I don't even know how to explain it. I don't even know how to tell him I'm jealous for no reason. I'm too embarrassed to tell him that I'm envious of Cameron; I have no reason to be.

"Wanna talk about it?" he pulls me close to him, and I relax under his touch.

"It's nothing," I sigh. "I'm just feeling the stress of senior year, I guess."

Why did I just lie to him?

"I'm sorry," I shake my head. "That's a lie. I'm just still feeling blindsided by your moving in with Cameron."

He opens his mouth to defend himself, but I cut him off.

"No, it's okay," I force a smile. "I knew you weren't going to live with us forever. I'm not crazy. I just thought your Mom would change her mind, I guess. I thought things would be different."

I thought we'd move out together. I thought we'd run away. We were always supposed to run away. I nearly laugh at how absurd it all seems; this is why I didn't want to get serious at 18 years old. I didn't want to imagine a future. I didn't want to be this hopelessly devoted to somebody this young. I've got a life of my own to build.

"It'll be easier for everybody," Isaiah smiles, nuzzling his face into my hair. "You'll see."

For both our sakes, I hope he's right.

Chapter Twenty-Seven

One good thing that comes from Isaiah moving in with Cameron is I finally have my bed back. I sleep better at night with him gone. Not because I was unhappy, but because there was a 6'9" dreamboat in my bed. We spend much less time together than before, but I fill that time with painting and studying. I keep up with my reading for class through audiobooks. I stay on top of chemistry. I take care of things around the house.

Another good thing is how special our time together becomes. Working around classes and Isaiah's work schedule makes us value the time we do have together. It makes me work more efficiently in my studio so that I can save time for him when he's off. It makes me plan time for my homework, and—by some miracle—I stay afloat in physics.

We hit a routine based on Isaiah's work schedule and fall comfortably into it. Isaiah and Cameron grow closer than Kayla and I ever were, and I feel her absence in a more painful way than I expected I would. Sometimes I even miss her. Some evenings I'm alone in my studio, I hear my parents and Thomas downstairs having fun, and I miss Kayla more than ever. Sometimes I hear my family having fun, and I feel more alone than ever. Introspection and solitude only work for so long before they consume you. Sometimes you have to step outside and experience the real world.

"I saw Martin Kimball today," Dad says one afternoon when he comes home from work.

Home. When did I start considering this place his home? He has a house that he goes to sometimes. We have rooms there. But he's spent considerably more time here.

Sometimes, I even forget my parents aren't actually married. Sometimes I forget that we're not a whole family. And sometimes, I remember that even when my dad was gone, we were more of a complete family than the Rosenthals ever were.

I wonder how my parents manage to hold things together when I choose to spend all my time with the son of the woman who broke them up. Sometimes I wonder if my dad and Betty Rosenthal still talk, and if so, in what capacity. Can they be just friends after everything they've gone through? If my parents could repair their relationship, maybe anything is possible.

"Earth to Cade," Dad waves his hands in front of my face and draws me from my thoughts.

"Oh, sorry, what?" I shake my head like I'm coming out of a trance.

"Martin Kimball," he says again. "I saw him today. He told me he was very impressed with the last piece you did for that charity art event."

I feel myself blush. I hadn't told my parents about it. On purpose. I was kind of embarrassed by it. I don't know why I was, but I was.

"Oh, yeah?" I'm unreasonably excited when Martin Kimball approves of my work. He knows good art when he sees it. He's staked his entire career on convincing people he knows good art.

"It was really good, Cade," Dad smiles and hugs me unexpectedly. "How do you do it? What made you think of putting the men's faces on the lions?"

I shrug. It's weird explaining my creative process to people. It's hard to explain that things just pop into my head, and I have to create them. I can't explain where the inspiration comes from. So, instead, I just shrug.

"It still weirds me out that you were an artist," I admit, trying to change the subject. "Why didn't I know that?"

"We used to do art when you were little, Bucko," Dad smiles but looks confused. Have I forgotten something else from my childhood?

"I don't remember that," I shake my head.

I don't remember much from before he left. Have I blocked out that much? He's only been gone for four years.

"I thought you hated my art," I confess.

He sits down next to me on the couch. His presence is comforting. Until recently, I hadn't realized how much I needed my dad's presence. How had I not missed him more? Did he miss me while he was gone?

I feel myself crying even when I don't mean to. I try to hold it in, but I can't. I never can. I've never been able to.

"What's wrong, Bucko?" Dad puts his arm around me and pulls me in.

I shake my head. I don't want to talk about it. I don't know how to say what's on my mind without it being offensive. And I don't want to offend him.

"If something's bothering you, talk to me," he sounds so kind, so soothing. "We can work through it together."

"Why didn't you miss us?" I heave before I've realized what I've said. "Why didn't you care how we were?"

I feel awful. I don't want to say these things to my dad. But at the same time, I need to say these things to my dad. It's like I've ripped off a bandage, and now I can really start to heal.

"What?" He asks so softly I can barely hear him. "Oh, Cade, no."

He holds me tight for a minute, and I hear his voice tighten. Is he crying?

"I wondered and worried about you two every day," his voice aches. I see him as a cat, stuck in a tree and afraid.

"I worried about your Mom every day," he's shaking. Is he facing his own demons?

"Then why didn't you call? Why didn't you ever come back?" I can't control the downpour of tears. I can't prevent the heaving that's taken residence in my chest. And I don't try to.

"It's complicated, Bucko," he says, and I think he's trying to dismiss me. But instead, he breathes in deep, trying to collect his thoughts into words.

"I was embarrassed," he says softly. "I don't have any good reason, Cade. I was embarrassed. I tore our family apart. And there was no way I could ever apologize or make it right."

"So, you just left?" I sniffle. I'm being ridiculous. He doesn't owe me an explanation. He doesn't owe me anything.

"It's more complicated than that," he says, but not angrily. "And it's exactly that."

Dad breathes in. He holds me close, and I'm not sure if he's supporting me or if I'm supporting him.

"Have you ever tried to ignore a problem until it goes away?"

I think of Kayla. I think of the growing chasm between us. I picture us on opposite sides of a bridge that's crumbled. That bridge has been broken for a long time.

"If you ignore it, it's something you can avoid dealing with," he explains. "But the longer you ignore it, the guiltier you feel when you finally confront the situation."

I know what he means. I know what he's saying. It is difficult to come back when you've ignored something for so long. It's like the hole in the floor of our old house. The landlord never fixed it. Because he'd ignored it so long, he'd distanced himself for so long that fixing it would be like admitting defeat.

"But we're your kids," I sob quietly. "I didn't have a dad."

"Oh, Cade," his shoulders slump. Now it's apparent I'm supporting him. "No. No. It was never about you. It was never about you guys."

"It was always about us, Dad," is all I can say. We wrap our arms around each other and mutually cry.

Suddenly, the magic comes back to me. I'm hit with a memory so vivid and vibrant and complete it surprises me.

"*Arrorró mi niño, arrorró mi sol,*" my mom sings softly. I'm in my parents' bed, holding tightly to a stuffed lion I ironically named Tyger.

"*Arrorró pedazo de mi corazón,*" She sings softly, running her hand through my sweaty head. I'm running a fever and can't keep my eyes open.

"*Este niño lindo, se quiere dormir,*" my dad joins in softly. They sing a beautiful duet. I feel a smile cross my face. I'm in a dreamy state. I'm the happiest I've ever been.

That was it. That was the special thing, the magic. Dad used to sing with my mother. They used to sing all the time. But that lullaby was their gift to me, sung in perfect harmony.

I smile through my tears as I'm drawn back to the present. Dad is through crying, but neither of us lets go. The years apart keep us together for longer than I'd have ever expected.

The door opens, and Mom and Thomas come in laughing. There we are, Yin and Yang again. I'm crying, and Thomas is laughing. Something about our duality is comforting. Something about us being opposites unites us. Dad and I pull ourselves together, and I catch myself smiling again. We're a family again. The Swansons may be broken, but we are whole.

"Is everything okay?" Mom asks when she sees me and Dad.

"Yeah," I smile, wiping my face. "We were just talking. You know me. I cry too much."

"No such thing," Mom says softly. She doesn't ask for any explanation, and I'm glad for it.

Mom and Dad look at each other for a long time, and I swear I can see energy spark between them. I stare at them, feeling embarrassed. It's like I'm seeing something intimate. And then I realize they're having a conversation. It is something intimate. They're not speaking, but they're communicating.

And then I realize they're talking about me. The smile that crosses Mom's face is so broad I can't help but be pulled into her magnetism. I'm crashing into the sun. I'm burning my retinas, but I can't stop looking.

"Boys," Mom says quietly as she sits beside me on the couch. "Your father and I have something we want to tell you."

Oh, God, I think. *They're pregnant. I cannot raise another brother.*

Thomas climbs onto the couch with us, squeezing himself into a space between Mom and me that doesn't really exist. We're cozy, and I feel warm, inside and out.

"We're going to Disney World?" Thomas asks excitedly.

"Well, kind of," Dad laughs. "I mean, that's part of it."

Okay, I think. *They're not pregnant.* But why are we going to Disney World?

Thomas cannot hold back his excitement. He shrieks with joy and laughs almost maniacally. He's overwhelmed by joy.

"What's the rest of it?" I ask, always the level-headed one.

"Well," Mom says like she's searching for words she can't find. "Your father and I have been spending a lot of time together lately."

Mom's stating the obvious. I just want her to tell me what is going on. It's driving me crazy. She's not usually one to talk in circles.

"And I think things have been going well," Dad interrupts, wrapping his arm around me and pulling me close. I feel six years old again when he pulls me tight. I feel too old to have my dad hugging me like this, but I don't say anything.

"Thomas hasn't had a single night terror since you've come back," I add, nodding. At first, it upset me. I wanted to be enough for Thomas. I wanted to be all he needed. I wanted to be enough for my family.

"And you've been smiling more," Mom runs her hand through my hair. "It's been so nice to see."

"Isaiah likes your smile," Thomas says matter-of-factly. "He told me one time when I asked him why he likes you."

I feel my cheeks warm. I'm smiling goofily, and I look from Mom and Dad to see my own smile reflected back at me on their faces.

"And you've been singing again," I tell Mom since we're pointing out all the things that are better. Who would have ever thought that Dad was the missing piece in all of this? After all that. After everything. Who would have thought I'd ever be able to forgive him?

"Well, I'm glad we're all in agreement that things are good," Dad laughs. "What your mother is trying to tell you is we're getting married."

"What?" I say over Thomas's excited wails.

"We're getting married," Mom says. She's practically glowing.

I don't know what to say. Are you supposed to congratulate your parents when they're getting married? The kid in me—that part that's reawakened since my dad returned to us—is incredibly happy. The skeptic in me—that part that's had to hold my family together for four years—is apprehensive. Part of me can't wait for us to be whole again. And part of me is afraid of what will happen when he shatters us again.

No, I think. *Not* when, *but* if. *Maybe he won't run this time.*

"I know it's a lot," Mom says, stroking my hair. "And it's all happening really quickly."

She's saying exactly what I'm thinking. But hearing it all in her voice somehow validates my fears. It feels okay to question things when Mom affirms me like this.

"We're going to wait until this summer," Mom sounds so happy, I don't want to ruin this for her.

"We've got a lot of things to talk about," Mom continues. The way she says it, I know that she means *we* as a family, not *we* as my parents.

"Where are y'all going to live?" I ask. "Dad's house is bigger. But it's not fair to make Thomas move twice in one year."

"What do you mean 'y'all?'" Dad asks, laughing. "You're moving with us."

"I'll be going to college in the fall," I explain passively. "It won't matter to me where you live."

What I really mean is *when I move out, I'm not coming back*. But I don't say this.

"Dad's house is bigger, but Thomas is comfortable here," I continue.
Mom raises an eyebrow at Dad.

"Cade," she asks softly. "Is this really about Thomas?"

"Yes," I say emphatically. But it's not.

It's about a lot of things. It's about nothing. It's about a world I can't describe and a problem that doesn't exist yet, but has always existed.

"Well, that's some of what we'll have to talk about," Mom says comfortingly. How does she remain so calm when I'm freaking out?

"Tell me about Disney World," Thomas says impatiently. "What does you getting married have to do with Disney World?"

So, Mom and Dad tell us their plans to get married at the courthouse and then fly us away on a family vacation, the first one since Thomas was three. I can't even imagine a world where Mom doesn't work for a whole week because she's on vacation, not because she's lost her job. I can't imagine a world where we throw all caution to the wind and take a vacation. I'm still stunned.

"We thought maybe Isaiah could come, too," Dad says. "If he can get the time off work, I mean."

I'm more shocked than I have any right to be. Who are these people? Are these really my parents?

"Are you sure?" I'm dubious, suspicious. "I mean, for real?"

"Sure," Mom smiles. "You guys will be sharing a room with Thomas. We've got nothing to worry about."

She gives me a knowing wink. I should I guessed my mom would have thought of everything. She always does. She's the smartest.

"I need some time to process this," I announce to my family. I go upstairs and grab my cell phone. It's Monday; Isaiah's not working. I text him asking if he wants to hang out. He nearly immediately responds. He can't. He's spending time with Cameron.

My vision goes red for just a minute. I have to calm myself down before texting back. I tell him that's fine and I'll see him later. I worry that my message sounds rude. I'm angry that he's choosing to spend time with Cameron over me. I fear that as my family is gluing itself back together, my relationship is falling apart.

I gather up my sketching supplies and throw them in my backpack.

"I'm going out," I tell Mom and Dad. "There's a sketching class at the Arts Council tonight."

And before they can agree, I'm in the car and blasting music as loudly as my old sound system will go. The February air is cold, and it's been dark for an hour already. Outside looks as awful as I feel. February is ugly. February is the worst month. T.S. Eliot was wrong. April is not the cruelest month.

When I pull into the Arts Council parking lot, I realize I have no idea what I'm in for. Will Thad, and Cathy, and Josiah even remember me? Were they serious about their offer to hang out? I need a friend in the worst kind of way. Would they even want to be my friends? They're in college. I decide I need to chill out and enter the building.

"Cade!" Cathy calls as soon as I enter the building. Her hair is lavender, and I almost don't recognize her. Josiah looks up from beside her, his septum ring glinting in the bright overhead lights. Thad smiles a crooked half-smile and waves me over. I feel oddly at home. I feel accepted.

"No cute guy?" Thad asks.

"This isn't really his thing," I explain.

I allow myself to be led around by them. They introduce me to several local artists. I recognize a couple of names who shared space with me at the *PRIDE* show. I recognize a couple of names of people who have had art on display at Kimball before my own show. I am surprised all of these successful artists still come to sketching class. I'm more surprised when they all recognize my name.

Before much time has passed, a woman with a sword takes place on a pedestal in the middle of the room. She's tall and curvy with long blonde hair that falls in waves down her back. We all get out our sketchbooks and begin sketching. Before I have the opportunity to draw anything comprehensible, she changes her pose. I find a new spot in my book and try again. Again, I'm not finished when she changes poses. One minute is not long enough to draw a person.

I look around me at the other artists, all hard at work. Everybody is churning out incredible sketches. They're all getting proportions perfectly. Cubist Cathy draws beautiful, crazy, crooked, unique versions of the warrior in front of us. I try harder. I work faster. I leave out details. But nothing I create looks like the girl in front of me. How am I failing so hard?

"It's okay," Thad says softly when he sees my frustration. "Quick figure sketching is a lot different than your photo-realism. Just loosen up and enjoy it."

I try to do as he says. Things get better, but not great.

Before I know it, 20 minutes have passed. The warrior steps off her platform and leaves the room. The artists all applaud her as she goes.

"This is hard," I say under my breath. Cathy smiles supportively.

"Now's the best part," Josiah stands and heads toward a coffee pot and a table of snacks.

"Is it over?" I raise an eyebrow. Did I drive all the way out here for twenty minutes of sketching?

"Of course not," Thad answers with a mouth full of brownie. "There'll be another model in a little bit."

When we've finished snacking, we again take our places in the circle. A male model takes the platform next. I reach into my bag and start looking for another pencil. By the time I look back up, the model has dropped his robe, and the most beautiful ass I've seen in my entire life is staring back at me.

I breathe in deep, steel myself, and start sketching. By the time the minute is up, all I've drawn is the beautiful ass, dimpled and muscular. I couldn't manage to see any of the rest of his body.

He changes poses, and I get to work, sketching the rippling muscles on his back, the strength in his shoulders. It is much easier for me to draw this model than it was the warrior princess, that's for sure.

"Much better," Cathy smiles, winking at me. Her cubist version of the model makes me giggle. Why would you draw this beautiful man in anything but realism?

Another couple of poses pass before the model turns his face toward us. I sketch a slender torso, the gentle line where his neck meets his shoulder. I sketch a strong jaw. Then I look at his face for the first time.

"Shit," I say before I realize I've said anything. "Dylan?"

This cannot be happening to me. Dylan? Of course, the model is Dylan. That's how my life always works. Of course, I've just filled a sketchbook with pieces of Dylan. All the pieces that add up to the whole that is the bad decision I almost made.

He winks at me, his smoldering eyes holding my attention longer than I'd like to admit. He changes to a new pose, placing his hands on his butt and thrusting his pelvis toward me. I close my eyes and try to clear my head. This is a sketching class. I have to be professional.

I sketch him cautiously. I look at him as little as possible. I never make eye contact with him. Until I do. He licks his lips slowly. I scribble so furiously I snap the lead out of my pencil. I don't think about his bronze skin. I don't think about his smile. I just find a new pencil and continue drawing as if my life depends on it. It's unreal how twenty minutes can feel like sixty years when you're uncomfortable.

"And time's up," somebody—an angel, maybe—says at last. I let out a deep sigh. How long have I been holding my breath?

Dylan bends over to grab his robe but does not don it. Instead, as I pack up, he walks over to me.

"Hey, Cade," he smiles, those smoldering eyes catching my attention against my will. "It was nice modeling for you."

He's standing uncomfortably close. He's naked. He's sexy, and he's cocky, and he's disgusting. I try to lean down to pick up my bag, and I'm face to face with his crotch. I sit up quickly.

"Yeah," I chuckle uncomfortably. "It was, um, it was nice drawing you."

It's not a lie.

"If you ever need a model, let me know," he leans in and kisses my cheek softly in front of everybody there. I grow rigid in my seat. I grow red. I grow four inches tall run away as quickly as possible, forgetting my bag and all.

"As you can see," he winks one more time in that way that only Dylans-with-a-y can get away with. "I think we could definitely go longer than twelve seconds."

I want to die. Somebody shoot me right now.

I expect Dylan to walk away once he's done making a scene, but he doesn't. He just hovers. Naked and confident and annoying. Most of the other artists are on their way out, none of them bothered by Dylan's blatancy or nakedness. Cathy, Thad, and Josiah, however, stare unabashedly.

"Do I have a chance with him?" Cathy asks Thad quietly. She's practically drooling.

"Nobody has a chance with him," Thad says, mesmerized. "Except apparently Cade. How is this even fair? I'm cute. I'm talented."

"Of course, you are, sweetie," Cathy says mocking comfort. She pats his face.

"Don't act like you're not impressed," Dylan smirks as I finally finish packing up, flushed and irritated.

"I've seen better," I lie. I've not seen Isaiah's body, but I know it doesn't look like Dylan's. Not that it matters.

"Where's that boyfriend of yours?" Dylan asks as I stand. We're inches apart. I can feel the heat of his body. I refuse to take a step back, though. This is a struggle for dominance, and I'm not going to be the first to back down.

"Why's it matter?" I sling my back over my shoulder. I'm staring into Dylan's smoldering eyes. I'm embarrassed that this is happening in front of everybody. I'm embarrassed that it's Dylan. I'm embarrassed that Dylan knows how sexy he is. I'm embarrassed that I know that Dylan thinks I'm hot. He told me so.

"I just figure he's not around," he's so close, I can feel his breath. "We could finish what we started at that party."

"I'd rather not," I sigh. "I made a mistake, okay."

Dylan pulls me close, and I struggle against him. He presses his body against mine, and his arousal grows obvious.

"Mistakes are meant to be made," he whispers in my ear.

I push away from Dylan, and at the same time, Thad pulls him away by his shoulder.

"That's enough, dude," Thad says protectively. "Put on your robe. Go take a cold shower. What the hell is wrong with you?"

I'm grateful for my new friends as Dylan stalks away, donning his robe. Cathy comes to check on me, and I am shaken but smiling. It's nice to have friends again. I agree to go with them to get dinner. I text my parents and tell them I'll be out late.

We decide where to go and make our way to our cars in the parking lot. Thad, Josiah, and Cathy pile into a beat-up Civic.

Dinner is nice. We laugh. I get to know my new friends. We bond almost immediately. And for the first time in my life, I'm with people like me. I'm with artists who see the world differently and grew up in dirty houses. I'm with people whose parents worked two jobs, and nobody had a private jet or owned a business. I'm with people who *get* me, and I feel completely accepted and completely me and completely free. And not once do I worry about Isaiah or Cameron or Kayla. And it's the most glorious feeling.

Chapter Twenty-Eight

Cameron and Isaiah are laughing obnoxiously loudly as I join them at the lunch table. Kayla makes eye contact with me and raises her eyebrows.

See, her look tells me. *I told you so.*

I ache because I haven't made Isaiah laugh like that in a long time. Maybe not since we started dating. I ache because Isaiah's always busy lately. I ache because I'm knee-deep in art when he's not busy, trying to finish my portfolio for the art show. I ache.

"Hey, hot stuff," Isaiah smiles as I take my obligatory seat next to him.

Has our flame burned out already? I feel like a Bangles song. I feel like I have no idea what's going on. Nothing has changed. Everything has changed.

"Hey, babe," I smile and lean into him. His presence is still comforting, even if I feel so unstable.

I know I should talk to him and sort things out. I know I should tell him how I feel. But I don't want to make things awkward if there's really nothing to worry about.

I wish I had somebody to talk to. Isaiah was usually my confidante, but the problem is him. Kayla and I haven't spoken since January. Thad, Josiah, and Cathy are friendly enough, but I can't confide in them. I'm more alone than I've ever been. I don't even have Mom anymore. Dad's taken her back.

"What's wrong?" Isaiah puts his arm around me. I don't pull away, even though I want to.

I notice Cameron out of the corner of my eye. He looks concerned for me. I must really look awful if the homewrecker is concerned.

You've got to stop, I tell myself. *Cameron is* not *a homewrecker.*

"Just tired," I sigh, which isn't a lie. I've been pushing myself hard to keep up with school and keep my art going. I've devoted every ounce of creativity in me to the *Kintsukuroi Boy* series, telling the whole story of a beautiful broken boy across mediums. I've shown the story evolve from humble beginnings in pen and ink to acrylics, watercolors, and pastels. I've mixed mediums and created cohesion in my pieces that I wasn't expecting. I've remade my portfolio completely since January. And my brain feels strained perpetually.

"I'm sorry," Isaiah looks concerned. His massive hand rubs my neck, and I melt into a useless puddle.

"You're tense," he kisses me just behind my ear. It sparks electricity through my body, and suddenly I'm wide awake.

"The title of my autobiography," I laugh.

"You guys are disgusting," Cameron laughs, throwing a napkin at us. "I'll find that one day, right?"

See, I tell myself. *Cameron's not a homewrecker.*

"You'll find that one day," I smile at Isaiah so broadly I feel my nose crinkle.

Why is it so hard to doubt his loyalty when we're together and so easy when we're apart? Am I projecting my insecurities? Am I trying to make our relationship fall apart because my parents did? What does it mean that theirs is repaired, but I'm still trying to break my own?

"Are we going to do anything for Valentine's Day?" I ask Isaiah. I've been trying to ask him in private, but he's always with Cameron lately. Cameron's our perpetual third wheel. Or maybe I'm the third wheel.

I see his face drop.

"I mean, we don't have to," I try to say quickly. "It's just you're my first boyfriend, and I didn't know, and I'm not really sure how this works."

It's just that I made you another flipbook, and those things take forever to make, and I know I've already made you a flipbook, but they're the best way I can show someone I love them, my brain rambles even after my mouth has stopped.

"I want to," Isaiah finally says when he sees I'm done. "But I have to work Valentine's Day. Can we go out for dinner on Sunday instead?"

I relax. He does want to see me. He does want to celebrate. I have got to learn to stop freaking out. Isaiah still likes me.

"That'd be great," I smile.

But it's not great. Because Isaiah's not working on Valentine's Day when I swing by to surprise him at his usual break time. Isaiah's scheduled to be off tonight, they tell me as I show up overdressed for a pizzeria. The rose and chocolates in my hand look ridiculous as I walk dejectedly back to my car. Why did Isaiah lie to me?

I sit in my car and try to pull myself together. I'm not going to cry. Not tonight.

I drive to Cameron's house, the house where Isaiah is temporarily boarding, and I sit in the driveway for a second. Only Cameron's car is here. His brothers are either at work or on a date. His dad must be at work. He's an executive chef at a restaurant; there's no way he has tonight off.

I ring the Mathis' doorbell and hear footsteps padding down the stairs. The door opens, and Isaiah stands there in a tank top and shorts. Cameron is not far behind wearing only shorts, his fit body glaring at me victoriously. I feel my mouth drop open. I look from Cameron to Isaiah and back again.

"Cade," Isaiah says, his voice shocked and embarrassed.

"Happy Valentine's Day," I throw the rose and chocolate at him. I reach into my jacket pocket, fish out the flipbook, and throw it at him for good measure.

I am going to cry tonight. I'm going to cry hard. I'm going to climb in my bed and curl up and pray never to see Isaiah Rosenthal or Cameron Mathis ever again.

"Cade, I can explain," Isaiah calls after me as I climb into my car and slam the door. I speed out so quickly my tires squeal.

My phone rings a hundred times as I drive. I ignore it every time. I can't believe this. I saw all the signs. Kayla warned me.

I can't believe Isaiah would do this to me. On Valentine's Day. It's not even an actual holiday. It's not even anything. But still. I can't believe he would do this to me.

My phone rings another time as I pull into my own driveway. I ignore it again. I can't talk to him. Every time I'm finally happy, something comes along to screw it up again.

I open the front door to my house. Chanel No. 5 wafts through the house, and Mom is standing in the living room in a red dress and pearls.

"Cade," Mom breathes. "We were worried. We've got to leave for our date, and you weren't answering."

"What happened?" Mom stops mid-thought when she sees me. She crosses the room and pulls me into her, but I pull away. I don't want to be held. I don't want to be comforted.

"Isaiah said he had to work tonight, so I went to see him. But he didn't have to work. He was with Cameron," I'm crying so hard I don't know if I even make any sense.

I try to pull myself together. I feel guilty for crying to Mom. She's happy. She's going on her first Valentine's date in four years, and she's going with the man she's loved since high school. I can't ruin this for her.

"Y'all go," I try to say calmly. "You're going to miss your reservations."

When Dad comes out, he looks as amazing as my mom. He's dressed to the nines in an Armani suit. His hair is slicked back. They look like movie stars. They look like the silver screen, just like they used to when I was little.

"No," Dad says firmly in a way that surprises me. "It's okay."

Dad pulls me into a hug, and I try not to get tears on his Armani.

"We'll go out another night," he says gently. "You shouldn't have to take care of your brother tonight."

I look to Mom apologetically, but she just smiles and nods.

"I'll make some hot chocolate," she smiles and disappears into the kitchen.

I don't want hot chocolate. I don't want anything. I want this empty feeling in the pit of my stomach to close. I want the ache to go away. I want Isaiah to be here. I want Isaiah to not be here.

I stalk up into my bedroom and fall face-first into my bed. I cry so hard I heave. I feel myself fall apart. I feel myself shatter, and there's nothing I can do to control it. Just as I was becoming whole, I'm in pieces again.

My phone rings several times in a row. I don't reach for it, but eventually, it stops ringing.

"Now's probably not the best time, Isaiah," Mom says gently into the phone. I don't know why she's answered it. I wish she would have just let it ring. I wish she'd have let Isaiah keep trying to call me. I want to know that he still wants to chase me.

"I won't give him that message," Mom says, her voice is stern. "You know our doors are always open to you if you want to come here and try to explain, but I'm not a messenger."

She ends the call and sits on the bed beside me. I hear the clink of a heavy mug of hot chocolate on my bedside table. She runs her hands through my hair, but she says nothing. I say nothing. I cry so hard I'm afraid I'll dehydrate. I cry so hard, I hope I'll shrivel up. I cry so hard.

"I hate him," I finally tell Mom when I've found words again. "I hate Cameron, and I hate him."

"You don't mean that," Mom says gently like she's talking to something frail and fragile, like a baby bird. "Maybe you misjudged what's happening."

"He lied to me, Mom," this is what I keep coming back to.

I argue with myself that maybe I did misunderstand. Maybe absolutely nothing was happening. Maybe Cameron really is just the best friend Isaiah's ever had. Maybe. But Isaiah lied to me. He lied to me.

"I know, baby," she says softly. "I don't know what to say. There's no handbook for things like this. You just have to trust your heart."

And we say nothing for a while. Eventually, I sit up and drink my hot chocolate. I don't say anything to Mom. She leaves me to myself after a while, and I walk into my art studio.

All around me are my Kintsukuroi Boy in various states of brokenness. He smiles a broken, beautiful smile at me. He surrounds me. But the Kintsukuroi Boy that flows out of me tonight is not happy or beautiful. He's pleased with himself. He leans against a croquet mallet, staring at the heap of porcelain behind him, a face sitting whole on the pile on top. The face belongs to the porcelain boy who has been repairing Kintsukuroi Boy the entire time.

I'm not sure how long I've been working when I hear a knock on my door.

CHAPTER TWENTY-EIGHT

"Who is it?"

"Can we talk?" It's Isaiah.

"No," I'm covered in paint. I've used watercolor, and pastel, and acrylic on this piece. There's gold paint everywhere. I'm as much of a wreck on the outside as I am on the inside.

"Please?" He sounds desperate.

"Go away, Isaiah," I sigh. I don't want to cry anymore over him.

"We'll run away," he says softly against the door. "We'll move to Hot Springs and drive the Duck tours."

"Stop it," I'm angry. "I don't want to run away with you."

I open the door, and he stumbles. He'd been leaning against the door, whispering.

"You lied to me," I say flatly. My voice is raw. My eyes sting. I'm covered in paint and pastel dust, and I must have a crazed look in my eye.

"I'm sorry," he says. He genuinely sounds sorry.

"I'm sorry doesn't fix this!" I slam my studio door. I don't want him in there. I don't want him to see my paintings. I don't want him to know how much of him is there.

"Cade," he sighs. "I'm sorry, okay."

"I can't do this," I sigh. I lean my back against the wall and slide down slowly.

"Listen to me," he's desperate, now. He slides down beside me. He doesn't try to touch me. He knows better than to touch me right now.

"What?" I've never been this mean to anybody, and it hurts. I've never been this mean to Kayla. How are people this mean?

"I didn't lie to you," he sighs.

"So, you and Cameron work from home, now, half-dressed?" I spit. "That's certainly a weird way to deliver pizza."

"We weren't at work," he admits. "But we were supposed to be. We were overstaffed, so we both got sent home."

"So, then you guys went home and stripped down and, what?" I'm being aggressive. I have no right to be. But I feel like I have every right to be.

"I was about to call you, Cade," he says softly. "I was about to see if you wanted to come over. Cameron was changing because he was going to go out to that new teen club. We were going to have the house to ourselves."

I feel bad. But I don't. He could have texted me before I made a fool of myself at the pizzeria. He could have texted me before I made a fool of myself at Cameron's house.

"What's going on?" Isaiah says this in the grand *what's going on in life* kind of way. Like he knows there's more going on than I'm letting on.

"I don't know," I finally say. Instinctively I lean in toward him.

"A lot." I sigh. "Everything."

"I miss having friends," I sigh.

"You have friends," Isaiah comforts me. He pulls my head close to his shoulder.

"I don't," I shake my head. "I have you and Cameron. But when I'm with you two, I feel like the third wheel."

Isaiah breathes in, about to defend himself, but I cut him off.

"No, it's okay," I say. "I'm having trouble with you and Cameron being friends. And I think the problem is me. I'm always the problem. Isaiah, I'm a time bomb."

"You are *not* a time bomb," he whispers. "Stop saying that."

"I am," I sigh. "That last time I talked to Kayla, she told me Cameron was trying to break us up. She said that Cameron wants to date you, and he thinks I'm not good enough for you."

"What a bitch," Isaiah laughs in disbelief. "That's not true, Cade."

I just shake my head. I don't know how to explain what's going on. I feel awful. I feel like a failure. I feel like I'm hurting Isaiah more than I ever realized.

"I know it's not true," I finally admit, because I *do* know it's not true. "But it feels true. And that's what worries me."

"You don't have to worry," he holds me close. "I'll let you know if I ever stop loving you."

I weep for a while into his shoulder. I don't know how to explain the feeling inside of me. I ache. All the time.

"I'm so sorry," I whisper. "I keep ruining everything. I keep ruining things."

"You don't ruin anything," Isaiah uses his fingers to pull my chin upwards, so I have to look at him. "I just wish you'd talk to me when there's something wrong."

"There's always something wrong," I say flatly. This is the first time I've ever articulated this, but it feels true. There is always something wrong. I'm not supposed to feel like a time bomb.

"I think I need help. I think I have depression or something," I tell Isaiah. I'm no longer an independent, sentient human being. I've crawled into his lap, and he's wrapped his arms around me, protecting me from the world. I want to stay here forever. It's the only place I feel safe.

"Then we'll get you help," he whispers, rubbing his hand on my back. "It'll all be okay. You can go see a doctor; it's not a big deal. I'll go with you if you want."

"Yes, please," I imagine us suspended in time like this. Forever. Me wrapped in Isaiah's arms. Me small and pitiful and meek, covered in paint and chalk, being held together by my beautiful, broken Kintsukuroi boy. I capture this image in my head to paint later. This will be the final piece in my portfolio. This will be how I end my four years of high school art.

"I loved the flipbook," he whispers in my ear.

It was a damned good flipbook. It shows Isaiah and me running off the edge of a cliff. As our feet leave the earth, we're transformed into massive eagles soaring above and beyond existence. We fly high into the sky until we break out of the earth's atmosphere. We make a sharp turn and dive into the earth, further and further down. We catch flame, tuck our wings close to our body, and dive into the earth's surface. We leave a crater from our impact. The scene pans down into the crater, and there we lie, hand-in-hand, laughing.

"Thanks," I smile and nuzzle my face into his neck.

"Isaiah?" I'm quieter than I mean to be, and at first, I don't think he hears me.

"Yeah?" He's holding me tightly, but also gently like he's afraid I will break.

"I love you."

"I love you, too, Cade." And I know he means it.

Days later, when the phone rings, I'm sitting in my art studio, working on my final piece for my state show entry.

"Mr. Swanson?" I don't recognize the voice, and at first, I think it's somebody trying to commission a piece of art. I've gotten two or three calls a week since my show.

"Speaking," I say, realizing how arrogant that sounds.

"Hi, Mr. Swanson, this is Denita Markham from Dr. Lacefield's office. We've got the results from your bloodwork. When can you come in for us to discuss them with you?" The nurse on the other line sounds pleasant, but that doesn't stop me from worrying. What if it's something worse than depression? What if I'm dying?

"Do you have any appointments available this afternoon?" I want to deal with everything now. I'm tired of being broken.

Forty-five minutes later, Isaiah and I are sitting in my doctor's office, holding our breath. We don't know what to expect, and it makes me nervous. I'm squeezing his hand too hard for comfort, but he doesn't say anything. His hand swallows mine, and I close my eyes to soak in the feeling. He fills me with warmth. He makes me feel safe.

"Cade," Dr. Lacefield smiles as he enters the room. I shake his hand and smile. "It's good to see you again. Thank you for coming in today. Do you mind if we discuss your lab results with Isaiah here, or would you like him to wait in the waiting room?"

"Oh no," I shake my head and take his hand in mine again. "He has to stay."

Dr. Lacefield smiles and says he understands. He begins to tell me about the tests he ran. He tells me about my lab results and that there are some surprises with my brain chemistry. He explains that I am experiencing depression because of that.

"The good thing," Dr. Lacefield smiles kindly. "Is that we have medicine today that can help most cases."

I feel relieved as he explains this.

"Sometimes people don't understand depression," he continues. "Because it's not something tangible, like a cold, people don't always get that it's a clinical problem."

He tells me how having depression is more than being sad. It's more than feeling blue. He tells me that it's something not to be ashamed of, and it's not something to be embarrassed by. He tells me that it may not be something I live with forever, but it also could be. He gives me hope.

He sends me home with a prescription for an antidepressant and a heart full of hope.

"I'm not a time bomb," I tell Isaiah excitedly when we're back in my car.

"I know you're not," he laughs. "I've been telling you that."

When I get home, prescription in hand, Mom and Dad are speaking in hushed voices. By the way they stop talking, I know that they were talking about me.

"Cade?" Dad calls.

"Yes, sir?" I answer.

Dad meets me in the living room.

"Is everything okay?" He asks, eyeing me and Isaiah and the white pharmacy bag in my hand.

"It will be," I smile.

Chapter Twenty-Nine

February passes, and with it, so do my mood swings. I'd forgotten what it was like not to be a time bomb. Maybe I've always been a time bomb. I apologize to Isaiah every day for my mood swings. I thank him every day for loving me through it. And I apologize to Cameron, which is difficult. Because I have to confess I was jealous of him for nothing. And he forgives me.

March brings rain, always rain. It brings gray skies and my finished collection for my art show. March brings commissions and work. But most importantly, it brings Spring Break. Seven glorious days with no classes. Seven days that Isaiah and Cameron don't have to work that they can come over and hang out. We spend the day at my house so that I can take care of Thomas, and on the nights when Cameron and Isaiah don't have to work, we stay out late.

When the sky blushes pink and orange, we become giants. We become masters of the realm. We grow a hundred times our size and own the world around us. We cram ourselves into mine or Cameron's tiny cars, and we're indestructible. The roads lay out before us like wilderness, waiting to be explored. In those twilight hours, in that In-Between, Isaiah, Cameron, and I become the people we want to be. We're the kings of all the lands.

"What are you guys planning on doing tonight?" Mom asks when she gets home from work. We're itching to leave already.

"We honestly don't have any plans," I tell her. "We just want to go explore, you know?"

"I remembered restlessness," she smiles. "Enjoy it while you can."

We cram ourselves into Cameron's car, feeling every bit as ridiculous as we look. My knees are practically folded up to my chin. Isaiah looks like he's dislocated limbs to fit into Isaiah's passenger seat. Cameron opens the sunroof, so Isaiah's head can poke out and not hit the ceiling. I laugh so hard at the ridiculousness of it all that I forget how to breathe.

"Where are we going?" Isaiah asks as Cameron heads out of town. The asphalt wilderness stretches out before us, waiting to be explored. The sky is going from pink and orange to deep indigo. I can't take my eyes off the beauty of it all.

"To my grandparents' farm," Cameron says nonchalantly. Of course, Cameron's family has a farm. That only seems appropriate for this All-American boy with the crew cut who only drives Fords and owns more camouflage than any person I've ever met.

"When I was little," Cameron says wistfully. "We used to go out to the farm with my mom. We'd go at night, hang out in the cattle pastures, and listen to the sounds. It was my favorite thing."

I've never heard Cameron talk about his family before, and it unsettles me to notice this.

"Before she died," he continues. "The farm was our haven. I haven't been out since she died last year."

My heart breaks for Cameron. Why didn't I know his mom died?

"Thank you for sharing your special place with us," Isaiah says softly.

I expect silence to settle over us, but it never does. We talk about everything and anything until we pull up to the gates of a sprawling farm. The night sky is velvety black, and the stars sparkle like jewels in the heavens. I'm in awe of how beautiful this place is. I'm sad that there are places too beautiful for me to paint.

Cameron's grandparents invite us in for dinner. We enjoy a hearty serving of red beans and rice, and homemade cornbread. It's all delicious and tastes like comfort and love. After dinner, we're treated to chocolate pie with meringue piled so high it looks like it's going to topple over. Cameron's grandparents regale us with tales of growing up and simpler times. At Isaiah's request, we hear the story of how they met, and when they married.

We listen to stories that involve cottonwood trees and fresh lemonade, and I imagine a world like that. I imagine a world without cell phones and social media. I picture front-porch swinging and people playing guitars. I imagine how beautiful a world like that must be.

Once we've eaten our fill and chatted to our heart's content, Cameron leads us to his haven, his special place in the pastures. We trek for what seems hours. The night air is calm and cool and quiet. Isaiah's hand holds tightly to mine, and I can't fight the ridiculous grin on my face.

"Careful," he says quietly. "Someone might think you're happy."

I elbow him and move in closer to him. I'm walking on clouds as we trek in the near dark. Our way is lit only by the glow of the full moon. Suddenly, we step out from the cover of trees and into an open field, and white light washes over us. Breath catches in my throat.

"Oh my God," I say so quietly it's lost in the breeze. "This is amazing."

The moon glitters on an open pond, the reflection broken and rippled by the breeze. The world stands still around us; it's like we've been transported outside of time. I try to capture everything in my mind. I try to remember every detail so I can recreate it.

I see my Kintsukuroi boy smiling as moonlight glints off his gold. I see him smiling into the face of the boy who fixed him, and for the first time, I realize it's not me. His hand is wrapped so tightly around mine we may fuse into one being, but I'm not the person who fixed him. For some reason, I'm okay with that. I'm grateful for Cameron and the magic he's worked to bring Isaiah's smile back. He's the gold-gilder. He's the hero.

We all stand in quiet awe before Cameron falls haphazardly backward onto the soft grass.

"It's chilly tonight," he comments, staring up into the sky. "But the sky is so clear; we can see every star."

Isaiah and I plop down beside Cameron. I can't control the smile on my face. This is the kind of night you read about. This is the kind of night when magic happens. There's something about the way stars sparkle that changes your life, even if just a little bit. There's something about the promise of a clear sky. There's something about this, about here, about now.

CHAPTER TWENTY-NINE

"What are y'all going to do for college?" Cameron asks, staring up at the sky.

"I don't know," Isaiah says. "I had a trust fund that would have paid for whatever I wanted."

I nearly sputter at the idea. I don't know why I'm surprised that Isaiah had a trust fund this big; it's just a world I don't think I'll ever understand. Even if it's a world I live in now. Even if it's a world to which Thomas will grow accustomed.

"You'll get scholarships," I rub his hand with my thumb. "You've got straight A's, and nobody is more deserving than you."

"Everybody's more deserving than me," he laughs, and I know this is modesty, not self-deprecation.

"What about you?" Cameron asks me.

"Well, hopefully, I'll win the art show and have my tuition to art school covered," it's been the goal all year, but I've never actually articulated it. I know it's not a surprise to anybody that this is the plan, but Cameron still seems impressed.

"You'll get it," Cameron says. "Nobody's more talented than you."

I don't respond with modesty because I know it'll come out as self-deprecation.

"And you?" I ask Cameron.

"Probably just Magnolia State," Cameron says passively. "It's a good school. It's close."

And so, we lie for a while, staring at the sky and pondering our futures. We're all wondering what's in store for us and how we'll all fit into each other's life when summer ends. None of us says anything else; none of us wants to be responsible for breaking the silence. The breeze blows past us, and the world starts spinning again. Time resumes while we lie there, but nobody cares.

"I don't want to go to college without you," I tell Isaiah as we walk back to the car. "I don't want to go to the store without you."

"You're going to go to art school," he kisses my temple. "Four years isn't that long."

"Four minutes is a long time without you," I smile and squeeze his hand.

"Can you two stop being disgusting?" Cameron jokes.

We tell Cameron's grandparents goodbye before we leave and cram ourselves back into Cameron's car. And we become giants again. We own the road and the world and everything in it.

"What do you want to do?" Cameron asks as we drive back toward the lights of the city. "The night is still young, my friends!"

So, we do precisely what three eighteen-year-olds with nothing but time do. We go to the city park. It's odd to see it at nighttime. The swings look like somebody just stepped off of them. I picture a kid swinging as high as possible and launching into the air, out of this world, and into another dimension. I picture us swinging in tandem, launching so high we fly into that other world. I imagine me and Isaiah and Cameron shrinking to our seven-year-old selves, climbing the rocket slide and blasting into space and discovering a new planet where everything is green and fresh and beautiful.

"I'll race you to the merry-go-round!" Cameron bails out of his car like it's on fire.

"Not fair!" I call out, struggling to dislodge myself from the back seat. "You got a head start!"

We collapse onto the merry-go-round once we're all there and laugh so loudly, I'm afraid we'll wake the neighborhood. We stare up at the sky and breathe in the chilly spring night. The world grows and shrinks around us as we alternate between giants and children. Isaiah gets up and takes hold of the bar beside him. He takes off at a sprint, running as fast as he can. He runs and runs until we spin into delirium. He leaps onto the platform with us, and we hold on for dear life.

Cameron loses his grip and flies off into the sand. He lies still for a minute before exploding into deafening laughter. I decide to follow suit, and I'm launched to the opposite side of the merry-go-round, knocking my head on a rock. It hurts, but I don't care; I'm having too much fun.

"Y'all are idiots," Isaiah laughs as he stretches out his arms and legs. His limbs take up the entire merry-go-round when he's splayed out like this. His rotations slow until he stops spinning completely. He stands and steadies himself against the dizziness.

"Swings next?" He asks as Cameron and I dust ourselves off.

We take off at a run again toward the swings. As I leap into the seat, I feel like Thomas and immediately start pumping my legs, trying to swing as high as possible. I haven't been on a swing set in years, and the feeling is exhilarating. I look at Cameron and Isaiah. We're swinging in perfect synchronicity. We're giants, and our motions are causing the rotation of the world, the pull of the stars. We're giants, and the night is ours, and the sky opens up to let us find our place that's green.

"3," Isaiah counts out loud.

"2," Cameron shouts into the night air.

"1," I laugh, and we launch ourselves into the sky.

We fly. We're suspended in time and space. I capture this moment a million times in my head. We're weightless. We're one with the stars. There has never before been and never again will be three people who belong to the universe the way we do right now.

And then I see white, and I hear the loudest crunch I've heard in my entire life.

I can't find words to say through the searing pain. My left arm is underneath my body and bent in a way I don't think it should bend. I grit my teeth and suck in hard, trying to form any words.

"Shit," Isaiah says, scrambling to me. "Babe, are you okay?"

Two hours later, I'm sitting in an exam room at the 24-hour urgent care center near the park. I wanted Isaiah to come into the exam room with me, but Mom and Dad insisted on coming with me. I left Cameron and Isaiah in the waiting room to take care of Thomas.

The doctor—a tall man who looks too young and too handsome to be a doctor—explains what the x-ray reveals to me.

"The good news is that it's really easy to read your x-ray," Dr. Singh smiles good-heartedly at me. "The bad news is it's undoubtedly broken."

He points to my x-ray, showing me obvious breaks in both arm bones.

"They're clean breaks. I'll have to reset them and cast them," he smiles a kind smile. "The best news is that you most likely won't need surgery. But you'll be in a cast for a good six weeks, maybe longer."

Six weeks in a cast. My senior year of high school. We're eight weeks from graduation. I laugh at the absurdity of it all. This seems par for the course in the comedy that is my life.

"I don't know if I should have people sign my cast or my yearbook," I laugh half-heartedly.

Isaiah is the first to sign it with a giant heart using a marker from the receptionist's desk at the urgent care. Cameron signs it next with a jagged, slanting signature. Thomas follows suit with an almost illegible version of his name.

"How're you feeling?" Isaiah asks. His eyes bore me, and I forget there's anybody here but him and me.

"Broken," I shrug. "But getting better." In more ways than one.

"I cannot believe you broke your arm jumping off a swing," Mom laughs as we leave the urgent care center.

"I can," Isaiah pokes me in the ribs playfully.

When school rolls back around on Monday, I haven't come up with a good cover story about my broken arm, so I just tell people the truth. I'm met with laughter all day, and I kind of like it. I've never been the type to make people laugh.

"Careful," Isaiah says for not the first time. "People might think you're happy."

"Maybe I am," I smile and look up at him.

"You know what's weird?" I ask him a few steps later. "Usually, when we walk through the hallways, everybody stops and talks to you, and they just look right over me. But slap a neon green cast on my arm, and suddenly people can see me."

"I don't think it's the cast," he says doubtfully. "I think it's you."

I shake my head. That can't possibly be right. I'm the same me. I tell Isaiah so. I ask him if he thinks I'm different.

"Not to me," he squeezes my hand, and I feel the familiar jolt of electricity I always feel when our skin touches. "But I've always seen this side of you."

"This side of me?"

"This happy, smiling side," he explains as we near my next class. "You usually walk the hallways scowling and looking down."

"I do not scowl!" I argue, even though I know it's true.

"When you're happy, nobody can stop looking at you," he smiles. "Your smile lights up the hallway."

I nearly laugh. There's no way that's true. It's his that's blinding. It's the first thing I ever noticed about him. But I don't argue; it's nice to be complimented.

Even Kayla notices. I feel her eyes on me before I see her. She looks awful. Her hair doesn't look like she's brushed it in days and her clothes are wrinkled. This is the height of Kayla's post-break-up slump. I can almost guess her diet at home, the secret pints of ice cream, the roll of cookie dough she hides in the back of the refrigerator. I know she's got cream soda cans underneath her bed.

I raise my arm in greeting, waving with my cast. She shrugs but doesn't wave back. It's the first time I've seen her and not felt anything. I'm not angry at her. I'm not happy to see her. Seeing Kayla across the school commons is like seeing a stranger.

Second hour is chemistry, like every day, and I have it with Kayla, like every day. We haven't acknowledged each other's presence since Christmas. We haven't spoken since the end of Christmas break. Apparently, our truce only lasted through Christmas. Kayla has been giving me the silent treatment, her worst form of punishment. But it's a nice escape for me; I haven't had to deal with her drama in nearly three months.

"Have a good class," Isaiah kisses me, and Kayla breaks character just long enough to look disgusted. I'm petty, but it makes me laugh.

"You're blocking the door," Cameron deadpans to break us up.

This is how it always should have been, I think. *Me, and Isaiah, and Cameron, and the in-between.*

Even broken and bandaged and gilded with gold, together we are giants.

Chapter Thirty

"Mr. Camplin," the school secretary calls over the intercom three days before my portfolio is due for the state art show.

Mr. Camplin and I are buried in paperwork, making sure we've taken care of everything for the portfolio review. I've printed photographs of my works. I've filled out a stack of paperwork detailing my creative process. I've written about artists I admire and feel inspired by. I've poured my entire existence into this portfolio. I've put all my eggs in this one basket.

"Mr. Camplin," the secretary calls again. "Will you please send Cade Swanson to the front office? Ask him to bring his belongings."

The room stills and everybody looks at me. Isaiah makes eye contact with me, but I don't know what to say. Terror runs through my veins. I've never been called to the principal's office, ever. I don't know what I've done to get called to the office.

"I'll hold onto this," Mr. Camplin smiles. "We'll finish it when you get a chance."

I nod. Tomorrow I'll bring all my finished pieces to the school so that Mr. Camplin can submit them to the exhibition. I can't believe this year is almost over. I can't believe that my future will be determined in five days.

"Cade," the secretary smiles sweetly as I enter the office. "Your mom called. Your father is on his way to pick up your little brother from school. She needs you to meet her at your house."

"What's going on?" I ask, worried.

"It's not my news to tell," she says softly. "But you need to go. I just need you to sign here to show you're checking out."

Panic rises up in me. Mom and Dad are both taking off work? There's something wrong. Is something wrong with Thomas? Is that why Dad is picking him up? I'm not in a stable place to drive. I don't know how I'll make it home, I'm so worried. I wish Isaiah could come with me. Or Cameron. Or, hell, at this point, I'd even take Kayla. I don't know how I'll stay focused enough to drive.

I drive home, running through possibilities in my head. When I get closer to my house, I notice a pillar of black smoke in the air.

"No," I say out loud. "No. That's not my house. That can't be my house."

I turn into my neighborhood and see my mom standing on the edge of the road—a firetruck, giant and red and hulking nearby. I park as close to my house as I can and get out and run to Mom.

I've never felt this helpless in my life before.

Everything is ruined.

Everything.

"Mom," I ask, my throat dry. "Are you okay?"

She doesn't say anything. She just wraps her arms around me and pulls me close. The heat of the flames causes me to sweat, but we don't move away. We're as close as we can safely be, and we're watching our entire lives crumble down.

"I'm so sorry, baby," she says as she holds me. "I'm so sorry."

And then I realize what she means.

Everything is ruined.

Everything.

Including my entire art studio. All of my paints. All of my pastels. Hundreds of dollars of materials ruined.

And every single completed painting.

Every. Single. One.

Every piece of my Kintsukuroi Boy. Everything I've done for this art show. Everything. My entire life is literally going up in flames.

"Mom," I gasp. "Mom. It's everything. I don't have anything to make for the art show."

I feel myself fall apart. I crash into her so hard she struggles to stay upright.

"I'm so sorry, baby."

And we just stand, watching the fire. Watching our lives and everything we've worked for be destroyed.

The worst part about a fire is whatever the fire doesn't destroy, the water does. When the firefighters finally have the blaze put out, the remains of our house are a soaked and smoldering mess. Dad and Thomas got here at some point, but I don't know when. Dad is holding Thomas in his arms. Thomas is sobbing uncontrollably. The sobs make me forget my own problems; all I want is to fix things for Thomas.

I see us standing outside the fire, our world strewn around us in ruins.

"What happened?" Thomas finally asks when he's through sobbing.

"We don't know, baby," Mom says gently. "We're going to be okay."

I don't know how she expects us to be okay. I don't know how she expects anything to be okay. My entire future just went down in flames. My entire world just burnt to a crisp. Every drawing pencil I own. Everything. Every canvas. Every shred of hope I had for my future.

Dad puts Thomas down just in time for me to wilt. My face crushes into his shoulder, and I cry harder than I ever have before.

"It's all gone," I sob. "Everything I've worked for. Everything is destroyed. I don't have anything to show. My entire portfolio was in there."

In this moment, I don't want Isaiah, or Cameron, or Kayla. All I want is my dad. All I can think that can make it better is him holding me like he did when I was six and afraid of thunderstorms. Like he did when I was eight, and my pet rabbit died.

"I'm so sorry," Dad repeats over and over.

"Aren't there any pieces you've got anywhere else?" Mom asks. She's always the first to try to fix a problem. She always looks for ways to make things better.

"Nothing at school is good," I shake my head. "All my best stuff is here. My Kintsukuroi Boy was here."

I feel so selfish, being concerned about my art. Everything is gone. All the pictures of our family. All of our clothes. All of our belongings and

Thomas's stuffed animals. My mom's family recipes in the recipe box I built her in the third grade. Everything is gone.

Mom, Thomas, and I weep for a moment, together, while Dad holds us together. He tries his best to gild us with gold, but our fractures may be too big this time. It's possible he doesn't have enough strength to keep us all together.

"Maybe there's a way," Dad says softly, his voice lost and ponderous.

"There's not," I sniffle and shake my head.

"Hear me out," he says; he's got his best fixer voice on. "Your mom has the pictures you gave her for Christmas in her office. I've got some stuff of yours at my house. I'm sure you've given Isaiah something you can use."

I'm surprised at how good this idea is. I do have a collection of work. It's all dispersed, but it exists. I try to think of everybody that has a piece of my art that may let me borrow it. There's Señora LeBlanc with the watercolor made from ash. There's my mom's yin yang. There's dad's pastel, which wasn't very good, but it's something. I gave Cameron and Isaiah flipbooks. Surely, I can't submit flipbooks.

I mourn the loss of all of the paintings I've sold. I don't even know most of the people who bought my pieces at Kimball Art. I might be able to borrow my *PRIDE in the Urban Jungle* piece; Martin Kimball bought it for his personal collection. I start ticking pieces off on my fingers. For the first time since November, I allow myself to dwell on the giant graphite piece I did of Thomas sleeping. His cherubic face could have won my art show.

"I need to make some phone calls," I announce and step away from my family.

I call everybody I can think of. I'm even so desperate as to call Kayla. She has a flipbook. She might even have the piece I did of her and Cameron from my exhibition. As expected, she doesn't answer, but I leave her a voicemail.

I talk to Mr. Camplin. I can't stop my voice from breaking when I'm on the phone with him. His voice sounds sad and distant. I can hear my own pain, my own shattered dreams reflected in his voice.

"I'm sorry, Mr. Camplin," I say. I feel like I've let him down. He was so excited for me to present in this show.

"No, Cade," he says back, sounding old and broken. "I'm sorry. I'm so sorry for you."

When I hang up the phone, hopelessness settles over me. I don't even have half a shot at winning the art show now. Nothing I've done compares to my Kintsukuroi Boy. Nothing I've created will be as good.

I'd put every hope I had into this, and I hadn't even realized it until it was gone.

"Isaiah," I'm saying to his voicemail before realizing I've even dialed his number. "I just wanted to hear your voice."

I breathe in deep; my voice is raw.

"My house burned down. Everything's gone. I just. I need you."

I hang up the phone.

Twenty minutes pass as Mom, Dad, Thomas, and I start to make a game plan for rebuilding and recovering. We'll be moving to Dad's house until we figure out what we're doing. We may live there long-term. It is bigger than our house, after all. Dad says I can use the fourth bedroom as a new art studio. Not that I'll have anything to put in it. It'll take me forever to build my collection up again.

Isaiah and Cameron pull up in Cameron's car. Before the car is stopped, I'm in Isaiah's arms. I feel safe in his arms. I still feel the heat of the flames in his arms. I crumple into a mess in his arms. He strokes my hair and lets me cry, and becomes my strength. In his arms, I am great and strong. With Isaiah and Cameron there, I am giant and indestructible.

"What can we do to help?" Isaiah asks when I've finally pulled myself together.

I put Cameron and Isaiah on art collection duty. I give them a list of people who have art I may be able to borrow for the show. I explain the plan to them. I ask them to talk to Martin Kimball and Señora LeBlanc, and everybody on my list.

"We'll go to the house and get our flipbooks, too," Cameron nods. I'm relieved that he's so ready and willing to help. I feel an odd peace settle over me. I've got my family and Isaiah and Cameron. There's nothing I can't overcome.

Just as quickly as they arrived, they pull away. I feel grateful to have one less thing to worry about.

The day is spent buying new clothes and essentials for our new living arrangements. The day is spent crying and feeling lost. The day is spent, and I am spent. We load Mom's minivan full of new clothes, and shoes, and toiletries. We've bought food and candles and picture frames. We've bought things to turn Dad's house into a home. And no matter what stores we go to, no matter the expense, Dad swipes his debit card without hesitation. I'm not used to this world where we're comfortable. I'm not used to this world where my family can afford to replace an entire house's worth of things in one shopping trip. My head reels over and over at the idea.

"Once we've unloaded all of this stuff, do you want to go to the art store and start trying to replace some of the stuff you lost?" Dad asks.

I consider this but shake my head.

"I can't even begin to think of what I want to replace," I shrug. I feel broken, still. I don't know how to start over again.

"Let me know when you're ready," he smiles. For the billionth time since Christmas, I'm thankful for my family. For the trillionth time, I feel my fractures sealed up and gilded. At what point do I stop being porcelain and become totally gold?

We try to turn Dad's house into a home. Thomas and I have spent a few weekends here, but not long enough to personalize our rooms. Both of our bedrooms are massive. They're so big we almost don't know what to do with them. Both of us have walk-in closets roughly the size of the bedrooms we lived in when our floor had a hole and the dishwasher didn't work. We share a bathroom that looks like something from a resort with a cavernous shower. The guest room is as big as my bedroom, and the closet is so big I could use it as my art studio and have room to spare. This is the life I have always dreamed of living, but it doesn't seem real.

I swallow my anger at my father. While we lived in squalor with dingy wallpaper and sunken-in carpet, he was alone in this giant house. Forgiveness is something you have to practice every day.

As the sun sets, Isaiah and Cameron let themselves into Dad's house. Our house. I practice calling it our house.

Their arms are full of pieces of art, some things I haven't thought about in ages. How did they locate all of this? They start laying out the pieces for me to see. They've both brought their flipbooks. Cameron has the charcoal piece I did of him and Kayla. I don't know how he got it, and I don't ask. Laid out on my bed is my art, a year-in-review. Many of my favorite pieces have been collected. Señora LeBlanc's ashen sugar skull watercolor sits in a beautiful frame. Mom picked up her Christmas present while we were in town. Thomas offers up his Christmas present, as well.

I try to control my emotions as my collection of pieces turns into the most eclectic portfolio known to humanity. But it's incomplete. It's missing my muse. It's missing anything inspired by Isaiah.

"I wish," I start to say, but stop.

"What?" Isaiah asks. His voice tells me he would do anything to make things right for me. He would always do anything to make things right for me.

"Nothing," I shake my head. How can I tell him what I want without seeming ungrateful?

"Just tell me," Isaiah laughs, pulling me close.

"I'm being ridiculous." I laugh. His eyes pierce me, and I feel the truth coming out of me.

"Most of my show had pieces of you," I sigh. "And now all I've got is this flipbook."

"Then let's go," Isaiah grabs me by the hand and leads me to Cameron's car. Cameron stays close on our heels.

"Where are we going?" I ask. Isaiah takes Cameron's keys and folds himself into the driver's seat. We cram in quickly; Isaiah's on a mission, and we don't want to be left behind.

"Where are we going?" I ask again as Isaiah turns onto the freeway. He doesn't answer. He grips the steering wheel with white knuckles. Wordlessly, he puts on his blinker and takes an exit, and I immediately know where we're going.

Before long, we're pulling into the driveway of Rosenthal Manor. It looks as insidious as it did the first time I came. The same fear bubbles up in me again. Is this the first time Isaiah's been back? Why are we here?

"What are we doing here?" I ask.

Isaiah doesn't answer; he just marches to the front door and opens it. I've never seen him so determined. It's oddly attractive.

"Mother," Isaiah calls angrily. Cameron and I are nearly immobilized by fear. We're not sure what will happen, but we don't want to miss whatever it is.

"Isaiah?" A deep voice calls from the kitchen.

A tall, handsome man with Isaiah's honey-and-amber eyes comes from the kitchen. I'm caught off-guard by how much alike Isaiah and his dad look. They have the same square jaw and powerful stance. They have the same smile. Every ounce of softness that Isaiah's face has comes from his dad. He's inherited very little from Betty Rosenthal, and for that, I'm grateful.

I can't turn my gaze away from this standoff between Isaiah and Mr. Rosenthal. They're staring at each other, smiling. Their eyes both shine with held-back tears, but neither of them takes a step toward each other. They're locked in this stupid power struggle that I don't understand.

"Isaiah," Mr. Rosenthal says, then his voice softens, and he pulls Isaiah into a tight hug. His long arms wrap all the way around Isaiah's narrow shoulders, and he holds him close.

"Dad," Isaiah's voice is choked. I feel like I'm watching something intimate and beautiful. I want to avert my gaze, but I don't know where to look or what to do with my hands.

"I'm glad you're home," Isaiah says softly, and I think it's a weird thing to say.

"I'm glad *you're* home," Mr. Rosenthal echoes.

They stand like this for a long time before stepping back and looking at each other again.

"Dad," Isaiah sniffles. "This is Cameron Mathis. I've been living with his family while you've been gone."

Has Isaiah's Dad been out of town this long? This is the first time I've seen him since Isaiah and I met, but I just assumed it's because he worked long hours. Not because he was always out of town.

Mr. Rosenthal shakes Cameron's hand, eyeing him closely. He's inspecting him the same way Mrs. Rosenthal inspected me. I cringe at the memory.

"And this is Cade," Isaiah grabs my hand and pulls me close. I'm embarrassed by the touch, but I don't pull away. "This is my boyfriend."

"Cade Swanson," Mr. Rosenthal extends a massive hand to me. "It's nice to meet you. I've heard a lot about you."

"It's nice to meet you, too, Mr. Rosenthal," I say quietly, my eyes wide in wonder.

"Call me Marcus," Mr. Rosenthal smiles a disarming smile. I can't stop staring into his honey-colored eyes; they're Isaiah's eyes set in someone else's face.

"I've heard only good things about you," he smiles before breaking our handshake.

"You have, sir?" I feel confused. Betty Rosenthal certainly hates me; I can't imagine who's told him these things.

"Your Dad is very proud of you," he explains.

I feel myself glow. And then I wonder how much my dad has talked to Isaiah's. They're business associates; it's not like they're friends.

"And you're very talented," he finishes.

We stand for a minute, saying nothing. We're all awkward: Cameron, Isaiah, Isaiah's dad, and me.

"Where's Mom?" Isaiah asks after a long silence.

"I don't know," his dad says somberly.

"We had an argument when I got home. She left about twenty minutes ago, and I haven't been able to get in touch with her."

He looks sad, but I don't know why.

"Son, can we talk in private?" Mr. Rosenthal says at last.

Isaiah and his father disappear into the study, leaving Cameron and me dumbfounded in the foyer. An hour passes while they talk in hushed tones in the library. I text my parents an update, so they don't worry. Cameron does the same.

We pass the time by telling each other about our favorite books and movies. We pass the time by telling each other knock-knock jokes. We pass the time doing nothing.

Finally, the door clicks open, and Isaiah and his father both come out of the room. Their faces are swollen from too many tears. Even crying, they look like strength personified.

I want to ask what happened. I want to ask what they talked about and why they're crying. I want to hold Isaiah and give him my strength the way he's always done for me. Not that he looks like he needs my strength. He seems stronger than ever.

"Okay," his dad straightens himself, standing taller than ever, and smiles broadly at Cameron and me. "Let's go get those drawings."

I don't understand what Mr. Rosenthal means at first. He disappears into a room and then into another. There's something comic-bookish about the entire experience. Eventually, he returns with two beautiful, obviously very expensive frames.

"I knew she wouldn't have gotten rid of them," he smiles. He turns the frames around, and I see the charcoals of Isaiah from my exhibition.

"Isaiah says these will help you win the art show," he holds them out to me like stone tablets holding ancient secrets.

"I wouldn't say win," I laugh. "But at least have a shot."

"Before you all go," Mr. Rosenthal says. "I'd like to talk to you, Cade."

I follow Mr. Rosenthal into the library, where he shuts the door again. This is the most terrified I've been in my entire life. And I don't want to be here. My house burned down today. Haven't I been through enough?

"I have to thank you," Mr. Rosenthal's honey-and-amber eyes stare through my soul. I'm still disarmed by them, by Isaiah's eyes on this older face.

"I'm sorry?" I'm confused.

"You took care of my son while I was gone," he smiles and offers me a seat.

I take it slowly, unsure of what's happening. Does Marcus Rosenthal like me? Is he the anti-Betty? I just don't understand.

"Listen," he says, sitting in a chair across from me. "Being a parent is tough. Sometimes you think you're doing your best, and then your kid doesn't turn out as you expected."

"I don't understand, sir," I shake my head. I'm tired of being told that parenting is hard. I'm tired of adults telling me how hard things are. It's not like things are easy for me, either. Life is hard. Get over it.

"Sometimes we don't handle things well," he continues, and I know he's talking about Isaiah's mom. "And in those times, we just have to hope that there's somebody in our children's lives who will help hold them together until we come around."

"Four years ago, Isaiah's brother and sister discovered their mom was having an affair," Mr. Rosenthal continues.

I feel myself grow rigid. The room runs cold. He knows? Is that what we're talking about? Something like relief washes over me. I hang my head in shame and relief. I close my eyes and breathe deeper than I have in a long time.

"So, you know?" I ask, raising an eyebrow. What's the endgame here? What's he getting at?

"I know," he nods. "And I want to thank you for not telling Isaiah."

"I feel awful that I haven't," I admit. "It makes me sick to my stomach. But it's not my story to tell."

"I know," Mr. Rosenthal nods slowly. "I'm going to tell him. There's a lot we need to talk about when he moves home."

"He's moving home?" I try to contain my excitement, but I don't. "But I thought Mrs. Rosenthal..."

"That's why I wanted to talk to you, just one-on-one," Mr. Rosenthal smiles Isaiah's smile. "I'm sorry for what she said to you. I'm sorry for everything she's done to you. I can't help but think if I'd been around more, that never would have happened."

"It's not your fault," I shrug.

"I'm not saying it is," he smiles a broken kind of smile. "I'm just saying I could have stopped it. My wife was out of line, and she should have never spoken to you that way."

"Isaiah told me how she spoke to you, and I want you to know that that is not how we carry ourselves," he smiles so kindly at me I almost break. "I don't care where you came from or what your family does. You make my son happy, and that's what matters to me."

I nearly hug him, but I can't imagine hugging this older, more severe version of Isaiah. I want to thank him, but I suddenly don't know how to speak. Instead, I just sit there and say nothing and do nothing.

"I suspect what she said had less to do with you than it did with her own embarrassment," he says softly.

"Isaiah's mother and I have separated," he finally confesses. "She has alienated all of our children from this family. It's probably inappropriate for me to tell you this, but Isaiah will need your strength as we work all of this out."

I nod, understanding. I don't know how I understand, but I do.

"Mr. Rosenthal?"

"Really, please call me Marcus."

"Yes, sir," I nod. "I've been kind of wondering."

I swallow. This is the most awkward thing I've ever asked. And I'm glad I'm asking Isaiah's dad and not my own parents.

"Things between you and my dad," I wince. "I mean. Considering the history between you two. And your wife. I mean. I really like your son."

I reconsider.

"I love Isaiah. And I don't want this to be weird."

He laughs a deep laugh, so resounding I think it may cause an earthquake.

"You don't have to worry," his voice is so kind, it warms me from the inside. "We're all working through our own things, right? Your dad and I have made amends. A long time ago. He's crazy about your mother, you know."

I do know.

"Everybody makes mistakes. He's owned his and asked forgiveness. What more can you ask?"

I want to hug him, this strong, gentle stranger who looks so much like the man that I love. I want to thank him for raising Isaiah and for forgiving my dad, and for existing. But I don't. I just smile and nod.

"I won't hold you any longer," he stands and gestures to the door. "You've got an art show to get ready for."

As I open the door, he calls my name.

"I should have started with this, but I'm sorry about your house," he looks embarrassed. "If there's anything I can do to help your family, tell your parents to let me know."

"We'll be fine," I nod appreciatively. "It's your son who needs help. He's been alone for four months. There's a lot of healing that needs to take place."

Chapter Thirty-One

"What time do you have to have all of your stuff turned in?" Dad asks cryptically as I get ready to leave for school.

"Mr. Camplin has to have it all by 1:00," I feel frantic and rushed. I spent all day yesterday tweaking my portfolio, trying to find some way to create cohesion. I was able to get the charcoals of Isaiah from Mr. Rosenthal, and I'm feeling better about things. But not great. I can't help feeling I could have an actual shot at winning if I had the portrait of Thomas that I sold in my art show. I wish I could get back the stippled piece of my mom. Regret fills me, and I think back to my mother's fear that I would regret selling my art. I don't want to admit that she's right, but she's right. Mom is always right.

"You'll make it," he smiles kindly, and I'm thankful for his support. "And the show starts Friday?"

I nod, shoving things into my backpack.

"The show runs all weekend," I explain, but the judges will give their statements and placings Friday evening at the reception.

I sigh in frustration, trying to load my backpack with one arm. Breaking my arm for the last two months of the school year is quite possibly the dumbest thing I've ever done. It's made everything more complicated. It's hard to get dressed in the mornings. It's hard to shower. It's hard to drive. It's hard to hold Isaiah's hand and do anything else. This is miserable.

"Would you like some help?" Dada laughs, offering his hand.

"No," I huff. "I've got this."

I struggle a little more before zipping my bag shut and throwing it carelessly onto my shoulder. Dad tries his hardest to hide a smirk, but I laugh with him. I'm sure I must look ridiculous. I feel ridiculous.

"Do you ever stop and just remember that you're 18 years old and broke your arm on a swing?" He laughs so hard I think he'll pull a muscle.

"Ha-ha," I deadpan. "Hilarious."

"I'm sorry," I apologize quickly. "I'm really stressed."

It's Wednesday. Two days from now, I will know whether I'm going to the art institute or not. Two days from now, I will see if I'm really as good as I believe that I am. Two days from now, my future will be revealed. And I'm not prepared for it.

"I understand," Dad puts his hand on my shoulders, forcing me to look into his eyes. "Relax, okay? Things will be okay. This isn't your only path to your future. Don't give it that much power."

I smile and shake my head. I want to tell him he doesn't understand. But he does. And he doesn't. I can't tell him I'm scared of him leaving again. I can't tell him I have to put all my eggs in this basket because I don't have anything else.

"Thanks, Dad," I smile, trying to play it cool. "I've just got a lot on my plate."

"Besides," Dad smiles. "There's nobody better than you. There's no way you'll lose."

I roll my eyes. I don't need his false reassurances. I don't need to get my hopes up. My Kintsukuroi Boy is gone, leaving only ash in its wake. I've no hope of winning now, and I don't know what I will do for college.

Mr. Camplin greets me when I get to school with a broad smile. If it were any other teacher, I'd think I must be in trouble, but not with him. He always lets us know what he's feeling. Mr. Camplin is transparent and trustworthy.

"Cade, I have good news," he leads me into his classroom. I wait for him to tell me what this great news is, but instead, he motions toward a stack of frames on a table in the corner of the room.

I answer his gesture with a confused look, but I cross the room to inspect it. As I get closer, I feel excitement bubble up in me. My entire show sits in beautiful frames. Glass gleams in front of my work. Something about framing everything makes it all seem so professional. Everything looks fresh and new, even my dad's subpar pastel. It all looks worthy of hanging in a state art show.

"Mr. Camplin," I start. "You shouldn't have."

Teachers can't afford the types of frames on these pieces. I'll never be able to repay an act like this.

"Not me," he smiles. "Look at the note."

Beside the stack of frames is a card. I open it and catch myself laughing.

"What does it say?" Isaiah asks, sneaking up behind me. How can somebody so tall and so beautiful sneak up unnoticed?

"'Mr. Swanson,'" I start, trying not to laugh. "'I wish you all the best this weekend in your show. Your art has been an asset to my gallery, and I want you to know you will always have space here whenever you'd like. I'm loaning you these frames, as well as your piece from my private collection for the show. I wish you the best of luck in everything; your future is bright and beautiful, and I feel personally and professionally lucky to be a part of it. Take care, Martin Kimball.'"

"That was so nice," Isaiah nearly shouts. "Why is it funny?"

"The P.S.," I laugh. "It says 'P.S. I do hope this changes your opinion of me and my manners.'"

Isaiah and I erupt into laughter, leaving Mr. Camplin as confused as I had been three minutes ago. I explain to him about my first interaction with Martin Kimball at the art supply store half a lifetime ago.

"And that, children," Mr. Camplin sighs. "Is why you always have to behave yourself. You never know what bridges you could be burning."

I can't help but feel elated. This is the nicest thing that anybody could have done for me right now. This is the most helpful thing anybody could have done.

"Your portfolio will be great," Mr. Camplin tells me, and I actually believe him. He doesn't lie.

"But is it going to be good enough?" I ask nervously.

"Of course, it will be," he smiles gently. I try to control the excitement that sparks up in me.

"That doesn't mean you'll win," he continues. "It just means your work is good enough. Your work is outstanding. But what's amazing about art is that everybody's work is good enough."

I open my mouth to say something, but he continues.

"Look at Frida Kahlo, her work is considered bizarre by many, but others are obsessed with her style. Compare her style to Odd Nerdrum, who is recreating the Baroque style today. Look at their differences compared to Picasso, Warhol, and Keith Haring. They're all so different, and they're all equally well-respected. Your art is good enough, Cade, because *you* are good enough."

I've never heard Mr. Camplin speak so passionately before. I feel the nearly overwhelming urge to clap for him after his speech. His eyes sparkle like he's inspiring the world. And for all I know, he is; one art student at a time.

We stand in silence for a moment, unsure of what to say after such an impassioned speech. Finally, I just nod and thank him. I didn't realize how badly I needed to hear that until I heard it. Isaiah takes my hand and strokes it with his thumb before he returns to his assignment; he still has a final piece to turn in. Mr. Camplin allowed anybody who wanted to enter the art show to turn in a portfolio in lieu of a final. I was the only person who took that option; it meant more work in the long run.

"Come by my room this afternoon, please," Mr. Camplin instructs me. "I'm going to need help getting things set up for the show. The other entries will be delivered this evening, and we've got to get everything ready."

I nod quietly. I can't believe this is happening. It's been my sole focus since September; what will I have to look forward to when it's over? What am I going to be working toward? Will I even know how to function without some lingering goal?

When the afternoon bell rings, Isaiah, Cameron, and I appear in Mr. Camplin's classroom, ready to set up shelves and display racks. The state art show will take over the entire fine arts wing of our school, Mr. Camplin explains. The hallways will be filled with paintings, drawings, and sculptures.

"Sculptures," I shake my head. "I don't have a chance against sculptors."

"They don't have a chance against you," Cameron laughs, carrying a large shelving unit by himself. I never realized he was so strong.

"Thanks," I smile, but I'm not confident. I grow less and less sure of myself as the minutes tick by.

"Cade," Mr. Camplin calls from his classroom. "Why don't you help me set up your portfolio? You can have your pick of location."

He and I pick a spot toward the front of the hallway. I want people to be intimidated by my art; I want to be the first thing people see. I want my work to be the thing everybody compares theirs to. It's a silly intimidation tactic, but I'll take every leg up I can get.

We begin hanging frames on a wire display. Together, in their beautiful glistening frames, my art actually looks like a collection. I can see a theme in my work. I can see similar techniques in all of my pieces. I hang my flipbooks in envelopes beside my portfolio and take a step back.

It's beautiful. I feel narcissistic to admit it, but this is a damned good portfolio. This is the culmination of four years of hard work. I catch myself smiling, hand on my hip, relief flooding through me. Maybe Mr. Camplin is right. Maybe I am good enough. Maybe my art is good enough. Even without my favorite pieces.

"Where do you want these?" Isaiah asks, pulling me from my moment of self-praise.

"What are they?" I'm confused. He and Cameron have two massive frames, but I've already hung everything I've included in my portfolio.

"I altered your portfolio after you left class this morning," Mr. Camplin brings more wire and hooks to add to my area. "Your father dropped these off for you."

When Isaiah and Cameron turn the frames around, I'm hit by a flood of tears. There they are, right in front of me. Staring back at me are my mom—stippled and beautiful and tired, a lifetime ago—and Thomas—asleep, a single moonbeam across his face, captured in graphite and love and admiration. How had I forgotten my dad had bought the piece of my mom. Why hadn't I asked him if I could use it? But has he always had this piece of Thomas, too?

I can't believe they're back in my life.

I can't believe they never really left.

I can't believe it.

I reach to grab the giant frames, but Isaiah shakes his head.

"Slow down," he laughs. "You haven't been able to hang a single thing because of that bum arm. You think I'm going to let you hurt yourself trying to hang these? Just tell me where they go."

When Isaiah and Cameron are done, my portfolio really is complete. It's all right there. It's exactly how I planned it. It's nothing like I planned it. There's not a single Kintsukuroi Boy in the whole thing, but there are two beside me. I am one. We are all broken. We are all giants. We are all indestructible and fragile.

"Mr. Camplin," I start, trying to pull myself together. "I can't thank you enough for giving me this opportunity."

"You earned this opportunity," he smiles. "You would have been the winner from this school regardless. Your classmates love art. They're very talented. But you live and breathe art. You'll be successful at it regardless of anything I've taught you. You'll be successful in spite of everything around you."

I shake my head, smiling. I don't think that's true, but I don't argue.

By the time we're through setting everything up, it's nearly 5:00, and Isaiah and Cameron have to go to work. I don't want to be alone tonight, for some reason. I don't want to spend any more time away from either of them than I have to.

"Oh," Cameron reaches into his backpack, remembering something before we part. "I was told to give this to you and make sure you give it back when you're done."

He hands me the flipbook I gave Kayla for Christmas. I hold it delicately like it's the holy grail like the Queen's Crown Jewels.

"Cameron, how did you get this?" It's clear he asked her for help. "You didn't have to go talk to her."

"It wasn't a big deal," he shrugs. But it is a big deal. And it's a big deal that she actually let me borrow it. All of this is a big deal.

"Thank you," I hug him tightly, kiss Isaiah goodbye, and help Mr. Camplin receive the incoming artists from other high schools in the state.

I try not to take notice of the art they bring in. I definitely ignore the beautiful fantasy piece that passes me, realistic mermaids swimming around a sunken Atlantis. Not once do I notice the ceramic soldier standing beside a flying flag. And I don't even glance at the giant marionette installation piece that stands 6 feet at the end of the hallway. No. I don't notice any of these things. I don't allow myself to be moved, shaken, or intimidated by any of them.

"Thanks for your help tonight, Cade," Mr. Camplin says at 8:00.

I shrug. I'm out of words to say. My portfolio will be judged in less than 24 hours, and my future will be decided. In less than 24 hours, my entire world will change one way or another. I'm preoccupied with the thought.

"Cade," he says gently, putting his hand on my shoulder. "What happens tomorrow doesn't matter. If you win, it doesn't mean you're any better than you are today. And if you don't, it doesn't mean you're worse than you are today. Don't think about it too much."

Telling me not to think on it too much is like telling the wind not to blow. Or telling the sun not to set. Or telling the Earth not to spin. It's not going to happen. I probably won't be able to sleep tonight. I probably won't eat when I get home. I'll probably sit in my new, small art studio with my graphite and my blank paper, stare into the middle distance, and imagine what life will be like when I don't win.

But when I get home, my house is filled with delicious smells, and I'm too distracted to ponder life. The smell of grilled hamburgers hangs in the air. Something sweet and vaguely chocolate hangs in the air just underneath the hamburger smell.

"I'm home!" I call as I make my way to the kitchen.

My family is already eating. Hamburgers and grilled asparagus, and bell pepper spears sit on the table. It looks delicious. I dig into my food almost immediately.

"I just finished frosting the red velvet cake," Mom smiles by way of greeting.

I can't control the broad smile that spreads across my face. Red velvet is my favorite. I know she's made it just for me.

We talk about our days. We try to make this new place, this new home, feel like home. I listen to Thomas talk about his exciting day and how he made milk spray out of a girl's nose. And I can't control the grin on my face to hear that Thomas is making friends.

We discuss the world's troubles. We talk about Disney World. We talk about anything but the State Art show. We settle into the unfamiliar familiarity of family dinner, and I feel my troubles slip away. I feel like we're a 90s sitcom. I feel like this is how it always should have been.

Somehow, I manage to fall asleep when I go to bed. I dream in vivid colors, in shapes like Picasso, and when I wake up in the morning, I feel refreshed and terrified. I don't know how I'm going to make it through the day. I don't know how I'm going to make it through the rest of the school year. Two weeks left until graduation. Two weeks left in this cast. Two weeks left, and I haven't picked a college yet. I haven't done anything for my future yet. I'm not ready to, yet.

I'm met in the parking lot by a beautiful boy with honey-colored eyes. He's leaning against the most beautiful car in the world. He's smiling the most beautiful smile in the world. The birds are singing the most beautiful song in the world. It's incredible how quickly perspective can change.

"You got your car back?" I nearly shout as I clamber out of my car to throw my arms around him.

"I think you're more excited to see my car than you are to see me," he laughs, then kisses me good morning.

"I mean, there are very few cars like this one," I wink and lace my fingers with his.

"How are things back with your dad?" I ask.

This. This is how I'm going to make it through this day. Through these two weeks. Through years and years and years. By holding Isaiah's hand, asking him about his life, and staring into his deep eyes.

"They're strange," he shrugs. "We've never spent a lot of time together, you know? It's weird. It's like trying to make friends with a distant uncle or something."

"I'm sorry," I move my body closer to his, trying to comfort him.

"It's okay," he smiles. "He loves me, and he supports me."

I nod.

"Have you heard from your mom?"

Isaiah shakes his head solemnly.

"She checks in with Dad every day," he explains. "But she never asks to talk to me. Dad says she's embarrassed, but I'm not sure."

I stroke his hand with my thumb. It feels like as soon as everything is coming together for me, everything is falling apart for Isaiah. Is that all life is? A series of breaks and repairs? Are we all just breaking at different times and trying to hold each other together?

"I don't think she's well," Isaiah finally says. "I think she's checked into some kind of hospital or facility for her mental health."

I open my mouth to say something, but I have nothing to say, so I shut it again.

"I hope she's getting the help she needs," I say at last, and I mean it.

Isaiah nods.

"Dad's agreed to stop traveling so much," he continues. "He's going to work from home more and try to make things right with the twins and me. I think he's divorcing my mom."

I want to say good riddance, but I don't. Isaiah loves his mother. And divorce is hard. It has many victims and leaves a lot of devastation. Divorce is a bomb, and everybody falls victim to its shrapnel.

"I'm sorry," I finally say. It's the wrong thing to say, but it's something.

"I'm just ready for some stability, you know?" He half-smiles.

I do know. I know exactly what he means. I've been craving stability for years. I still am. Maybe we're never really stable. Perhaps nothing is ever really fixed after we're ten years old. Is Thomas nearing the end of his own stability?

"Good luck," I finally smile. "We're about to start college. Nothing's ever going to be stable again."

"Speaking of," Isaiah changes the subject as quickly as possible. "Have you decided where you're going yet? It's April. We've got two weeks left of high school."

He's been hounding me. He wants me to decide where I'm going if I don't win the art show. He never says *when* I don't win the art show, and I silently thank him for that. I don't say anything, just shake my head. I'm trying to ignore it.

"I'll decide this weekend, I guess," I shrug.

"Are you excited for tonight?" Isaiah squeezes my hand tightly as we enter Mr. Camplin's room.

"I'm just ready for it to be over," I admit.

Art passes by sluggishly. I don't have anything to work on; my portfolio is on display by the auditorium. I float around the room, helping my classmates with their projects. I help Nicole adjust values on her oil pastel piece. It's embarrassing to be in the same room as her; I've never gotten over the awkwardness of being near her after that awful party.

"Dylan told me about the drawing class," she says sheepishly.

"I don't want to talk about it," I shake my head. "Not today."

"I just wanted to tell you that I know he's a creep," she says softly. "I know you don't want to talk about it, but I wanted to tell you that. You're the first person who's ever turned him down, you know."

I shrug. I didn't exactly turn him down. I puked. I might have gone ahead with it if it weren't for that. I tell her as much.

"Well, there's that," she laughs. "But also, at the drawing class. He's not used to people standing up to him like that. I just wanted to say that was really cool. Isaiah's cute, but I don't know many people who wouldn't jump at the opportunity to sleep with Dylan."

"Now I really don't want to talk about it," I laugh awkwardly.

"Fair enough," she takes a step back from her oil pastel and gives it a hard look. "This is terrible."

"It's pretty awful," I laugh and nod.

When art is over, I pass Kayla in the hallway. Against my better judgment,

CHAPTER THIRTY-ONE

I stop her to talk to her.

"Hey," I say. It catches in my throat like I've swallowed sand. I wish it weren't so hard to talk to her.

"Hey," she says, half annoyed, half embarrassed.

"I just wanted to," I try to gather my words, to wrap them in a soft, Kayla-appropriate tone. "I mean, thank you. For letting me borrow your flipbook. It means a lot to me."

"It's whatever," she shrugs awkwardly. "You can keep it if you want."

"I don't want to," I argue. I wrap armor around myself to protect myself. She's trying to hurt me, but I won't let her. "I'll give it back when the judging is over. I just wanted to say thank you."

"You can throw it away when you're done," she says shortly and then marches away without giving me the chance to respond.

I feel a hand on my shoulder, offering support. I turn to see Cameron. He looks angry; he looks protective.

"Why does she hate me?" I ask, shaking my head.

"She doesn't," he smiles kindly. "She hates everything. That's different."

"Are you ready for the best day of your life, Cade Swanson?" Cameron asks as we walk to chemistry together in Kayla's wake. I wonder if he knows that that's what Kayla used to ask me at the start of every day. I wonder if he's trying to take over as my new best friend. I wonder if he realizes he already has. And I wonder why I didn't realize it before

"This is not the best day of my life," I shake my head. "But I'm definitely ready for it to be over."

And so, after seven more sluggish hours, it is. I avoid the fine arts wing at all cost. I know the judges are busy at work, looking over our portfolios one last time. I know the ranking is happening as I make my way to my car. I wonder what they think when they look at mine. I wonder how it compares to everybody else's. I wonder how you can compare what I do to what other people do. I'm not an Impressionist. You can't compare Monet to Renoir. You can't compare Michelangelo to Diego Rivera.

By the time I get home, I've nearly hyperventilated twice and taken three wrong turns. I'm distracted. I'm a wreck. And I can't see how the judges ranked us for another four hours. I don't know how I'll survive.

Chapter Thirty-Two

"You look so handsome," Mom smiles at me as I enter the living room. Dad insisted on buying me a new suit for the judging tonight. I highly suspect I will be highly overdressed, but I'm grateful for it nonetheless.

I wish I had had something this nice for my gallery show. I wish I had been able to appreciate my dad's presence at the gallery show. It's almost hard to remember a time before Dad came back. It's almost difficult to remember that there was a time before we were all shiny and gilded in gold. I've almost forgotten there was a time when we weren't giants.

"Is Isaiah coming here, or is he meeting us there?" Mom asks as she inspects Thomas's clothes. She wants to make sure everything is perfect for the evening. I just want to make sure I don't barf everywhere.

"He and his dad are going to meet us there. And Cameron, too."

I'm grateful she doesn't ask about Kayla. I think my parents have figured out that Kayla and I aren't the friends we used to be. Mom's stopped asking me about Kayla. Even Thomas hasn't mentioned her lately. I'm sad about how things have played out, but not as sad as I would have anticipated.

"That'll be nice," Mom smiles. "Can you believe this, Cole? Our son is all grown up."

I see her eyes start to sparkle with tears. I wish she wouldn't cry; it always makes me feel uncomfortable.

"He's going to graduate soon," she smiles an off-center smile. "And go to college and move away from us and grow into this amazing man."

"Mom, stop," I smile. "I'm not grown yet. I can't even tie my tie."

I wave my neon green cast around to indicate to my dad that I need help.

I'm almost embarrassed that I have to ask him for help. Almost.

"I've got this," Dad laughs, standing in front of me to tie my tie.

Looking at him is odd; it's like looking into a mirror, only aged. It's like seeing a paler, older version of myself, all furrowed brow and serious face. I make a mental note to draw my dad. The last time I drew him was years ago, a lifetime ago. The last time I drew him, I didn't understand shadows or tonal value. The last time I drew him, his face was disproportionate. And he framed it anyway. The last time I drew my dad, he still supported me. Just like tonight.

"Are you ready?" Mom asks, fastening her pearl earrings.

"No," I shake my head. I feel sick. I've spent so much time and energy trying not to hope, not to expect, not to dream about winning. Now that the night has come, I'm willing to admit to myself that I have a shot.

Even though my original portfolio burnt down, I have amazing things hanging at the school. I have two photorealistic drawings of my family. I have incredible flipbooks. I have lifelike charcoals of the man of my dreams. I've seen my competition. I know what other students turned in. I know that there are good pieces of art, but I'm confident that mine is one of the best portfolios.

We load ourselves into Mom's car—it's much bigger and more comfortable than Dad's Porsche, even if it is less flashy—and I try to keep my mind off of the show. I try to quell my uncomfortable excitement by thinking about school and graduation. I try to think about the past and all of the awful things I've gone through. I try to think about Betty Rosenthal and how much I hate her.

But I'm also grateful for her. Before things fell apart, she gave me my start. She gave me my first big break. She opened the doors to my future. I don't know if it was out of guilt for breaking up my family or because she wanted Isaiah's friend to be successful, but either way, I'm grateful.

I try to think about Kayla and how things started out and how things ended up. She was the best friend I thought I'd ever have. She helped me through some of the roughest times in my life. And even if our friendship did end up one-sided in the end, it hadn't always been that way.

I try to think about Cameron and how our friendship has changed, too. I think about how ambivalent I had been of him at first, but how I've grown to love him. How he's grown to be closer to me than Kayla ever has been. And how he was so quick to accept the person that I am. That I love Isaiah.

Before I can try to think of anything else, we're in the school parking lot. People are flooding into the school in their nicest clothes. Isaiah is waiting outside in his nicest clothes, standing next to his Dad, his several-years-older twin. Isaiah looks so handsome, I can't stop myself from kissing him the moment I'm with him, even with our families around.

"Ew," Thomas cries exaggeratedly. Our families chuckle.

"You look amazing," Isaiah tells me softly, sliding his fingers between mine.

"Nothing compared to you," I squeeze his hand.

I realize that this is the first time my Dad and Isaiah's Dad have been together, in this capacity, as the dads of boyfriends. At a big event. I wonder how uncomfortable they must be. I wonder if I'm the only person who's uncomfortable.

"Cole," Marcus Rosenthal says, extending his hand in a business-like gesture. "It's good to see you."

His tone isn't as formal as I would expect, considering the history between them and the circumstances surrounding things tonight.

"It's good to see you, too, Marcus," Dad smiles and pulls Mr. Rosenthal into a hug.

"Hey, can we talk real quick?" Isaiah pulls me away from our families as they catch up.

"My Dad told me," he says softly, wincing like he's in pain.

For a moment, I don't know what he's talking about. And then I do.

"I'm sorry I kept it from you," I apologize immediately, hanging my head. "I didn't want to. I just. I didn't want to hurt you. I"

"No," he cuts me off. "I'm not mad."

I look into his honey-and-amber eyes.

"Thank you," he kisses my forehead. "I'm sorry you felt like you had to hold it in. I could have taken it. But I know you were just thinking about me."

Something in my neck loosens for the first time in millennia, and my shoulders relax. I didn't realize I'd been carrying so much tension.

"In the future," he laughs. "You don't have to protect me. I can take it. Besides, I have to protect you. That's my job."

I don't argue with him. He has done an awful lot of protecting and saving me. Will he always be my knight in shining armor? I certainly hope so.

"Thank you," he says again, kissing my cheek. "You're the best."

I feel myself melt into a puddle. I run all over the ground, and glow with warmth and become lava. I synch with the turning of the earth. Being with him makes me this way. I hope it always will.

"Alright, you two," Dad jokes. "Break it up. Let's go inside."

I squeeze Isaiah's hand tightly and walk with him into the school. The hallways are buzzing with chatter and are packed with well-dressed families fawning over artwork. Other kids my age are presenting their portfolios to the families.

I see people proudly displaying their watercolor paintings, their charcoal portraits, their mixed media canvases. I see artists telling people about their oil paintings, their sculptures, their pastel works.

Everybody here is good. Everybody here is talented. Everybody at this show, like me, is the most gifted artist in their school. Everybody, like me, is proud of what they're done. Everybody, like me, is nervous about the outcome of their portfolios.

"Will you present your show to us?" Mom says delightedly. She's glowing. She looks so young and vibrant. She looks like the most beautiful piece of art at this show.

So, I lead my posse to my display, standing proudly amidst all of the phenomenal collections around me. I talk about every piece I created. I talk about the time and love I gave to every piece. I tell them about what was happening in my life whenever I created each piece. I tell them about watching Thomas sleep and his night terrors and how no night was too terrible for the angelic face in the picture to fix. I tell them about the stippled piece of my mom and how she gave me strength whenever I was weak. I tell them how she was my rock through so many tough times. Mom cries as I talk about it.

I tell them about Isaiah in his multiple forms. About how before I knew I loved him, my art tried to show me that I loved him. I tell them about his inspiration and influence on my art. I try not to be too sappy.

As I talk, I notice a group of people forming around us. I recognize some of the faces, like Cathy, and Thad, and Josiah. I nearly ask them what they're doing here, but I know they're here to support me and see my work. I feel bad that I don't have in Kintsukuroi Boys to show them; they'd have loved them.

Some of the faces, though, I don't recognize. Other artists are gathered around me with their families. Mr. Camplin joins them, as well as a group of professional-looking men and women wearing judges' badges. I recognize one of the judges as Cynthia Reid, the dean of fine arts at Magnolia State. I expect nerves to come as I draw a crowd, but they never do. I'm in my element.

As I talk, I talk about the difficulties of each medium I work in. I talk about the complexities of developing your own style and the hardships of watching your entire show burn down in a fire. Judging is over; I know this won't sway the judges' decisions.

I notice my flipbooks start to float around the crowd; people flip through them, looking impressed and surprised as they flip. I talk about animation as a lost art form. And before I know it, it feels like I'm giving a lecture. People are hanging on my every word. People are listening so intently. I feel empowered and encouraged.

A hand goes into the air unexpectedly, and I'm briefly stunned. I was not prepared for a question and answer session.

"Um, yes?" I ask, confused. "Do you have a question?"

"Yeah," says a girl with dark hair pulled back into an intricate braid. "Would you say it's harder to work in your photorealistic style or this animation style in your books?"

I consider this; it's something I've never really thought about.

"I don't know that any one style is harder," I say after thinking about it. "I think they all have different skill sets. Photorealism takes a lot of patience and meticulous review of your reference. But animation takes bringing things from your imagination to life. It takes thinking about physics and the way things move in the real world. They're both a challenge. Just like impressionism makes you think beyond what you see and translate what you're feeling into a visual medium."

"Mr. Swanson," Cynthia Reid asks next. "What medium is your favorite? If you could only work in one medium for the rest of your life, what would it be?"

"Graphite," I respond without hesitation. "You always have a pencil with you. You can create art anywhere with it. There were a few years in my life when I couldn't afford any other medium. I think that's what caused me to work so hard to be good at my graphite work. I was always able to afford a pack of #2 pencils."

I see a few members of the crowd nodding their heads in understanding or agreement. I see my dad grimace. I don't apologize for telling the truth, even if it hurts.

I answer a few more questions from the crowd, feeling awkward and powerful. I am a giant. I own this realm. I can't help but notice Isaiah and Cameron's impressed looks. I can't help but notice Mr. Camplin's approving nod. I can't help but see my parents looking at me with pride, and respect, and love. I can't help but beam as the judges are beaming at me.

"May I have your attention, please," Cynthia Reid says into the quiet crowd. "If you'll follow me to the auditorium, we'll begin the awards presentation for the night."

We file into the auditorium. The air is charged with electricity, anticipation, and nerves. Thomas is glued to me, chattering excitedly and nervously. Isaiah is stroking my hand with his thumb, comforting me.

We say nothing. My parents say nothing. Marcus and Cameron say nothing. Only Thomas is steadily telling me how proud he is of me, and how he knows I'm going to win, and how I'm going to be a famous artist like the "Pictasso" guy, and how he hopes we can go out for dessert when this is over, and he can't wait to tell all of his friends that I won, and that he's going to miss me when I'm in college, and I can't for the life of me figure out how he can talk so much without breathing.

"Good evening, everybody," Mr. Camplin says into the microphone. "Welcome to Riverside High School. We are so happy to be able to host this event tonight. And we are so honored that so many of you brought in such tremendous artwork. As you all brought in your portfolios, all I could think was how grateful I am that I'm not judging. I don't know that I'd be able to pick just one winner."

The audience applauds respectfully. Mr. Camplin is nervous and comes across as flat and flustered onstage. The stage lights make him look pale and sickly.

"I'm happy to introduce Dr. Cynthia Reid, the dean of the College of Fine Arts at Magnolia State University. She will be announcing tonight's judges and tonight's winners."

Another round of polite applause as Dr. Reid appears onstage.

"Cade, wasn't she at your show at Kimball?" Mom whispers as she takes the mic. I nod slowly; I don't want to miss a thing Dr. Reid says.

"Good evening," Dr. Reid smiles broadly. "I have had the pleasure tonight of judging with some of the most gifted artists and art educators I have ever met. Let me introduce them to you first."

Dr. Reid introduces an oil painter whose work has been displayed at galleries in Paris. She introduces a sculptor who teaches at a college on the other side of the state. She introduces a watercolorist whose work is featured in the textbook Mr. Camplin teaches from. She concludes by introducing the dean of the Art Institute.

"Mr. Camplin was not lying when he said our jobs were tough tonight," Dr. Reid smiles kindly. "Many years, we have gotten together to judge this art show, and there is one portfolio that stands out far above the others. Those years, our work is practically done for us."

The parents in the audience laugh politely. The students don't. We're all on edge.

"This year, that was not the case," she continues, adjusting her thin-framed glasses. "This year, there were so many good portfolios. We've spent hours deliberating and trying to pick a clear winner. Our decisions were split. We each found something amazing in every portfolio. This year, we had to narrow it down to five. And then three. And got stuck between two. It was unprecedented."

Dr. Reid opens a sheet of paper and starts to look over it.

"In fact, it was so unprecedented that we've evoked a rule we haven't used in years to create individual awards, aside from the overall portfolio award. Each of these individual awards will also be given a monetary award to help defray some of the expenses associated with attending university."

I want her to shut up already and start reading the names. I want her to stop talking and just tell us who won. I just want to know what my next step in life is.

Dr. Reid begins reading the categories and announcing the winners. There is an award for the best mixed-media piece, which goes to an artist who used reclaimed wood to create a three-dimensional painting of a forest on a large canvas. The digital media award goes to someone who recreated iconic posters throughout the years with modern-day political figures. The acrylic award goes to the artist who created fairy and mermaid landscapes, whose work I noticed when she brought it in. Her work is impressive; I won't be surprised if she wins the entire competition.

I'm shocked beyond words when I receive the animation and graphite awards. I finger the $500 worth of checks in my hand as I await the end of the individual awards.

"Now's the time you've been waiting for," Dr. Reid says gently once the applause has died down from the final individual awards.

"I am happy to announce our top five portfolio finalists. Please make your way to the stage as I call your name."

"In fifth place, receiving a $500 scholarship to any state school is Ana Marsden from Richland Heights High School," Dr. Reid announces.

As Ana takes her place on the stage, she's beaming. She's not upset about getting fifth place. She's joyous that she's placed.

Her portfolio consisted almost entirely of pet portraits done in different styles of great artists. They were brilliant. Funny and charming and personal.

"Fourth place, with a $1000 scholarship to any state school is Drake Thomas from West High," Dr. Reid announces.

Drake's family shouts in excitement as he takes the stage. Drake was the artist who used reclaimed wood. His works all had an industrial feel, sometimes incorporating used screws and bolts to create dimensionality in his art. His family is so proud. He can't help but smile broadly.

"In third place, receiving a $2,500 scholarship is Helen Prescott."

Helen Prescott takes the stage. Her art is the fantasy art with the realistic fairies and mermaids. She uses colors reminiscent of Thomas Kinkade's and is skillful with a palette knife in ways that I never will be. I'm surprised she didn't win.

I squeeze Isaiah's hand hard. I'm nervous. What if I didn't place at all? All of the artists were amazing. I found myself longing to create art like everybody there. Everybody has their own statements, and their own voices, and their own styles. I wanted to be as talented as everybody in the room with me.

"Don't worry," Isaiah whispers. "Yours is the best here. Just chill out."

"You have to say that," I sigh softly. "You're my boyfriend."

"I don't have to say anything," he laughs.

"In second place," Dr. Reid says once the applause stops. "Is one of the most amazing portfolios I've ever had the privilege of seeing."

My heart stops. My stomach drops. I know it's not me. My portfolio was good. It wasn't amazing. I didn't place.

"Cade Swanson of Riverside High School."

I applaud politely, looking around for the artist she just called. Why is nobody standing up?

"Cade," Isaiah laughs, pushing me. "That's you."

My parents are on their feet as I climb the steps, whooping and cheering. Isaiah, Thomas, Cameron, and Marcus follow them. They're clapping so proudly and cheering so loudly I can't help but be overtaken by joy. I'm smiling as broadly as if I'd won. I'm smiling more broadly than if I'd won.

Something in me tells me I did win. I may not be first place, but I did it. I won. Bright green cast and all, I am a giant. I won.

As I stand at the front of the stage, people in the audience begin to stand until everybody is up. They're on their feet, clapping loudly for me. A standing ovation? I don't even know how to accept that. I feel tears stream down my face. I'm crying in front of 500 people, all standing to acknowledge me. I'm in a green cast, and I'm glittering with gold, and I'm a giant. And they're applauding me. They're clapping for me as if I'm the winner. And I'm not.

"Our final award tonight is the overall portfolio award," Dr. Reid announces, trying to get the crowd under control again. "This artist had a wonderfully cohesive portfolio. Every piece fit with each other. Every piece felt like a natural flow from the one before it. It was impressive and an honor to get to see. Let's hear it for Ayah Haddad from Lincoln High."

I clap proudly for Ayah as she approaches the stage. Her portfolio was inspiring. She had a lifelike sculpture of a woman in a hijab running. She had an oil painting of the hijab-clad woman lying with her face on a mat in the middle of the desert, sand blowing furiously around her. There was a watercolor piece of the same woman hiding in the dark, a baby in her arms. Her entire portfolio told the story of a woman running and hiding and surviving and fighting. It was beautiful. I was moved to tears when I saw it.

"Congratulations," I tell her, offering her my hand.

"And you as well," she's smiling broadly.

In a blur, we're off the stage and smiling for pictures beside our portfolios. We stand beside each other, all five of us wearing the same proud, victorious smile. We all feel like winners. We are all giants. We are all champions.

"Cade, can I speak with you and your parents when you get a moment?" Dr. Reid asks once things have calmed down.

I search through the crowd and find my parents, Thomas, Isaiah, Marcus, Cameron, Thad, Cathy, and Josiah. I'm swallowed in hugs, and praise, and congratulations. I'm high-fived, and my hand is shaken, and my cheeks are kissed.

"Will you hang on just a moment?" I ask everybody. "I want to celebrate with you, but Dr. Reid wants to talk to my parents."

I lead my parents to Dr. Reid, who awaits with a very business-like look on her face.

"I wanted to congratulate you," Dr. Reid smiles at me. "And your parents for raising such a successful, well-spoken, and talented son."

We accept her congratulations and praise. My parents are glowing, both in love and in pride. They look like kids on their first date.

"I didn't announce it on stage, and it was on purpose and for my own self-serving reasons," Dr. Reid smiles kindly. "But your award is a $10,000 scholarship to any state school."

I choke on nothing. $10,000? I can't even imagine what $10,000 in scholarships looks like. That's an entire car. That's almost what I paid for my car, and that was after saving for months.

"And you're more than welcome to accept it and attend any school," she continues. "But I'm willing to offer something better to get you at Magnolia State University."

I feel myself shaking with excitement. More than $10,000? What is going on? I cannot believe this is happening to me.

"I want you so badly at our school that I'm willing to offer you a full scholarship," she continues. "We will cover your books, living expenses, and classes. We will cover anything. I think you will be a good asset to our program."

"What's the catch?" I ask, dubious. "Why would you give me all this money?"

"You're probably the first person who's ever been suspicious of a scholarship," she laughs kindly. "One day, Mr. Swanson, you're going to be a successful artist. You already are. One day you will be an animator, or a fine artist, or an art teacher. And people will want to go where you've gone and do the things you've done. Quite simply, Mr. Swanson, you're an investment. But I believe you are the right investment. And I'm willing to bet as much money as it takes to make sure we get to invest in you."

I consider this for a long time before saying anything.

"Can I call you later this week?" I ask finally. I can't make this decision tonight. I've got too much on my mind as it is.

"Of course," Dr. Reid laughs. "Take your time. But please call me and let me know no matter what you've decided."

"I will," I nod once. "Thank you."

"Your portfolio really is one of the best I've ever seen. I was wowed at your show at Kimball Art, and I'm wowed now. You've got a gift, Mr. Swanson. I know you've worked hard at it; nobody knows that better than I. But what you've got is also a gift. And I'm so happy to see you're using it and sharing it."

The night ends in a blur of hugs and a congratulatory dinner. My dad and Marcus Rosenthal agree to pay for everybody, including Thad, Cathy, and Josiah. They buy us expensive steaks and crème brûlée. I look around me at the people who are here to support me, to celebrate me. These people are my family. These people are in my life for a reason.

Sculptors say that their sculpture is inside the clay all the time, Mr. Camplin once told us as we learned to work with clay. *It's their job to reach into the clay and pull out all the extra and all the unwanted stuff and what's left is their art, their beautiful finished thing.*

If you were to reach into this crazy year and pull out all the extra stuff, all the unwanted stuff, this is what you'd be left with. These people, this moment, my life is the beautiful finished thing.

Epilogue

"Papa, tell me about how you and Daddy met," Aiden asks me as I grade a stack of projects beside me.

I laugh, looking up from my stack. I've told him this story a thousand times, but it never gets old for me.

"He was my best friend in high school," I answer. "He rescued me when I didn't know I needed saving."

"You saved me too," Isaiah calls from the kitchen where he's cooking dinner.

"And now Daddy's a hero, right?" Aiden smiles brightly, looking from me to Isaiah.

"That's right," I put down my pen. "Your Daddy helps people every day. He's the best social worker who's ever existed. Because he has such a big heart, and he loves everybody."

I look at our son, six years old and king of the world. He's still young and unbroken, and I hope every day that he will be spared as long as possible from being broken and gilded with gold. I hope that he will feel like a giant in the world every day.

"You help people every day, too, Daddy says," Aiden giggles the most infectious giggle; he reminds me of Thomas when he was that age. "Did you always know you were going to be a teacher?"

"I didn't," I shake my head. "In fact, your Daddy always thought *he* was going to be a teacher. I was going to be a graphic designer or an animator."

"I don't know what that is," Aiden laughs. I decide not to explain graphic design to him; I'm tired, and it'll make him ask a thousand more questions.

"How is Uncle Cameron my uncle? He's not your brother, like Uncle Thomas, or Daddy's brother, like Uncle Logan." I want to know why he's asking so many questions tonight, but I don't want to quash his inquisitive nature. He loves to learn, and I don't want to shut that down.

"Sometimes your family is the people you pick," I explain to him.

"Like how you and Daddy picked me?" He bats his long eyelashes at me, and I pick him up and kiss him all over his face. Sometimes I can't help it. Sometimes he's just the most adorable thing in the entire world.

"Just like that," I throw him over my shoulder and bring him into the kitchen where Isaiah is chopping vegetables.

"You're so sexy when you cook," I kiss him before pushing Aiden into his face.

"You're just saying that, so I'll keep cooking," he laughs before putting down his knife and taking our son into his arms.

"I am," I laugh. "But that doesn't mean it's not true."

Watching him swing Aiden around takes me back to high school and the way he used to wrestle with Thomas. I can remember the first time he let Thomas crawl all over him, and I knew right then that that was the man I wanted to raise kids with.

"What's got you asking so many questions tonight?" Isaiah asks in my stead.

"Our teacher had a baby," Aiden says through giggles as if we didn't know this. "And our new teacher came today. And she said she knew you."

"Oh yeah?" I ask, standing back to watch Isaiah spin Aiden around playfully. I can't control the smile on my face.

"Do you remember her name?" Isaiah asks. It would be out of character for our son to forget his teacher's name.

"Ms. Albright," Aiden announces proudly. "Kayla Albright."

"Really?" I suddenly stand up straighter. It's been 15 years since I thought about Kayla. I haven't seen her since graduation. In fact, I thought she'd moved away. Maybe she's moved back.

"She knew you were an artist," he continues. "And she says she has a book you made for her, but I don't know what she means. You don't write books."

"I'll show you one of my books tonight," I tell Aiden. "Why don't you go read until dinner's ready?"

Isaiah puts Aiden on the floor and smiles as he runs to his bedroom to read.

"He has so much energy," he laughs as Aiden runs away. "How do people have multiple kids? I can hardly keep up with one."

"So, Kayla's back," he wraps his arms around me just as he has for 15 years. Like he has forever.

"Apparently," I shrug. "Maybe I'll email her and see if she wants to get coffee and catch up."

"You sure you want to do that?" Isaiah raises an eyebrow at me. "She was pretty awful."

"Time changes people," I shrug. "And if she's not interested, she'll say no."

"You're a nicer person than I am," Isaiah returns to chopping vegetables. "But you're also still trying to be nice to my mom like that's ever going to make a difference."

"Maybe it won't," I laugh as I set the dinner table. "But at the end of the day, what matters is how we treat people, not how they treat us. It's what I tell my students every day, so I have to live it out, too."

"I wish you'd been my art teacher," Isaiah laughs as he stirs whatever's in the pot on the stove. "Mr. Camplin was good, but I would have learned better from you."

"What makes you so sure?" I laugh.

"I would have had the hots for the teacher," he winks. "I would have tried much harder."

I laugh inappropriately loudly.

When you pull out all of the extra stuff and all of the unwanted stuff, this is the beautiful, finished piece of art that's left. Me and Isaiah against the world. Just like it's always been. Just like it always will be.

We are gilded in gold, and we are giants.

About the Author

Paul Randall Adams is an author of young-adult and new-adult stories. He is a husband, father, professional musician, amateur artist, and former teacher. You can find him online at www.paulrandalladams.com or on Twitter and TikTok (@pauladamswrites).